THE PROBLEM OF
THE
EVIL EDITOR

Also by Roberta Rogow

The Problem of the Missing Miss
The Problem of the Spiteful Spiritualist

THE PROBLEM OF THE
EVIL EDITOR

Roberta Rogow

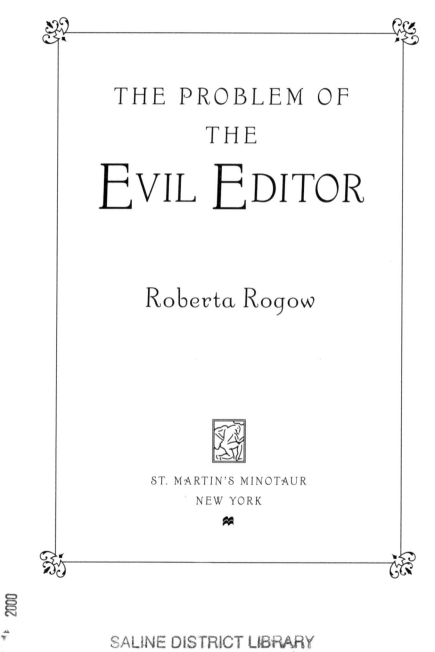

ST. MARTIN'S MINOTAUR
NEW YORK

Design by Nancy Resnick

Library of Congress Cataloging-in-Publication Data

Rogow, Roberta.
    The problem of the evil editor / Roberta Rogow—1st ed.
      p. cm.
    ISBN 0-312-20903-7
    1. Carroll, Lewis, 1832–1898—Fiction. 2. Doyle, Arthur Conan, Sir, 1859–1930—Fiction. 3. Authors, English—Fiction. 4. London (England)—Fiction. 5. Editors—Fiction. I. Title.

PS3568.O492 P69 2000
813'.54—dc21

                                  00-029675

First Edition: June 2000

10   9   8   7   6   5   4   3   2   1

To my daughters, Miriam and Louise,
who put up with my mishegoss.

Special Dedication:
To Peter, Bob, Howie, Bob, and Andre:
The staff of *Youth's Companion* wouldn't have been
the same without you.
Thanks for twenty years of Fandom.

CHAPTER 1

W orkers of London! Listen to my words!" The man on the wooden box that still gave off the aroma of its previous contents, disinfectant soap, waved his arms at the crowd and shouted into the rising wind.

"England is in dire straits! The forces of labor have been ground down by the capitalist dogs!"

Indeed, the people filling Fleet Street were aware that the previous three months had seen weather the likes of which had not been met in England since the reign of Charles the Second, when the Thames froze solid enough to hold a fair on the ice. The Gulf Stream had unaccountably been derelict in its duty of providing moderating warm winds that would keep the British Isles green, resulting in a disastrously cold winter. From Christmas of 1885 to Candlemas of 1886, the temperatures had been well below freezing all over England, Scotland, Wales, and Ireland.

The fall in the temperature had resulted in a decline in the working place. The ground froze hard as iron, leaving agricultural workers unable to break ground for the winter planting. Road construction was impossible under the severe conditions, which left the gangs of casual laborers without labor to do. Coal mining came to a halt, and coal became more and more expensive. Those men who were out of work could no longer afford to heat their shanties, shacks, or hovels, and even the fortunate few who could find work had to make do with scraps of wood gleaned from rubbish heaps.

"My brothers, have you heard the results of the debates? Do you know that the division has resulted in the complete defeat of the Poor Aid Bill?" The speaker on the soapbox waved his arms, causing his black cloak to flap in the quickening wind and nearly losing his high black hat in the process.

If the crowd on Fleet Street had not heard the news, they were now informed. Already, cabs were pulling into the narrow street with reporters scrambling to give their hastily scribbled notes to their city editors to be worked into the late editions. There had been more heat than light in the words of the honorable gentlemen of the House of Commons, and what it amounted to was the information that the poor are always with us, that the House had no control of the weather, and that there would be no national alleviation of the general misery. Any assistance given to the destitute would have to come from the parish, town, borough, or village in which said paupers abided. In the case of London, that meant the Lord Mayor's Fund, which, according to the reporters coming from the eastern end of Fleet Street, was at an all-time low. Clearly, the good people of London had been dilatory in their consideration of those less fortunate than themselves in this year of disasters.

Even as the reporters were bringing their stories in, the news had gotten out through the greater medium of gossip. The cleaners and porters at Westminster were more vociferous than the gentlemen of the press. The version of the goings-on in Parliament that filtered down the chain from Whitehall through the Strand and into the back alleys of Soho and Seven Dials was far more inflammatory than anything that would be printed in the *Daily Worker*.

The speaker drew a crudely printed handbill out of his cloak and waved it at the crowd. "My brothers, the Fair Trade League has organized a meeting tonight in Trafalgar Square to demand work for those willing to do it. I tell you, friends and brothers in labor, this is not enough! We must unite and throw off the chains of oppression! The time is now!"

The time was nearly three o'clock, and the men of Fleet Street had better things on their collective minds than the words of radicals like Henry Hyndman on his soapbox. The afternoon editions had to be printed so that every literate Londoner could be informed of the latest news. Huge wagons with rolls of paper took up most of the space in the road, blocking omnibuses and cabs, while the horses whinnied and the drivers vented their displeasure in language that turned the air about them blue. Brawny men in knitted jerseys wrestled the rolls into the cellar printing plants, where compositors had already set the type and the steam was up, firing the rotary presses that would eventually spew out the afternoon editions of the London newspapers.

"Workers of London!" Hyndman shouted into the rapidly increasing crowd. "Do not be led by those who would compromise with your oppressors. Do not follow the Fair Trade League, who would delay the inevitable. Today, London; tomorrow, the world!"

Hyndman's words were faintly heard in the offices of *Youth's Companion,* in the building just opposite his stand. It was a tall, narrow brick building that had been built at the time of the present queen's coronation, when gas lighting, water mains, and basic chimneys had been considered adequate amenities for the workers therein. A paneled door surmounted by an elaborately carved lintel led to the upper three floors devoted to the business of the publication, while the ground floor held a small bookshop.

At the moment, only one of the upper floors was occupied, since the only fires lit in the building were those in the offices of Mr. Basset and his assistant, Mr. Andrew Levin. One writer, two copy editors, and an artist huddled around Mr. Levin's fire, warming their hands and effectively shielding anyone else from getting the benefit of what little heat the fire provided.

Mr. Levin, a darkly handsome young man, whose classic profile belied his less-than-classic accent, tried to move the others out of the way, but the bulk of Chief Writer David Peterson was considerable, and Staff Artist Edgar Roberts was too tall to be easily removed. The two copy editors, Roberto Monteverde and Winslow Howarth, had squeezed in next to the others, soaking in what comfort they could.

Mr. Levin looked around the office at the two men waiting to see Mr. Basset and sighed. It was not an office conducive to waiting. Mr. Basset preferred to conduct his business by mail rather than in person, and Mr. Levin had to agree that this was probably better for all concerned. If the full force of Mr. Basset's personality were felt, potential contributors might never return, let alone send in stories or drawings for *Youth's Companion*. Mr. Levin felt that while Mr. Peterson could undoubtedly provide enough material from his fertile imagination to propel the magazine into the next century, subscribers might be attracted to the idea of buying *Youth's Companion* in hopes of finding a story or poem by some well-known author. Mr. Levin was especially proud of having solicited and received several puzzles and conundrums as "filler" from the well-known children's author, Mr. Lewis Carroll. He hoped that a few more would answer his requests for material suitable for children.

He glanced at the elderly gentleman and his more youthful companion, who had been sitting on the wooden settle (the only seating in the anteroom other than Mr. Levin's own chair, behind Mr. Levin's rolltop desk). The elderly gentleman, a tall man in clerical black, had laid aside his old-fashioned high silk hat but had retained his long ulster against the cold. The other man, a stalwart redheaded young man with a bristling mustache, sported a dashing balbriggan plaid with a cape collar, and a tweed cap of the double-billed deerstalker variety.

The older man had apparently had enough of the punishment dealt out by the settle. He marched over to Mr. Levin's desk and stood over it with an accusing glare at the unfortunate young man. He fished out a large pocket watch from under his coat and consulted it, then addressed Mr. Levin. "Sir," he said, carefully controlling his tendency to stammer in moments of stress, "I have been waiting for forty minutes to see Mr. Basset. Is he or is he not in?"

4

From the sounds emerging from the closed door at the end of the office opposite the stairs, it would appear that Mr. Basset was in. Mr. Levin smiled weakly. "If you would give me your card, sir . . ."

"I have given you my card. I am Mr. Dodgson of Christ Church, Oxford. Mr. Basset sent me a kind note stating that anytime I found myself in London, he would be pleased to see me. I have the note here."

"Are you sure you have it with you?" murmured the man next to him.

The older man fumbled in his pocket. Out came an astonishing pile of oddities to be laid on Levin's desk: a brightly colored silk handkerchief, a length of string, a paper bag of lemon drops, and finally, a much-folded letter.

"Here it is," Mr. Dodgson said, waving the letter under Levin's nose. "As you see, it is a request for a small contribution to the magazine, originally addressed to my representative at Macmillan Press. They sent it on to me, and I sent the requested material, with the stipulation that it be used without payment and that the magazine be sent to charitable organizations free of charge." He frowned at the assistant, who picked up the letter carefully as if it might explode in his hands.

Mr. Levin examined the letter and returned it to the scholar with a condescending smile. "This, sir, is the letter I send all prospective contributors. It is a formality, not an introduction. I did not know that we had a contributor by the name of Dodgson."

The younger man spoke up for his friend, who was rendered speechless with mortification. "Mr. Dodgson is also known by the name of Lewis Carroll," he told Mr. Levin.

"But I do not usually acknowledge letters sent in that name," Mr. Dodgson added. "In this case, since Mr. Macmillan vouched for the authenticity of the publication, I made an exception."

The men huddled around the fire turned around at the sound of the name "Lewis Carroll." Mr. Peterson, the rotund and balding chief writer, stared at the older man. He ran a hand over the stringy remnants of his hair in a vain attempt to make himself presentable and uttered the words *Alice in Wonderland* in a voice of mingled awe and admiration. He buttoned his gaping waistcoat over his shirt and approached Mr. Dodgson with the reverence of one who is in the presence of a master of the craft.

"The precise title is *Alice's Adventures in Wonderland,*" Mr. Dodgson corrected him. "But I am the author of that work."

Mr. Howarth and Mr. Monteverde acknowledged the genius in their midst by bowing. The two men were both slight and bearded, and could have been mistaken for brothers, save that Mr. Howarth was dressed neatly in a tweed sack suit of dittos, while Mr. Monteverde sported a frock coat, dark trousers, and dandified embroidered waistcoat. The tall artist, Mr. Roberts, dressed in artistic velveteen trousers and jacket, with a woolen scarf around his neck in lieu of cravat, said nothing, but shook his mane of chestnut hair out of his eyes and sketched on his ever-present drawing pad.

As soon as he heard the name, Mr. Levin's face, so bland and superior, crumbled. "Oh, dear," he whispered, a guilty flush reddening his cheeks. "I had no idea you would actually come . . . very few of our outside contributors take the time . . ."

"I thought I might introduce my friend Dr. Arthur Conan Doyle to Mr. Basset," Mr. Dodgson said carefully. "He has written several stories that I consider worthy of publication in this magazine. His works have been published in *Cornhill* and *The Boy's Own Paper.* And he's Dicky Doyle's nephew, you know."

The last recommendation was offered as a final sop to Mr. Levin's conscience. Mr. Levin tried to soothe the agitated scholar. "Mr. Basset is occupied and may not be available for some time. He is, after all, a very busy man."

"Perhaps we should come back at another time," Dr. Doyle murmured with a rueful smile.

Mr. Levin had thoughts of the notable author escaping, disparaging *Youth's Companion,* and refusing to offer any more of his works to the publication. He rose, displaying a dashing checked waistcoat under his impeccably tailored frock coat. "I shall tell Mr. Basset that you are here," he said, approaching the inner office door with an air of trepidation. "He rarely sees anyone without an appointment, but in your case, sir, I am sure he will make an exception."

"And if he doesn't, we will," Mr. Peterson added. "If nothing else, sir, we will stand you to a drink at Ye Olde Cheshire Cheese down the street. Mr. Lewis Carroll, sir, you have been my inspiration! I just read *The Hunting of the Snark* for the third time. It's a masterpiece! And my oldest girl is just the right age for *Alice.*"

Before Mr. Dodgson could cope with his admirer, a young woman entered the office carrying a box tied with twine. Her high cheekbones and long sharp nose were flushed with her exertions, giving her features a rosy glow that was echoed in her red woolen hat and mittens. Her shabby but serviceable gray cloak covered a drab dress with only a token bustle instead of the enormous gathering of fabric at the base of the spine demanded by fashion.

"Good afternoon, Mr. Levin," she said, setting the box precariously on top of the front of the desk.

"Miss Harvey!" Mr. Levin rescued the box and placed it on the desk itself. "Manuscripts typed already? How efficient of you."

"Well, sir, if I must earn my living, I must do it well," she said with a rueful smile that revealed a dimple at the corner of her mouth. "And I can do the typing at home, where I can be within call of Mama."

"How is your mother?" Mr. Levin asked, as he untied the string and opened the box of typed manuscript.

"As always. Some days she is quite well enough to go out, but with this dreadful cold, she has not been outside the house for nearly a month." Miss Harvey looked over the top of the desk. "Are the pages all right? There were a few small errors, but I think I corrected them all. . . ."

Mr. Levin smiled weakly. "I shall inform Mr. Basset," he said, rising and moving to the door to the office as he did so.

"And inform Mr. Basset that we are waiting," Mr. Dodgson added.

A tall man in worn and patched trousers and knitted jersey sweater covered with an ink-stained apron stamped into the anteroom. His hands, covered in fingerless woolen gloves, were smeared with ink, and a paper cap covered his curling red hair. He advanced on the shrinking Levin and thrust his jaw out pugnaciously.

"I want a word with His Lordship," he stated in a ripe Irish brogue.

"O'Casey!" Mr. Levin look shocked. "How many times have you been told that you are not to appear on this floor unless you are called?"

"Well, I have been called." O'Casey looked around the room for supporters and found only an interested audience. "Me men have called me to speak up for them. Is Mr. Basset in, or has he gone off to tea with the friend of his bosom?"

Mr. Levin tried to regain control of the situation. "Mr. Basset is occupied," he said primly.

A muffled roar from the inner office made that obvious.

"Occupied with what? He sits in his office, warm as toast, and me and me men freeze our . . ."

"O'Casey!" Mr. Peterson nodded in the direction of Miss Harvey.

"Sorry, Miss, I didn't see you." O'Casey nodded at the young woman, then turned back to Levin. "How am I supposed to print when the ink's frozen in its jars? How's Monahan supposed to set type, with his fingers sticking to the very pans? Not a coal for the fire, not even a few sticks of wood, and not a man of us don't have the cough." He sniffled into a large bandanna for emphasis.

"I am a doctor," Dr. Doyle announced. "I would be glad to . . ."

O'Casey was not seeking treatment. "When can we get a fire?"

"You were given an allowance for coals at the beginning of the year," Levin reminded him.

"Aye, and we've used it up," O'Casey countered. "And what we want to know is, when do we get more?" He advanced upon the helpless secretary.

Mr. Peterson interposed his considerable bulk between the printer and the secretary. "Steady on, O'Casey," he said firmly. "There's no point in beating on poor old Levin here. He's not

8

the one who won't spend the shilling or two on coal. He's just the errand boy."

"He keeps the books, don't he?" O'Casey was not to be mollified. " 'Tis his hand doles out the pay packets. He could cook the books for a few extra pounds of coal if he wished, and why not?"

"Because it would not be right," Mr. Dodgson said, but his clerical whisper went unheard in the general mumble of agreement.

"Mr. Levin," Miss Harvey said, adding her voice to the din, "I really must have my payment. Mama is waiting for me, and it was beginning to snow when I got off the Underground."

"The money box is kept in Mr. Basset's office," Mr. Levin pointed out. "If Mr. Basset is otherwise occupied, I dare not interrupt him."

"Then you can damned . . . that is, you can print your own magazine," O'Casey said furiously. "Either me and me men get a fire, or we go on strike!"

"But . . ." Levin looked for support. He found none in the faces of Peterson, Monteverde, or Howarth. Roberts glowered fiercely, shook back his hair, and began another sketch, staring at Miss Harvey as if he had never seen her like before.

"I shall speak with Mr. Basset," Levin said, giving way to popular sentiment.

Before he could move, the door to the inner office flew open. A tall man swathed in a long fur coat, topped with a slouch hat, emerged and strode dramatically across the anteroom. He paused for effect at the top of the stairs.

"You are being quite shortsighted," he told the enraged editor in tones of icy contempt. "I am going to be very famous shortly, and you will only be remembered as the man who refused to hire Oscar Wilde. Good day, sir!" He swept grandly out the door, leaving the rest of the company staring at him open-mouthed.

Mr. Basset glared at the assemblage in the anteroom. He was a tall stout man with a short beard, whose few gray hairs betrayed the advance of middle age, dressed in the frock coat, black waistcoat, and black trousers demanded by his position. He peered

9

through his spectacles at the group and demanded, "What are all these people doing in here, Levin?"

"Well, Mr. Basset . . ." the young assistant began. His voice was drowned by those of the other petitioners.

O'Casey stepped forward. "I've got seven men down in the cellar, and the printing press is frozen solid, along with the inks," he declared. "How're we to work if there's no fire? A pound'll buy us coal. . . ."

"I have finished your manuscripts, Mr. Basset," Miss Harvey interrupted the printer. "And I really must be paid for my work so that I may get on home before the snow gets any worse."

"And we're down here because we have no fires upstairs," Peterson said, speaking as the representative of the staff. "How can we write about African safaris and the jungles of the Amazon when our pens are freezing in our fingers? And Eddie can't do the woodblocks properly if his hands are so stiff he can't hold the knife." He looked at the artist for agreement. Mr. Roberts's scowl deepened as his pencil danced over the pages of his sketchbook.

Mr. Basset looked at his staff, as if trying to assess which of their requests to deny first. Then his eye fell upon the two strangers. "What are these men doing here?" he demanded of Levin.

"Mr. Dodgson and Dr. Doyle," Levin performed the necessary introductions. "Mr. Dodgson has come from Oxford to persuade you to look at some of Dr. Doyle's stories. I suppose he has heard that you are considering taking on another staff writer and has come to apply for the post."

"If he's anything like that lunatic who just left, I won't like him," Basset grumbled. "Well, come on in, and I'll take a look at what you've brought me. The rest of you"—he glared around the anteroom once again—"get back to work!"

"Back to work, is it?" O'Casey tilted his paper cap over one eye. "Until me and me men get a fire, we're out on strike! And don't think you can get scabs from the Portman Penny Press, because I'm going to have a word with them. Workers unite!" He could be heard stamping his way down the stairs, punctuated by a slamming door.

"Ungrateful Irish wretch," Mr. Basset muttered. "Well, Dodgson, or whatever your name is, come on in, since you're here. Doyle, I hope you write something besides fairy tales. That last fellow turned my stomach."

Mr. Basset marched into his office, with Mr. Dodgson and Dr. Doyle behind him. The rest of them huddled together in front of the fire and waited until he should emerge from his lair again.

CHAPTER 2

M r. Samuel Basset's private office filled most of the first floor of the narrow *Youth's Companion* building. It was a long narrow room with tall windows fronting onto Fleet Street, whose paneled walls held cherished mementos of Mr. Basset's youthful exploits in Africa. Photographs of a young Sam with his dearest friend, Mr. Nicholas Portman, standing over assorted dead animals, with their native bearers obediently looking on, were placed between the stuffed and mounted heads of antelopes with curved and twisted horns. The roaring fire was surmounted by a mantelpiece of black marble that held carved wooden statues of African deities. The door itself was flanked by a pair of African tribal spears.

There were two chairs, upholstered in leopard skin, in front of Mr. Basset's desk, for use by visitors. The desk itself was a large, well-made piece of furniture, whose surface was covered with untidy piles of manuscripts, galley proofs, and correspondence, each held down by a separate artifact. A short brass dagger served as a paperweight on one pile of printed proof sheets, while a longer, thinner knife was laid across the pile of accounts receivable. An oddly curved clublike object held down a pile of handwritten manuscripts to be read, and a knife with a curved blade lay atop the written correspondence to be answered.

Mr. Basset took his own chair, large and well-upholstered but not particularly ostentatious, and regarded his unexpected visitors with an exasperated sigh.

"I am a very busy man," he stated. "I can give you," he consulted his pocket watch, "twenty minutes. We have a magazine to put out."

"Then I will be brief," Mr. Dodgson said. "This is my friend, Dr. Arthur Conan Doyle. Dicky Doyle's nephew," he added, as Mr. Basset's frown appeared to indicate total incomprehension.

"I have sent some manuscripts to you," Dr. Doyle reminded him. "However, I have not received any indication one way or another as to whether you intended to publish any of my stories, and when Mr. Dodgson invited me to London to meet some of his literary friends . . ."

Mr. Basset held up a hand for silence while he delved into the pile of handwritten manuscripts.

"That's mine," Dr. Doyle said, pointing to one packet.

Mr. Basset grunted an assent and frowned as he scanned the stories. "Oh yes," he said, in a voice that left no doubt of his total dismissal of the product before him. "I remember these. I thought I had told Levin to return them. You say you're a doctor, young man?"

Dr. Doyle nodded modestly.

"In that case, I suggest that you cease polluting your mind with such thoughts and resume your medical practice. You will do more good and less harm!" He tossed the manuscripts back to their author with a sniff of disdain.

"I beg your pardon!" Dr. Doyle's mustache bristled.

Mr. Basset continued his tirade. "I have never read such a perverse tale in my life! An ancient Egyptian mummy coming to life! Or this one, *Captain of the Polestar*. What sort of thing is that for a young man to read? Mysterious doings in the Arctic? Female forms drifting out of the mist?"

"I have been in the Arctic," Dr. Doyle protested. "Such things occur!"

13

"And the tales are quite well-written," Mr. Dodgson added, in defense of his protégé.

"I will not publish this sort of thing in *Youth's Companion,*" Mr. Basset proclaimed. "I want stories of adventure, stories that will rouse the spirit of young Englishmen to take the banner of Empire and fly it across the globe!" Mr. Basset fairly swelled with patriotic pride as he regarded the signed photograph of His Royal Highness, the Prince of Wales, which had been given a prominent place on his desk. "The stories I want will encourage boys . . ."

"And girls," Mr. Dodgson put in.

Mr. Basset glared over his glasses at the person who had the audacity to interrupt him. "Girls do not read *Youth's Companion,*" he stated flatly.

"I beg to differ," Mr. Dodgson said. "Miss Alicia Marbury, the daughter of Lord Richard Marbury, has confided to me that she was sustained during her ordeal last summer by the recollection of stories she had read in your excellent publication and others like it."

Mr. Basset stroked his beard and harumphed loudly. "Miss Marbury may be an exceptional young lady. Her father is, after all, a noted Liberal and something of a firebrand. However, I maintain that these stories of Dr. Doyle are not suitable for any publication and certainly not one meant for the entertainment of the young. I might as well have published those mawkish effusions of that Irish popinjay who just left."

"Do you refer to Mr. Wilde?" Mr. Dodgson asked.

"Do you know him?" Mr. Basset's eyes narrowed in suspicion.

"I do not number him among my acquaintance," Mr. Dodgson admitted. "But he was most conspicuous when he was up at Oxford. He was not at the House. . . . that is, at Christ Church," he explained, "but he was noticed. That was, after all, his intention."

"Oh, he's noticeable," Mr. Basset snorted. "I have no patience with that sort of tomfoolery. And what did he offer as proof of his ability to write for young people? Two of the most mawkish fairy tales I have ever read, one about a giant in a garden and the other about a talking statue. Disgusting pap!"

Dr. Doyle looked confused. "Sir, if you reject tales of horror and suspense, and you also reject fairy stories, what do you want?"

"I want stories of valiant young men fighting Nature and the Elements," Mr. Basset roared out. He grabbed a copy of *Youth's Companion* from the pile on his desk and thrust it at Dr. Doyle. "Read this, young doctor, and then you will understand what I want. In the meanwhile, go back home to Yorkshire ..."

"Portsmouth," Dr. Doyle corrected him.

"... and try not to kill too many of your patients. Good day!" Mr. Basset rose in dismissal. Mr. Dodgson stood, bowed, and accepted the rebuff with as much grace as he could. As he opened the door, Messrs. Peterson, Howarth, Monteverde, and Roberts piled in, shoving Mr. Dodgson and Dr. Doyle aside in their eagerness to have a word with their editor in chief.

"Haven't you got anything better to do than to stand about in the anteroom?" Mr. Basset demanded of his loyal staff. "We're supposed to go to press tomorrow, and from what I see we aren't half ready." He indicated the galley proofs on his desk with a sweep of one hand.

"It's too cold upstairs," Peterson complained. "Besides, we've just come up with a grand idea, standing about, as you put it."

"What sort of an idea?" Mr. Basset took refuge behind his desk.

"A new sort of magazine," Peterson explained.

"A new way of telling the story," Monteverde enthused.

"A combination of text and illustration," Howarth added.

"In color!" Peterson finished for the quartet.

"In color?" Mr. Basset echoed.

"It works this way," Peterson told him. "Eddie, here, does the illustrations for our stories. The illustrations further the action, so that the reader sees the action instead of having it described to him. The story is laid out, frame by frame, with the dialogue as captions, under the illustrations ..."

"Or, perhaps, written over the characters' heads, like a ... a ..." Howarth fished for a word.

"A balloon?" Mr. Dodgson provided the answer, fascinated by the concept.

"That's it! A balloon!" Peterson turned to the editor. "We've got some dandy story lines, and Eddie thinks he can come up with the illustrations. We could try one out in the next issue, and perhaps do it as a serial, have the hero hanging over a cliff or something like that, so that the readers would have to buy the next issue to find out what happens next."

Basset considered the idea. "It has some merit," he admitted. "But what about literary content? We have to assure the parents of our subscribers that their children are receiving the best literary efforts for their shillings. A story told largely in pictures is hardly new!"

"But not the kind of story we're going to tell!" Peterson fairly climbed over the desk in his enthusiasm. "Have you read M. Verne's stories? Flights to the Moon or to the planet Mars! Explorations into the heart of the Amazon jungle to discover dinosaurs still living! Think of that! And in color . . ."

"Color!" Basset's voice rose from basso to countertenor. "Color printing?"

"It wouldn't be that much more," Peterson argued. "I hear there's a new process just developed, and O'Casey's men can handle anything we give them." He leaned over the desk again, dislodging a set of galley proofs from the top of one pile. He automatically bent to retrieve the pages, then looked harder at the top sheet.

His round face grew crimson. "Isn't this my story?" he said, flipping his way through the pages. "It is! This is 'King Arthur Comes to London.' " He shook the offending pages in Basset's face. "This is the story you told me wasn't good enough for *Youth's Companion*. I lined that story out for you at the summer picnic, and you said it would never go over, that I should forget about it, and here it is; you've taken my idea and run with it!"

"And he's put his own name on it, too," Monteverde pointed out, peering at the offending pages over his friend's shoulder.

Howarth took the pages out of Peterson's hands, looked them over, then passed them on to Roberts.

"And it's illustrated!" Roberts's voice shook at the thought of someone else illustrating a story for *Youth's Companion*. "With

16

color plates! You never let me do color plates!" He slammed the pages down on the desk in fury.

"You only told me the story," Basset grumbled, shifting uneasily in his chair. "You never wrote it down."

"Only because you told me not to waste my time with it," Peterson retorted. "Then you loaded me up with so much other work that I never did get back to it. And here it is, under your name, to be published by Portman Penny Press, by your good old friend Nicky, to be sold across the length and breadth of England, wherever the Penny Press can get a foothold! I should have you up on charges!" He fairly panted in his rage.

"Of what?" Basset smiled nastily over his beard. "One cannot steal an idea. How do you know that I didn't make it better than anything you could have written, you helpless hack! If I hadn't taken you in here you'd still be scribbling penny dreadfuls over at the Penny Press!"

"I ought to leave you flat, Basset!" Peterson snarled. "See if you can get someone else to write to order for one pound ten a week!"

Basset leaned back in his chair and said smugly, "You won't, Peterson, because you've got two children, and there aren't many steady positions open for a mediocre writer with a taste for the finer things and a wife with social ambitions. As for the rest of you"—Basset looked them over, like a schoolmaster chastising an unruly class—"be glad you are not like those ruffians out there, starving in the streets! None of you could manage to support yourselves without me. Call yourselves editors! A failed playwright, a menu-writer, and as for you"—he turned to Roberts—"if it weren't for me you'd still be in that shop turning out comic Valentines and vulgar Christmas cards!"

Roberts lunged over the desk, his hand clutched around one of the daggers. Howarth and Monteverde clung to each of his arms, trying to control their unruly comrade-in-arms.

Basset continued his tirade. "I could find another staff in a minute. Anyone on the street would be in here like a shot if they knew they could bring down a steady wage."

"Not if they have to put up with these conditions," Peterson shot back. "At least at the Penny Press we had a fire in the work-

17

room and a cup of tea in the afternoon. I've half a mind to join O'Casey and the rest of the men out on the streets in protest."

Basset's face turned red at the thought of such a defection. Dr. Doyle stepped forward, to be ready when Mr. Basset's impending apoplectic fit should manifest itself. "I suggest you breathe deeply," the young doctor said, "and that you open your collar and waistcoat."

Mr. Basset looked up, chagrined as he realized that Mr. Dodgson and Dr. Doyle had witnessed the whole scene and echoes had undoubtedly reached as far as the anteroom.

He took the deep breath prescribed by Dr. Doyle, and said, "I do apologize, Mr., er"—he glanced at the card on the desk—"Mr. Dodgson. And your attentions will not be needed, Dr. Doyle. I am quite all right. Levin!"

Mr. Levin edged into the office. "Yes, Mr. Basset?"

"I want to have a word with you." Mr. Basset's tone was ominously calm.

"Yes, sir. Mr. Basset, the typewritten copy for next week's issue is here, and the young woman expects to be paid. If you please, sir, I must get the cash box." The secretary sidled over to the desk and attempted to reach the sacred drawer where the ready money was kept.

"What's this about women in the office?" Mr. Basset's voice rose again. "I thought I told you . . ."

"Miss Harvey is a skilled typewriter, who works from her home," Levin explained. "She placed an advertisement in the newspapers. I thought it might be useful to have the handwritten manuscripts typewritten before they went to compositors."

"A good compositor can work perfectly well from manuscript," Mr. Basset stated flatly, as if this argument had already been won.

Mr. Levin disagreed. "There have been too many typos," he objected. "The last one was really bad. The story dealt with a farm winch, and the compositor printed it as farm wench. We can't have that sort of thing in *Youth's Companion.*" He lifted his eyebrows in disdain at the vulgarity of typesetters.

"And how much am I supposed to pay this female?" Mr. Basset

grumbled, as he fumbled on his watch-chain for the keys to the strongbox.

"She gets twopence per page; she has typed 120 pages, which would mean twenty shillings, or a pound for the entire manuscript," Levin reeled off.

"A whole pound?" Basset looked up from his labors. "I want to see this typing before I part with that kind of money."

He strode back into the anteroom, where Miss Harvey sat on the wooden bench, stubbornly waiting for her money. Before he could say anything more, yet another young woman timidly knocked on the office door, a plain-looking girl barely out of her teens, in a fur jacket and hat, clutching a cardboard portfolio.

"I was told I could leave some drawings off," she said hesitantly.

"Who are you?" Mr. Basset roared at her.

Mr. Roberts explained, "This is Miss Potter. I think she shows promise. We met at the Natural History museum. I suggested she bring her portfolio in." For Mr. Roberts, this was an oration, and the others gazed at Miss Potter with renewed respect.

"And I suppose this is the work in question?" Mr. Basset pointed to the portfolio the young woman held under her arm.

Miss Potter nodded wordlessly, undid the strings of the portfolio and pulled out a few pencil drawings. Mr. Dodgson drew near, for a better look.

"Quite nicely done," he said approvingly. "Charmingly domestic. I especially like the rabbit."

Mr. Basset was not in the mood for charming rabbits. "If this is the best you can do, young woman, I would suggest you go home and take up another form of recreation. You will never be an artist, Miss Potter, and anyone who told you you could was lying to you. Good day!"

Miss Potter's eyes filled with tears. Mr. Roberts glowered at Basset, as if to say, You know nothing about art and less about teaching it!

As Roberts led the stricken Miss Potter down the stairs, Basset turned on Miss Harvey. "As for you," he declared, "you are a wretched typist. I detect typographical errors on the first three pages. I will not pay more than a penny apiece for these, and I will not pay at all until they are redone."

"But I must have something. . . . I must get back to Mama . . ." Miss Harvey sputtered. She looked about for support and found none.

Mr. Basset gave a final glare around the room and stalked into his office, slamming the door behind him.

"What shall I do?" Miss Harvey said miserably. "I spent my last penny on the Underground, and I cannot walk all the way back to Chelsea."

Mr. Levin fumbled in his pockets and came up with a few coins. "This will get you back home," he said apologetically. "I shall see to it that you are paid as soon as Mr. Basset is satisfied."

"Ha!" Peterson gave a crack of mirthless laughter. "You won't stand up to the Hound. And don't think you're any more important to him than the rest of us poor slaves, Levin. You may put on a clean collar every day and sport a dandy waistcoat, but you're still just office staff, the same as any of us."

"Perhaps," Levin said, nettled. "But there is always Mr. Portman. I can always go to him and . . ."

"And do what? Tell him that his old Winchester schoolmate is a bully and a thief? I'd like to see you try!" Peterson turned to Mr. Dodgson with an apologetic smile. "Sorry you had to see all that, sir. Basset's not always so bad."

"Oh yes, he is," Howarth muttered, and Monteverde nodded in agreement. They heard Roberts's tread on the stairs and looked at each other knowingly.

"Eddie's in another pet," Peterson said philosophically. "And I suppose I'll have to pour the oil on troubled waters once Basset finishes with Levin." He turned back to the fire again.

Mr. Dodgson turned to his friend and said, "Dr. Doyle, I fear I have dragged you to London on a fool's errand. I apologize for wasting your time as well as mine in making the acquaintance of Mr. Samuel Basset. Perhaps we will take some tea, and then I can see you to your train for Portsmouth."

Dr. Doyle nodded in agreement, and the two moved toward the door as an outraged yell came from the direction of the inner office. "Levin! Get in here at once!"

Mr. Levin jumped like a startled deer. "At once, Mr. Basset."

Miss Harvey stared after him as he bolted into the inner office.

"What's gotten into him?" Monteverde asked the world in general.

"I think Basset just read the ledgers," Peterson said, with a malicious grin. "I don't think they quite match with what Basset thinks they should be."

"Cooking the books, is he?" Howarth commented.

"Paying people under the table, more likely," Monteverde said with a shrug. "Basset's such a squeezer, he resents every penny spent."

"Well, our salaries won't make or break the bank," Peterson said philosophically. "Pity he's in such a mood because I've just heard I'm to be a father again. . . ."

"Really? Congratulations!" Monteverde and Howarth chimed in.

"All very well for you two, you're bachelors," Peterson sighed. "Myrna's having a hard enough time now making ends meet, and when I tell her about Basset stealing my book idea she'll be livid. I thought I could negotiate a rise, but with Basset in this mood, it's impossible."

"You don't suppose he'd really fire the lot of us, do you?" Howarth asked anxiously.

Peterson smirked and shook his head. "You saw how he treated Wilde, and Wilde's a coming man. The Hound won't have anyone on the staff who's a better writer than he is, except for me and you, of course. As for getting line and copy editors from Portman Penny Press, Nicky might have a thing to say about that. No, he'll do what he's always done, make a good deal of noise and come around in the end. I just wish he'd do it faster, that's all."

Levin emerged from the office, breathless and pale. His hands shook as he placed a pile of ledgers on his desk. He ran one hand over his hair, then twitched his cravat back into place.

"Mr. Basset wishes to speak with you, Mr. Peterson," he said formally.

"Mr. Levin, what has happened?" Miss Harvey asked.

"Mr. Basset has discovered that I have been, as he puts it, usurping his authority. His reaction to my hiring you to do our typewriting was not what I had expected it to be. He was not pleased at all that the manuscripts were being typed outside the confines of the office, and when I suggested that you might be hired to do the typing here, the words were, 'Over my dead body.'"

"I had no idea he was so . . . so against females," Miss Harvey said, with a glance at the door behind which the ogre lurked.

"What is more, he was particularly upset about my contacts with our contributors, which he claimed was his business and no one else's. And he's been counting the money in the box and claims there are certain discrepancies."

"Been nicking the pocket change, have you?" Peterson asked jovially.

Levin ignored him. "I have never heard such language," he sputtered. "I have been compared to Brutus and Judas, when all I wanted to do was to make the magazine better by attracting more contributors. Mr. Basset took it in bad part that I had taken the liberty of corresponding with them myself."

"Oh dear," Mr. Dodgson fussed. "I thought I was welcome here, but it seems I have made a dreadful mistake. I should never have come in unannounced, and I shall never do so again."

Levin managed to smile at the scholar in his distress. "It was not your fault, sir. It would have come out eventually. I did not think Mr. Basset would react quite as strongly as he has done."

"Why? What's he done?" Howarth asked.

Levin's voice shook with emotion. "He is talking about prosecution on criminal charges!" he announced dramatically.

"What? That's absurd!" Miss Harvey exclaimed.

"According to Mr. Basset, there is a certain sum in the ledgers that is not accounted for, and if I do not come up with the money, I will be prosecuted!"

"That old . . ." Peterson bit back the words. His normally jovial expression darkened. "He's gone too far this time. I'd better have a word with him and remind him of old times, toiling in the staff room at Portman Penny Press."

"Please, do not put yourself out on my account," Levin said curtly. "I will not remain where I am not wanted."

Peterson tried to soothe the agitated young man. "Look here, Levin, you know how we all depend on you to keep the old Hound sweet. Let me have a go at him, make him see reason . . ."

"No!" he shouted out. Then his voice lowered. "Mr. Peterson, you have had enough of Mr. Basset's ill will this afternoon. I will, no doubt, find some other position."

"Not if he makes you face criminal prosecution," Peterson stated. He knocked resolutely on Mr. Basset's door.

Mr. Dodgson would have stayed, but Dr. Doyle had heard more than enough of domestic squabbles. "There must be a pub where we can get some hot buttered rum," Dr. Doyle said, dragging his older friend down the stairs to the street. "And then I'm off home. It's not your fault, sir, that Samuel Basset is such a crosspatch, and cannot recognize a good story when he sees it, but that is that. There are other editors who will take my stories if he won't, I'm sure of it."

Mr. Dodgson looked up at the sky. "It is snowing," he observed. "I sincerely hope you will be able to reach Portsmouth before midnight."

In that, as in so many other things during that evening, he was to be disappointed.

CHAPTER 3

The snow that had started as a few stray flakes when Miss Harvey had mounted the stairs to the offices of *Youth's Companion* had increased in intensity, so that by the time Mr. Dodgson and Dr. Doyle emerged from the offices of *Youth's Companion*, Fleet Street was veiled in a sheet of white that whirled and eddied in the wind. Much to Dr. Doyle's dismay, Mr. Dodgson would not take his prescription of hot toddies.

"I cannot be seen in a common tavern," Mr. Dodgson said, as he dragged his companion up and down Fleet Street in search of a respectable establishment where the two of them could drink tea, and only tea. Alas for Dr. Doyle, Fleet Street catered to the hard-drinking Fourth Estate, and no suitable tea shop could be found. They struggled against the wind, up and down the street, and Mr. Dodgson was still unsatisfied, while Dr. Doyle wished heartily that he had found a less persnickety companion.

They were back at the Strand end of Fleet Street, in front of *Youth's Companion*, still without tea, when Mr. Dodgson called a halt. The two men stopped in the nearest doorway. Mr. Dodgson gripped his hat with gray-gloved hands, while Dr. Doyle seriously considered tying the flaps of his deerstalker cap under his chin to protect his ears from the cold. Around them surged men in caped greatcoats, long ulsters buttoned to the chin, or dramatic cloaks. Necks were swathed in everything from fine cashmere scarfs to hand-knitted mufflers wound around freezing faces. All up and down Fleet Street the umbrella vendors did a thriving business, as the passersby tried to protect their expensive headgear from the weather. Hardier souls in cloth caps or woolen hats and women in voluminous skirts and shawls hawked hot pies or steamed shellfish from barrows and carts. Mingling with the crowd were the men from the Fair Trade League, passing out handbills announcing the Grand March and Meeting in Trafalgar Square, in protest of the bill just defeated, at seven o'clock that evening.

The sight of the Fair Trade League drove Mr. Hyndman to new heights of rhetoric from his position of authority on the soapbox. "My brothers in labor, you have heard, as I have, that the members of Parliament have decided to deny you the pittance you request for common aid. Shall you stand by and wait for them to dole out the few pennies you need to buy coals for your fires and bread for your wives and children?"

The assorted reporters, street vendors, businessmen, and loungers muttered their agreement.

"He has a point," Dr. Doyle observed. "It has been a wretched winter. Even the dry docks at Portsmouth have had to lay off day laborers, and the fishing fleet's been iced in for a month."

"The weather has been frightful," Mr. Dodgson agreed. He fussed about, looking first in one pocket and then in another for the small sums he had put aside for cab fares. He edged closer into the doorway of the shop and noticed for the first time the wares exhibited in the window.

"A bookshop!" he exclaimed in delight.

"So I see, sir." Dr. Doyle looked up and down Fleet Street for transportation, while Mr. Dodgson was drawn like a magnet towards the shop.

The front window held an enticing variety of printed matter, displayed to entice the passersby to stop and examine and, eventually, to buy. The right-hand shelf contained the collected works of the Portman Penny Press: small paper-backed volumes, each an eye-catching yellow, with a woodblock illustration on the cover to entice the passerby to sample the adventures of *Dangerous Dan the Highwayman* or share the sorrows of *The Virtuous Chambermaid*. On a more serious note were the series of books that would instruct the reader in *The Mysteries of the East* or explain *The Monuments of Ancient Egypt*. The Portman Penny Press was ready to provide reading matter for every taste at the cheapest possible price.

The other side of the shop clearly catered to a different audience, as evinced by the quality of merchandise in the left-hand window. Here were books with embossed or painted covers, opened to reveal illustrations of fairy palaces and exotic creatures, Arabian Nights' genies, or elfin dancers of English folklore. More prosaic volumes showed maps of the world, unusual animals, or diagrams of mechanical marvels. Here, too, were educational toys: telescopes for budding astronomers, butterfly nets for young naturalists, globes for future explorers.

Mr. Dodgson smiled happily as he regarded the shop window. He beckoned to Dr. Doyle. "I see they have copies of *Alice*. I shall go inside. Perhaps they will permit me to sign a copy. It sometimes helps sales," he added, to justify his sense of pride.

Dr. Doyle had more or less given up hope of finding a cab in the snowy street. As soon as a hansom or a hack was empty, it was immediately commandeered by one of the reporters or editors emerging from the many newspaper offices that made Fleet Street synonymous with the British press. Dr. Doyle decided that the shop provided some protection from the weather and followed Mr. Dodgson into the shop, brushing the snow off his shoulders as he did so.

Mr. Dodgson had picked up a copy of *Alice's Adventures in Wonderland* and was frowning at it. "This book should not be here," he declared.

"This is a shop that specializes in books for children," Dr. Doyle pointed out.

"Of course it is," Mr. Dodgson said querulously. "But this particular printing was not to be sold. I shall speak to the proprietor." He called out imperiously, "Is someone there?"

A fine-boned balding man in a cutaway coat and striped trousers approached, eager to make one last sale before closing time.

"May I be of assistance, gentlemen?" he asked, assessing the sales potential of his two customers.

"What do you know of this book?" Mr. Dodgson shook the offending volume under the shopkeeper's nose.

"*Alice's Adventures in Wonderland.* A charming fairy tale, written, I believe, by an Oxford don, especially for a young lady of his acquaintance. It has been in print for many years and is considered acceptable for all children. Have you a complaint to make of it?" The shopkeeper looked anxiously from one man to the other.

"I do indeed," Mr. Dodgson said. "Where did you get this copy?"

"I beg your pardon?" The shopkeeper stared at Mr. Dodgson as if he had just sprouted horns and a tail.

"This is the first p-printing!" Mr. Dodgson shook the book fiercely in the shopkeeper's face. "This p-printing was d-defective and was n-not to b-be sold." He turned to Dr. Doyle and took a deep breath, to keep his stammer under control. "Tenniel felt the illustrations were not properly engraved and insisted on doing them over," he explained. "On reflection I agreed, but decided that rather than destroy the books, which I had, after all, paid for, this printing was to be recalled and the copies distributed among village libraries and institutions for poor children who could not afford the price of a good copy. I know these illustrations perfectly, and this is the first printing, not the one to be sold. Therefore, I ask you, sir, where did you get it? And why is it being sold for full price? And why," he continued, advancing on the hapless shopkeeper, "if it is being sold at full price, am I not receiving full royalties on it?"

"Are you Mr. Lewis Carroll?" the shopkeeper asked, taking refuge behind his counter.

"In this case, I am!"

"Then I must inform you, sir, that I am not the proprietor of this shop. It is Mr. Basset who controls the stock, not I. In fact," he added, seeing Mr. Dodgson's grim expression, "these copies turned up when we cleared out the stockroom. Mr. Portman seemed to think that they had been given to his father when Sir William Portman used the building and ran the shop himself. It is possible that, having given some of the copies to worthy institutions, Mr. Nicholas and Mr. Basset decided to appropriate them and sell them, thinking, no doubt, that the minor imperfections in the printing of the illustrations would go unnoticed by the general public. And, to be quite truthful, Mr. Carroll, no one has noticed. The book sells quite well, and those imperfections in the illustrations that seem so dreadful to you are overlooked in the excellence of the writing. I am very sorry that you are not pleased, sir, but do not take offense with me. You must speak with Mr. Basset. I had nothing to do with it."

Dr. Doyle had been peering out of the window at the snow while the battle raged. Now he called out, "Here's your chance, Mr. Dodgson. It looks as if Mr. Basset is leaving the office. He just came out the door."

Mr. Dodgson retained his hold on the book. "I shall not pay for this copy," he fumed. "Remove the rest of them from your stock. If you like, you may send the bill to me at my Oxford direction. I shall instruct Macmillan to send replacement copies, of a better printing than this, suitable for sale. As for Mr. Basset, I shall confront him myself."

"If you want to speak to Mr. Basset, you had better be quick," Dr. Doyle called to his mentor from his position at the door. "I think he's just flagged down an omnibus."

"We must catch him before he mounts it," Mr. Dodgson declared, bustling out the door. Dr. Doyle cast a look of apology over his shoulder at the clerk and followed Mr. Dodgson into the snowy street, where Mr. Basset stood on the sidewalk, hanging onto the handles of the doorway, apparently arguing with someone while the omnibus waited, trapped between a cab and a dray.

"Mr. Basset!" Mr. Dodgson called out, "May I have a word . . ."

Mr. Basset was already having words with the large person in front of him, who had pulled him away from the omnibus and was now confronting him with upraised fist.

"Mr. Basset, I must speak with you!" Mr. Dodgson shouted, as the omnibus lurched away. Basset turned slowly, as if to see who had addressed him. He put out a hand, reaching blindly for support. Mr. Dodgson automatically steadied the man with one arm, while he tried to control his stammer long enough to make his wishes known.

Before he could speak, Mr. Basset sagged downward, his knees buckling under his weight. Dr. Doyle leaped forward to ease the stricken man to the snowy pavement.

For a moment the incident was not noticed. Then someone realized that a man had fallen. Reporters in battered hats and patched greatcoats, vendors of apples and hot pies, newsboys in tattered castoffs waiting for their evening wares, all stopped to see what was going on. Even the street-corner orator stopped haranguing the crowd long enough to come down from his soapbox and have a look.

"I am a doctor!" Dr. Doyle announced. "Stand back and give this man air. And someone fetch the police! This man has been injured."

One of the reporters waved and shouted at someone on the Strand. Another ran toward Ludgate Circus. Dr. Doyle looked wildly about to find some place out of the wind and snow where Basset could find shelter.

Basset seemed to recover consciousness for a minute. He clutched at Dr. Doyle's coat, his mouth working, spittle dribbling from one corner of his mouth. Mr. Dodgson leaned over him as the man tried to speak.

"What is he saying?" Mr. Dodgson asked anxiously.

"Wi——" Basset breathed, his eyes focussing on something just beyond Dr. Doyle's shoulder. Then he gave a spasmodic gasp and his body went limp.

A large constable shoved his way through the crowd. "Wot's all this, then?"

"This," Mr. Dodgson said, "is—or rather, I fear, was—Mr. Samuel Basset, a publisher of children's books and magazines."

"He's dead," Dr. Doyle pronounced, as he checked the man's neck pulse and tried to hear his breathing.

29

"How?" The bobby peered at the fallen man, who was already being covered by a thin down of snowflakes. "Who done it then?" He glared suspiciously at Mr. Dodgson and Dr. Doyle.

"I saw some bloke run off down the Strand," one of the apple vendors offered.

"Big feller, too," added the nearest newsvendor.

"Anyone see 'is face?" The bobby looked around the crowd. The reporters already were scribbling in their notebooks. Here was a juicy story, a vicious attack on one of their own, and on his front doorstep, as it were!

"Can't see yer own feet in this muck, let alone the face of sum-mun runnin' away," observed the apple woman.

"May I suggest that you exp-pedite matters by summoning your sup-periors as quickly as p-possible?" Mr. Dodgson said testily, his stammer threatening to overcome him in his agitation. "It is quite cold, and if you do not hurry, any indications of who the assailant might be will be covered by this snow."

"Aye, that's so," the bobby agreed. He tweeted his whistle to alert his comrades in Ludgate Circus to send reinforcements.

By this time, the members of the Fourth Estate were busily interviewing as many people as they could find who would admit to knowing the deceased. One approached Dr. Doyle.

"A doctor, you said?"

"Dr. Arthur Conan Doyle," was the reply, and the spelling of the name was carefully checked.

"Did you know the man well?"

"I only met him this afternoon," Dr. Doyle stated.

"And you, sir?" The young reporter turned to Mr. Dodgson, who had risen to speak to the policeman and was now edging away from the stiffening form on the pavement.

"I do not wish to be interviewed," Mr. Dodgson told him. "My association with Mr. Basset was brief and was about to be broken off. I was sadly misled."

The reporter was about to follow this promising lead when the loud clanging of a bell announced the arrival of the police am-bulance and a squad in the blue jackets and helmets with the badge of the City of London, led by a tall and burly individual in a bowler hat and caped greatcoat. At the same time, a short, spare man draped in a long overcoat, also wearing a bowler hat, made his way through the crowd, followed by a second squad with the badge of the Metropolitan Police on their helmets.

"MacRae, Metropolitan Police," the shorter of the two announced curtly. "Constable, what's all this about?" At the same time, the taller, burlier officer declared, "Calloway, City of London Police. What's going on here?"

The bobby saluted, including both inspectors in his greeting. "Gentleman assaulted, sir. According to this gentleman, he's a Mr. Samuel Basset."

Mr. Dodgson peered through the snow at the new arrival. "Good heavens," he exclaimed, "Inspector MacRae!"

"Aye, that's me," Inspector MacRae glared at Mr. Dodgson and Dr. Doyle. "Don't I know you?"

"We met in Brighton last summer," Mr. Dodgson reminded him. "The matter of Miss Alicia Marbury's abduction."

Comprehension dawned, and MacRae's scowl deepened. "I recall now," he said. "Aren't you supposed to be in Oxford? And you," he turned to Dr. Doyle, who had relinquished the body of the late Mr. Basset to the uniformed authorities. "Brighton, wasn't it?"

"Portsmouth. Southsea, actually," Dr. Doyle corrected him.

Inspector MacRae seemed to take Mr. Dodgson's defection from the realm of academe as a personal insult. "What're you doing here?"

"What are you doing here, Inspector?" Mr. Dodgson asked. "As I recall, you are in the Special Irish Branch, not the Criminal Investigation Department. And I believe this is the City of London, which means . . ."

"Hit means 'e don't 'ave no right to be 'ere," Calloway stated. "So wot's the Met doin'? This 'ere's my patch, MacRae. 'Ands off!"

Inspector MacRae glanced down at the body of the late Samuel Basset. "If this is the work of Fenians, Calloway, then it's my body, not yours. I've had word that there's a meeting called for tonight in Trafalgar Square, and some of the lads gave me the wink that there's to be more than words flying in the Strand. The Fenians may try to take advantage to do mischief, and when they do, we'll be waiting for 'em!" MacRae rubbed his hands, partly to combat the cold, partly in anticipation. "We'll teach 'em to run riot in the streets!"

"Haw!" Calloway expressed his opinion of the Special Irish Branch and their relentless search for Irish terrorists. "This 'ere's no Fenian bomb, MacRae. This gent's been struck by some bloke out fer 'is pocket watch and purse. None of your affair, so go off and chase Fenians and let the rest of us get on with it."

"Mr. Basset said something before he died," Dr. Doyle said, conscious of his duty. "It sounded like the letter 'y' . . . as in, 'Wi . . . ' or 'Why'. . . ."

"Could he have been naming his killer?" MacRae asked.

"I have no idea what he meant," Dr. Doyle replied. "In fact, it may only have been his expiring breath. Take no notice of it."

"I take notice of everything, sir." MacRae took out his notebook and glanced at his rival, who glared back and produced a notebook of his own. "Now, sir, for the record, what were your relations with the deceased?"

"Is there no more sheltered place where we can pursue these inquiries?" Dr. Doyle asked, looking about him. Most of the stalls had closed. The taverns were nearby, but crowded.

A familiar voice broke into the hubbub. "What's going on here?" Mr. Levin shoved through the crowd, to see why the police ambulance was blocking the street. "Oh my!" Levin's too refined tones broke into purest Whitechapel. "Ow, it's Mr. Basset! Is 'e . . . ?"

"Who're you?" Calloway asked, his eyes narrowing in suspicion.

"I am Andrew Levin, and . . . is that Mr. Basset? Is he unwell?" Levin's voice trembled.

"He is dead," Inspector MacRae said bluntly. Mr. Levin closed his eyes and murmured something under his breath. Behind him, the rest of the staff had edged into the crowd, joining their fellow journalists on Fleet Street. Howarth and Monteverde bowed their heads in respect as the police lifted the body of the late Samuel

Basset up into the waiting ambulance, while Peterson and Roberts touched their hats. Calloway and MacRae eyed each other, neither one willing to give way to the other, while the ambulance driver awaited further orders. All traffic on Fleet Street had ground to a halt while the driver of the police ambulance, the driver of the next omnibus, and the driver of a huge dray cursed and edged their horses back and forth.

"Where are you taking him?" Levin asked Inspector Calloway, who looked, in turn, at the ambulance driver.

"St. Bart's is the nearest," the police ambulance driver said, looking to Calloway for approval. MacRae nodded.

"Get the poor soul under cover," he agreed. "We can sort this out later." Calloway gave the signal, and the ambulance driver edged the horse up to the Strand, the better to turn around and head back into the City, to the venerable hospital of St. Bartholomew's. The flow of traffic resumed, and the attention of the police was turned to the staff of *Youth's Companion*.

CHAPTER 4

※※※

The staff stood on Fleet Street huddled together, still shaken by the event. Monteverde and Howarth seemed to look to Peterson for guidance, while Roberts scanned the crowd to see if Miss Harvey had made her escape. He caught her eye and beckoned to her to come closer. Calloway and MacRae glared at the assembled staff, who looked blankly at each other, while Mr. Dodgson and Dr. Doyle lurked at the edges of the group.

Finally, the senior member of the group managed to find his voice. "Poor old Basset Hound," Peterson said. "Did he have a stroke? Apoplexy?"

"It seemed to me that he just fainted away," Dr. Doyle stated. "Although I thought there was someone with him just before he collapsed. They might have been having some sort of argument."

"Didn't see any sign of an attack, did you?" Calloway asked.

"I couldn't be certain, what with the snow and the crowd on the pavement," Dr. Doyle confessed. "I thought I saw a large man, in some sort of cloak or cape, standing near him, but I could not swear to it in a court of law. Inspectors, is this going to take very long? I am supposed to be on the late train to Portsmouth."

"Is there no place where we can get out of this weather?" Mr. Dodgson complained.

Mr. Levin spoke up. "Excuse me, Inspector, but I hold the keys, and the offices of *Youth's Companion* are right behind us. If you like, I can open the door, and we may step into the vestibule. As soon as you have finished with our statements, these people can be on their way." He indicated the staff, who were fascinated by the interplay between the City of London and the Metropolitan Police.

Calloway hunched his shoulders against the wind while Levin fumbled with the keys. Once the door was open, MacRae and Calloway plunged in out of the weather, leaving Mr. Dodgson, Dr. Doyle, and the rest of the staff to crowd in behind them. Two constables of each persuasion held back the curious onlookers. Only Mr. Roberts noticed that Miss Harvey had turned back to hover near the door and hear what was being said, and he kept his own counsel.

"Now then," Calloway began, with notebook at the ready. "Wot 'ave you got to say for yourselves?" He glared at Levin, then at Monteverde and Howarth, and finally at Peterson, who decided to take up the position of spokesman for the staff.

"I'm David Peterson, chief writer and senior staff member," Peterson stated, with a glance at the others, who seemed content to allow him to take the lead.

"Were you out on the street when Mr. Basset was attacked?" MacRae asked.

"Just got out of the office," Peterson said cheerfully.

"Did you see anyone with Mr. Basset?" Calloway took over the questioning.

"Couldn't see your hand in front of your face in this snow," Monteverde commented unoriginally.

"I saw even less," Howarth put in. "I was right behind Monte on the stairs when he told me that Basset was down."

"Then you're no 'elp to us," Calloway said in disgusted tones. "Give yer directions to the constable, get on 'ome, and we'll be around to take your statements in the morning."

"Certain it's a simple robbery, are ye?" MacRae said.

"Hit's clear to me wot 'appened," Calloway retorted. "One of the usual bunch, out to nab a quid or two in the snow. There's a scuffle, Basset gets 'it, and chummy takes off before we can clap eyes on 'im."

"I think there is more to it than that," Dr. Doyle spoke up.

Inspector Calloway did not want to listen to him. "No Fenians in this business," he told MacRae. "I'll 'ave me men keep their eyes on the lookout, but this is one we'll never solve."

"If you will let me speak . . . ," Dr. Doyle began again.

Mr. Peterson interrupted him. "Levin, you'll let us know the drill? Black bands on arms, black gloves?"

"I shall speak with Mr. Portman as soon as I finish with these, um, gentlemen," Levin said.

"They're not gentlemen; they're coppers!" Peterson snickered.

"Were you acquainted with this Mr. Samuel Basset?" MacRae turned to Levin.

"I am . . . was . . . his assistant." Levin swallowed several times. "This is quite, quite shocking. What happened? You said he was . . . dead? How? Why?"

"That's an interesting question, sir, to which at present we have no answers," MacRae told him, with a speaking look at Calloway, who ignored him. "He appears to have been attacked by some kind of ruffian. A tall man, seemingly, with a name that starts with 'Wi———' ."

"Surely not Mr. Wilde!" Levin exclaimed. "He would not have done such a thing!"

"Wilde? Not that fellow who parades about in velvet knee breeches, mocking his betters?" MacRae bristled at the thought.

"He's not as effete as he looks," Dr. Doyle spoke out. "In fact, he's quite tall, and according to reports, he gave as good as he got when he toured America. I've attended some of his lectures. He's a very good speaker," he added to Mr. Dodgson.

Inspector Calloway turned to Levin. "Had Mr. Basset any family?"

Levin thought a moment. "I never heard of any. He had a flat

36

on Baker Street." Levin swallowed hard. "I . . . I suppose I shall have to go to the Press Club and tell Mr. Portman of Mr. Basset's . . . accident."

"Accident, my eye!" MacRae snorted. "What did this Wilde have to do with Basset?"

"Mr. Basset declined to employ him as staff writer," Mr. Levin said carefully. "In fact, he threw him out of the office."

"And the fellow took his revenge by knocking the blighter on the head," Calloway said gleefully. "Well, that's assault and battery, and, perhaps, murder."

"Just because he was refused a position?" Peterson scoffed.

"There are a few chaps out in the street who would kill for a good job," Howarth said somberly. "Mr. Basset was right about that."

"And this 'un gave 'im a dick on the nob," Calloway pronounced.

"I thought you'd decided that this was a simple robbery," MacRae snapped at Calloway.

"Could be that I was mistook and too 'asty," Calloway conceded. "There might be more to this than meets the eye."

"I suggest you wait until after the autopsy . . . ," Dr. Doyle began. The wind blew the door open and the sound of the orator was heard once more.

MacRae's attention was distracted from the business at hand. "There goes Hyndman again. He's Inciting to Riot! Well, this is one time I've got him dead to rights! He'll not spout that Socialist nonsense very much longer!"

"I do not believe that Mr. Wilde . . . ," Dr. Doyle began.

MacRae settled his bowler more firmly on his head, and prepared to face the elements. "As soon as I've taken care of Mr. Hyndman and his friend John Burns, I can get a warrant for Mr. Oscar Wilde. A man like that shouldn't be too hard to find."

"But . . . ," Dr. Doyle tried once again to get MacRae's attention.

"Not now, young man. You'll stop by the Yard and give your statement in the morning," MacRae said. "And stay indoors tonight. This is no place for youngsters, or old codgers." He gathered himself together, settled his spectacles firmly on his nose, and dove out into the street once more.

"Now," Calloway took out his notebook, "I'll just take your names and directions, and let you gentlemen be on your way. MacRae's got a bee in 'is bonnet about the Irish."

"Then you don't think Wilde is in any danger?" Peterson asked.

"As to that I cannot say," Calloway declared. "I'll expect statements from all of you in the morning." He carefully took Mr. Dodgson's and Dr. Doyle's cards, winked, and stalked off after bigger game than aesthetic poets.

Mr. Levin looked shaken to the core. "I must inform Mr. Portman," he muttered to himself. "I'm sorry, Mr. Dodgson, Dr. Doyle, but I must close the door now. Mr. Monteverde, Mr. Howarth . . . If you don't mind, Mr. Roberts . . ." He edged everyone outside into the snow.

Roberts scowled at Levin and strode after Miss Harvey. Peterson looked at his fellow sufferers. "Anyone for a quick one before we have to face the weather?"

Howarth looked at Monteverde and the two adjusted their hats (a neat bowler for Howarth, a dramatic velveteen trilby for Monteverde).

"Mama's waiting dinner for me," Monteverde said.

"And I've got to get home to Post-Office Polly," Howarth explained.

"You spoil that hound!" The two men set off in opposite directions, one towards Saffron Hill, the other to Pimlico. Levin touched his bowler hat and disappeared into the snow, leaving Mr. Roberts speaking earnestly to Miss Harvey.

Once again Mr. Dodgson and Dr. Doyle found themselves in the crowded street.

"Dear me," Mr. Dodgson said. It seemed inadequate to the occasion.

Dr. Doyle was more forceful. "That idiot MacRae is off on a wild-goose chase, and Calloway's not much better. Wilde had nothing to do with Basset's death."

38

"Indeed?"

"Of course not. I was trying to tell them that the cause of death wasn't a blow to the head. The man had been stabbed in the back, as they'll find out soon enough when they do the autopsy."

"Really? But why did Mr. Basset say, 'Wi—'?" Mr. Dodgson asked.

"If he said a name at all," Dr. Doyle objected. "And what is that object you've been clutching all this while?"

Mr. Dodgson looked down at his hands. Sure enough, he was holding a long scarf, made of undyed wool, knitted in a curious twisted pattern. "Mr. Basset was holding this as he fell," Mr. Dodgson said. "I suppose I must have taken it when you laid him on the ground."

"Shouldn't we give it to the police?" Dr. Doyle asked.

Mr. Dodgson considered, then said, "If Inspector MacRae is determined to follow his own course, there is little we can do to stop him. He would probably ignore this very important clue. He has already decided that Mr. Oscar Wilde is the culprit and will think of nothing else. As for Inspector Calloway, he would probably use it to fix the blame on some miscreant who had nothing to do with Basset's death, if only to clear the case from his records." Mr. Dodgson considered his course, then declared, "We must find Mr. Wilde before Inspector MacRae does and warn him."

"But . . . if Wilde had nothing to do with the assault . . . ," Dr. Doyle objected.

"Whether he did it or not, his career will be ruined," Mr. Dodgson said. "I am not personally acquainted with Mr. Wilde. He was at Magdalen not Christ Church. However, he is an Oxford man, and as such, he deserves my support. I have also read some of his remarks on art. He has much to say that is to the point. It would be a great pity if a promising young writer should be stifled at the very outset of his career by a false accusation such as this. It can blight all hopes of advancement. No, Dr. Doyle, we must take matters into our own hands. The problem is, how to find Mr. Wilde before Inspector MacRae obtains his warrant."

Mr. Dodgson thought a moment, while the snow piled up on

top of his high silk hat. Then he set out along Fleet Street, dragging Dr. Doyle with him.

"Where are we going?" Dr. Doyle asked, struggling through the crowd that was pushing in the opposite direction, towards the Strand.

"Today is Wednesday, is it not?"

"I believe so."

"Good. Tenniel will be at the *Punch* dinner. He always attends on Wednesdays. Tenniel knows everybody, and if he doesn't, du Maurier does. I will call on Tenniel at *Punch* and find Mr. Wilde's direction from him. Come along, Dr. Doyle, there is not a moment to lose. We must find Mr. Wilde and warn him to keep out of MacRae's way until this matter is settled and the true murderer is brought to justice."

Mr. Dodgson and Dr. Doyle disappeared into the snow. Behind them, the rotund figure of Mr. David Peterson stepped out of the doorway of the bookshop, where he had taken the opportunity to light a cigar before heading back to the domestic bliss waiting for him in his small attached house in Sloane Square.

So, Peterson thought to himself, Basset was dead, and not from a blow to the head, as had been assumed, but from a knife wound to the back. How appropriate! The old bugger had stabbed enough of his writers and artists in the back himself, stealing their work and peddling it as his own, paying coolie wages, and blaming the declining circulation of *Youth's Companion* on everything but his own lack of talent and refusal to hire better.

Well, thought Peterson, that would change. Nicky Portman would have to find himself another editor in chief, and the most likely person for the job was one David Peterson. Hadn't he provided most of the content of the magazine for the last five years? He would never have thrown a sweet little thing like Miss Potter out, whether her fuzzy rabbits were worthy of publication or not. He certainly wouldn't have insulted a master of fantasy like Mr. Lewis Carroll!

Peterson puffed on his cigar as he slowly walked towards the Strand, considering what he had overheard. Basset had been stabbed, but by whom? When? And where? Basset had been alive when he left the office. They had all heard his heavy tread on the stairs. He hadn't been in the street for all that long, and who, in all that crowd, would have taken the time to shove a knife into a complete stranger?

Peterson stopped in front of a small tavern and sniffed the air, redolent of beer and onions. He looked up and down the street. He could, of course, take the Underground, but before he did, he wanted more fortification. He ducked into the tavern and ordered a hot rum toddy. He wasn't sure, but there was something nagging at the back of his mind and he would not be satisfied until he had worked it out.

CHAPTER 5

The dramatic collapse and violent death of one of its own members could not go unnoticed by the Fourth Estate. Samuel Basset had conveniently perished on Fleet Street itself, the very hub of the British press. He had perished surrounded by reporters, all eager to record his passing in the most sensational terms permissible by their individual editors. On the other hand, he had timed his death imperfectly. The afternoon and evening editions had already been made up; the death of a mere editor in chief of a periodical devoted to children did not warrant the expense of making up an extra edition. Samuel Basset's obituary, like his autopsy, would have to wait until morning.

Meanwhile, reporters interviewed everyone on the street at the time of Mr. Basset's dramatic death: apple women, newsboys, hot pie men, and even each other. Only the orator on the soapbox went unnoted and unnoticed as he continued to exhort the printers and compositors on their way home from their labors.

"I tell you, my brothers, that the time has come to let those fine gentlemen know that the franchise is not enough. We want more than the chance to vote for whoever is assigned to us. We want bread for our children, we want coals for our fires, we want the right to earn our bread with honest labor!"

A knot of men stopped in front of the speaker. Towering over them was O'Casey, the chief printer of *Youth's Companion*, who had pushed his way to the front of the crowd and now stood belligerently in front of Hyndman.

"And how are we supposed to do that, my fine fellow? You with your top hat and fine coat, you've never worked a day in your life, have you?" O'Casey shouted truculently.

"I've spent my life fighting for the rights of fellows like you to provide me with these fine clothes," the speaker retorted. "You are in the forefront of history, my good man. The Social Democratic Federation will fight the good fight, but first you must get the ear of those gentlemen in their warm clubs, the well-fed ones who begrudge a penny to warm an honest workingman's home. . . ."

"He has the right of it there!" O'Casey shouted. "Just this very day, me and me men were denied the use of a fire in the printing plant, while the master sat warm in his office!"

The mutter of conversation grew into a growl of anger as the speaker took up the chorus. "And what do our elected representatives, the Council and the Lord Mayor have to say? They tell us that there is no money in the Lord Mayor's Fund! The members of Parliament will not come to our aid. They say we must ask our own town council, the City of London. But the Mayor and Council will not help us because, they say, there is no money in the fund set aside for poor relief! I say, my brothers, that the time has come to take what is rightfully ours! We must show those well-fed gentlemen in St. James's that we will not stand for this neglect!"

The mutter grew to a roar. O'Casey leaped onto the box, shoving the speaker into the snow-filled street.

"I'm a peaceable man, but this fellow is right. No fine gentleman can tell me that me children should starve because it is the will of God that they should go hungry. They did it to us in forty-eight and forty-nine, and they'll not do it again!" O'Casey's arms were raised in outrage or prayer.

There was another roar of approval. The high-hatted speaker fought for the place of authority atop the soapbox, pushing O'Casey off and regaining the initiative and his place as Leader of the Pack.

"Call your friends, call your enemies! Tonight we will make our will known!"

"You tell 'em, 'Enry!" one of the reporters called out.

" 'Enry 'yndman, the Worker's Friend!" someone else jeered.

Hyndman ignored the sarcasm. "Yes, I am the workers' friend," he retorted. "I fight for justice! I fight for those who have no one else to fight for them!"

O'Casey glared at the speaker. "Who says we don't fight for our own?" he demanded.

"You're standing there like cattle!" Hyndman called back.

"I say we can fight for ourselves," O'Casey shot back at him. "We don't need some jumped-up toff in a high hat to tell us how to get our own back."

"Then why don't you do it?" Hyndman yelled at the crowd. "Because you're afraid, that's why! You'll take whatever the high-and-mighty will deign to give you, but you won't lift a finger to save yourselves!"

The muttering in the group grew louder, as Hyndman's words were repeated. The men of Fleet Street began to spread onto other streets. The word was out in the Temple, where scriveners and clerks, porters and cleaners joined the crowd. Costers with their barrows were attracted by the mass of people. As soon as they realized what was afoot, they, too, were added to the crush of humanity slowly moving towards the Strand.

The reporters in the crowd recognized a news event when they saw one. Already they were mentally forming their stories: Mass Demonstrations in the Strand! Mob Riots! Next to this, the death of an editor, particularly the editor of a mere children's periodical, was nothing. This was history in the making, and no reporter worthy of the name would want to be left out of it. The press was added to the press of people, edging their way towards the monument that marked the dividing point between the City of London and the rest of the metropolis.

Mr. Edgar Roberts was tall enough to stand out even in that mob. He set his broad-brimmed hat solidly on his head and pulled his long knitted scarf around his neck. He scanned the crowd for a red hat and gray cloak. Two or three long strides were enough for him to catch up to his quarry. "Miss Harvey? I thought you had left Fleet Street."

"Mr. Roberts?" Miss Harvey peered through the snow at the tall figure in front of her. "What happened to Mr. Basset? I saw him fall, and I thought you beckoned to me, so I tried to come over to the door, but there were so many people out on the streets . . ."

"Miss Harvey, would you let me buy you some tea?" Roberts interrupted the flow of words.

"Now?" She looked around at the crowded street.

"Twining's is still open. I believe they have a small eating place in the back of the shop, where one can get a cup of hot tea and a scone." The artist fixed her with a gaze of burning intensity. "I have a . . . proposition I would like to put to you."

Miss Harvey looked about her again. The crowd was becoming threatening. Mr. Roberts was very tall and the thought of hot tea was suddenly very appealing. "I don't suppose anyone could object," she said.

Mr. Roberts took Miss Harvey's arm and led her to Twining's. He would have his Queen Mab or know the reason why!

Mr. Levin paid no attention to the crowd or the speakers. He made his way through the snow down the Strand, which by now was so choked with people, horses, and carriages that walking was the fastest means of transportation. The snow had begun to pile up against the corners of the buildings, while the crossing sweepers had their hands full keeping the intersections free for pedestrians. Mr. Levin marched on, head down against the wind, past the shops, hotels, and fine restaurants that marked the Strand as one of London's most fashionable thoroughfares.

His destination was Trafalgar Square and St. James's Place beyond it, where the most exclusive men's clubs lurked behind discreet oak doors. Here were the sanctuaries where gentlemen could read newspapers, play cards, argue politics, or just sleep the day away. No visitors were allowed in the best of these clubs; even the worst of them had a cachet that was maintained by the strict use of blackball rules.

The Press Club was the newest of these institutions, the brain child of Mr. Nicholas Portman, the son of the founder of Portman Penny Press. Nicky Portman had the reputation of being a man who got things done. When the more venerable clubs refused him admittance because of his ancestry, he stated boldly that a man's grandfather had nothing to do with said man's accomplishments and had proceeded to use an unexpected legacy from a wealthy relative to take over the moribund Players' Club and turn it into a haven for literary figures of all types, particularly journalists. Not content with that, he had instituted such radical reforms as to make the Press Club unique.

It was the Press Club that had instituted a ladies' entrance, for use by female members of the Fourth Estate, who were actually allowed to eat in the dining room on alternate Saturday afternoons. It was the Press Club that entertained visiting Americans, such as the vociferous Mr. Clemens and the less vociferous Mr. Harte, when they came to London for lecture tours. Under the leadership of Mr. Portman, the Press Club was willing to extend hospitality to anyone who could prove that they were a published author and could behave like a gentleman.

As befitted the founder and chief benefactor of the Press Club, Mr. Portman had filled the place with his own souvenirs. His African ventures were recalled by an assortment of wooden idols and fetishes, lined up on the shelves of the library. A trip to the Caribbean had yielded a conservatory full of exotic plants. India was represented by the brass trays and vases in the lounge, while Chinese porcelain and Japanese prints adorned the members' dining room.

Mr. Nicholas Portman himself still retained the boyish good looks of his early photographs. His round face bore a habitual expression of surprise that hid a determination to outdo his father and grandfather in the world of publishing. His blue eyes looked out on the world as if seeking ever wider horizons. If his blond curls were slightly less exuberantly curly than in former years, if his slender waist tended to burst out of his tailored waistcoat, well, this was only to be expected of a man entering his fourth decade.

Nicky Portman was anxiously waiting when the Press Club's majestic butler showed Levin into the club library, a book-lined corner room permeated by the smell of old leather and musty pages. Here one could find a copy of every book ever printed by the Portman Penny Press, the source of the fortune laid down by the first Nicholas Portman, who had begun life as a bookbinder's assistant and had ended it as a millionaire, thanks to the newly literate working classes and their demand for cheap, readable books. Mr. Portman's father, Sir William Portman, had managed to gain a knighthood largely by giving books to schools and charitable institutions. Nicky, as he was known to London society, had followed the family trade, expanding the Portman Penny Press into the area of children's publications.

Mr. Portman had apparently delayed his tea; a tray with a teapot and a covered dish that might contain muffins was on the table in the middle of the room. He eyed Mr. Levin as the taller man dripped melting snow on the figured carpet. "Where is Sammy?"

"Mr. Basset is not coming," Mr. Levin said miserably. "Mr. Basset has . . . He has met with an accident."

"What sort of an accident?" Mr. Portman asked sharply. "Spit it out, man!"

"Sir, he's dead!" Levin blurted out.

"What! How . . . ? When . . . ?" Portman sputtered.

"It happened about an hour ago," Levin said. "In the street, in front of the office. The police . . . the police think someone might have knocked him on the head. There are a number of ruffians about tonight," Levin added. "I thought I saw Mr. Hyndman making one of his usual ranting speeches, urging them to take matters into their own hands, after the rejection of the Poor Aid Bill."

"And you think one of these workingmen decided to hit my dear Sammy on the head? I never heard such nonsense," Mr. Portman snapped out. "What else can you tell me?"

"Not much, sir. Mr. Basset had already left for the day, and I was in the process of locking up before leaving the building. The rest of the staff writers were on their way down when I heard the police arrive."

"Police? Already?"

"I believe there was already an inspector from the Special Irish Branch on the scene," Levin explained. "Because of Mr. Hyndman, I expect, and the unpleasantness over the vote. Then someone from the City of London Police showed up, too."

Mr. Portman thought this over. "It's all very strange," he said at last. "Who would want to hurt poor old Sammy?"

"As to that, I could not say," Levin said, his voice trembling. "He was not in a good temper, sir. There had been a few . . . altercations earlier today, but I do not believe that either Mr. Wilde or O'Casey meant what they said in the heat of anger." Levin shook his head sadly.

"Wilde? You don't mean Oscar was there?" Mr. Portman looked up at Levin. "I sent him over, you know. I thought Sammy could find a place for him on the staff."

"You should have said something to Mr. Basset about Mr. Wilde being your particular friend," Mr. Levin said. "As it was, Mr. Wilde did not mention any connection, and Mr. Basset was not pleased with his, um, writing style. To be blunt, sir, Mr. Basset would not hire Mr. Wilde, and Mr. Wilde left the office in what can only be described as high dudgeon."

"Hmph!" Mr. Portman made a noise between a snort and a laugh. "I can just see Oscar doing it, too. And what did O'Casey want?"

"Mr. Basset would not permit any more expenditure on coals, and there was no fire in the printing plant. O'Casey was upset."

Mr. Portman sighed. "That was Sammy all over. Penny wise, pound foolish. He'd been so poor as a lad, you know, he watched over every penny, even when I told him I'd stand the gaff. He was my oldest friend, Levin. We were at school together."

"So he told me, sir. Several times." Levin eased his coat open. "Er . . . What shall I do, sir?"

"Do? What do you mean, do? Do about what?" Mr. Portman asked irritably.

"Mr. Basset's . . . um, remains . . . have been taken up by the police," Mr. Levin reminded him. "According to the inspector in charge, Inspector Calloway of the City of London Police, the . . . Mr. Basset has been taken to St. Bart's for examination by the police surgeon. There will be an inquiry and an inquest. Then there is the procedure at the office. The staff know about Mr. Basset's death. That is, they were on the street in the crowd when the police were summoned. Shall I call them in tomorrow? Will they be expected to attend the funeral? Who will take care of the, um, arrangements?" Mr. Levin stopped in confusion.

Mr. Portman answered the last question first. "Sammy's people are all gone now. His mother died some years ago, and his father . . . he never really knew his father. There were no other children, no brothers or sisters. I suppose I was all the family Sammy ever had." He sighed deeply. "The office will open tomorrow, and you may put a black wreath on the door of the office and of the shop downstairs. Black armbands, of course, but nothing more for the staff. I shall take care of the funeral arrangements. The staff will have the day to attend. I only hope that poor Sammy will not be totally anatomized."

"Anatomized?" Levin squeaked out.

"Standard procedure, unfortunately. There will, of course, be an autopsy. . . ."

"Autopsy," Levin whispered, going white.

"But if, as you say, the cause of death is so obvious, that should be a mere formality. I will inform the staff of the date of the funeral." Mr. Portman shook his head sadly. "Poor dear Sammy. To end like this!" He looked up at Levin. "What are you standing about for, man?"

"The magazine," Levin said, through dry lips. "Our new issue is not yet printed. We will miss our mailing deadline. And how shall we break the news to the children? Should I write the editorial?"

Mr. Portman shook his head. "No, Levin," he decided, "I shall do it. Sammy was the children's dear, dear friend, their Uncle Basset, who always had their best interests at heart. Death is no stranger to our readers, unfortunately, but we need not dwell on the manner of it. As for *Youth's Companion*, I shall come down to the office and take charge myself. I often thought that Sammy had become somewhat hardheaded in his selection of material, and now that I hear he rejected Oscar's lovely stories, I am sure of it. Perhaps a fresh approach is needed. We shall see."

"Of course," Levin said faintly.

"Well, Levin," Mr. Portman said, rising and patting the taller man on the shoulder, "you must be quite distressed. Have a drink at the bar downstairs before you go home. You must have had a dreadful day."

"Thank you, sir," Levin said. "In fact, the snow is quite thick, and I should be getting on home. And the people on the street are becoming very unruly."

"In that case, you'd best be on your way. Thank you for coming to me directly. I would not have liked to learn of Sammy's death by reading it in the morning papers."

"No," Levin said. He picked up his bowler hat and sketched a bow. "I thought you should know, sir. Things being what they are, I felt it important to see you in person."

Mr. Portman had sunk into thought. He waved absently at the other man, who had no choice but to bow and leave.

Levin paused outside the study. Should he have mentioned the argument with Mr. Basset about the discrepancies in the accounts, and the threat of prosecution? No. Now that Basset was gone, why upset Mr. Portman with such minor difficulties?

Levin pulled his overcoat about him and headed out into the snow again. There were rough men all around, shaking their fists and shouting. It could not be a cab, then; it would have to be the Underground. Levin turned his steps eastward. He might be able to convince his landlady to let him have some hot soup tonight.

Edgar Roberts left Miss Harvey near the Temple. They had not quite reached an agreement, but he was certain he could get around her ridiculous scruples about posing for Queen Mab. The noises of the riot drew his attention. Everyone in London seemed to be heading towards Trafalgar Square. Why not go there himself and see what was happening? Queen Mab could wait another night! Mr. Roberts joined the crowd, his eyes bright with mischief, his pencil at the ready.

David Peterson had emerged from his tavern spot with several hot rum toddies under his belt. His head felt pleasantly fuzzy, but he grinned to himself as he looked about for a cab and found none. The snow was swirling about, eddying about the venerable buildings of the Temple, covering the tops of high hats with a fine film that had to be knocked off before it soaked into the silk.

The snow had not deterred the crowd. All around him, angry men were gathered, shaking their fists at imaginary employers. A few women had joined the mob, carrying baskets of shriveled flowers or battered fruit, and they added shrill soprano and alto cries to the basso rumble of the workingmen. Some of the navvies had shovels and picks with them, carried in the vain hope that someone would offer employment.

"Let's 'ave up the stones!" someone bawled over the muttering. Picks and shovels were used to pry up cobblestones, to the delight of the crowd.

Peterson sighed inwardly. He would have to walk home. There was not a cab to be had and the thought of the Underground was too daunting in his present state of inebriation.

Peterson plodded along the Strand, going over his options. He had formulated a theory, one which would explain what he had seen. Now what should he do about it? He could say nothing and wait for the police to get around to him, or he could come forward and present what he had thought out to Inspector Calloway or Inspector MacRae. Of course, the two policemen could then discard what they had been told. MacRae seemed to be a hasty type, rushing here and there without first considering what was logical and what was not. Calloway, on the other hand, was unimaginative and would take the most comfortable explanation. He'd already decided that Samuel Basset had been the victim of a random attack and would let it go at that.

"Watch where you are going!" A familiar voice broke into his internal reverie.

Peterson stopped short, nearly running into another person just ahead of him. "Oh, I beg your pardon," he said. Then he recognized who it was. "What on earth are you doing out this late?"

"Everyone else is out tonight. Why not me?"

"Never mind that. Look, I wanted a word with you."

"Oh?" The other man ducked into a narrow alley, a narrow street left over from the days when the Strand had been a little stream and the streets were lined with brick houses.

Peterson followed, eager to put his theory to the test and happy to be out of the wind.

"I've been thinking about what happened this afternoon on the stairs."

"I don't know what you're talking about!" The other man tried to step around Peterson, but there was a lot of Peterson to step around, and the alley was very narrow.

Peterson grabbed the other man by the arm. "I think you do. I don't have to say anything to anyone, but you'll have to give me a good reason not to go to the police."

"What do you mean?"

"Did you really think you'd get off that easily?" Peterson chortled happily. "Oh, we're going to have some fun, you and I. Portman's bound to put me in Basset's place, and when he does, we can discuss where we go from here."

"You're mad!"

"Do you think so? I can always come forward and say that I hadn't quite realized what happened. We can talk about it in the morning. I have to get home to Myrna. Ta-ta . . ." He turned to go.

Behind him, the other man touched the wall, as Peterson burbled on. One of the bricks in the ancient wall had been loosened by the cold. He wriggled it out of the mortar, hefted it, and slashed down with all his might. Twice more and then he merged into the mob, just another figure in the Strand.

The crowd surged around him, yelling obscenities up at the lighted windows of the hotels. One of the cobblestones was heaved in the direction of the lighted window, and a bloodthirsty howl went up from the crowd, as the glass broke with a satisfying tinkle.

It was all that was needed to turn the crowd into a mob. Eager hands grabbed at small and large stones, while others pushed and pulled at the wooden shutters on the shops. Pieces of wood were used as crowbars, as the men and women who had been denied such luxuries descended on the wares offered for sale to the wealthy.

None of this mattered to David Peterson. His body lay bleeding in the alley, as the crowd passed by, down the Strand towards Trafalgar Square.

CHAPTER 6

❦

While Mr. Levin was informing Lord Portman of the death of his old friend, Mr. Dodgson was leading Dr. Doyle through the crowd in quite the opposite direction, eastward on Fleet Street, past the muttering crowds of poorly dressed people who had joined the growing mob. His destination was Bouverie Street, one of the twisting alleys that led out of Fleet Street towards the river. A hall porter in a vast ex-military greatcoat stopped them as they tried to enter the stairwell that led upwards to the offices of *Punch* and looked them over with suspicion in his eyes while Mr. Dodgson fumbled for his card.

"Business hours is over," the porter said loftily.

"I am quite aware of that," Mr. Dodgson told him. "I wish to speak with Mr. Tenniel. Has he come in?"

"I shall take your card up and find out." The porter disappeared up the stairs, leaving Mr. Dodgson and Dr. Doyle to gaze at the reproductions of famous illustrations that had been hung on the walls. Here were the well-known works of George du Maurier and Dr. Doyle's own relation, the incomparable Dicky Doyle. Here, too, were caricatures of statesmen, beginning with Palmerston and Russell, the Iron Duke and Sailor Billy, through "Dizzy" Disraeli and "The People's" William Gladstone, to Lord Salisbury, the current prime minister. Britannia, in all her glory, ruled over Marianne of France, Brother Jonathan of the United States, and the caricatures of Russia, Germany, and the newly united Italy. This was the vestibule of *Punch,* and Dr. Doyle drank in the atmosphere like fine wine.

The porter returned and announced with a sniff of disdain, "Mr. Tenniel will see you, gentlemen."

Dr. Doyle followed his mentor eagerly up the stairs anxious to view the hallowed scene of his uncle's glory. He remembered the one time he had been allowed to come to London, when Uncle Dicky had taken him to see the *Punch* offices. Had they been larger then, or did he simply recall the rooms from a child's point of view?

The porter led them up a second flight of stairs to a small anteroom that led, in turn, to the celebrated dining room. Dr. Doyle could just see the famous mahogany table through the partly open door to the dining room. He had heard that those lucky few who had been accepted as permanent staff writers and artists for *Punch* were allowed to carve their names into the woodwork. It was here, in this dining room, that the Wednesday night dinners were held, during which the content of the magazine would be laid out for the coming week. It was rumored that the conversation at these dinners was filled with wit and salacious gossip in equal part and that the food was only of the best. The delectable aromas coming from the dining room gave at least the second part of the rumor the benefit of truth.

Dr. Doyle suddenly remembered that he had not eaten since his quick lunch on the train from Portsmouth. It would be too much to ask that he be allowed to remain for dinner . . . wouldn't it?

A tall white-haired gentleman with a sweeping walrus mustache greeted them with a raised eyebrow and an outstretched hand. "Dodgson? What are you doing here? If you've come to ask me to illustrate for you again, I won't do it. I thought I made myself quite clear about that. . . ."

"My dear Tenniel, that is not at all why I came," Mr. Dodgson said, fussing with his gloves. "The fact is, I have had a shock."

"Could we have a chair for Mr. Dodgson?" Dr. Doyle stepped forward to take charge of his older companion.

"Oh yes. May I introduce Dr. Arthur Conan Doyle. He's Dicky Doyle's nephew, you know." For once Dr. Doyle did not writhe in embarrassment when Mr. Dodgson insisted on including his uncle's name in the introduction.

Tenniel turned his penetrating gaze onto the younger man and extended a hand ceremoniously. "How do you do, sir. I knew your uncle well. In fact," he frowned, searching his memory, "I believe we have met. Of course, you were much younger then."

"My uncle took me up to see the dining room table once when I was a boy," Dr. Doyle said shyly. "He was very kind to me. Unfortunately, my father's brothers did not approve of his marriage to my mother, a feeling that led to a difference between the two sides of the family. Since they lived in London, and we remained in Edinburgh, we did not see much of them."

Mr. Dodgson had been given a chair, from which he looked up at Tenniel with an apologetic air. "I realize that you are about to sit down to dinner, but it was quite necessary that I see you. I must have the direction of Mr. Oscar Wilde."

"Eh?" Tenniel's mustache quivered. "What on earth makes you think I know the fellow?"

"He is constantly being talked about," Mr. Dodgson said. "Certainly, if you do not know him, one of the others does."

"He's du Maurier's target, not mine. Du Maurier!"

A dapper-bearded gentleman poked his head out of the dining room. Tenniel beckoned him over. "Here's Dodgson come to ask us where Wilde is."

George du Maurier looked puzzled. "What do you want with him?" he asked.

"He is in danger of being taken up by the police on a charge of murder," Mr. Dodgson explained. "Not an hour ago, Mr. Samuel Basset was attacked in Fleet Street. He died there, on the street, in front of his own offices . . ." Mr. Dodgson could not continue, overcome with emotion.

"Could you provide Mr. Dodgson with a glass of water?" Dr. Doyle asked.

"A stiff brandy would do more good," du Maurier observed.

"Sherry will do nicely," Mr. Dodgson whispered.

"But this is nonsense," Tenniel said, as du Maurier provided the necessary stimulant. "Wilde is notorious, but hardly homicidal."

"Nevertheless, there is a policeman who has some animus against him, and since Mr. Basset's dying utterance seemed to be the name 'Wilde,' this policeman has gone to Scotland Yard to obtain a warrant for his arrest."

"And you think that if Wilde makes himself scarce . . . ," Tenniel mused.

"We can find evidence that will certainly clear him," Dr. Doyle said proudly. "For instance, this scarf." He produced their trophy. "Does that look like something Mr. Wilde would wear?"

Du Maurier chuckled. "It's not 'Aesthetic,' " he said. "But it might be one of those 'handicrafts' he's always going on about. As it happens, I do have Wilde's direction."

Tenniel's eyebrow raised higher. Du Maurier reddened. "He's moved into a house in Tite Street, in Chelsea, down the street from where old Whistler used to live before he had to take smaller quarters."

"I thought you and Jimmy weren't on terms," Tenniel murmured.

"That's not my fault," du Maurier said. "If the old . . . painter"—he glanced at Mr. Dodgson and reworded his pejorative phrasing—"wants to pretend he's still a Bohemian in Paris, that's his lookout. Some of us have moved on." He straightened his natty waistcoat and smoothed his beard, conscious that he, at least, looked like someone who would be received in all the best salons.

Du Maurier scrabbled in his pockets, then realized his drawing materials must be in the offices downstairs. "I shall write the direction for you. You may get there by cab. . . ." He bustled out of the anteroom in search of writing materials.

"It's snowing hard," Dr. Doyle informed them. The news was

57

reinforced by the entrance of a rotund balding man, whose normally cheerful face had taken on a peevish expression.

"Furniss!" Tenniel reproved the latecomer. "We were holding dinner for you."

"What a night!" Harry Furniss brushed snow off his bald head. "Not a cab to be had, and there's a mob outside in the street. Hyndman's been working them up, and it looks like a riot is in the making."

"Well, you can't blame them," Doyle said defensively. "The word on Fleet Street was that the vote went against poor relief, and the Lord Mayor has announced that the funds for distribution to the unemployed are dangerously low."

The distinguished gentlemen of *Punch* regarded the young man as if he were about to heave a brick into their midst.

"And then, if you can believe it, there was a police ambulance in the middle of Fleet Street as well," Furniss complained. "It blocked all traffic between here and the Strand, until they moved it on and got things going again. Between that and the mob, I could barely get through."

"That would be for poor Mr. Basset," Mr. Dodgson explained.

"Not Sammy Basset?" Furniss turned to Mr. Dodgson. "Dodgson? I thought you were safely in Oxford!"

"I have not come up to ask you for the illustrations," Mr. Dodgson said with a guilty smile. "In fact, I have not even begun on the next chapter of our book. I thought I could introduce my young friend, Doyle . . ."

"Dicky Doyle's nephew, you know," Tenniel added, by way of elucidation.

". . . who has written several excellent tales," Mr. Dodgson went on, ignoring the interruption, "to Mr. Basset. I did not realize that Mr. Basset was not the sort of man to be dropped in on."

Tenniel gave a snort of laughter. "I should think not! The only person who could deal with Basset was Nicky Portman. I believe they were at school together."

"What is worse," Mr. Dodgson fumed, "he was selling this in his . . . his confounded bookshop!" He produced the offensive volume of *Alice's Adventures in Wonderland* and shook it at the illustrator.

Tenniel grabbed the book and scanned it with a frown. "This is the first printing," he said severely. "I thought we were agreed that this printing was not acceptable for sale and should be distributed to charitable institutions."

"Apparently, Mr. Basset discovered a box of them in a storeroom and was offering the books for sale in his shop. At full price!" Mr. Dodgson fairly sputtered in his indignation.

"The cheek of it!" Tenniel gasped.

"What is worse," Mr. Dodgson went on, "Mr. Basset was a thief. He stole an idea for a story from one of his staff writers and published it under his own name."

"Reprehensible, but typical," Tenniel commented. "Still, hardly a reason to strike a man down in the street. Everyone on Fleet Street knew about Samuel Basset and his economies. He couldn't get anyone to work for him but those hacks from the Portman Penny Press."

"I did some illustrations for *Youth's Companion,*" Furniss said. "What a mistake!"

"I thought Basset never used outside contributions," Tenniel said. "How did you come to work for him? You're not that hard up, are you?"

Furness shrugged. "Oh, I had a nice letter, I think it was last summer, requesting a few small things, as fillers, you know. Well, as it happened, I had a couple of small items that had been rejected by you lot so I sent them along. I had to wait for months for payment, and there were endless letters back and forth arguing every line of every drawing. In the end I wrote it off as a bad job and let it go at that. But you won't catch me doing anymore work for Basset."

"He sounds very much like someone else of my acquaintance," Tenniel murmured, with a glance at Mr. Dodgson, who was gradually recovering from his exertions. "I can understand why someone should wish to strike the man down. He could be thoroughly provocative. But why should the police hit upon Wilde?"

"Oscar?" Furniss looked at Tenniel in astonishment. "Being wanted by the police?"

"Someone thinks he may have been the one who struck Mr. Basset," Dr. Doyle explained. "We wanted to find him to warn him. If he can provide a suitable alibi, there will be no arrest."

"Well, you can find him at . . ."

"Here's his house direction," du Maurier burst in, drowning out his rotund colleague. "I have written a short note of introduction to Mrs. Wilde, explaining who you are and what your errand is. I sincerely hope you find Oscar and keep him out of the hands of the police. He makes very good copy, and it would be a pity to lose him."

Mr. Dodgson stood, bowed to the assemblage, collected the scarf and his gloves and hat, and beckoned Dr. Doyle to follow him. Tenniel escorted the two men to the landing.

"See here, Dodgson," he said, "I don't understand why you have to mix yourself up in this matter. Let the police do their work and leave the detecting to them. You have no responsibility to Sam Basset. . . ."

"Oh, but I do," Mr. Dodgson said. "Mr. Basset spoke to us as he lay dying. I cannot rest until I have understood what it was he was trying to say."

"In that case, do it indoors. If, as Furniss says, it is snowing, you must find yourself a warm spot for the night. Ask your young medical friend if I am not right." Tenniel pulled at his mustache, shook Mr. Dodgson's hand, and let the hall porter lead the way to the exit.

Dr. Doyle smiled wryly as Mr. Dodgson made his way down the stairs. "I am pleased to make your acquaintance, Mr. Tenniel. Your illustrations have given me both pleasure and enlightenment. As for Mr. Dodgson"—he glanced down the stairs, where Mr. Dodgson waited for him—"you have worked with him yourself, sir. He can be a most determined man."

Tenniel nodded and returned to the dining room. He and du Maurier turned on Furniss with ferocity.

"What were you thinking of, man? Were you actually going to

send that sweet old gentleman over to the Café Royal?" du Maurier asked, aghast.

"But that's where Wilde holds court," Furniss protested. "You've sent him off to Chelsea on a wild-goose chase."

"Not necessarily," du Maurier said. "If the snow is as bad as you say and there are rioters out in force, Oscar just might decide to grace his family fireside with his presence. As for the Café Royal, if Dodgson were to go there he might suffer a fatal seizure, and then you'd have the death of a beloved figure on your conscience."

"Humph!" Tenniel snorted. "Beloved figure indeed! That cantankerous old don was very nearly the death of me. I have no idea why, after working with him once, I ever was persuaded to do so again. Furniss, if you will take my advice, get out of that contract if you can. The man will drive you mad."

Harry Furniss smiled. "I wanted the fame of having worked with the great Lewis Carroll and survived with both wits and wallet intact," he said. "Now, Tenniel, what are you going to do about the big cut? With all the doings on the streets, perhaps you should do a take on Dickens. . . . You know, have a laborer, and a farmer, and a miner holding out their begging bowls, asking the Lord Mayor and Parliament for 'more.' "

Tenniel pulled at his mustache. "Certainly not," he declared. "Hyndman and his lot are leading the way to perdition. This week's cartoon will depict the dangers of such a path: anarchy, death, and the ruination of the British economy." He led the way into the dining room, where a good dinner awaited him.

Outside the snow continued to fall, while the crowd grew louder and Mr. Dodgson and Dr. Doyle pursued their quest for the elusive Mr. Wilde.

CHAPTER 7

※※

Once more Mr. Dodgson and Dr. Doyle made their way through the crowd on Fleet Street, pushing their way through the crowd of eager reporters, disgruntled laborers, and assorted stray vagabonds who had been drawn to the scene in hopes of finding excitement or warmth or a pocket to pick. The leather aprons and paper hats of the printers had been augmented by knitted jerseys and caps of the rough characters who had straggled up the hill from the piers below London Bridge. Billingsgate fish market women added their shrill voices to the hubbub. A number of highly painted women, underdressed for the intense cold, had also joined the mob in hopes of distracting some of the participants from their avowed purpose of teaching the upper classes a lesson.

A few bobbies watched the crowd warily. So far there seemed to be more words than missiles flying about, but sounds of battle from the direction of the Strand ignited the crowd on Fleet Street. They surged forward, carrying any odd passersby with them, including Mr. Dodgson and Dr. Doyle.

The two struggled to the edges of the crowd, somewhere near the ancient buildings of the Temple. Members of the legal profession and their hangers-on were now added to the throng: attorneys in sack suits, some barristers, still wearing their wigs, and even a judge or two. Most of the men were wrapped in cloaks or greatcoats, and all were loud in their condemnation of the approaching mob.

The meeting of the two groups was not harmonious. The navvies brandished their tools. The clerks took refuge in shrill accusations and defiance. One of the younger, more giddy clerks went so far as to heave a snowball into the middle of the mob, causing loud yells and a barrage of missiles, some of which were not snowballs.

"This won't do," Mr. Dodgson fussed. "I thought we could find a growler, but Furniss was right. Between that mob and the snow, there is not a cab to be had. What shall we do? Mr. Wilde lives in Tite Street, in Chelsea, according to the direction given me by Mr. du Maurier. I have visited the district in the past. It is quite a distance away, past Sloane Square, as I recall. We must get to him quickly before that policeman can find him!"

"I should think Mr. Wilde might relish being arrested," Dr. Doyle said with a grin. "It would certainly attract notice, if that is what he is after."

"Very likely," Mr. Dodgson replied, "but a murder charge is no laughing matter, Dr. Doyle, and it is far easier to be arrested for a crime than to be exonerated. Where are we?" He peered around through the falling snow.

"Near the Temple, I believe." Dr. Doyle looked about him. Where the Strand met Fleet Street, the mob milled about, as if looking for a direction in which to proceed. The falling snow nearly obscured the ancient walls of St. Mary's in the Strand, sitting in the middle of the road like an island in the stream of traffic. Omnibuses threw up sprays of muddy slush, drenching the trouser legs of passersby. Horses added their protests to those of the rioters.

Those who preferred to remain aloof from the fray turned towards the river and the newly constructed embankment that was supposed to hold back the floodwaters of the Thames.

"There's the Underground," Dr. Doyle announced, pointing to

63

a flickering light at the end of Arundel Street. "Doesn't the new line go to Sloane Square?"

"I believe it does, but . . ." Mr. Dodgson held back, but Dr. Doyle was more enthusiastic about the new mode of transportation. He led Mr. Dodgson down to the Embankment, eager for a new treat, while the elderly don fumbled in his pockets for coins.

"I don't believe I have ever ridden the Underground," Mr. Dodgson said, allowing himself to be led onward by his energetic young companion.

"Now is as good a time as any," Dr. Doyle told him. "It's supposed to be one of the marvels of the age. A steam train, running on a regular schedule, under the streets. And I understand that there is a scheme afoot to electrify the rails so that the smoke and soot are totally eliminated."

They crossed the road and entered the station, allowing themselves to be carried onward with the rest of the passengers. A stout man pointed to a booth where they purchased tickets, then they continued down into the very bowels of the earth to the platforms.

The two men descended the stairs to find themselves in the crowd of office workers returning to their homes in the far reaches of Chelsea, Kensington, and Bayswater. The uniformed conductor checked their tickets as they joined the throng.

Mr. Dodgson seemed to shrink into himself as he realized there were no first- or second-class passengers. This was, indeed, mass transport: cheap, reliable, but not particularly clean. The arrival of the train was heralded by a blast of sound and soot.

Along with the rest of the riders, Mr. Dodgson and Dr. Doyle were pressed into the carriage. Dr. Doyle managed to find an empty seat, in which he graciously installed his mentor. With a lurch and another blast of sound, the train moved forward, jerking a young woman into Dr. Doyle's arms.

"Miss Harvey!" Dr. Doyle recognized the young woman. "I thought you had already gone home."

"Mr. Roberts took me to tea," Miss Harvey explained. "He wished me to sit for him."

"Indeed?" Dr. Doyle tried to retain his dignity, which was

difficult when being jolted back and forth by the action of the train.

"I was somewhat surprised," Miss Harvey went on. "I have never considered myself a beauty or worthy of being painted. However, Mr. Roberts said that he thought I have an interesting face, and that he wished to use me as a model."

"And what did you tell him?" Dr. Doyle asked.

"I said I would have to consult my mother," Miss Harvey replied, trying to keep her footing as the train jolted its way westward. "Mr. Roberts is quite intense, even for an artist. He was most insistent that I pose as Queen Mab." Another jolt nearly sent her into Mr. Dodgson's lap.

"Do take my seat," Mr. Dodgson attempted to rise. Miss Harvey smiled but shook her head.

"It is only a few stops, and I am really quite capable of standing for a few more minutes."

The train lurched again. Conversation was impossible as the whistle shrieked, announcing the next stop.

Miss Harvey waited until the train started again before resuming the conversation. "I thought I saw some disturbance in the street," she said. "There are a number of roughs out tonight."

"There are indeed," Dr. Doyle told her. "I must say, Miss Harvey, this is no night for a young lady to be abroad. Between the snow and the riot . . ."

"Riot? Is it really so bad? Mother will be most distressed." Miss Harvey's face clouded over. "She can be quite difficult, you see, and since Father died, she has been quite dependent on me for support. He left very little. That is why I placed the advertisement in the newspapers to offer to type manuscripts. It was very kind of Mr. Levin to allow me to do my work at home instead of at his office."

"Mr. Basset may have had something to say about that," Dr. Doyle said. "I wish you well in your endeavors, Miss Harvey. Here is our stop."

"And mine," she said, as she followed them onto the platform and presented her ticket to be punched. "Mother and I have lodgings off the King's Road."

"Then you know this area?" Mr. Dodgson asked.

"We have lived here since I was a child," Miss Harvey said with a sad smile. "My father was once much in demand as an art critic and consultant in the design of buildings. Mr. Wilde once said . . ."

"Was your father an architect?" Mr. Dodgson asked sharply, trying to place Miss Harvey in the social scheme of things.

"He was consulted," Miss Harvey corrected him. "Unfortunately, my poor father was not in good health in recent years, and when he died, his friends were not as forthcoming as they might have been. I do not like taking charity, gentlemen, and typewriting is as good a way as any to provide a few small comforts for my mother."

By now they had left the Sloane Square station and were proceeding westward along the King's Road, a well-paved, well-lit thoroughfare, lined with shops and eating places. The shutters had already been put up, closing off the glass windows of the shops from thieves, but the pubs and taverns were full of eager diners and gesticulating debaters.

Miss Harvey led them along the byways of Chelsea. The snow was settling on the railings of the houses, making little caps on the fireplugs that interspersed the streets. There was no echo in this corner of London of the mobs that were gathering in Trafalgar Square. Here were tidy little streets, with neat rows of houses, tucked behind the shops of King's Road or across from the bulk of the Chelsea Hospital.

Mr. Dodgson frowned as he tried to understand Miss Harvey's social status. "Are you acquainted with Mr. Oscar Wilde?" he asked.

"Not really," Miss Harvey demurred. "But my mother has left cards with Mrs. Wilde, and Mrs. Wilde kindly came to call on her. Of course, Mrs. Wilde is presently"—Miss Harvey paused, trying to find the right words—"Mrs. Wilde is not in a condition to receive visitors at the present time."

"Eh? Is the woman ill?" Mr. Dodgson asked. "I would not like to bother her if she is . . ."

Dr. Doyle smothered a laugh under his mustache, as he recognized the current euphemism. "Not ill, sir, but expectant."

"Of what?" The older man was still befuddled.

"Of a new arrival," Dr. Doyle said. "Which explains why Mr. Wilde is so eager for a position. If he is to be a father, he must be able to provide for his growing family."

"I see," Mr. Dodgson said. "Dear me. That would make it even more imperative that we clear his name."

"Mr. Wilde? What has he done?" Miss Harvey asked.

"He may have assaulted Mr. Samuel Basset," Mr. Dodgson told her.

"Oh no!" Miss Harvey gasped. "I cannot believe that! Why, he is such a charming man and so very gallant towards his wife!"

"I only hope he is gallant enough to come home in a snow-storm," Dr. Doyle said. "Miss Harvey, you have been very kind, but you should be returning to your own lodgings. Your mother will be expecting you. . . ."

"I will accompany you to Tite Street," Miss Harvey insisted. "You will never find it otherwise. And then I will go home to Mother." The thought did not seem to cheer her.

Miss Harvey led the way around Burton's Court, down Smith Street, around Tedworth Square, and into Tite Street, a prosaic street with a row of small brick houses, each with its railing, each with its covered set of steps leading up to the front door. It was at one of these modest dwellings that she knocked, while Mr. Dodgson and Dr. Doyle waited impatiently on the stairs.

The door was opened by a young woman dressed in the so-called "Aesthetic" style of high-waisted, long-sleeved dress, without the tight-boned waist or bustle demanded by fashion.

"Good evening, Mrs. Wilde," Miss Harvey greeted her.

"Miss Harvey?" Mrs. Wilde looked through the snow towards the King's Road. "Has Oscar come with you? He told me he was going to the city . . ." Her voice trailed off as she saw the two men standing on the front steps.

"My card, madam." Mr. Dodgson passed it to her.

"These gentlemen were looking for Mr. Wilde, and I thought I had better come along to introduce them," Miss Harvey said.

"Do come in then," Mrs. Wilde said, peering at the card, as

the two men and Miss Harvey stepped out of the snow and into the front hall.

"We do not wish to inconvenience you," Mr. Dodgson said diffidently, as Dr. Doyle removed his plaid greatcoat and deerstalker hat.

"Do come to the fire, gentlemen; you must be quite cold," Mrs. Wilde said, leading the way into the sitting room. "I am always at home to my neighbors, Miss Harvey, but I do not understand why you two gentlemen are here on such a dreadful night."

"Perhaps this note will explain." Mr. Dodgson scrabbled in his pockets and produced the note from George du Maurier. He looked about the room, trying to gather his thoughts, while his hostess scanned the brief message. The sitting room had been painted white and decorated with examples of Mr. Morris's furniture. The ceiling had been embellished with white peacock feathers, which held Mr. Dodgson's interest for so long that Dr. Doyle was almost ready to jump into the conversation.

"As you see, madam, it is your husband we are seeking," Mr. Dodgson said, as Mrs. Wilde folded the note again and looked up with a puzzled expression.

"Oscar?" Mrs. Wilde frowned. "He is not at home, although I expect him shortly. He often is late to dinner, and if the snow outside is very deep, he may be very late."

"In that case, madam, have you any idea where he may be found? Is he at a particular club, for instance?" Mr. Dodgson persisted.

"Please sit down, sir, and warm yourself." Mrs. Wilde drew her unexpected guests closer to the fire, where a small table had been set with teapot, teacups, and a plate of bread and butter.

Dr. Doyle's stomach reminded him once again that he had had nothing to eat since the sandwich he had consumed on the train from Portsmouth. That had been nearly six hours ago. His mouth watered at the sight of the humble slabs, ready for toasting.

Mrs. Wilde seemed instinctively to recognize hunger. "Do sit down, gentlemen," she said, indicating the wooden chairs drawn up to the fireplace in a semicircle.

"This is Dr. Doyle," Mr. Dodgson introduced his companion, who was trying hard not to ogle the platter with its slices of bread and butter.

"Is Oscar ill?" Mrs. Wilde passed the platter to Dr. Doyle, who restrained himself from grabbing the lot and merely took one slice.

"I have no idea. I must find him before the police do." Mr. Dodgson ignored the offering of bread and butter.

"The police?" Mrs. Wilde was thoroughly alarmed. "It is not the bailiffs, is it? Because everyone will be paid as soon as Oscar finds employment. He went to Fleet Street this very day . . ."

"Yes, ma'am, we know," Dr. Doyle soothed her. "But Mr. Samuel Basset did not employ your husband, and he was heard to threaten Mr. Basset. Then, when Mr. Basset was attacked . . ."

"Mr. Basset attacked!" Mrs. Wilde gasped.

"In the street, outside the offices," Mr. Dodgson told her. "And a large man, very like your husband, Mrs. Wilde, was seen on the scene of the crime. He dropped this scarf."

Mr. Dodgson had picked up a slice of bread and butter and was absently munching on it. Now he pulled the woolen scarf from around his neck and passed it to their hostess.

She looked at the homely object carefully, passing it through her fingers and tracing the design.

"This is not Oscar's," she stated firmly. "It is Irish, of that I am quite sure. The women of the Aran Isles knit jerseys and mufflers in these patterns, each one unique to a particular clan or family. This one has been used often. See, here, where the yarn is nearly worn through?" She pointed to the flaw in the scarf.

"But it is of Irish manufacture," Mr. Dodgson repeated.

"The design certainly is Irish," Mrs. Wilde reiterated. "Whether the wearer is Irish is, of course, another matter. It does not belong to my husband. Of that I am quite, quite sure."

Mr. Dodgson nodded several times. "It is a pity that you cannot tell me where you husband is," he said. "It would help convince the policeman in charge that he had nothing to do with the death of Mr. Basset if he could produce a viable alibi."

69

"Death?" Mrs. Wilde gasped. "You said Mr. Basset was attacked."

"He was," Dr. Doyle explained. "But the cause of death was not the blow to the head, but a stab in the back. That would indicate some other person, with a great deal of animus against Mr. Basset, thrust a knife into him before this mysterious Irishman hit him on the head. Unfortunately, the police inspector on the case seemed quite determined to bring Mr. Oscar Wilde in, and we are just as determined that he should not."

Mrs. Wilde frowned. "Oscar sometimes meets Mr. Whistler for tea," she said slowly. "Sometimes at his studio, and sometimes at the Café Royal."

Mr. Dodgson stood up, shook out his coat, and adjusted his hat. "The Café Royal," he repeated. "I shall have to find it."

"There is a cab stand near the Royal Hospital at the end of the street," Mrs. Wilde said helpfully. "One of the cabbies will be able to assist you. And if you find Oscar, do send him home," she added wistfully.

"We most assuredly shall remind him of his familial responsibilities," Mr. Dodgson told her. He turned to Miss Harvey. "You, too, must get yourself home, my dear. This is no night for a young woman to be abroad."

Miss Harvey nodded. "I wish you luck in your search, sir."

Dr. Doyle once again donned the plaid greatcoat and adjusted the deerstalker hat, with an inward sigh and a wistful look at the platter of bread and butter.

"Shall we walk with you, Miss Harvey?" Mr. Dodgson offered.

"I live only around the corner," Miss Harvey demurred. "And you must find a cab, and get to Mr. Wilde before that dreadful policeman does. Think of poor Constance . . . Mrs. Wilde, that is . . . if Mr. Wilde should be taken into custody."

"Nonsense," Dr. Doyle protested. "We can't possibly allow a lady to walk out unescorted on a night like this, especially with mobs out in force. Miss Harvey, you must allow us to see you safely to your door."

"If you insist on it," Miss Harvey said. "But you must not come in. My mother can be somewhat . . . tedious," she said with a small smile. "If she sees me escorted by two gentlemen, she may decide that one or both of you should make me an offer."

Dr. Doyle chuckled. "That would be difficult, since I am already married, and Mr. Dodgson is not in the running."

The three of them maneuvered down the steps and back to the broad expanse of the Royal Hospital Road. A lone cab and horse plodded down the road on its way back to the shelter of a warm stable.

Mr. Dodgson hailed the cab and thrust Miss Harvey and Dr. Doyle into it before the cabby could protest.

"We shall go to"—Mr. Dodgson turned to Miss Harvey, who gave the required directions—"and from there to the Café Royal."

Dr. Doyle frowned. "If that mob in Fleet Street is any indication of what's afoot," he said, "MacRae may have other fish to fry tonight. The death of one editor, no matter how evil, may be as nothing if those workmen decide to take matters into their own hands."

"In that case," Mr. Dodgson said, "once we have discharged our duty to Mr. Wilde, I will treat you to dinner, Dr. Doyle. I owe you at least that much for bringing you to London under false pretenses."

CHAPTER 8

T he snow was still falling gently as Mr. Dodgson and Dr. Doyle let Miss Harvey out in front of one of the brick row houses that lined Holbein Gardens.

"Thank you for taking me up," Miss Harvey said, eyeing the large front windows, where a form could be seen hovering behind the lace curtains eagerly observing the cab.

"It was nothing more than common courtesy," Mr. Dodgson told her. "Give my regards to your mother and explain that you were well-protected all evening."

Miss Harvey scurried up the steps, while the two men turned to more important matters.

Dr. Doyle called up to the cabby, "Do you know the Café Royal?"

"In Regent Street? Aye, that I do." The cabby seemed to snigger unpleasantly as he clicked his tongue at his horse.

"Take us there," Mr. Dodgson ordered.

The cabby made a noise that could have been a cough or a laugh, and Mr. Dodgson and Dr. Doyle settled back into the growler as it bumped and slid along the snow-covered streets.

Mr. Dodgson muttered to himself, "This makes no sense. No sense at all."

"Why do you say that, sir?" Dr. Doyle asked.

"Why should anyone wish to dispose of Mr. Samuel Basset?" The question was not rhetorical. Mr. Dodgson really wanted to know.

"He wasn't very pleasant," Dr. Doyle said.

"He was not. He was rude to his subordinates; he stole ideas from his staff and published the results under his own name; he sold books that were defective and meant for those who could not afford better copies. None of these defects of character were dire enough to lead someone to kill him."

"As to that, Mr. Dodgson, we cannot be certain," Dr. Doyle protested. "You and I have seen the extreme measures that have been taken by persons in the grip of some obsession."

Mr. Dodgson nodded. "Quite true. Obviously, Mr. Basset had offended someone so grievously that the person felt driven to murder. We must discover more about him. We cannot proceed without facts."

Mr. Dodgson huddled himself into his overcoat, while Dr. Doyle peered out the window of the cab at the passing scene, or as much of it as he could see between the smears of dirt on the window and the swirling snow in the streets. He wondered if they could get something to eat at the Café Royal. It was well past teatime, and while Mrs. Wilde's bread and butter stayed the pangs of hunger for an hour, he looked forward to something more substantial.

The growler slogged on, as the horse picked its way from King's Road to Sloane Street, around Hyde Park, and through the exclusive areas of London used by the aristocracy as their particular domain. Here the streets were kept free of snow by crossing sweepers plying their brooms vigorously in hopes of a penny or two doled out by the servants in the elegant establishments that lined the streets of Mayfair and Belgravia.

The cab went on, around Grosvenor Place and onto the broad avenue known as Piccadilly. Here they met with traffic headed in the opposite direction: private carriages and cabs rather than omnibuses and drays. The cab lurched eastward until it reached the great crossroads marked by the statue of Eros, where the slow march came to a dead halt.

Mr. Dodgson stopped muttering to himself and came back to reality. "Cabby," he called, banging on the roof of the growler, "why are we stopping?"

"Seems to be quite a crowd in the road," the cabby reported.

Dr. Doyle opened the door of the cab and peered through the snow. Just as the cabby had said, the street was filled with people, somewhat better dressed than those in Fleet Street, but just as angry.

"Apparently, the evening papers have been distributed," Dr. Doyle told his mentor. "I do not think these people liked what they read."

From the noise of angry voices raised in protest, that seemed to be an understatement. Shop assistants, waiters from restaurants and taverns, and loungers of various sexes and degrees of gentility were merging with the printers and workers from Fleet Street and the Strand until the whole road was filled with people. Well-dressed ladies and gentlemen found themselves jostled by the mob as they tried to get into their hotels and restaurants. Horses reared and plunged, as daring men and boys grabbed at the reins and banged on the sides of the carriages.

A speaker had mounted another soapbox under the statue of Eros: a brawny individual with a broad Scots accent, who echoed the words of Hyndman as he exhorted the crowd around him. "Brothers in labor! It is time to rise up and take what is rightfully ours, earned by the sweat of our brows and the sinews of our arms!"

"Go to it, John Burns!" yelled someone in the crowd.

"Give 'em what for!"

"This will never do," Mr. Dodgson fretted, as the cab was rocked by one of the rioters.

"Where are the police when one needs them?" Dr. Doyle scanned the crowd ahead of them.

"More importantly, how far are we from the Café Royal?" Mr. Dodgson called up to the cabby.

"It's down Regent Street aways, but I can't speak for your safety if you leave this yer cab," the cabby warned them.

"I can't guarantee that an innocent man will not go to jail if I don't," Mr. Dodgson retorted. He handed the cabby his fare and left the haven of the cab, pushing through the crowd to the pavement, while Dr. Doyle fended off possible attack from behind.

If anything, the crowd in Piccadilly was more volatile and diverse than the marchers in Fleet Street. Not only were there workingmen and food vendors, but a number of villainous-looking characters had joined the throng, looking for trouble and finding quite a bit of it. Small children whose sex was disguised by dirt and rags were running about in the street, picking up whatever scraps of food were dropped by the pie vendors, apple women, or fish-and-chips barrows. Gaudily dressed young women and men sauntered along the edges of the crowd on the theory that any large group of people would generate some business.

The falling snow was soon trampled into a thick mush as the crowd surged around Piccadilly Circus, across the Haymarket and lower Regent Street and into Trafalgar Square, where they joined the mob that had already come through the Strand. John Burns carried his soapbox as he marched along, ready to add his voice to Hyndman's in their quest for social justice.

Mr. Dodgson looked wildly about him as he was pushed this way and that by the crowd. Dr. Doyle grabbed the nearest passerby, a young man in ragged trousers and oversized patched jacket, with a packet of newspapers under his arm.

"Here, laddie!" Dr. Doyle's Scottish burr became more distinct. "Can ye direct us to the Café Royal?"

The newsboy eyed the pair and whistled between his teeth. "Never would've took yer fer that lot, guv'nor!"

Dr. Doyle felt vaguely offended. He was beginning to suspect there was something unsavory about the Café Royal, something that would make it an unsuitable place for Mr. Dodgson to be seen in. The mere mention of the name had caused an unseemly reaction earlier, and the gentlemen at *Punch* had clearly felt it would not be a good idea to send Mr. Dodgson there (for they must have known it was Mr. Wilde's favorite haunt). Dr. Doyle followed Mr. Dodgson and the newsboy around the corner to Regent Street, where the boy indicated a large and imposing structure, lit up by electric lights.

"Over there, guv'nor," the boy said, pointing across the street and pocketing the coin Dr. Doyle offered him.

"Too much traffic to risk crossing the road?" Dr. Doyle hinted.

The boy shook his head. "You don't catch me in there, guv'nor. I got me reputation to consider!" He waved cheerfully and dove back into the crowd, bawling out, "Getcher *Standard*! Latest news!"

The Café Royal fairly dominated Regent Street, one of Nash's more elaborate additions to the London scene during the Napoleonic era. There was no subterfuge about the Café Royal. It stood out, well lit and elaborately decorated, with a muscular doorman on hand to turn the revolving door that welcomed the traveler into the lobby.

Mr. Dodgson and Dr. Doyle were duly swept up by the doorman and deposited in the aforesaid lobby, where Mr. Dodgson blinked in the glare of the electric lights, and Dr. Doyle took in the full grandeur of the scene. Ladies in elaborate gowns, blazing with jewels, ascended the grand staircase that led to the private rooms, accompanied by escorts in full evening dress or brilliant dress uniforms of the armed services. Young boys in tightly buttoned page boy uniforms trotted up and down the stairs with messages or orders. Only the waiters were missing; their services were rendered almost invisibly, through a network of stairs in the back of the building.

"Where is Mr. Wilde?" Mr. Dodgson asked aloud, regarding the three doors that led to the public rooms on the ground floor. One appeared to lead to the reception room, where a young woman in a modest black dress cared for coats, capes, and other outdoor wraps. One led to a small, dark bar. The third door led to a public dining room, from which the sounds of laughter seemed to echo and reecho.

"May I be of assistance?" An imposing figure in the full-dress garb of a headwaiter approached them.

"We are looking for Mr. Oscar Wilde," Mr. Dodgson said. Once more he produced his card. "I was told he dines here frequently. Is he here now?"

"Mr. Wilde is one of our noted patrons," the maître d'hotel admitted reluctantly. "I will see if he is here at present." He left the two men to observe the passing scene, while he removed himself to the inner recesses of the dining room.

Dr. Doyle sniffed the air hungrily. Perhaps, after they finished their business with Wilde, he and Mr. Dodgson could sample the cuisine.

A pair of young men in loud checked suits pushed by the two, happily entering the sacred hall without hindrance.

"Do you think we might just go in?" Dr. Doyle suggested. "It is, after all, a public restaurant."

"I would not like to give the impression that we were planning to dine here," Mr. Dodgson objected. "And our message to Mr. Wilde is of a personal nature."

"Dining here might not be so bad an idea," Dr. Doyle said.

"I prefer the Holborn," Mr. Dodgson said firmly. "I had not thought to be in London at all tonight. I am supposed to dine in Hall. All this rushing about, looking for Mr. Wilde . . ."

"Did I hear my name mentioned?" The ubiquitous Irishman poked his head out from behind the glass partition. "Mr. Dodgson? It really is you! I thought that card was some sort of prank. Whatever are you doing in London?"

"I came to introduce my friend Dr. Doyle to Mr. Samuel Basset," Mr. Dodgson explained. "In fact, we were in the office of *Youth's Companion* when you made your dramatic departure."

"Dramatic indeed!" Wilde laughed heartily. "Come, Mr. Dodgson, you must sit down and have a drink."

Wilde led the two of them to a table at the farthest end of the room, where several young men were sitting, smoking cigarettes, and drinking various beverages, none of which was tea. Mr. Dodgson sat down on the edge of the chair that was offered to him, while Dr. Doyle took a better look at his surroundings.

The Café Royal had been designed for luxury. The restaurant was lavishly decorated in burgundy and white, with a painted ceiling that might rival that of the Palace of Versailles. Round tables were placed around the floor, while banquettes against the walls provided some measure of privacy for those parties that had decided to use the public rather than the private rooms. Wilde's coterie occupied one whole corner of the room and made enough noise to equal the rest.

The clientele of the Café Royal's public restaurant seemed to be exclusively male, consisting of older men in dress suits and younger ones in dinner jackets or sack suits. Dr. Doyle sniffed the air, then frowned. Over the aromas of good food was the odor of patchouli. Could it be, he wondered, that the men in this room were using scent?

His eyes narrowed as he observed the patrons of the Café Royal. The gentleman with the silvery hair was positively stroking the hand of his young companion, who was gazing soulfully into the older man's eyes. Two younger men in sack suits in a corner banquette were holding hands, while the male couple next to them seemed to be having some sort of polite argument. The only women he could see were two ladies in severely tailored dark dresses bending over their plates at one of the tables in the middle of the room.

It suddenly came to Dr. Doyle what sort of place he and his scholarly friend had stumbled into. He had heard about such things from the sailors on his two sea voyages, but it had never occurred to him to explore them while he was away from the constraints of English society; and as a happily married man, he was not about to start now. What sort of man, Dr. Doyle asked himself, would desert a charming young wife to enjoy the dubious charms of these young men, with their sidelong glances and twisted smiles? Would he be able to smash a man down with a blow simply because he had been refused a position?

The subject of these ruminations had made a place at the table for Mr. Dodgson by jocularly ousting the young man with the dark curls and intense black eyes who had previously held the seat.

"Ern, be off with you," Wilde said, tapping the young man on the shoulder. "I'll have you know this is a true gentleman and a scholar, although what he is doing here I cannot tell you. Waiter, a glass of something for Mr. Dodgson. What can I offer you, sir? Champagne?"

"Considering that you have no employment at the moment, since you did not get the position at *Youth's Companion,*" Mr. Dodgson said stiffly, "and that your wife is waiting dinner for you and is quite anxious about your whereabouts, I shall not impose upon your time or your resources. I only came to warn you that a policeman is coming with a warrant to arrest you on a charge of assault and battery. Possibly even murder."

The result of this melodramatic announcement was a thunderous peal of laughter from Wilde and a round of tittering from his companions.

"Arrest me for what? Who am I supposed to have assaulted and battered?" Wilde asked when he had recovered from his laughing fit.

Mr. Dodgson's testiness brought out his stammer. "Mr. Samuel B-basset was struck d-down in front of his very offices in Fleet Street this afternoon," he declared. "A man of your description was seen arguing with him and striking him down. The man then ran away down the Strand."

"Is that all?" Wilde made a noise that might have been a snort of disgust or a suppressed giggle.

"It is no laughing matter, Mr. Wilde," Mr. Dodgson reproved him in the tones used to correct obstreperous undergraduates. "Inspector MacRae of Scotland Yard, who has charge of the case, apparently knows you, or knows of you, and has taken you into dislike. Mr. Levin, Mr. Basset's assistant, blurted out that you had been in the office that day and had had words with Mr. Basset that had led to Mr. Basset, in effect, throwing you out of the premises."

"But that does not mean that I wanted to kill him," Wilde said. "He refused me employment. So have a number of other people. If I were to bash in the head of every man who refused me employment, I would be the greatest murderer since Bluebeard.

What evidence does this Inspector MacRae have that I was any-where near Fleet Street at the time . . . When did all this assaulting and battering take place?"

Mr. Dodgson consulted his pocket watch. "It was just on five o'clock," he said. "And it is now nearly eight."

"Is that Christ Church Time or Greenwich Time?" Wilde asked innocently.

"It is London time," Mr. Dodgson said severely.

"Surely, you have not been here for three hours!" Dr. Doyle exclaimed.

"Has it really been that long?" Wilde said innocently. "My dear fellows, it was snowing!"

"It still is," Dr. Doyle muttered.

"Well, what would you have me to do?" Wilde looked around at his audience. "Shall I make a dash for the Continent? Fly, all is discovered?"

"You might consider going home," Mr. Dodgson told him.

"Of course. Anyone who knows me will tell these meddling policemen that if you wish to find me, you should look for me anyplace *but* at home." He took a sip from his wineglass, then said, "It really doesn't matter. Your Inspector MacRae can get as many warrants as he likes. I have been here from four-thirty onwards, as these fine lads can tell you. Isn't that right, boys?"

There was a chorus of assent from around the table.

"So you see, Mr. Dodgson, it was very kind of you to take the trouble to warn me of impending doom, but it was quite unnecessary. I have an alibi that will stand up in any court in the land." Wilde gestured towards his entourage.

"Nevertheless, Mr. Wilde, I strongly suggest that you make yourself scarce until this matter is resolved," Mr. Dodgson said. "Now, I have done my duty. You have been warned."

"Oh, warning me does no good. I always give into temptation," Wilde replied with an expressive shrug.

Mr. Dodgson stood up and bowed stiffly. "In that case, Mr. Wilde, I will leave you to dine with your friends."

"But won't you join us?" Wilde smiled winningly at the older man. "There's plenty of room."

Mr. Dodgson looked over the company and shook his head. "I thank you, but no. My friend Dr. Doyle must catch his train. His wife will be worried about him," he added, with emphasis on the word "wife."

The intended rebuke went unheeded. Mr. Dodgson looked about him for his hat. The young man whose seat he had usurped retrieved the unfashionable high black hat from the floor and handed it to Mr. Dodgson along with the Irish knit scarf.

Wilde fingered the scarf with a quizzical look. "Is this yours, Mr. Dodgson? It's not at all your style. Do you have an Irish servant at Christ Church?"

"I beg your pardon?" Mr. Dodgson's voice rose shrilly.

"I meant this scarf," Wilde said. "Where did you get it? To my knowledge, they are not made for sale. They are given to a loved one, to protect him from evil."

"This was found on the person of Mr. Samuel Basset," Mr. Dodgson said. "I am of the opinion that the one who dropped it might well be the one who struck him in the street. It is, as you have noted, of Irish manufacture."

"This was never made by a machine," Wilde corrected him. "It was knit by hand to the ancient Celtic pattern. It is an art that is becoming scarcer as the machine takes over the task of the skilled worker." Wilde's air of flippancy left him as he examined the scarf carefully.

"Observe!" Wilde pointed to the scarf. "There are slight imperfections in the thread, which is undyed. As I said, this sort of scarf is not made for sale. You cannot obtain one in a shop. Only a female member of the family, a mother or sister—"

"Or a wife," Dr. Doyle put in.

"If you say so. Now, as to the owner. There are traces of dark powder in the threads of this scarf, and there is a distinct odor of printer's ink. If I were asked, I would say that the owner of this scarf is a printer, Irish, and probably has red hair." Wilde indicated two tiny filaments caught in the fibers.

Dr. Doyle whipped out the little magnifying glass that went with him everywhere. "You are quite right," he said. He looked at Wilde, then at the entourage, and decided he would never un-

81

derstand how a man with such acuity and such taste could desert a charming wife and cozy home in Chelsea for the dubious delights of the Café Royal.

"If I were your Inspector MacRae, which thanks be to God I am not," Wilde said, "I would seek out an Irish printer with red hair and ask him what he was doing at five o'clock this evening."

"O'Casey!" Dr. Doyle exclaimed. "He was in Fleet Street, ranting against his employer."

"Then we must find him," Mr. Dodgson decided. "I have warned you, Mr. Wilde, and I only feel it fair to warn O'Casey of his fate. I am sorry, Mr. Wilde, but I cannot dine with you tonight. I trust you will go home to your wife before the snow makes the roads impassable." He looked around the table and shuddered. "Boys," he muttered to himself, just loud enough to be heard. "I dislike boys intensely."

"Now that is a pity, Mr. Dodgson," Wilde responded. "You are going to miss a good dinner, and I *do* like boys. Intensely!"

The laughter followed Mr. Dodgson and Dr. Doyle out the restaurant door and back into the lobby.

"What do we do now?" Dr. Doyle asked, almost wishing that Mr. Dodgson had taken Wilde's offer of dinner.

"We find Mr. O'Casey and return his scarf to him," Mr. Dodgson said firmly. "And then we shall dine at the Holborn Hotel. It is far too late for you to get the train back to Portsmouth, even assuming that the trains are running at all. As for your room, do not worry about the charge. You were kind enough to provide for my lodging when I visited you in Southsea last year. I insist on returning the favor."

This settled, the two men buttoned their coats and dove back into the snowy streets in search of the errant printer.

CHAPTER 9

Inspector MacRae had had a bad day.

He had reported for his shift that morning with every intention of ferreting out information on the Fenian miscreants who had bombed the offices of the Metropolitan Police some fifteen months previously. He felt sure that he was closing in on the gang. He had already made contact with several persons who swore they knew members of the Irish revolutionary societies that had been making their grievances known in newspapers, manifestoes, and rabid speeches at Hyde Park Corner on Sunday afternoons.

One of his informants had shown him the handbills that were being spread around the docks and through the East End. "If the Poor Relief Bill don't go through, we're on the march!" said the informant with the air of one determined to sacrifice himself for the Cause. Since MacRae had every reason to believe that the informant's usual occupation involved removing objects from vacant houses while the owners were on holiday, he took the handbill to Scotland Yard, where he was called into the offices of Chief Inspector Warren.

"What do you make of this?" Warren had a selection of handbills on his desk, all calling for a meeting in Trafalgar Square at seven o'clock in the evening of that date.

"Just the usual, sir. But it might be prudent to have some constables at the ready," MacRae said.

Warren, a veteran of more than one Indian skirmish on the Northern Frontier, nodded. "I don't think this will amount to much. There was no end of fuss about the Chartists back in my grandfather's day, and they washed out with the rain, hahaha!" He chortled gleefully, recalling how the revolutionary ardor of the mob had cooled in a violent rainstorm. "But perhaps you'd better take a squad out, just in case of trouble."

Accordingly, MacRae had stationed twenty constables at intervals along the Strand, and had taken ten more to Fleet Street, where his mission to halt Irish terrorism had been sidetracked by the inconvenient death of one Samuel Basset, possibly at the hands of the Irishman Wilde.

MacRae did not approve of Oscar Wilde. He had never met the man, had never heard him lecture, and knew only what he read in *Punch* about his affectations. However, he had heard from fellow officers that Wilde had been seen with dubious companions in the neighborhood of the Café Royal and that, combined with his national origin, was enough for MacRae to put him on the list of possible suspects. As soon as the matter of the riot was dealt with, MacRae decided, he would get a warrant and arrest Oscar Wilde. It would not be difficult to find the man; if he were not at the Café Royal with his associates in crime, he would be at his house in Chelsea. Wilde could wait.

The riot could not. The ubiquitous handbills had been distributed around the barrows in Covent Garden and up and down Piccadilly, urging all good workers to join their brethren in Trafalgar Square in protesting the miserable wages paid to day laborers, and the heartless manner in which charity funds were doled out to the indigent. The poverty-stricken Londoners who could read spelled out the information to those who could not. One or two, then three or four, then in the dozens, they streamed out of the side streets and tangled alleys to join the mob in the Strand that had flowed out of the East End via Fleet Street.

No one had sent handbills to the ultraexclusive enclaves of Belgravia and Mayfair. None of the inhabitants of the houses of the aristocracy or the merely rich would be informed that the poor were on the march demanding social justice in Trafalgar Square at seven o'clock in the evening. The veritable battalions of servants who ministered to the owners of the houses in Belgravia and Mayfair were not interested in protesting their lot, since they considered themselves lucky to be employed in such comfortable surroundings. None of the cooks, butlers, housekeepers, maids, grooms, valets, or kitchen slaveys would have taken the time to appear amongst the unwashed masses in Trafalgar Square, not on a Wednesday night and certainly not while it was snowing.

It was, therefore, a shock to the wealthy and well-dressed crowd descending on the West End theaters and restaurants for a night of amiable diversion to find a mob of poor and ill-dressed people barring their way on Oxford Street, Piccadilly, and the Strand. The result was chaos.

Men in corduroy trousers and patched jackets, women in flannel skirts and petticoats, children whose picturesque tatters masked very real hunger and cold collided with the well-dressed ladies and gentlemen draped in the best woolen suiting (if male) or fur and velvet (if female). Carriages were rocked back and forth, while horses reared and kicked in terror at such handling. Through it all the snow kept falling, making it difficult to tell friend from foe, except by the quality of their clothing.

The press was well represented, with reporters marching along with the ragged workers, scribbling madly as they recorded the sights and sounds of combat for their morning readers. Was this to be the much-heralded and feared revolution preached by Herren Marx and Engels? Would England suffer the same fate as France and be forced to endure a commune of the workers? The reporters shivered in their thin jackets or overcoats and huddled in doorways, peering at their notepads by the light of flickering gas jets that diffracted through the falling snow and gave an eerie glow to the proceedings. Sketch artists tried to capture the mood of the crowd in a quick drawing that would be sent for engraving in time for the morning editions.

The wooden blocks of the pavement were prized out of their places. Some enterprising soul had discovered a cache of bricks to be used in refacing the façade of one of the larger shops. These missiles were joyously seized and shaken fiercely by large rough hands bent on destruction of the status quo.

The fountain at Trafalgar Square was now the center of the action. Henry Hyndman had taken his soapbox and joined his larger and rougher companion, John Burns, at one side of the square. They had been joined in leadership by the Irish printer, O'Casey, who took up a position between the two official leaders of the Social Democratic Federation. Tom Mann, the perpetrator of the handbills from the Fair Trade League, found himself outnumbered and outshouted by the other three, who subverted what was supposed to be a peaceful demonstration with their calls for social action.

The ringing tones of Hyndman were echoed by the mellifluous Irish brogue of the printer, O'Casey, and the gruff Scottish bark of Burns.

"My brothers, we must take back what is ours by right!" Hyndman exhorted the crowd.

"The gentlemen sit in their fine clubs, drinking wine and eating meat, while our children starve for a crust of bread!" O'Casey roared out. "Their wives wear warm furs, while ours shiver in a shawl! Shall we allow it?"

"Never!" Hyndman glared at the printer, not willing to share the spotlight.

"It's the right of every man to be fed and clothed," Burns insisted.

"Then let's get fed and clothed!" someone in the crowd shouted out. There was the sound of heavy boots on the bricks of the pavement, and the sucking sound of mud underfoot as the newly fallen snow was transformed into slush by the press of feet. A whoop and a tinkle of glass set off a chain of similar sounds. Those shops that were not shuttered were being looted.

"Do not be distracted, my brothers!" Hyndman shouted, waving his arms. No one paid him the least attention. The crowd had seen the shops in Bond Street, their glass windows barely concealed by wooden shutters. There were goods for the taking, and taken they were!

Once started, the looting grew in intensity. Market women squabbled over ready-made shirts on display in shopwindows. Longshoremen discovered the wine shops and began sampling their wares. The broken glass made for painful going for the barefoot children scrambling amongst the debris for whatever they could find. One child was pushed out of the way, while a larger adult grabbed at the luscious fruit in the shopwindow of a luxurious greengrocery. The sounds of fists on flesh were added to those of breaking wood and glass. Over all, the snow whirled and spun, giving a magical air to the scene.

"No! No!" Hyndman screamed into the crowd. It was no use. Neither the Fair Trade League nor the Social Democratic Federation could stop the mob any more than the blue-coated Metropolitan Police could. The London mob was a force to be reckoned with, as elemental as the wind and the snow, and just as controllable.

Inspector MacRae watched with horrified fascination as the orderly protest disintegrated into a full-blown riot. His twenty men were clearly no match for the multitude now thronging the Strand, let alone the others in Trafalgar Square. He beckoned one of the constables to his side.

"Send to Bow Street, Constable. We'll need some reinforcements."

"Aye," the constable said, casting an eye over the crowd. "And a Black Maria as well."

"On your way," MacRae ordered. He wiped the snow off his spectacles and tried to assess the situation. He had not expected the violence, in spite of what his informant had told him. After the vote in the House, it was only to be expected that the more vocal elements of the Irish and radical (to MacRae, they were synonymous) communities would take to the soapboxes and air their grievances. It was their right as Englishmen to do so, although MacRae wished they had chosen a more clement evening to vent their feelings.

What they did not have the right to do, and would not be

allowed to continue doing, was to put their fierce and fighting words into action. This so-called political meeting had crossed the line into criminal activity, and MacRae sent another message to Scotland Yard for more constables to be stationed in Piccadilly and Regent Street. It was becoming obvious to MacRae that the police vans had better be alerted as well. There would be arrests, many arrests, and the Bow Street Police Station would have to be ready to hold them against the morning magistrate's court sessions.

One of the ragged youngsters pulled at the inspector's long coat. "Hoy! Copper!"

"What's amiss? What do you want?" MacRae turned to look at the boy.

"There's a dead 'un back there yonder." The boy's eyes were huge in his blackened face.

"What do you say?" Inspector MacRae tried to peer through the falling snow to see if the reinforcements from Kensington had arrived yet.

" 'E's lyin' there in 'is gore," the boy said, quoting one of the more vivid terms used by the press.

"Where? Show me!" MacRae motioned the nearest constable, a tall stalwart with the brass number of the Bow Street Station on his helmet. "Come with me, Constable. Boy, where is this body?"

The boy shoved his way against the press of people, dodged several stones, and found the alleyway where the body of the late David Peterson lay.

"Nasty way to die," commented the constable.

MacRae frowned. "Any way's nasty, Constable. This changes everything. There's murder done here, and someone's going to pay for it."

"What shall we do with 'im?" the constable wanted to know.

"You stay with him until the ambulance can take him over to St. Bart's," MacRae decided.

"And how are we to find who flung the stone that knocked this poor chap on the head?" the constable asked. "Which of 'em will say, 'I done it'?"

"We haul 'em all in and sort 'em out later," MacRae declared. "Constable, have you a good, loud voice?"

"I've got a bass that's the pride of Zion Chapel," the constable confided.

"Then, my lad, you get to do the honors." MacRae fumbled in his coat and drew out a much-folded paper. "You read that, and do it properly."

The two of them stood under the nearest gas lamp, while the constable scanned the paper. "Is this correct?" he asked his superior.

"It is," MacRae said grimly. "And we cannot make an arrest until it is read; so, Constable, read them the Riot Act!"

"Aye, sir!" The constable took a deep breath. "In the name of the queen! By the Act of Parliament of 1715, this gathering is declared an unlawful assembly; all herein assembled are ordered to disperse at once!"

There was no reaction to this announcement. The looting continued unabated.

MacRae smiled grimly. His steel-rimmed spectacles fairly glittered in the lamplight.

"The Riot Act having been duly read, this gathering is now declared an illegal assembly. All persons on the streets are now declared subject to arrest and imprisonment! Constables . . . do your duty! And you, boy," he added, scribbling a note on his ever-present notebook and tearing it out. "You get to Scotland Yard and have a police ambulance sent round. Here's a shilling for you, and the thanks of the Metropolitan Police."

"Aye, sir!" The ragamuffin saluted and trotted off on his errand.

MacRae pulled his coat collar closer to his neck. It was a pity about this unknown man, but he had obviously been in the wrong place at the wrong time. The man's pockets had been turned out, and his few belongings had been removed . . . watch and chain, wallet, coins. The body was covered with a thin layer of snow; he would have been killed at least two hours ago. That was before the Riot Act had been read and the order had been given, but it made no difference. Whoever the unfortunate man was, his death would be put down to the disorder and that was that.

MacRae nodded to the large constable, who raised his brass whistle and blew, signaling his forces to counterattack. It was the order the blue-coated officers of the law had been waiting for. They waded into the crowd, batons at the ready, flailing at anyone who might be holding anything of value.

The cries of the wounded were added to the deep shouts at the front of the procession. Police wagons were drawn up along the Strand, further blocking the traffic of carriages, horse cars, and cabs. Cabbies and coachmen vented their vocabularies on the rioters on foot, slashing at them with their whips and urging the horses forward. The horses, on the other hand, decided that they would express their discontent in the most visible way they could. The odor of steaming manure was added to that of unwashed bodies in the street.

The bricks were now directed at the policemen, who reacted with vigor, thrusting anyone within arm's reach into the nearest Black Maria to be hauled off to the Bow Street Police Station.

The sounds of battle were faint on Regent Street, where the revelry of London society proceeded unabated. Mr. Dodgson and Dr. Doyle walked from the Café Royal towards Piccadilly, unaware that the disturbance had turned into a major riot. There was a distinct coolness between the two that was not necessarily the fault of the weather.

Dr. Doyle muttered angrily, "We might have learned something if we had joined Mr. Wilde and his friends for dinner. It is getting late, sir, and I have missed both my luncheon and my tea. Could we not stop and have something to eat?"

"I did not quite like the look of the place," Mr. Dodgson said testily, as he adjusted his hat. "There were far too many boys. It seemed somewhat peculiar."

"Well, sir, what shall we do now that we have warned Mr. Wilde?" Dr. Doyle asked.

"We must find the printer, O'Casey, and ask him about this scarf," Mr. Dodgson decided. "And then, Dr. Doyle, you must find a telegraph office, if one is open, and send a wire to your wife informing her that you will be detained for at least a day. The policeman from the City of London, what was his name?"

"Calloway?"

"Yes, he said he would take our statements tomorrow."

"The police may have more to deal with at the moment than the death of a mere editor," Dr. Doyle said, as the true magnitude of the scene before him sank into his consciousness. They had, by now, reached Piccadilly Circus, the confluence of Piccadilly with Shaftesbury Avenue.

The street was full of shouting, gesticulating, running people: men in workmen's corduroys and leather aprons, rough woolen jackets, and battered felt hats; and women in the full skirts and patched jackets of the market stalls who added their voices and arms to the din. Ladies and gentlemen leaned out of their carriages, demanding that the crowd make way so that they could get to their assigned boxes at Covent Garden and the Savoy Theater. Blue-clad constables tried to clear the streets of both high and low society, while overhead the skies opened up once more, sending the snow indiscriminately down on rich and poor alike.

Hyndman waved at Burns, while O'Casey continued his harangue. "We must plead our cause before the high and mighty ones, who take their ease in their gilded palaces!" O'Casey roared out.

"The clubs!" A shout came up out of the crowd. O'Casey jumped off his soapbox. Hyndman and Burns, loath to relinquish leadership to this Irish upstart, flanked him as they led the crowd out of Trafalgar Square and towards the bastions of privilege, the exclusive clubs that lined Pall Mall and St. James's Square.

The uniformed porters and doorkeepers of the clubs were not about to allow their sacred precincts to be overrun by such rabble. They might have been deemed too old for active service in Her Majesty's armed forces, but they could still raise their fists (not to mention clubs, cudgels, and horsewhips) in defense of Queen, Country, and the right of a gentleman to take his ease without being disturbed by the great unwashed.

St. James's took on the aspect of a battlefield. Bricks, stones, and wooden blocks were the chosen missiles of the crowd outside, while the defenders plied whatever they could lay their hands on to keep the enemy at bay.

Inside the Press Club, Nicky Portman availed himself of the latest in technology. He used the telephone to inform his dear friend Chatsworth, the Undersecretary to the Home Secretary, that the Press Club was under attack and could he send some policemen to put down the rioters?

"Rioters? What rioters?" Chatsworth, safe at home in Grosvenor Place, had not heard of any rioters.

"The ones outside in St. James's," Portman told him.

"Good Lord! Buckingham Palace must be protected!" Before Portman could say another word, the connection was broken. Chatsworth had done the unthinkable: he had taken independent action and decided to notify Scotland Yard himself, without the knowledge of the Home Secretary, who was, in any case, not available at the moment and would undoubtedly agree that whatever happened to the tradesmen on Piccadilly and the Strand was unimportant compared with the protection of Buckingham Palace!

The message arrived at Scotland Yard and was duly logged in by the sergeant at the main desk. He passed it on to the inspector on night duty, who wrote out another order and handed it to the breathless constable who had just arrived from Inspector MacRae.

"New orders," the inspector told him. "Get over to Buckingham Palace and make sure all's safe there."

"But what about the shops in Piccadilly?" The constable looked affronted. Leaving shops unprotected seemed to be giving in to the mob.

"Orders from the Home Secretary," the inspector said with a grimace.

The constable saluted and prepared to face the storm once more. He would prefer the worst of the weather to MacRae's temper when he received this order to break off his defense of Piccadilly to guard the empty palace.

By now, MacRae was furiously trying to organize a plan of attack. A squad had arrived from Bow Street, and MacRae ordered everyone on foot in Piccadilly, the Strand, or Oxford Street to be pulled in, on the assumption that anyone in a carriage or cab was, ipso facto, not a rioter, and anyone on foot was.

It was at this point that Mr. Dodgson and Dr. Doyle joined the crowd. Dr. Doyle tried to pull his older companion out of the way of the rioters and the police.

"Mr. Dodgson . . . ," Dr. Doyle began.

Mr. Dodgson looked up at the crowd and asked, "Where did all these people come from?"

A large constable accosted the two men. "What're you doin' 'ere?" he demanded.

Mr. Dodgson began to sputter, "W-we are w-walking to our hotel."

"A likely story!" The constable grabbed at Mr. Dodgson's arm.

"This is Mr. Dodgson, a learned gentleman from Oxford," Dr. Doyle protested. "We have every right to walk the streets of London, on this night as any other. Let us pass!" He tried to pass the constable, who was at least six feet tall and several stone larger than Dr. Doyle.

The constable decided that these must be the ringleaders of the crowd. Hyndman, he had been told, dressed in black with a top hat. John Burns was large and Scottish. Here were two men, one in black with a top hat, the other large, with a Scottish accent. The constable glowed at the thought of having brought in the leaders of the rebellion.

"Stop, in the name of the queen!" He grabbed Dr. Doyle's arm to turn him around.

Dr. Doyle responded automatically with a boxer's instinct. The blow was blocked, and the blue-clad figure proceeded to land a "facer" on Dr. Doyle's cheek.

Dr. Doyle countered with another jab towards the other man's midsection. His assailant folded, while a third man arrived to separate the combatants.

"You're under arrest for breaking the Queen's Peace in accordance with the Riot Act!" the second constable announced, while the first man gasped in agony.

"What?" Dr. Doyle realized with a sinking heart that he had just assaulted an officer of the law. Before he could explain anything, he and Mr. Dodgson were thrust with the rest of the rioters into the nearest police wagon.

"But we just wanted to . . . What are you doing? Where are we going?" Mr. Dodgson stared wildly about him, as he was shoved into the back of the vehicle.

"I believe we are being arrested," Dr. Doyle told him.

"Arrested?" Mr. Dodgson's voice sank to a whisper. "Oh, no! Whatever will Dean Liddell say?"

"We seem to be one of a multitude," Dr. Doyle consoled him. "I expect we will be sorted out tomorrow morning, and nothing more will be said."

"I sincerely hope so," Mr. Dodgson said, as a constable closed the doors and the wagon began its jolting trip over the cobblestones to Bow Street.

From the safety of his cab, Oscar Wilde watched the scene with detached amusement. The words of the Oxford don had stung him, and he had decided to return to the family fireside after all. He had found a cab on Regent Street, but all traffic was tied up on Piccadilly, thanks to the riot. To his amazement, he saw dear old Dodgson being carried off in the paddy wagon with a selection of rough-clad rioters.

"This will never do," Wilde said to himself. "The old gentleman took the trouble to warn me of impending disaster. The least I can do is rescue him from the arms of the law."

But how? Wilde mentally ran through the list of his friends and acquaintances. Whistler? The old charlatan had been more waspish than usual these days, with Oscar taking the limelight away from him. None of his other acquaintances could muster the kind of support that Whistler could, except for Nicky Portman. Between his father's good works and his own cheerful curiosity, Nicky Portman had acquired an astonishing collection of friends and acquaintances in almost every sphere of public life. Somewhere in that group should be someone who could get old Dodgson out of jail.

"Forget what I said about Tite Street," Wilde called up to the cabby. "Take me to the Press Club on St. James's."

"There's a mort o' folk out tonight," the cabbie objected.

"In that case, I shall walk," Wilde decided. He left the safety of the cab and strode confidently through the crowd towards St. James's and the Press Club. Perhaps he could find a drink there and a few choice companions. He forgot about going home to Constance. She was used to his vagaries by now, and poor old Dodgson needed rescuing.

CHAPTER 10

B ow Street had once been the very heart of law enforcement
in London. When Sir Henry Fielding had established his
famous Bow Street Runners in the previous century, the basis of
the Metropolitan Police had been laid. An elaborate building had
been erected to house this elite force, and Sir Robert Peel had seen
fit to take it over for his Metropolitan Police without making any
changes in the exterior. A grand marble façade graced the street,
opposite the back entrance to the Royal Opera House, while alleys
on either side of the building allowed police vehicles to pull up
and discharge their passengers. The effect was one of both grace
and power.

Once inside the building, matters were quite different. The
wooden floors were black with the mud of a century of use. The
walls were grimy with soot. The bare walls of the individual cells
in the basement were scarred with graffiti left by hundreds of
nameless felons, prostitutes, and assorted riffraff, who insisted on
making their marks before being led to the Bow Street courts.

On this particular night, Sergeant Morris, the night warder, had
thought to have a quiet evening. Midweek was not particularly
busy; except for the usual petty thieves and prostitutes, crime

seemed to wait for the weekends. Sergeant Morris was ready to settle down with a cup of tea and his favorite newspaper to wait out the evening.

Then came the deluge! He greeted the first group of laborers with bored disdain, taking their names and assigning them to a cell apiece. Then came another shipment, and a third. With only a limited number of cells, two or more prisoners had to be assigned to each cell in violation of the ruling that each prisoner must be isolated. By the time the fourth wagonload had been discharged, Morris had had to call in a pair of constables to help him sort them out.

By ten o'clock, the rotund Sergeant Morris was thoroughly put out. The cellar seemed to be packed with men, women, and children, all shouting, cursing, screaming at the tops of their lungs. The cells were filled, the cellar was filled, and yet another wagon-load was discharged into Sergeant Morris's custody.

"Wot d'ye expect me to do with this lot?" the warder exclaimed, as Mr. Dodgson, Dr. Doyle, and the rest of their wagonload of strollers on Piccadilly were handed over to be incarcerated.

"Hold 'em till the magistrate gets around to 'em," Sergeant Hoskins told him. "In case you 'aven't 'eard, there's merry 'ell breakin' loose out there."

" 'Ow am I supposed to look after 'em?" the warder protested.

"Jest 'old 'em," Hoskins told him, leaving the beleaguered warder to find places for this last shipment of malefactors.

Sergeant Morris looked them over. None of them looked particularly dangerous. Apart from several men in heavy woolen jackets and a young woman in a gown much too thin for such a cold evening, there were a young man in a natty new suit that had been spoiled completely with muck, an elderly gentleman in a top hat, his companion in a plaid balbriggan overcoat and deerstalker hat, two exquisitely dressed young men in evening clothes, and a newsboy. As far as Sergeant Morris could tell, none of these were about to run amok or flourish weapons.

"You be quiet," he ordered, herding them into the open aisle between the rows of cells, which was already filled with people who had been swept up by the minions of Inspector MaeRae.

"Whatever are we doing here?" one of the young exquisites complained.

"Inspector MacRae'll be along to sort you out," Sergeant Morris promised, slamming the door to the cellar shut and leaving his prisoners to mill about unhappily with the rest of the crowd who had not been locked away behind the solid doors of the individual cells.

Mr. Dodgson edged away from the press of humanity into the corner between the wall and the barred door, too terrified to look about him. He did not like being this close to so many people all at once, especially those who might have been characterized as "the great unwashed." To be thrust into a basement room with so many rough people was not what Mr. Dodgson liked or expected of life. He closed his eyes and tried to pray for rescue. Divine Providence was being sent an urgent summons.

Dr. Doyle, on the other hand, was drinking in the thrill of having been arrested, sure in the knowledge that he would soon be exonerated of all wrongdoing. He touched his eye and winced. He would have a spectacular souvenir of the night's adventures to show Touie when he got home . . . if he got home! He sincerely hoped he would not have to spend any more time at the Bow Street Police Station than it took to see the magistrate, pay a fine, and take his leave. This was an exhilarating experience, but not one that he would like to extend indefinitely.

Another load of prisoners was thrust into the cellar. The ringleaders of the demonstration had been arrested. Hyndman and Burns swaggered into the cellar, to be greeted with cheers and catcalls.

Mr. Dodgson opened his eyes and recognized the third man in the group. "You are O'Casey." It was a statement, not a question.

"Aye, that I am." O'Casey looked at Mr. Dodgson suspiciously. "And what is that to you?"

"We were in the office when you had words with Mr. Levin. We saw and heard everything," Dr. Doyle put in. "I'm Irish myself, by way of Scotland. I know what temper is, and Mr. Basset's actions would have provoked Saint Patrick himself to

98

anger. If you did accost him, it is entirely understandable."

"Accost him, you say?" O'Casey echoed. "That I did! I do not deny it. I wanted a word before I called me men off on strike. 'Tis no light thing to give up a good position, and *Youth's Companion*'s steady work."

"And so you went and had a dram . . ." Doyle went on, with a sniff.

"A wee whiskey," O'Casey confessed. "To chase the cold out."

"And when you saw Mr. Basset come out of the office door . . . ?"

"It fair made me blood boil!" O'Casey said fiercely. "There he was, in his fine fur collar and his warm hat, and me Molly shivering in her shawl at home." He choked with indignation at the unfairness of a universe that gave warm clothes to some and denied them to others.

"And you accosted him," Doyle finished.

"If by that you mean did I ask to have a word with him, that I did. And I put our terms to him, fair and square. A ten-hour shift, a small fire in the composing room, and a rise of a shillin' a week."

"And the response?" Mr. Dodgson asked.

O'Casey's wrath began to build. "Not a word did he say to me! Just stood there and would not answer, as if I was shoutin' to the wind. *Too proud to answer,* I thought, and I raised me fist to him, to get his attention, you might say."

"And then he tried to mount his omnibus," Dr. Doyle prompted the printer.

"He held onto the rail," O'Casey recalled. "But now that you mention it, it is in me mind that he staggered like a man in drink. But it was coming on to snow, and I was not meself, so to speak. I tell you, sir, it was a black rage come over me."

"I see." Mr. Dodgson nodded. "You would not have noticed, for instance, if Mr. Basset were pale or appeared to be suffering from some pain . . ."

O'Casey shook his head. "All I could think of was me wife and children back in Whitechapel, and me with no work, and that . . . that . . ." Words failed him. He choked on his indignation. Suddenly his eyes narrowed as he looked at the two men. "What's all this pother really about, then?"

Dr. Doyle said, "After you had your altercation . . ."

"Me what?"

"Your, er, spat with Mr. Basset, what did you do then?" Dr. Doyle continued the questioning, while Mr. Dodgson fingered the knitted scarf.

"I went back to the pub and had another drink," O'Casey confessed. " 'Twas then I heard yon fellow in the black coat and hat tellin' the bosses off, him what had never worked a day in his life!"

"And that is when you joined Mr. Hyndman on his podium," Mr. Dodgson said. "Did you not notice the police ambulance in the street?"

"In that snow I couldn't tell an omnibus from the Lord Mayor's coach," O'Casey said with a laugh.

"Then you were not aware that Mr. Samuel Basset is dead," Mr. Dodgson stated, watching the printer closely for his reaction.

"Dead?" O'Casey's bravado leaked out of him. "I barely tapped him!"

"You did strike him though?" Dr. Doyle asked.

"He was provoking, as you said. What right had he, a bachelor, to question me and refuse me a living wage? Me, what has a wife and three children depending on me to put the bread on the table?" O'Casey's voice rose to orator's pitch. The prisoners, less riotous than before, grumbled an agreement with the sentiments, if not the details.

"But you claim he was alive when you struck him and alive when you left him," Mr. Dodgson mused. "This is most puzzling. Dr. Doyle, are you aware of any means by which someone could be stabbed in the back and yet continue to remain alive for some time after being injured?"

"Stabbed?" O'Casey looked from the older man in black to the younger one in the tartan coat. "As God is me witness, all I did was hit the man with me fist! I had no knife on me, nor would I do such a thing as to stab a man in the back."

"I believe you," Dr. Doyle said. "Besides, if you had just

stabbed a man, you would hardly have stood up in the middle of the road, inciting your fellow workers to riot and rebellion."

"Riot and rebellion indeed!" Mr. Dodgson echoed. His hands twisted the knitted scarf.

O'Casey stared at the long knitted object. "Where did you get that?" he demanded.

"Is it yours?" Dr. Doyle asked, with a speaking look at Mr. Dodgson.

"Aye, that it is. Made by me very own Molly herself as a token afore we was wed. Where did you find it? It would have been the last straw to have come home with the ill news of me bein' discharged and then to have lost the one thing she made for me into the bargain."

Mr. Dodgson took a deep breath. "It was put into my hands by Mr. Basset," he told the printer. "I should have taken it to the policeman in charge of the case, but he would not have listened to me." He thought for a minute, then handed the scarf back to its owner. "Here, O'Casey, take your scarf, and let this be a lesson to you. Do not presume to take by force what will come to you in due time through diligence." Mr. Dodgson straightened his coat and adjusted his hat. O'Casey accepted the scarf and touched his forehead in the manner deemed appropriate for a member of the working classes when addressed by a superior.

Dr. Doyle allowed himself a small smile at the miniature sermon. Then he turned back to O'Casey with the air of one who is willing to step down a rung on the ladder of society in the name of universal manhood. "Tell me," he said in a confidential tone, "what did you think of Basset and his staff?"

"Basset was a skinflint, no doubt about it," O'Casey stated. "Ye see, him and Mr. Portman started the magazine back when I was just a printer's devil at the Penny Press. Mr. Portman put up the money, but he and Mr. Basset shared in the takings. The more profit shows on the books, the more Basset gets to take home; but where he puts it, I cannot say. No wife has he, nor like to have, from what I've heard of him."

"Really?" Mr. Dodgson was drawn into the discussion. "How long have you worked for *Youth's Companion*, my man?"

"I've been head printer and compositor there these six years. Come over from His Lordship's Penny Press, as did most of me men, savin' young Wiggins, who's the apprentice."

"Of course, being in the printing plant, you wouldn't have anything to do with the writers or editors," Mr. Dodgson mused.

"Now there you're wrong," O'Casey stated. "They come down now and again, especially Mr. Roberts, the artist fellow. Mr. Roberts is picky about the illustrations, but he's an artist. Let one line be amiss, and he'll be down in a flash. He even comes in of a Sunday to work up in his garret, making sure all's well with his pictures. Mr. Peterson, now, he's a cheery sort, always a jolly word and a shilling or two at Christmas. The other two are well enough. They don't bother me, and I don't mind them."

"And Mr. Levin?" Mr. Dodgson hinted.

O'Casey snorted in disgust. "Dresses fine and talks fair, but he's no gentleman, no matter how many fine waistcoats he sports, and that's the truth."

"I noticed that waistcoat," Dr. Doyle said with a knowing grin. "Not cheap, is it?"

O'Casey winked. "O'course, for them as has friends in Petticoat Lane, waistcoats like that is easy to come by."

Mr. Dodgson frowned. "Petticoat Lane? Isn't that where the ragpickers have their stands?" He turned to Dr. Doyle. "There has been a great deal of discussion in charitable circles about the sad state of poverty in such places. How odd that Mr. Levin, who seems to be a respectable young man, should be known in Petticoat Lane."

O'Casey winked again. "Fine feathers don't make fine birds," he stated. "Levin's always up and down, in and out, with the galleys and the page proofs, and the messages from Mr. Basset. He's the one hands out our pay packets each week."

"And he keeps the books," Dr. Doyle commented. "That would indicate that Levin was something of a dogsbody, not an editor at all."

"But he took it on himself to communicate with contributors," Mr. Dodgson reminded Dr. Doyle. "And he arranged for Miss

Harvey to typewrite the manuscripts. He seems to have assumed a great deal of authority, with or without the knowledge of Mr. Basset."

Before they could continue the conversation, Sergeant Morris appeared with three well-dressed gentlemen in tow. One of them was Oscar Wilde, instantly recognizable by his long fur coat and slouch hat. The other two were in evening clothes, both tall, but one was more of a weedy build and the other appeared to be more robust. Oscar Wilde had obviously found rescuers for the gentleman from Oxford and his Scottish friend.

"In 'ere, gentlemen," Sergeant Morris announced, displaying his catch. Mr. Dodgson looked through the bars and cried out in mixed alarm and exasperation.

"Mr. Wilde!" Mr. Dodgson exclaimed. "What are you doing here? I sincerely trust you were not caught up in the riot as Dr. Doyle and I were. Particularly since we went to a good deal of trouble to tell you to stay away."

"In point of fact, I have come to get you out," Wilde said. He looked about the squalid quarters and shuddered.

"Good heavens!" The tall and weedy man peered at the crowd in the basement. "Sergeant! What is that gentleman doing here?" He pointed a trembling finger at Mr. Dodgson.

Sergeant Morris consulted a handwritten list. "According to this, 'e's been brought in on charges of Inciting to Riot."

"Mr. Dodgson?" The weedy one gasped out. "You must release him at once! This is Mr. Dodgson, a noted scholar, Fellow of Christ Church, and all that. I don't think he's ever incited anyone to anything in his life!"

"Do you know the gentleman?" Sergeant Morris asked with a frown.

"I should say I do! He was my brother's tutor at the House . . . that is, Christ Church. I say, Mr. Dodgson!"

Mr. Dodgson looked up. "Do I know you, sir?"

"Chatsworth," the weedy one introduced himself.

"Chatsworth." Mr. Dodgson regarded the earnest young man on the other side of the bars. "I know the name, but not the face. You were not one of my students."

"That was my brother, Michael," Chatsworth reminded him. "I was up in 'Eighty. You'd just stopped teaching."

"Then you can vouch for this gentleman's good behavior on release?" Sergeant Morris sounded hopeful. Perhaps he could get rid of some more of these unwanted guests.

"I certainly can," Chatsworth said fervently. "Release Mr. Dodgson at once, Sergeant."

"And my friend, Dr. Doyle," Mr. Dodgson insisted, beckoning his companion to join him.

"What's he down for?" Wilde wanted to know.

Sergeant Morris consulted the list again. "Assaulting an officer and resisting arrest."

Wilde looked at Chatsworth, who looked at the third member of the rescue squad.

"By the look of that eye, Dr. Doyle had good reason to assault the officer," the taller man said. "If he promises never to do it again, we will guarantee that he keeps his word. Will that suit you, Sergeant?"

Sergeant Morris considered the situation. He already had more prisoners than he knew what to do with. He would have to account for all of them to the magistrate, but this Chatsworth claimed to have come from the Home Office. If he took responsibility for them, Sergeant Morris was ready to sign them off into his custody.

While Sergeant Morris was negotiating with Chatworth for the release of the two prisoners, Oscar Wilde performed the necessary introductions.

"Nicky, you haven't had the pleasure of meeting Mr. Dodgson, the noted author and mathematician, and his, um, companion. . . ."

"Doyle. Arthur Conan Doyle." Dr. Doyle extended a hand.

"Gentlemen, this is Mr. Nicholas Portman, the proprietor of *Youth's Companion* and Samuel Basset's oldest and dearest friend," Wilde continued with a flourish.

"I must thank you, sir, for obtaining my release," Mr. Dodgson said. "And, of course, for releasing Dr. Doyle. It is quite important that he get to Victoria Station. He must go home to his wife in Portsmouth."

104

"That he will not," Mr. Portman stated. "All trains out of London have been stopped until the tracks can be cleared.

Dr. Doyle shook his head. "Touie will be worried," he said. "I think we will go on the telephone as soon as it is laid into Southsea. Perhaps I should remain here, Mr. Dodgson, until the magistrate comes in the morning." He turned to the printer, who was standing next to him, staring hopefully at his employer. "And what about O'Casey here? His wife must be worried about him, just as Touie would worry about me."

"Eh?" Portman raised his eyebrows in inquiry, as Dr. Doyle indicated the hulking printer next to him.

"He's the chief printer at *Youth's Companion*," Dr. Doyle reminded Portman. "You can't get your magazine out without him."

"Of course, of course," the publisher muttered. "I heard you were a troublemaker, always arguing with poor Sammy."

"We had words," O'Casey admitted.

Once again they were interrupted by the police. Inspector MacRae and Sergeant Hoskins had descended the stairs and were now at the cellar door.

"There 'e is, sir," Hoskins said, pointing to O'Casey. "That's the man. 'E were in Fleet Street, and again in Trafalgar Square, and 'e were at the 'ead of the mob in St. James's."

MacRae's eyes glittered behind his spectacles as he approached O'Casey, who glared back at him in fury.

"This man is not to be released on any account," MacRae ordered. "He's been identified as one of the ringleaders of this riot, and he shall pay for it! There's a dead man to your credit, and you'll swing for murder, me lad!"

O'Casey's fury turned to horror. "I never did more than tap 'im!" he protested.

"It was a tap that laid him out on the street," MacRae said grimly. "What's your name, man?"

"Seamus O'Casey, but . . ."

"Then Seamus O'Casey, I arrest you on a charge of murder, in the name of the queen. It is my duty to inform you that anything you say will be taken down and used against you in a court of law. Warder, get this man a cell of his own. He's got a lot to answer for."

105

O'Casey looked despairingly at Mr. Portman.

"Surely, sir, you must help him," Dr. Doyle protested. "He is one of your employees, and he is being accused of a crime he did not commit."

Mr. Portman interrupted him, ending all argument. "O'Casey, I shall send my solicitor to see you tomorrow morning. If you are innocent, as you say, then you shall be set free. As for you, Mr. Dodgson, I insist that you stay at the Press Club for the night. We have some rooms that are set aside for distinguished visitors, and I can imagine no one more distinguished than the author of *Alice's Adventures in Wonderland.*"

Mr. Dodgson was rendered speechless. Dr. Doyle was not. "We thank you, sir, for your kindness," he said, as Sergeant Morris opened the barred door to allow them to leave the cellar. "We have had a very active evening, and a hot bath and a meal would be most welcome."

Oscar Wilde sauntered past Inspector MacRae, who was consulting with Sergeants Hoskins and Morris. "Are you the policeman who thinks I committed murder?" he asked disdainfully.

MacRae glanced up at the dandified figure before him. "And who might you be?"

"I might be almost anyone, but I am, in fact, Oscar Wilde. And I am here, in person, to inform you that I have a cast-iron alibi for the time at which, according to Dr. Doyle here, the murder of Samuel Basset was committed. Therefore, I strongly suggest that you go find out who actually did it and leave me and my family alone." Wilde adjusted his hat smugly and sauntered back towards the stairs.

Mr. Dodgson sputtered. "After all we went through to find him! That man is quite impossible!"

"But he is amusing," Mr. Portman said, leading the other two back up the stairs, past the crowded anteroom, and back into the street, where his carriage was waiting. "And now that I have you to myself, Mr. Dodgson, there is a favor I wish to ask of you."

"Anything that I can do, I certainly shall," Mr. Dodgson said.

"It is really quite simple. I want you to find out who killed Samuel Basset."

CHAPTER 11

The snow was still whirling about as the group left the Bow Street Police Station. Mr. Dodgson settled his high hat more firmly on his head, while Dr. Doyle finally gave in and tied the strings of his deerstalker cap under his chin. Mr. Portman beckoned towards the carriage that had been waiting for him amongst the police wagons.

"Take us to the Press Club, Thomas," he ordered the coachman. "And then you may take Mr. Wilde to his house in Chelsea."

The coachman waited while Dr. Doyle assisted Mr. Dodgson into the carriage, then inserted himself into the seat beside him. Mr. Portman and Mr. Wilde followed, and the carriage moved off, slowly and carefully, as the horses picked their way along the slippery, slushy, icy streets.

Inside the carriage, Mr. Dodgson sputtered to Mr. Portman, "I thank you for your d-deliverance, b-but I really do not understand why you think I can discover who k-killed Mr. B-basset. Surely, it is a matter for the p-police."

Mr. Portman snorted his opinion of the police. "You saw that man, MacRae. First he goes after Oscar here, and now he's lit on my printer."

"Neither of whom could possibly have done the deed," Dr. Doyle stated. "As will be demonstrated as soon as the body is examined. If they had asked me—"

"But they didn't," Wilde interrupted him. "Policemen have very limited minds. It comes of associating with the most obvious of criminals. Now a really ingenious criminal could probably develop a whole network of activities under the noses of Scotland Yard simply because no one would believe in such a thing."

Mr. Dodgson frowned. "Do you really think that O'Casey is in danger of being hanged for this crime, which he assuredly did not commit?"

"A case could be built up, circumstantially, of course," Wilde said with a shrug. "And if the jury are stupid enough, they will convict him on the strength of his being Irish and impassioned, a state that is far too common these days."

Mr. Portman shook his head at his young friend. "I could say the same of you, Oscar."

"What were you thinking, sir, to come into the police station yourself?" Dr. Doyle admonished his more successful colleague. "Mr. Dodgson and I have been exerting ourselves on your behalf, trying to warn you about MacRae, and what must you do but flaunt yourself in front of him!"

Wilde laughed gleefully. "Oh, it was worth it just to see the man's face! There is nothing like being able to prove oneself in the right when someone else wishes to prove you wrong."

"Nevertheless, it was dangerous," Mr. Portman agreed with Dr. Doyle. "It might have been you in those cells instead of poor O'Casey, and then where would you be?"

"In the cells," Wilde said airily. "But you would have come along to get me out. Someone always does get me out of trouble."

"Someday," Portman warned him, "you will get into trouble, and no one will be able to get you out."

Wilde waved impending doom away with an expressive gesture. "Here we are," he announced. "Nicky, do you happen to have a drink for me at the Press Club?"

"Oscar," Portman said sternly, "you are going home. Right now!"

Wilde pouted like a sulky schoolboy. His mentor was not to be mollified. As soon as Mr. Dodgson and Dr. Doyle had descended from the carriage, Oscar Wilde was thrust back into it, and the coachman was given his instructions.

The carriage disappeared into the falling snow, and Mr. Portman ushered his two guests into the Press Club, passing through a row of six stout porters in green coats, each armed with a large and knobby cudgel, prepared to defend the building from the rioters, most of whom had already been arrested and removed from St. James's.

Mr. Portman noted the battered appearance of the leader of the pack, a six-foot specimen with a spendid pair of military side whiskers, who opened the door to the Press Club with a flourish.

"There's word that the Fenians and the Socialists are behind the ruckus," this individual informed his master.

"And I see you have been active on our behalf," Portman noted. "I hope you gave as good as you got."

"That we did!" The door was opened, and Mr. Portman led the way into the anteroom, where they were relieved of their hats and outer wraps by a butler of the most superior sort, who had to keep reminding himself that in this establishment being a member of the Fourth Estate did not automatically exclude a person from the title of "gentleman."

"Have two rooms prepared, Norwich," Portman instructed him. "And send up something hot for late supper, eh?"

"There is a good broth tonight, sir," Norwich said, as the footman bore the muddy coats off to be brushed. "And, if I may say so, a beefsteak."

"Beefsteak? At this hour?" Mr. Dodgson consulted his watch, then the large clock ticking in the hallway.

"Er . . . for the gentleman's eye," the butler hinted.

Dr. Doyle grinned, and touched his bruised face. "A raw beefsteak compress is the accepted treatment for a black eye," he admitted, "but I think I would prefer it internally rather than

109

externally. And cooked, if you please." But by this time, Norwich had left for the kitchen, and Dr. Doyle's request went unheard.

Mr. Portman was eager to show off his latest toy, a small elevator that would take them to the top floor, where he kept his personal apartment. "I've installed a small generator in the basement," he confided. "And I have had the electric light put in, as well as the telephone. I want the Press Club to be modern, not like those old fogies down the street. Some of those fellows still have the outside offices, simply because their grandfathers did. No, Mr. Dodgson, this is the nineteenth century, and we must move ahead!"

"Does that include modern presses and the new American machinery for setting type?" Dr. Doyle asked. "I read of it in the *Illustrated London News.* According to the information I received, the machine can replace three typesetters and can set the type faster and more neatly than the human hand. I don't think O'Casey and his crew will be pleased with that."

Portman nodded. "It is true, sir, that modern methods often leave some men jobless, but on the other hand, those who are willing to learn the new techniques will find themselves more in demand. It's a devil's bargain, to be sure, but one must move forward, Dr. Doyle!"

"You, at least, seem to be most forward-looking," Mr. Dodgson observed, as he took in the private sitting room. Here William Morris had been given a free hand. The walls were covered with dark green wallpaper, picked out with a gold floral design. The chairs were straight-legged, simple, and unadorned, set around a small table. Two upholstered chairs in dark green and gold matched a chesterfield sofa, set in front of a tiled fireplace with a green-veined white marble mantelpiece. There were no extraneous ornaments, no whatnots or small tables covered with photographs, no stuffed animals leering down from the walls. Instead, Mr. Portman had hung a few paintings that seemed to be mere dabs of color against the wallpaper. Only by standing back and observing did the impressions resolve into shapes of flowers.

"I see you have a painting by Mr. Whistler," Mr. Dodgson

observed, noting at least one painter he could identify on the walls. "And this is by Mr. Turner, is it not?"

"Yes, indeed," Mr. Portman said with pride. "And I picked these up in Paris last summer. What do you think, sir?"

Mr. Dodgson cleared his throat. His opinion of the French paintings was clearly not that of his host, and he did not want to be so uncivil as to disagree with him.

He was saved from that embarrassment by the arrival of Norwich and the footman with a steaming tureen of broth, a fresh loaf of bread, a round of Stilton cheese, pats of butter, and a pot of hot tea. On a separate platter was the raw beefsteak, meant to be applied to Dr. Doyle's rapidly swelling eye. The tray was deposited on the stark wooden table, and the butler was dismissed.

"We'll serve ourselves, Norwich," Mr. Portman told him. The butler retreated, reserving his opinion of those who would usurp the position of their servants for his private journals, into which he regularly inscribed all such thoughts.

Once the butler and footman had withdrawn, Portman was able to get to the point.

"If you do not mind," Mr. Dodgson told him, "I do not speak while I eat. It leads to choking."

"Then I will speak while you eat," Portman said, as Dr. Doyle broke off a piece of the loaf and munched hungrily and Mr. Dodgson spooned up his broth as if each mouthful were liquid gold. "I had no idea that you were in London at all, but when Oscar told me that you had been present at Sammy's death, I realized that you, of all people, could best discover who killed him."

Mr. Dodgson swallowed carefully, took a sip of tea, and asked, "Why? What do you know of me that would make you think that I could undertake such a task as to uncover a murderer?"

Portman smiled and said, "Lord Richard Marbury is one of our members, by virtue of his articles and tracts. He has told me how useful you were last summer when his daughter was abducted."

"But that was quite different," Mr. Dodgson protested. "The child had been placed in my care. It was my duty to see her returned to her parents."

"And in this case, you were present when Sammy died," Portman countered. "You were on the street."

"There were any number of people on the street," Mr. Dodgson objected. "Including, I might add, Inspector MacRae."

Mr. Portman helped himself to a piece of cheese. "I do not think that any of them killed poor old Sammy. What I want you to do is to act as a . . . consultant. You would only have to discover the facts of the case and lay them before the police. It would then be up to this MacRae, or the fellow from the City of London, to act on what you tell them."

Mr. Dodgson considered the proposal. "It would be interesting," he said finally. "And I suppose I do owe something to Mr. Basset. The difficulty will be in narrowing down the field of suspects."

"You agree that it was neither O'Casey nor Wilde?" Dr. Doyle asked around a mouthful of bread and cheese.

"I refuse to believe that Oscar Wilde could kill anyone," Portman stated. "As for the printer, if, as you seem to think, Sammy was stabbed, it is most unlikely that he would do it. Bashing someone on the head is more O'Casey's style, especially if there was drink taken."

"It would seem," Mr. Dodgson said slowly, "that if we eliminate the impossible, that is, Wilde and O'Casey and the people on the street, we must deal with what is left, however improbable. In other words, unpleasant as it may be, one of the staff at *Youth's Companion* must have killed Mr. Basset."

Mr. Portman nodded. "And that is why I would much prefer a private inquiry to a police investigation," he said with a sigh. "Inspector MacRae now seems satisfied that Sammy was killed by O'Casey and will look no further, but I don't like the idea of having a murderer on my magazine. If one of those men knifed Sammy, I want him exposed, removed, and hanged!" Portman's voice raised to a shout.

Mr. Dodgson regarded his host with a look of concern. "Were you and Mr. Basset very close friends?"

Portman took a deep breath and lowered his voice. "Sammy and I met in school. Winchester, it was. My father had begun to rise in the world, although his fortune was not what it was to become, and he thought it would do the family good if I received the benefit of a first-class education. Eton and Harrow were out of the question, but Winchester was acceptable, and I was accepted . . . but not by the rest of the students, if you take my meaning. The son of a bookseller, however wealthy, was not to be considered the equal of the sons of country squires and clergymen. I was very lonely until Sammy came along on a scholarship from some maternal relations. His father's family were, let us say, not interested in acknowledging him, and he never talked about them."

"But you hit it off?" Dr. Doyle adjusted the raw steak and focussed the other eye on Lord Portman.

"We had common interests. We both enjoyed a good book and devoured anything by Mr. Dickens or Thackeray. We both liked swimming and hated horses; we both longed to get away from England and explore the rest of the world. I remember how the two of us read the reports from Burton and Speke about their discoveries in Africa, and how we planned that as soon as we finished our schooling we should run away together." He stopped, then added, "Do not misunderstand me, gentlemen. It often happens, you know, that young men develop friendships—deeply passionate friendships—that may or may not be carried forward in later life."

Mr. Dodgson nodded sagely. He had seen much the same sort of friendships among undergraduates in his years at Oxford. "So you were Mr. Basset's friend at school," he summed it up. "And afterward?"

"I went on to university," Portman said. "Cambridge, not Oxford, Mr. Dodgson. My father was busy turning out small volumes through the Portman Penny Press that could be sold for under a shilling to workpeople. He had a stable of writers, who could turn out exciting tales or useful manuals for workpeople. What he needed were editors, who could take the manuscripts and make them up into readable material that could be printed and sold in the thousands, if not the millions. I asked him to take on Sammy, and Sammy came into the Portman Penny Press. He wasn't all that innovative of a writer himself, but he knew how to make a good story better, and that got him moved into an editor's seat."

Mr. Dodgson's face twisted in a grimace. "The Portman Penny Press!" he uttered in tones of the utmost loathing.

Mr. Portman lifted his chin in a gesture of defiance. "Do not scoff, sir, at the Portman Penny Press. What with the new education laws and the national schools, literacy is on the rise. A workingman or a shopgirl deserves a good yarn to make life a little more exciting as much as anyone in Mayfair or Belgravia does. And remember, many of our titles are educational as well as entertaining. In fact, that's why Sammy and I were sent to Africa in the first place."

"Really?" Dr. Doyle took another cup of tea and removed the beefsteak from his eye.

"That was my father's idea. We would go to Africa, once the trail had been blazed, and write a series of books about our adventures, aiming them at young boys, you see."

Mr. Dodgson was fascinated. "And did you have adventures?"

Mr. Portman smiled to himself. "Oh yes, we certainly did. We were attacked by native tribesmen, we were lost for a month in the bush country until some missionary chap found us and dragged us back to the Nairobi settlement, we shot all sorts of animals, and drew pictures of more, and on the boat home Sammy came up with the idea of publishing a magazine for boys. You see," Portman explained, "Sammy thought that if we could catch the boys when they were young, they would become readers for life, and what better to read than the books from Portman Penny Press?"

"What indeed," Mr. Dodgson echoed faintly.

"So your father put up the money for *Youth's Companion?*" Dr. Doyle asked.

"He offered me the use of the old building, since he'd planned to move to larger quarters, farther down Fleet Street," Portman explained. "I'd come into some money when I turned twenty-one, and I put it into *Youth's Companion*. The old treadle-run presses were still there, since my father was installing the motor presses in the new building, but I had to come up with the salaries for staff, furnishings, and so forth."

Mr. Dodgson frowned to himself. "And what did Mr. Basset offer to the new enterprise?"

Mr. Portman cleared his throat, embarrassed to discuss such a mundane matter as money. "Sammy was to do all the writing, and I was to find the subscribers. Then he and I were to share and share alike in any profits the magazine made. Of course, for the first two years, there weren't any profits. We were sharing digs then, so I footed the bills for our living expenses; but after the third year, we were out of the red ink, and Sammy insisted on paying me back every penny I'd advanced. He was a fanatic about getting into debt. I've often wondered if there was some story attached to it, something that he could not discuss, not even with me."

"Well, that explains one thing," Dr. Doyle said. "He had every reason to curtail expenses if it meant more money in his pocket and kept him out of debtor's prison. Had he no other interests? No other friends but yourself?"

Portman's embarrassment deepened. "Of late, Sammy and I had grown apart," he confessed. "I came into some more money, from one of my mother's relations. Once I started the Press Club, I had little time for Sammy. He ran *Youth's Companion*, and I let him get on with it."

Dr. Doyle glanced at Mr. Dodgson, then asked the one question no one had dared ask. "What about Mr. Basset's private life? Did he have any, um, particular friend? A lady, perhaps? Had he no companions, no one with whom he might have quarreled . . . ?"

Portman sighed. "You must understand something," he said finally. "When we were younger, Sammy and I were very close. Especially in Africa. But we move on, gentlemen. Sammy and I were drifting apart, and perhaps it was my own fault. I do tend to get enthusiasms!"

"That is quite understandable," Mr. Dodgson said.

"And then I moved out of our digs and took up my flat here," Portman went on, "so I couldn't tell you who Sammy was seeing. We had tea once a week to discuss matters concerning *Youth's*

Companion, but aside from that . . ." He paused and frowned to himself. "I saw him at the Café Royal with a good-looking lad once and took him to task about it. He explained to me that he'd been given a good start by my father and me, and he felt it his duty to do the same for other poor chaps. I accepted that at face value and never questioned him again."

Mr. Dodgson laid his spoon aside and poured a cup of tea. "If, as we suspect, one of the staff at the magazine is the culprit, we must examine their backgrounds closely," he said. "How were they hired? Did you or Mr. Basset make the selection? How long have these persons been there?"

Portman thought it over. "David Peterson was one of my father's writers at the Portman Penny Press," he said at last. "He brought in the other two, Monteverde and Howarth. There's an artist, too, I think. . . ."

"Roberts," Dr. Doyle said helpfully.

"That's the chap. Sammy saw some of his work in a shop and asked about it. He was doing comic valentines, Christmas cards, that sort of thing. Sammy thought he'd do well for us and gave him the position of staff artist."

"He seems to be somewhat, um, temperamental," Mr. Dodgson remarked.

Portman shrugged. "Well, he's an artist, after all. I believe he is trying his hand at oils. Sammy mentioned something of the sort to me, but he seemed to think that Roberts was not quite up to it and that he had best remain as he was. I accepted his judgment."

"The staff worked well together, as far as you know?" Mr. Dodgson asked.

"As far as I knew. Of course, Sammy would never bother me with petty office squabbles." Portman's frown deepened. "I'd hate to think of any of them being so vicious as to stab poor old Sammy in the back. What sort of a man does that?"

"Or a woman," Dr. Doyle put in.

"Eh?" Portman stared at the young doctor.

"I'll have to see the wound, but a very determined young woman, particularly one who is strong and muscular, could have inserted the knife," Dr. Doyle continued. "There were two young women in the office that day, a Miss Helen Harvey and a Miss Potter. Mr. Basset was unpleasant to both of them."

"I do not think Mr. Basset was killed because he was unpleasant," Mr. Dodgson said firmly. "There must have been some other, compelling reason that would drive a man into such a frenzy that he would resort to so evil a deed."

"Then . . . why?" Portman asked, his face a mask of confusion.

"Why indeed," Mr. Dodgson echoed. "Exactly what Mr. Basset asked. Why?"

"What did he mean by that?" Portman was more confused than ever.

"When I know that," Mr. Dodgson said, "then I shall know who killed him. Until then, I believe I shall take your offer of a room for the night. Dr. Doyle, I suggest you do the same. By tomorrow morning, things will appear much clearer."

All over London, lights were being turned out. Only the press rooms of Fleet Street were lit, grinding out the morning editions that would inform the good citizens of the riot in Trafalgar Square. Until those editions reached the newsstands, most of London would remain in ignorance of those momentous events.

In the Ristorante Monteverde in Saffron Hill, Roberto Monteverde regaled his family with the description of the shocking death of Samuel Basset and wondered whether this meant that he would be able to rise to the chief writer's chair.

In his bed-sitting room in Pimlico, Winslow Howarth patted his little corgi and wondered if he could convince the new editor to let him write more and edit less.

In an attic studio in Bloomsbury, Edgar Roberts looked over the sketches he had made and hoped that Miss Helen Harvey would sit for him as Queen Mab.

In a meager flat in Chelsea, Miss Harvey tried not to listen to her mother's whining voice as she doggedly typed the manuscripts handed back to her by the late Samuel Basset and wondered if she dared to go against her mother's whims and pose for Mr. Roberts (although not, he assured her, in the altogether).

117

In a second-floor bedroom near Baker Street, Andrew Levin carefully brushed the mud off the legs of his trousers and hoped that the police investigation would be over quickly and Mr. Samuel Basset could be laid to the rest he had denied others.

And in the neat little row house in Holbein Place, Myrna Peterson sat and waited anxiously for the step that never came, rehearsing a speech of recrimination that she would never have the opportunity to deliver.

CHAPTER 12

The snow stopped in the early hours of Thursday morning, leaving London blanketed in white. Broad expanses of lawns in Hyde Park glistened in the dawn. Noble oaks that stood where the second Charles had entertained his boisterous friends now had branches that bowed down to the ground. Each railing bore its own little white cap, like frosting on a cake. Unfortunately, none of this glory could be seen through the dense fog that covered London like a blanket, sealing in the soot of thousands of coal and wood fires, and making traffic worse than ever. Cart horses, cab horses, omnibus horses, all had to pick their way carefully along the main highways, which were covered with frozen slush. A few desultory efforts had been made to clear the roads, but the snow remained on the pavements.

Neither fog nor snow, however, halted the spread of news. The mob had left Fleet Street to its own devices, and the presses had been running all night long. Now the morning *Times* gave a full and fulsome account of the previous night's doings. According to the reporters on the scene, the West End was at the complete mercy of the mob, while the police had been called off to guard the homes of the rich and famous. The names of Hyndman and

Burns appeared at the head of the columns, together with their vehement words. Shopkeepers were warned to stay home so that the police could arrest whichever rioters dared to show their faces in the daylight.

The gentlemen of the Press Club read their newspapers eagerly at breakfast, commenting sarcastically or pompously, depending on whose newspaper they were reading.

Mr. Dodgson was pleased to note that his black coat and trousers had been brushed and pressed by the club's ever-efficient staff. Hot shaving water and a newly honed razor had been provided for his morning ablutions. Enticing odors lured Mr. Dodgson downstairs, where the breakfast table had been set in the Members' Dining Room. A groaning sideboard was covered with chafing dishes containing eggs, bacon, porridge, and assorted muffins, toast, and breads overseen by Norwich, the butler, and his staff of footmen.

Dr. Doyle was already there, his plate full of scrambled eggs and bacon. Mr. Dodgson contented himself with a bowl of porridge and a cup of tea and joined his young friend in scanning the morning newspapers.

"I have been considering our course of action," Dr. Doyle said, as his mentor took the place next to him. "Even though Mr. Portman has vouched for us, we must appear at the early session at the Magistrate's Court at Bow Street, if only to get O'Casey out of the cells."

"I do hope there will not be too many reporters present," Mr. Dodgson fussed. "It would be dreadful if our last night's adventure got into the press and from there to the Senior Common Room at the House."

"I've already seen the papers." Dr. Doyle patted the stack next to him. "Depending on whose account you read, there were a thousand bloodthirsty savages abroad in the streets of London murdering people in their beds last night, or there were five hundred honest Englishmen exercising their God-given right of peitition."

"Any mention of the unfortunate Mr. Basset?" Mr. Dodgson scanned the columns of print.

"He seems to have been overlooked in the press of events. I

spoke to some reporters in the crowd last night, and they would have made sure to get the story into the morning editions. Try the obituary columns." Dr. Doyle nodded to two gentlemen of dignified demeanor, who gravely nodded back and continued to eat their kippers. "This is the most marvelous place, Mr. Dodgson. Do you know, Mr. Portman actually has a copy of Mr. Poe's *Tales of Terror*? I have been longing to read it. . . ."

"Perhaps at another time," Mr. Dodgson said kindly. "Ah, here we are." He quoted the *Times*: " 'Suddenly, at his offices, Mr. Samuel Basset, distinguished editor in chief of *Youth's Companion*.' "

Dr. Doyle snatched the newspaper away and frowned at the brief announcement. "Nothing about the manner of his death? That's odd."

"Quite odd, considering the number of reporters on the scene," Mr. Dodgson agreed. "I suspect the hands of Inspectors Calloway and MacRae have fallen upon the press. It is fortunate that the events of last night seem to have overshadowed Mr. Basset's death."

"What are you going to do about Mr. Portman's request?" Dr. Doyle asked. "I, for one, am quite sure that someone in that office killed Mr. Basset, but who it was and how it was done I cannot tell. Whoever did it must be quite dangerous and should be stopped. When I think of Mr. Basset, gasping away on the street . . ."

Mr. Dodgson shuddered and closed his eyes. "I prefer not to think about it," he said. "However, I agree with you that something should be done, and neither of the policemen involved in the case seem to wish to pursue the matter further."

Nicholas Portman had taken his role of chief mourner very seriously. He now joined his overnight guests decked out in a black tailcoat, black cravat, and black waistcoat, with a black band around his arm and another around the hat, which he held in one hand.

"We must be at Bow Street early," he reminded them. "I've already sent for my solicitor to take on O'Casey's case. I'll pay his bail, of course, and see to it that his family does not suffer. And then, I suppose, I must tell the staff at *Youth's Companion* what I have decided to do about Sammy's position."

"As editor in chief?" Dr. Doyle asked.

"I have given it a good deal of thought," Portman said, "and I have decided . . ."

What he had decided would have to wait. The butler announced, "Mr. Levin has come, my lord."

Andrew Levin looked haggard and worn. His clean-shaven cheeks showed several tiny cuts where his hand had shaken. Like Mr. Portman, he had found time to have a black band sewn onto his jacket and had put a black ribbon on his hat. He frowned slightly when he recognized Mr. Dodgson and Dr. Doyle.

"I beg your pardon, sir, for disturbing you at your breakfast, but I thought you might want to give me some orders as to what to do at the office. Mr. Dodgson, I had no idea you were still in town."

"I had little choice in the matter," Mr. Dodgson said. "What with the snow stopping all the trains, and the rioters in the streets, I was most grateful for Mr. Portman's offer of house room for the night. I do hope the trains will run soon. I really ought to be back in Oxford."

"Let's hope the magistrate will be in a generous mood," Portman said. "Levin, I want you to get back to the office. I want to speak to the entire staff."

"Including the printers?" Levin asked.

Portman thought a minute, then nodded. "If you can find them. O'Casey was taken up last night, and will be at the Bow Street Police Station until I can bail him out, but the rest of them should come in this morning. If not, round up some of the unemployed printers on the street and have them there by eleven o'clock."

"I sincerely hope you have not decided to give up *Youth's Companion,*" Levin said, as he followed Mr. Portman and the other two into the hall, where Norwich oversaw the retrieval of their outer wraps.

"Not at all," Portman told him. "Quite the contrary. *Youth's Companion* was Sammy's life. I wouldn't want to destroy it. However, Sammy had become somewhat, um, stiff-necked in his attitudes. A fresh approach may be needed."

Levin nodded. "I see, sir. May I point out that there are still a number of rough-looking men about, and the police have been warning persons not connected with government businesses to remain in their homes until the disorder is resolved."

"We have a magazine to get out," Portman said loftily. "If the staff does not choose to come in to work, they must be brought in or replaced."

Levin bowed and bustled out. Mr. Dodgson and Dr. Doyle exchanged glances.

Mr. Dodgson drew Dr. Doyle aside while Mr. Portman was helped into his fur-trimmed greatcoat. "Should we inform Mr. Portman of Mr. Levin's disagreement with Mr. Basset?"

Dr. Doyle glanced at their host. "Levin doesn't seem to regard himself as discharged," he pointed out. "With Basset dead, I don't see how it could make much difference."

Mr. Dodgson donned his long black ulster, and Dr. Doyle shrugged himself into the garish plaid balbriggan overcoat. The Portman carriage was waiting to transport the trio back to the Bow Street Police Station.

It was slow going. Neither snow nor fog would deter the ever-present omnibuses from their rounds, and the owners of the ransacked shops had come to find out what was left of their merchandise. Rough-looking men lurked on street corners, while constables marched up and down the Strand and Piccadilly. Glum looks on all faces showed discontent on all sides. The news vendors up and down the streets shouted the headlines: " 'Rioting in the West End! New attacks expected!' "

The Bow Street Police Court was packed with humanity, most of it in full cry. Inspector MacRae's Special Division had done its work well. Most of the rioters of the night before were jammed into the area set apart for the accused, while the public consisted largely of reporters, all jotting down their impressions of the dangerous radicals who had dared to destroy the West End.

The magistrate, one Mr. Gosport, was a wizened gentleman with a pronounced wheeze, who clearly felt himself ill-used, being called upon to render justice upon such a multitude so early in the morning on such a miserable day. He sat in his seat of justice and regarded the mass of humanity in front of him through eyes bleary with age, fog, and a vicious head cold.

One by one the men filed by him and told their stories, most of which went like this: "I was standing in the Strand, minding me own business, guv'nor, when this copper comes up and bangs me on the 'ead and locks me up!"

"And what were you doing in the Strand at that hour?" the magistrate asked, pointing at the nearest prisoner.

"Goin' 'ome, to me kiddies," the man responded, to the applause of the crowd behind him.

The magistrate eyed the crowd. "Ten shillings fine each, and go home to your families," he declared.

There was a muttered protest from the crowd. The magistrate glared at them. "Be grateful that it is only a ten-shilling fine and not prison for breaking the Queen's Peace," he told them severely.

"Ten shillin's a week's pay!" yelled one of the rioters.

"Ten shillings or ten days," the magistrate snapped out. "Constables, get this lot out of here. Who's this?" He stared at Hyndman, who managed to look elegant in spite of a day's growth of beard.

"The ringleader," Inspector MacRae spoke up. "Mr. J. Henry Hyndman. And this," he hauled out the brawny longshoreman next to the dapper Socialist, "is Mr. John Burns. The pair of them started the riot, with their speechmaking."

"I shall not pay a penny of this unlawful tribute," Hyndman announced grandly.

"Nor shall I!" Burns glared at his rival for the position of archagitator.

"Then you'll go back to your cell until you do," the magistrate decided. "And who's this one?" He eyed O'Casey, who stood defiantly beside Burns.

"Seamus O'Casey, printer and agitator. He's wanted for murder," MacRae said.

"Really? He looks murderous enough for two," the magistrate observed. "Who is he supposed to have murdered?"

"An unknown person in the Strand." MacRae consulted his notebook.

"If the person's unknown, why charge this fellow with his murder?" the magistrate interrupted MacRae.

"And Mr. Samuel Basset," MacRae finished, with a scowl at the magistrate for interrupting him.

"Eh? Who's this Basset person?"

"Editor of a magazine for children," MacRae explained.

"And how was he killed?" Mr. Gosport asked, with ghoulish relish.

"The deceased appeared to be suffering from the results of a blow to the head," MacRae stated.

"And what evidence do you have against this prisoner?"

"He was seen at the scene of the crime, and he admitted to having struck the deceased." MacRae had recourse to his notebook again.

"When did he admit to the crime?" Mr. Gosport asked.

"He was heard by the persons incarcerated with him to state that he had struck Mr. Basset," MacRae told him.

"Was that before he had been warned?" Mr. Gosport peered over his spectacles at MacRae. "If so, that evidence is inadmissible." Mr. Gosport looked over the crowd. "Who heard the man O'Casey confess to the crime?"

No one wanted to admit to overhearing O'Casey's confession. Finally Mr. Dodgson struggled to the front of the mob. "I was present when O'Casey spoke of accosting Mr. Basset," he said diffidently. "And I was present when Mr. Basset died."

"And who are you?" Mr. Gosport asked.

"I am the Reverend Mr. Charles Lutwidge Dodgson, of Christ Church, Oxford." Mr. Dodgson offered his card as proof of his identity.

"I see." Mr. Gosport peered at the visiting card, then at the black-clad scholar before him. "And did you see the man O'Casey strike down this Basset?"

Dr. Doyle could stand it no longer. "He was not killed by the blow to the head!" he exclaimed.

"Who's this?" the magistrate wanted to know, while the bailiff shoved Dr. Doyle aside.

Dr. Doyle would not be shoved. "I am Dr. Arthur Conan Doyle, of Portsmouth. I, too, was present when Mr. Basset breathed his last, and I can assure you that he was not killed by the blow to his head but rather by a stab wound in the back, as the autopsy report will prove."

"What autopsy report?" The magistrate blew his nose loudly into a large red-and-white handkerchief.

"Ah . . . there has been no autopsy yet," MacRae admitted. "However, the police surgeon at St. Bart's will have one on my desk, and as soon as he does, this matter will be resolved one way or another!" He glared at Dr. Doyle, who glared back, mustache bristling with indignation.

"You!" The magistrate beckoned O'Casey forward. "Is what this officer says true? Did you strike this Basset person?"

O'Casey looked wildly around the court. There was no assistance in sight. "I hit him, Your Honor, but he was alive when we parted, on me mother's honor!"

"Unfortunately, I am not acquainted with your mother," the magistrate said dryly. "I must remand you into custody until this matter is settled. Bailiff, take him back to the cells and let him sit and repent."

"One moment!" Mr. Portman called out.

"And who are you?" Mr. Gosport regarded this interruption with the same jaundiced glare as he had bestowed upon Mr. Dodgson.

"I am Nicholas Portman, and I am this man's employer. I have my solicitor here, and I am willing to offer bail, if the court will permit."

"No bail in murder cases," Mr. Gosport ruled.

"But he did not commit this murder!" Dr. Doyle exclaimed.

"What about the other fellow, the one in the Strand?" MacRae demanded.

"If this man, O'Casey, was seen by hundreds of people in Trafalgar Square, he could not have been knocking someone on the head in the Strand," Mr. Dodgson said.

Mr. Gosport considered this, while Mr. Portman consulted with the solicitor, a tubby young man in a soft hat and long overcoat, who had been hauled out of bed at the behest of his superiors to handle this distasteful situation.

"The man, O'Casey, led the mob," MacRae reminded the magistrate. "He was seen and heard inciting the crowd to riot and rebellion."

"In that case, he cannot be guilty of murder," Mr. Gosport decided. "He remains in custody until such time as he, Mr. Hyndman, and Mr. Burns can be properly tried on the charges of Inciting to Riot and Breaking the Peace."

O'Casey looked at his employer, who looked at the solicitor, who shrugged.

"I'll get a good barrister for him," young Mr. Redburn told Mr. Portman. "Until he's stood his trial, I think you'd better find another man to run your printing press."

Portman watched helplessly as his chief printer was led back to the cells by a uniformed warder. Then he turned to Mr. Dodgson and Dr. Doyle. "You see how it is? They will have that man in prison whether he is guilty or not. It is infamous!"

"He is guilty of Inciting to Riot," Mr. Dodgson pointed out.

"But he is not a murderer," Dr. Doyle countered. "And whoever this unknown man is, O'Casey most certainly did not kill him, nor did he incite anyone else to do so. All I heard were the usual whirling words, accusing the rich of neglecting the needs of the poor. Nothing about murder, one way or the other."

The three men walked out into the fog and peered about for the Portman carriage, while the young solicitor hovered in the background, waiting for further orders.

"Redburn, you get back to your office and find a barrister to take on O'Casey's defense," Portman told him. "Dr. Doyle, do you think you can get into the autopsy at St. Bart's?"

Dr. Doyle nodded. "I think there's an Edinburgh man on the staff," he said cheerfully. "As for the other fellow, he may well be there as well as poor Basset. It was a dreadful night last night, and there're few places they could have taken him."

"In that case," Portman stated, "we shall go to St. Bart's and find out what we can. The sooner we can find the real murderer, the sooner I can get my printer back, and the sooner I can get *Youth's Companion* out."

CHAPTER 13

M r. Portman and his two guests stood for several minutes until the brougham tooled up to the door of the Bow Street Police Station, with Thomas apologetically explaining that the bloody bobbies wouldn't let him stay there, and in any case, he wanted to walk the horses, lest they take a cramp by standing about in the cold.

"Quite all right, Thomas. We want to go to St. Bart's Hospital. Do you know where it is?"

"Smithfield, I believe," Dr. Doyle put in. "It was considered quite a plum to get a position there when I was a medical student."

Mr. Portman mentally ran a map of London through his head. "High Holborn, then, Thomas."

"If you say so, sir," The coachman waited until the three men mounted the carriage, then carefully made his way through the press of police vans, delivery carts, and cabs, and headed eastward towards the City.

"Are you certain we can gain admittance?" Mr. Dodgson fussed.

"I think Ogilvie is in Pathology," Dr. Doyle said, after a mo-

128

ment's thought. "He was a class ahead of me, but he'll remember me. Dr. Bell was very pleased with his work. Of course, now his patients are all dead, which helps enormously in diagnosis." Dr. Doyle laughed heartily.

Mr. Dodgson had other things on his mind. "I noticed you did not mention Mr. Levin last night, when we were discussing the staff of *Youth's Companion*," he reminded Mr. Portman. "Is he not to be considered as staff?"

Portman looked blank. "I suppose he is," he said at last. "He was Sammy's discovery."

"How so?"

"You recall, last night I told you about how Sammy had taken to charity work," Portman explained. "We heard Mr. Barnett lecture on his scheme for bringing University people down to Whitechapel to educate the poor children and bring young men into a more respectable way of life. Sammy was especially impressed by Mr. Barnett's ideas, since he'd been a poor lad himself. I'd just started the Press Club, and I suppose he wanted something of his own to do, so he took to bringing books over to Mr. Barnett's church, St. Jude's, even though it wasn't his parish. Far from it!"

"I have heard Mr. Barnett myself," Mr. Dodgson murmured. "He is a most enthusiastic speaker."

"He certainly impressed Sammy," Mr. Portman said. "He even started a little lending library, using the books from Portman Penny Press. As I understand it, young Levin hung about St. Jude's to help in the library, and so they became friendly."

"An odd sort of friendship," Mr. Dodgson mused. "They did not seem to get along at the office. Mr. Basset was quite rude to Levin in the presence of the rest of the staff."

"That was Sammy's way." Portman sighed. "He was very touchy about being respected. I never understood it myself; but if, as I suspect, he was born on the wrong side of the blanket, he might take any encroachment on what he considered his prerogatives in bad part."

"Which would certainly explain why he was so upset when he found out that Mr. Levin had been conducting correspondence with contributors to *Youth's Companion* in his name." Mr. Dodgson gripped the strap inside the window of the carriage as the horses lurched along.

"Sammy was upset with him?" Portman's eyebrows rose. "Levin said nothing about this to me last night. So he was taking on a few new chores, was he?"

"Apparently, he was. He wrote to me, soliciting material, and I sent a small selection of puzzles and conundrums," Mr. Dodgson said. "And Mr. Harry Furniss of *Punch* seems to have done the same. I have no idea how many others were approached, nor how much material of this sort found its way into the magazine."

Mr. Portman frowned. "One of the things Sammy was insistent on was that everything in *Youth's Companion* should come from our own writers and artists. In that way we could be certain of the quality of both the material and the source. We didn't want any of our readers or their parents to be exposed to anything that would offend or shock."

Dr. Doyle grinned under his mustache. "If that's so, I can understand why Mr. Basset was so upset at the idea of hiring Mr. Wilde for the staff position. I'm surprised you considered him, sir."

Portman laughed. "There's no harm in Oscar, in spite of his poses and airs. He's a talented young man, and I thought I could give him a hand up, as it were. Besides, I like his wife. Thomas!" He leaned out the window. "Where are we?"

"Just about there, sir!" The carriage arrived at a vast pile of a building, like a square box of stone, with Georgian lintels over the doorways.

They pulled up into a large cobbled yard, where ambulances stood at the ready, their drivers muffled against the fog, and the horses harnessed and blanketed.

"Walk the horses and find yourself something hot to drink," Mr. Portman ordered. "Be back here in half an hour."

The coachman flourished his whip, leaving the three men to deal with the uniformed porter at the hospital door. A brief exchange of coins, and the porter led them through dank and malodorous halls, down a flight of steps, and into a stark gaslit chamber presided over by a stout young man with sandy hair, thick spectacles, a snub nose, and an infectious grin. He wore a heavy knitted jersey under his bloodstained apron to keep out the cold, and he greeted his old schoolmate with a wave of his hand and a look of astonishment.

"Hello, Doyle," he caroled. "Didn't expect to find you in London. I thought you'd gone to sea."

"I did, but I didn't like it. I'm in private practice now."

"Come for a busman's holiday, eh?" Young Dr. Ogilvie waved at the sheeted bodies that filled the morgue. "We're full up this morning."

"I heard you had taken on the job of police surgeon and wanted to compare notes. I've done a few autopsies myself down in Portsmouth," Dr. Doyle told him. "And since I've been trapped here in London, thanks to the snowfall that's stopped the trains, I thought I'd drop by."

"And 'oo let you in, eh?" snarled the second man in the room. Dr. Doyle looked up to see Inspector Calloway bearing down upon him.

Ogilvie shrugged and said, "Look here, Doyle, I know you're anxious to get on, but bringing observers in is strictly against the rules!" He glanced at the other two men, who tried to look as if they were just passing by.

"And you bein' a witness, the last person we want is you!" Calloway rumbled.

"Nonsense," Dr. Doyle retorted. "They used to open autopsies to paying observers—"

"Not now they don't," Ogilvie interrupted him.

Dr. Doyle smiled with bluff charm. "See here, Ogilvie, this is a particular favor. The man who was brought in last night was a . . . a sort of acquaintance."

"Which one?"

"Eh?" Dr. Doyle's mustache quivered in perplexity.

"It's been a busy night," Ogilvie said grimly. "What with the cold and the rioting, we've got five bodies on the table."

"The one I want is a man—"

"That lets out the poor old biddy over in the corner and the little missie yonder." Ogilvie gestured towards a pathetic bundle of rags that had once been a beggar woman and her far younger associate.

"About forty years of age," Dr. Doyle continued. "Rather stout, with a beard—"

"And that lets out the old gent with the long hair and side whiskers taken out of the Thames," Ogilvie said. "What color was the beard?"

"Brown, with some gray," Dr. Doyle said after some consideration.

Ogilvie shook his head. "We've got two of them," he said.

Mr. Dodgson had been straining to hear the conversation. Now he heard Dr. Doyle's sharp exclamation.

"Two!"

"Aye, that's right," Ogilvie said with a grin. "As I said, last night was a busy one. We got the two gentlemen in, one just on six o'clock, and another at around eight. I don't suppose either one of 'em's the one you're looking for."

Mr. Portman stepped forward. "I am here to make the identification of my friend Samuel Basset," he declared. "I shall do so. After that, you may release the body to me for proper interment."

"I haven't done my autopsy yet," Ogilvie objected.

"That's what I'd hoped for," Dr. Doyle said. "I was there when Basset died, so I can fix the time of death. As for the means, that's what I want to find out."

"We know the means," Calloway told him. " 'e were struck down."

"I don't think so," Doyle said, his mustache bristling. "I tried to tell you that last night, but you would not listen to me. I told the magistrate in court this morning that I suspected that Basset had been stabbed, but—"

"Well, let's have a look." Ogilvie interrupted his old classmate's tirade and indicated the two bodies lying on wooden tables, their faces covered with canvas sheets. The smell of putrefaction lay heavy over the room, mingling with the odors of disinfectant and human waste products. Mr. Dodgson cringed away from the tables while Dr. Doyle and his friend stepped closer to the two male bodies. Neither of them had been undressed, an oversight that Ogilvie was about to correct.

"Which one?" Ogilvie asked.

"I think this one." Doyle indicated the sheet that covered the less rotund of the two. "Mr. Basset was wearing black trousers, I believe."

"He usually wore black trousers and a frock coat to the office," Mr. Portman said.

"And 'oo might you be?" Calloway demanded.

"I am Nicholas Portman. I was Sammy Basset's oldest friend," the publisher said.

"Portman Penny Press?" Ogilvie asked with a wry twist of the mouth.

"The same." Mr. Portman nodded. Calloway was not impressed. Dr. Ogilvie turned back the cover over the face of the corpse. "Mr. Portman, can you identify this person as Mr. Samuel Basset?"

"Of course I can!" Portman snapped out.

"I say, Doyle, can you take the notes?" Ogilvie asked. "I'm supposed to keep records on all autopsies. New orders from on high." He gestured expressively with his lancet towards a sheaf of cheap paper attached to the table with a cotton string.

"Not a bad idea," Dr. Doyle said, fumbling for his pencil and notebook.

"Just means more work for the likes of you and me," Ogilvie groused. "Well, then, let's see what we have here. A male, identified by friend as Samuel Basset, age forty or thereabouts . . ."

"He would have been forty-one on his next birthday," Portman murmured. "Poor Sammy!"

"Very well, age forty. Weight, sixteen stone; height six feet; in good physical condition . . ."

"Sammy liked to keep fit," Portman said. "He walked everywhere and enjoyed swimming."

"Difficult to do in London," Mr. Dodgson observed.

"There are swimming baths and clubs," Portman said. "And I believe he skated during the winter."

Oglivie went on: "Clothing: one greatcoat, frock coat, black trousers, waistcoat, shirt, combinations, socks, shoes. Watch and chain in waistcoat pocket. Wallet in breast pocket of greatcoat, contents"—he glanced at the wallet, before handing it on to Calloway—"twenty pounds in notes. Pocket change: ten pennies, two shillings, and a couple of sovereigns. Cardcase in waistcoat pocket, penknife in trousers pocket—"

"Robbery was not a factor," Dr. Doyle observed with a glance at Calloway. "No street ruffian would have left a full wallet or a watch like that one."

"Time of death—" Ogilvie droned on.

"I can give you that to the second," Dr. Doyle announced. "I was on the spot. Five-fifteen precisely."

"All the easier for me," Ogilvie said with a nod. "Observations include bruise on left temple—"

"But that's not what killed him," Doyle insisted.

"Doesn't seem to have done more than break the skin," Ogilvie agreed. "Not unless the old boy was exceptionally thin-skulled."

"I think he must have been stabbed some time before we even got to him. Let me help you lift him up and you'll see what I mean."

Carefully the two men turned the body over. There, in the middle of Basset's back, was the aforementioned wound: a barely noticeable slit in the coat, with a thin crust of dried blood around it.

"One for you, Doyle," Ogilvie said. "Let's have the coat off and see how deep this goes."

It took some time to remove Mr. Basset's greatcoat, frock coat, waistcoat, linen shirt, and woolen combination underwear. Whatever had stabbed him had gone through all that and still entered his body. Most of the blood from the wound had been absorbed by the layers of his clothing. By the time they got down to the skin, the bloodstain was distinctly wider.

"Narrow entry wound," Doyle said with some satisfaction. "And a slit, not a round hole. I'd say the man was killed with some sort of long dagger, a stiletto, perhaps?"

Mr. Dodgson had been edging farther and farther away from the late Mr. Basset. He now bumped into the table that held the sheeted figure of another man, whose damp shoes projected over the edge of the table.

"I beg your pardon," he stammered. He peered at the shoes, then at the edges of the trousers that flapped over them.

"Dr. Ogilvie!" Mr. Dodgson called imperiously. "Who is this?"

"Unknown, brought in about eight o'clock last night," Ogilvie mumbled. "Look here, Doyle, I think you're right, and this chap died of internal bleeding. This wound itself doesn't look deep enough to cause death instantly."

Dr. Doyle bent over the body to examine it more closely. "What I suspect is that the knife, or whatever it was, nicked an artery, maybe the renal artery, and Basset bled to death in half an hour, maybe less. He may not even have known he was dying!"

"Poor chap!" Ogilvie allowed himself a moment of human feeling, then picked up his scalpel and applied it to the body, laying open the thoracic cavity. "Here you are, Doyle! Full of blood, just as you said. Whoever bashed this fellow was bashing a dead man, although neither of them knew it."

"Wot!" Calloway exclaimed. "You mean this 'ere bloke was dyin' when 'e 'it the street?"

"So it would appear," Oglivie said. "Whoever did for this fellow, he didn't do it on the street itself. It would have taken at least fifteen minutes for him to die."

Mr. Portman's face took on a greenish tinge, only partly because of his gruesome surroundings. "Then he must have been stabbed inside the office," he said slowly.

"Which completely exonerates O'Casey, who was well out of the place before we left," Dr. Doyle said, as he scribbled assiduously at the report, which would, in time, find its way into the files of a new and improved Scotland Yard. "You'd better inform Bow Street. Whatever else he's accused of, O'Casey's no murderer."

"Dr. Doyle! Mr. Portman!" Mr. Dodgson's voice trembled with emotion. "I believe we know this man!"

He lifted the sheet off the face of the second man in the dead room. Mr. David Peterson's balding head and line of chin beard were revealed.

135

"How did he die?" Mr. Portman turned on the medical examiner.

"A blow to the head, and this time, it really was the cause of death, no doubt about it," Ogilvie said, pointing to the congealed mass on the back of the skull. "There is a definite break in the cranium, and gray matter was spattered in his hair."

"Was the weapon found?" Mr. Portman asked.

"In this snow?" Ogilvie shrugged. "He was found half-frozen. No telling how long he'd been lying out there. I heard he was in the middle of the riots. He must have been clipped by one of the stones those idiots were tossing right and left at the shopwindows."

"But that wouldn't have left brains all over him," Dr. Doyle objected. "And look here, Ogilvie, there are at least two marks on his noggin. This man was hit at least twice, and that makes it murder, deliberate and possibly premeditated. What's more, he wasn't hit with a stone. Look at the wound; it's regular, not rounded, and there are flakes of brick dust in it." He produced his magnifying glass to prove his point.

"But why should anyone take a brick to Peterson?" Mr. Portman asked. "He could be extremely tiresome, cracking senseless puns and playing cruel pranks. He was always short of money, and he could be thoughtlessly unkind to his poor wife, but that's no reason to bash him like that."

"Nothing in his pockets, nothing on his waistcoat," Calloway said sagely. "This pore chap were robbed, sure enough. 'E must 'ave been in that riot, and one of the lads took advantage, as you might say."

"Unless," Mr. Dodgson said thoughtfully, "Mr. Peterson knew, or thought he knew, something about the death of Mr. Basset. He seemed to be a very clever man, with a taste for puzzles and conundrums. Perhaps he recognized something or thought he had discovered who had killed Mr. Basset. If, as you say, he was always short of funds, he might have tried a bit of extortion on the murderer."

"But that would be very dangerous," Dr. Doyle pointed out.

"A man who has just killed is in a delicate state of mind. Mr. Peterson must have been mad—"

"Or drunk," Mr. Portman put in. "David liked his glass."

"We shall not learn anything more here," Mr. Dodgson announced. "Mr. Portman, I believe we will have to question the staff at *Youth's Companion* if you wish me to discover the true killer."

"And 'oo gave you the right to question anyone?" Calloway demanded. "You're nothin' but a bloody hamateur!"

"Possibly so," Mr. Dodgson said with great dignity, "but I am willing to proceed with an open mind, whereas you, Inspector Calloway, are bound by your so-called system. If you wish to continue your investigation, you would be well to do it at the offices of *Youth's Companion*. That is where Mr. Portman's staff is gathering, and that is where the answer to the question asked by Mr. Basset in his death throes will be."

"Wot question?" Calloway followed the trio through the corridors and back to the yard, where the carriage was still waiting.

"Mr. Basset asked, 'Why?' " Mr. Dodgson explained. "I am now certain that he was not naming Mr. Wilde or anyone else. He wanted to know why he had been stabbed. He must have known his killer, which means it must have been one of the men at the office. Ergo, we must go there to find the answer."

"What do you think you will find at the office?" Mr. Portman asked.

"It is elementary," Mr. Dodgson said, picking his way across the hospital yard to where the coach waited for them. "As Dr. Doyle has just proven, Mr. Basset must have been stabbed within the confines of that building before O'Casey ever spoke to him in the street. The killer was one of those who was in the office between four and five o'clock."

"If we have come to this conclusion now, Mr. Peterson must have reached it last night," Dr. Doyle stated. "He must have approached the killer, who used the disorder in the streets to mask his deed. The killer must have hoped that Peterson's death would be put down to misadventure and blamed on some unknown rioter."

"Instead of which," Portman said, "you have now convinced me that one of the staff at *Youth's Companion* harbored such hatred for poor Sammy that he took a knife to him and then whacked old Peterson when he taxed him with it! I cannot believe it!"

Mr. Dodgson shook his head sadly. "Dr. Doyle and I have discovered that there is murder even in the best of families," he said. "Mr. Basset had nurtured a snake in his bosom."

"And I depend on you to remove it," Portman said firmly. "Thomas! Fleet Street!"

Behind them, Inspector Calloway fumed. He was not going to let either the Metropolitan Police or some interfering amateur get the better of him. He would obtain the necessary warrant and conduct his investigation properly, by the book, as per the system, while MacRae and Scotland Yard ran after radicals, and the amateur sleuthhounds chased phantoms.

With these thoughts, Inspector Calloway headed for the headquarters of the City of London Police on Jewry Street to obtain the necessary warrants. He'd show that scrawny pipsqueak from Scotland Yard how a proper investigation should be run!

CHAPTER 14

By the time the Portman carriage reached Fleet Street, the early traffic had eased somewhat, so that Thomas the coachman could actually maneuver his vehicle between the omnibuses, drays, carts, and cabs. Reporters who had been out all night observing the activities in Trafalgar Square had filed their stories and were now enjoying their "elevenses" at the many pubs patronized by the Fourth Estate. The presses were even now steamed up and running off the afternoon editions, which would be on the streets by lunchtime.

The street was still covered with the remains of the last night's snow, which was now in the process of melting down into slimy slush. The only sign of trouble on Fleet Street was a gang of tough-looking men lounging about the stone griffin, where Mr. Hyndman had taken his stand the night before. The presence of blue-clad constables ostentatiously wielding their batons left no doubt as to the fate of the toughs should they try to repeat the previous night's adventures.

Mr. Portman descended from his carriage in front of the *Youth's Companion* building, with his two guests close behind him. "I don't think I'll need you anymore today, Thomas," he said carelessly. "I have no idea how long this is going to take, and I can find a cab when I'm ready to leave."

"Aye, sir." Thomas touched his high hat with the butt of his whip in salute and eased the horses back into the traffic, while Mr. Dodgson and Dr. Doyle followed Portman through the door to the offices, which had already been embellished with a large black bow.

Mr. Portman noted this with a satisfied nod. "Good. Levin's here, I see." That individual had apparently been busy on Portman's behalf. The coal fires had been lit in the two offices on the first story, and Howarth, Monteverde, and Roberts were in Levin's anteroom, waiting for orders. Only one of the staff, David Peterson, was conspicuously absent.

Portman nodded affably to Monteverde and Howarth, and shook hands with Roberts.

"I cannot say how sorry I am—" Mr. Portman began to speak, his normally cheerful face clouded with grief.

"I do not know where Mr. Peterson is," Levin said, before his employer could remark on the absence of the chief writer.

There was a knock at the downstairs door. Levin darted down the stairs to let in a well-built dark woman, on the sunny side of thirty, dressed in what must have been her best fur jacket and matching hat. She made her way laboriously up the stairs, panting with the effort of negotiating the stairs in her bustle and tight corsets.

"Myrna? What are you doing here?" Winslow Howarth sprang to her side to support her as she tottered into the office, with Levin at her heels. He turned to Mr. Portman. "You remember Mrs. Peterson, sir."

"Win, Monte, something dreadful must have happened to David. He didn't come home last night. I thought he might have spent the night with one of you because of the snow, but this morning's newspapers said there was a riot . . ." She looked from one of her husband's friends to another, seeking an answer. Howarth and Monteverde gazed back at her blankly.

"There was some trouble in the streets," Monteverde said. "But

I was going home in the other direction, so I didn't have any difficulties."

Howarth shook his head. "David did ask me to join him in a drink, but I had to get on home to Post-Office Polly. Dogs must be taken out, snow or no snow. I left Peterson here in the Strand."

"I thought I saw him coming out of a tavern," Roberts put in. He glared back at his comrades' accusing eyes. "Well, he might have been having a short toddy against the cold. I wanted to see what was forward in the square, along with everyone else." He tossed his hair back out of his eyes and stood in his favorite spot, leaning up against the fireplace as if daring anyone to accuse him of anything else.

"And then, this morning, this note came," Myrna said, producing a folded piece of paper. "Delivered by hand, by some boy from the streets, who told me it came from the Press Club."

She suddenly recognized the proprietor of the magazine. "I do beg your pardon, Mr. Portman, but I am quite overset by all this. It's not like David to stay out all night and not even send me word."

"A most faithful and diligent spouse," Mr. Dodgson commented.

"Usually," Mrs. Peterson amended. "Once in a while, when he was with friends, he'd come in late, but he's never been out for a whole night." She looked anxiously at her husband's coworkers, then at Mr. Portman. "I do hope he was not taken up by the police in the rioting last night. This morning's newspaper said that any number of innocent persons found themselves in the cells, all through being on the Strand or in Piccadilly when the police vans went by."

"Oh dear," Portman moaned, "this is going to be worse than I thought." He turned to the woman, who was becoming more and more distraught with every delay. "Mrs. Peterson, I have bad news. Your husband met with an . . . an accident last night."

Myrna gasped and looked about her for some place to sit. Howarth and Monteverde eased her onto the wooden settle, where Dr. Doyle and Mr. Dodgson had waited so uncomfortably the day before.

"Where is he?" Myrna whispered.

"At St. Bart's Hospital," Portman told her.

"Is he injured? When can I see him? I must go to him at once!" Myrna tried to rise. The two men beside her exchanged glances. Clearly, their friend and colleague had met with more than a mere "accident."

"Mrs. Peterson," Dr. Doyle said gently, "your husband is beyond your help. I very much regret to tell you this, but Mr. Peterson is dead."

"David? Dead? How?" Monteverde and Howarth exclaimed, while Levin fussed with the fire, poking it into a higher blaze.

"He was apparently struck by a missile during last night's disturbances," Mr. Dodgson said carefully.

"Dreadful!" Mr. Levin murmured into the fire. "Left in an alley, in the snow!"

Myrna's wails drowned out Levin's soothing voice. "He can't be dead. He can't be!" she shrieked suddenly. "What am I going to do? What am I going to do now?" She began to weep noisily.

Monteverde produced a large handkerchief and handed it to Myrna, while Howarth clutched her hand to offer silent solace. Roberts looked at the trio from his vantage point, drew out his small sketchpad, and expressed his concern with his pencil instead of his voice. Clearly, this death meant far more to the staff of *Youth's Companion* than the shocking demise of the editor in chief.

Portman drew Mr. Dodgson and Dr. Doyle to the fire, leaving the staff to deal with the widow. "This is dreadful," he said. "I had hoped to break the news to her gently, under more propitious circumstances."

"What should we do?" Howarth asked, looking in the direction of Mr. Portman, as befitted the most senior member of the staff present.

"We should take her home," Monteverde declared. "And I suppose someone should notify David's brother. They didn't get along, but he'll have to know. And there's the funeral and all that."

"She'll have to identify the body first," Howarth reminded him. "And there're the kiddies to think of." He turned to Mr. Portman.

"David had two little girls, and he told us there's another on the way. He was going to hit old Basset . . . that is," he stopped in confusion.

"He was about to ask for a rise in pay," Monteverde stepped in. "But it wasn't the right time for it. Mr. Basset was in one of his economical moods, and he'd had some odd visitors." He stopped suddenly, recalling that Mr. Dodgson and Dr. Doyle were among the odd visitors.

Mr. Dodgson was drifting about the room, poking at the papers on Mr. Levin's desk, much to that gentleman's annoyance. "Has anything been touched here since last night?" Mr. Dodgson asked.

Levin blinked in confusion. "I do not believe so. Mr. Basset would not pay for a daily charwoman, so I hired a porter to come in twice a week to remove wastepaper from the dustbins, sweep the floors, and so on."

"No night porter? No watchman?" Mr. Dodgson pursued the issue.

"There's an old chap who has a sort of kennel in the yard behind us," Monteverde explained. "Mr. Basset did not believe it was necessary to hire a watchman, since there was precious little in here to steal, barring the presses, and it would be a job and a half to get them out of the basement!" He turned around to see if this witticism had drawn any laughter. It had not, and he went on, "It was David's idea to find some old geezer to stay in the yard, rent-free, to keep an eye on the place for us. We'd give him a penny or two for food and a fire and a dram of gin."

"But who lays the fires in the mornings?" Mr. Dodgson asked, still puzzled by the domestic arrangements at *Youth's Companion*.

"Er . . . I do," Levin said reluctantly. "I have the responsibility of opening in the morning and locking up at night. Although," he added, after a moment of thought, "Mr. Roberts also has a key to the front door. He occasionally comes in to complete his cuts for the following day." Levin gave Roberts a sniff, which Roberts greeted with a snarl.

"I see." Mr. Dodgson started drifting about the room again. "In that case, Mr. Levin, you must have been the last one out the door last night."

"I was," Levin said proudly. "At five o'clock precisely I told everyone to go home and locked the doors. As you recall, sir, I let you and Inspector MacRae into the vestibule to get out of the cold and snow."

"And you locked the door behind us when we left," Mr. Dodgson said.

Mr. Portman frowned. "Five o'clock? I thought our business hours were from eight-thirty until six-thirty."

Mr. Levin reddened. "Mr. Basset had already left for the day," he said defensively. "For his weekly meeting with you, sir. He left at four-fifty, by my watch. The snow was beginning to fall quite heavily, and I felt that it would be better for all concerned if I let the staff return to their homes before it got too deep for navigation. Between that and the agitation in the street, I took it upon myself . . ."

Portman's frown deepened. "It was not your place to do so," he scolded. "However, it happened, and you were probably right to let the staff leave early. I might well have done the same thing had I been here. Sammy, of course, would have insisted on everyone's staying until the exact hour, but he wasn't here, was he?"

Levin's handsome features were flushed with chagrin at being berated in front of the rest of the staff. "I did what I thought best," he repeated.

The uncomfortable moment was interrupted by a feminine voice from the stairs.

"Mr. Levin, I worked all night to finish these . . . Oh dear, am I interrupting?" Miss Harvey appeared at the office door, her red woolen hat and gloves making a bright spot of color amongst the drab blacks and browns of the rest of the office staff.

Mr. Levin hurried forward to take the packet of manuscript from her hands. "Miss Harvey! I had no idea you would come all the way into town today! What with the cold, and they say the rioters will be out again . . . and I am sure you have heard of the unfortunate accident that befell Mr. Basset . . . and now it seems that our Mr. Peterson was also attacked in the riot . . . Mrs. Peterson is here . . ." Levin fussed about, putting the typed manuscript on his desk, pushing one of the ledgers aside to make room for it.

The ledger fell to the floor, its pages splayed open. Mr. Dodgson retrieved it, smoothed the folded page, closed it, and laid it back on top of a pile of similar ledgers.

Mr. Portman stepped forward, eager for any distraction from the sad news of two deaths in one evening. Mr. Levin hurried to make the proper introductions: "Mr. Portman, this is Miss Helen Harvey, our manuscript typewriter. I thought it a good idea to have the copy typewritten before sending it on to the printing room, rather than making our compositors suffer with the dreadful handwriting of some of our writers." He glared at Monteverde and Howarth, who were still sitting with Mrs. Peterson.

Nicky Portman smiled down at the young woman. Not badlooking, he decided. Not a child, but definitely not an old maid either. Aloud he said, "You are not related to the Harvey who wrote those pieces in the *Illustrated London News* about decorative arts in Japan? The fellow who bought all that blue-and-white pottery and fobbed it off on Whistler for his study?"

"I should not say that my father 'fobbed off' anything," Miss Harvey said sharply. "He was considered an authority on Oriental and Classical pottery and the decorative arts."

"Was?" Portman picked up on the verb.

"He died last year," Miss Harvey explained.

"I am sorry to hear it," Portman said. "What have we here?"

"Last night Mr. Basset told me to retype these manuscripts. I have done so. If you please, Mr. Levin, I would like to collect the money that is owed me. My mother is waiting for me at home." Miss Harvey raised her chin in an attempt to gain dignity.

Portman raised his eyebrows at Levin, whose flush deepened. "I made the arrangements with Miss Harvey," he explained. "She was to be paid for piecework, from our petty cash. However, in light of his unhappy experiences during the afternoon, I felt it best not to disturb Mr. Basset with so minor a matter. In fact, I made Miss Harvey a small loan to tide her over until such time as Mr. Basset would allow me access to the cash box."

"In that case, let's pay Miss Harvey what is owed her," Portman said expansively. "And Mrs. Peterson, you must not remain here. It's unfortunate that I have already dismissed my coachman, or I would have had Thomas take you home. However, the least I can do is provide a cab. Mrs. Peterson, have you any relations to turn to at this sad time?"

"My mother's in Hereford," Myrna said between sobs. "I'll have to go home to her, I suppose; but she's only got the small cottage, and how we'll manage I do not know. David was not the most provident of men. I suppose his brother will help . . . Oh, what am I going to do?" She started to cry gustily, while Monteverde and Howarth looked helplessly about them for someone to take over the duties of providing solace for the widow.

Portman tried to bring order into what had become a scene fraught with emotional turmoil.

"Mrs. Peterson, I am truly sorry for your loss. If you will give Levin, here, your brother-in-law's direction, I will send a note immediately and notify him of this sad event. And I suppose I had better get into Sammy's office, Miss Harvey, and give you what is owed you."

Mr. Portman smiled at Helen Harvey. She smiled back, and her face took on an elfin sort of beauty.

Mr. Portman opened the door to the inner office and gasped, bringing everyone else to the door to see what was amiss.

The inner office was in total disarray. Papers were strewn over the floor. The mounted heads of antelopes and leopards had been wrenched from the walls, apparently with the aid of one of the African spears that had originally been stationed on either side of the doors and were now ranged in a grisly row under the windows.

"What on earth . . . ," Portman gasped, as he took in the destruction.

Mr. Dodgson followed him into the room. "Dear me," he murmured. It seemed inadequate to the occasion.

As always, Dr. Doyle came to the point. "Is anything missing? The cash box, for instance?"

Levin darted forward and made for the desk. "It's here," he announced, removing the metal box from the bottom drawer of the desk. "But I don't have the keys. Mr. Basset kept them on his person, attached to his watch fob."

"How like Sammy," Portman muttered. He turned to Miss

Harvey. "I see I shall have to turn banker and make you a brief loan until such time as I can recover Sammy's keys and pay you for your trouble."

"All I want is what is owed me," Miss Harvey said resolutely. "And I hope the manuscript is satisfactory."

Levin was making an effort to collect the papers from the floor.

"Do not touch anything!" Mr. Dodgson snapped out. "The police will wish to examine this room."

"The police!" Mr. Levin's flushed cheeks turned pale.

"It is possible that Mr. Basset was stabbed here in this room and not out on the street at all," Mr. Dodgson pointed out. "In any case, this room has been ransacked. By whom and for what purpose I cannot say at this time. Where is Dr. Doyle?"

"I'm here," Dr. Doyle called from the stairwell. "Look here, Mr. Dodgson."

The group followed Mr. Dodgson to the stairs. Dr. Doyle had opened the door to allow more light into the dark cavity of the stairwell. A ray of watery sunlight illuminated the wooden stairs. There, clearly outlined, were reddish brown stains.

"He must have been stabbed here in the stairwell," Dr. Doyle announced.

The shadow of a man fell on the stained stairs. The group looked up to see Inspector MacRae standing in the doorway, with Inspector Calloway looming behind him.

"Good morning, gentlemen," MacRae said, touching his bowler hat. "I'm glad to see that everyone's here. Now we can get on with finding out who killed Mr. Samuel Basset."

CHAPTER 15

I nspector MacRae stamped the snow off his feet in the vestibule, while two large constables and Inspector Calloway lurked behind him. Dr. Doyle sprang up from his crouch to guard his find against the vandals who would grind it into the wooden risers.

"Inspector, mind where you step!" Dr. Doyle cried out. "There are bloodstains on these stairs!"

MacRae peered at the rust-colored drops and nodded at Calloway. "They might be bloodstains," he conceded. "Step carefully, lads," he warned his men, as they edged up the stairs and into Mr. Levin's office.

Mr. Portman had recovered some of his composure when the two policemen emerged from the stairwell. He frowned at Inspector MacRae. "Aren't you the inspector who charged my printer with murder?" He turned to Calloway. "And you were at the autopsy."

The two men, one large and red-faced, the other small and bespectacled, glared at each other in mutual loathing, then turned to the civilian in front of them.

"Inspector MacRae, Metropolitan Police," MacRae snapped out. "I was the first officer on the scene when Mr. Basset died."

"Inspector Calloway, City of London Police," the other man said, with a look of disdain at his smaller colleague. "Because Mr. Basset met 'is end on Fleet Street, this case is officially the business of the City of London," Calloway explained.

"But it has been turned over to the Metropolitan Police, since the City of London is not equipped to deal with crimes of violence, such as this murder," MacRae stated. "Therefore, I am in charge of the case, and Inspector Calloway here will conduct the interviews as per my orders." He settled his spectacles firmly on his nose. "And now that you know who we are, sir, who are you?"

Portman looked affronted. How dare this policeman not know the face of the publisher of Portman Penny Press! "I am Nicholas Portman," he said, "and Samuel Basset was my oldest and dearest friend."

"In that case," MacRae said briskly, "maybe you can tell me who hated him enough to stick a knife in his back. Aye, Doyle," he turned to the young doctor, "Calloway gave me the news. I'm man enough to admit when I'm mistaken. You were right, and it was not the blow to the head that killed him."

Dr. Doyle smiled smugly under his mustache, then remembered the second death of the night before. "And what about Peterson?"

"Who?" MacRae took a moment to recall the second unhappy victim of the riot. "Oh, that fellow. The fat one who stopped a brick."

A wail from the settle drew the attention of the two policemen to the two ladies and their protectors.

"Be more careful, Inspector!" Howarth scolded the policeman.

"This is the wife, or, I should say, widow of that unfortunate man," Portman explained. The two inspectors removed their hats in deference to Mrs. Peterson and Miss Harvey, then turned back to Mr. Portman.

Portman had other things on his mind. "Where is my printer?" he demanded. "Where is O'Casey? Now that it's been proven that he could not have killed Sammy, he should be freed at once. I'll have my solicitor post his bail."

MacRae glared at the publisher. "O'Casey is to be remanded

to the court on the charge of Inciting to Riot, in defiance of the reading of the Riot Act. He'll be tried, along with his friends, as soon as we can clear the streets of the rabble."

"Nonsense!" Portman exclaimed. "O'Casey's been with the Portman Penny Press for years. He's no agitator!"

"O'Casey was rather, ah, vocal," Mr. Dodgson reminded him. "And he was certainly in the forefront of the disturbance in the Strand last night."

"He's also charged with the murder of one David Peterson, as identified by you, Mr. Dodgson," Calloway took over.

MacRae looked the scholar over with a frown. "I am surprised to see you still here, Mr. Dodgson. I thought you'd be on your way to Oxford by now."

"The trains have been delayed," Mr. Dodgson said frostily. "Besides, Mr. Portman has asked me assist him in getting his magazine through the press. As for O'Casey, Dr. Doyle's examination proved that Mr. Peterson's wounds were inflicted by several blows to the head. This is not at all consistent with the activities we observed in the Strand during the, um, agitation. O'Casey was plainly in sight of the crowds during most of the evening. Whoever struck down Mr. Peterson, it was most certainly not he."

Myrna shrieked in anguish. Helen put an arm around the sobbing woman and turned on the men with righteous indignation. "Gentlemen! Have some consideration for Mrs. Peterson's feelings! If you must discuss horrors, do it somewhere else!"

The other men made consoling noises. Monteverde and Howarth arranged themselves on either side of the grieving widow, while the artist, Roberts, took his place against the mantelpiece again and sketched the scene with a cynical smirk.

It was Levin who made the decision as to how to proceed. "The fire has been made up in Mr. Basset's office, gentlemen. Perhaps this discussion would be best done in privacy."

Portman nodded. "Good thinking, Levin. Come along, Inspector. I can give you my statement in the office." He started to move, then turned back to the secretary. "Levin, if we're going to press today we will need a press crew. Better get over to Portman Penny Press and see if Hannegan can spare some of his men."

"Should I not remain here, sir, in case some of the printing crew should decide to come in?" Levin's face was white and drawn, making him look more than ever like a classic Greek statue.

"Sammy should have hired an office boy to run the errands," Portman grumbled.

"There are plenty of boys in the street," Howarth said. "One of those lads can do your errand for a penny. Have him run over to the Penny Press."

Portman looked for paper and pen on Levin's desk. The obsequious secretary provided them. The note was written, and Levin descended the stairs to dispatch it. He returned with Mr. Smythe, the proprietor of the bookshop below. The delicate-looking shopkeeper was dressed in his usual black frock coat and striped trousers, but had added a small black ribbon to the lapel of his coat in token of mourning.

"Mr. Portman," the shopkeeper said with a low bow. "I had no idea that you had decided to honor us with a visit. I wish to know what is to be done about the shop. I have ordered a wreath, of course, but do not know where it is to be directed, and I have placed a crape bow on the door, as Mr. Levin ordered."

Portman stopped the flow of words with a grand gesture. "By all means leave the bow upon the door," he ordered. "I have not decided where to hold the funeral, but the shop will be closed for that day, when I shall announce the time and the place. As for the shop and stock, I have not yet decided what to do about it."

"Who actually owns the shop downstairs?" Mr. Dodgson asked sharply.

"It was my granddad's shop, when he first started," Portman said with a shrug. "My father expanded the business and took over the rest of the building; and when he moved over to the new place down the street, he made it over to me. Sammy thought it would be a good idea to keep it up, to sell *Youth's Companion* and Portman Penny Press books for children and young persons, so I let Sammy run it, and we split the profits. Sammy was always one to turn a penny."

Mr. Dodgson's expression grew stern. "I only wish to know because he was selling, at full price, merchandise that had been removed from the active market as defective, to wit, the first printing of *Alice's Adventures in Wonderland*. I wish that merchandise to be removed from the shop at once, to be distributed, as I and Mr. Tenniel had originally decided, to village schools and institutions that could not afford a perfect copy."

Portman looked blankly at the shopkeeper.

"I believe the gentleman is referring to the copies of *Alice's Adventures in Wonderland* that Mr. Basset discovered in the storeroom when he did inventory last summer," Smythe said. "They must have been given to your father for his charitable donations. Mr. Basset was of the opinion that although the books were twenty years old, they were in good condition and should bring a tidy sum when sold. If the gentleman is adamant in his request, I can remove them from the stock; but I assure you, sir, the imperfections are so minute that no one could detect them."

"*I* can detect them," Mr. Dodgson said stubbornly.

Mr. Portman sighed. "If you like, I can turn the entire box over to you, Mr. Dodgson," he said. "I can't answer for Sammy's behavior, except to excuse it on the grounds that he was somewhat careful about money."

Inspectors Calloway and MacRae exchanged looks. Clearly, they considered Mr. Dodgson's distress over the sale of a book that was twenty years old unimportant when compared to the deaths of two men yesterday.

MacRae glared at the assemblage. "Don't anybody leave," he ordered. "I'll want Calloway here to have a word with each of you."

"Is there somewhere else where we can conduct our interviews?" Calloway asked. "This 'ere office is too public fer my taste."

"I want to use Sammy's offices myself," Portman stated. "Levin, have you built up the fires upstairs? Perhaps Inspector Calloway can use the writers' room."

"I can build up the fires now, if you wish," Levin said, holding the office door open for Mr. Portman to enter Mr. Basset's office. Portman led the way into Basset's private office, while Levin fussed behind them, and the two constables took up positions next to the door to the outer office, preventing Monteverde, Howarth, and Roberts from entering. The two writers and the artist had to peer into the office around their shoulders.

MacRae stopped in the doorway and took in the scene of chaos. "What happened here?" he asked.

"That should be obvious," Dr. Doyle replied. "Someone tore the place apart."

"Whatever for?" MacRae shook his head at the damage.

"More to the point," Mr. Dodgson said, "when did this occur?"

"Eh?" MacRae swiveled his head to look at the scholar, who was picking his way around the room, carefully examining the debris.

"This building was locked last night by Mr. Levin. You and I were present at the time, Inspector. There is no night porter, but there is a man who has been allowed to use the yard behind as a place to sleep in return for watching the building. You will, of course, question him."

"Teaching your granny to suck eggs, sir? I'll have my men on it," Calloway said with a nod at MacRae.

Mr. Dodgson went on, ignoring the interruption. "However, between the snow and the disturbance in the street, it is unlikely that he would have seen anything. The question remains: When was this destruction done?"

"And why?" Dr. Doyle shook his head. "Look at those heads! Wrenched off the walls, mounting boards and all!"

"It would take a strong man to do that," MacRae observed.

"Or a madman," Mr. Portman put in. "What could he expect to gain by this?"

"I don't suppose Mr. Basset had been in India and stolen some exotic jewel," MacRae said sarcastically.

"Oh dear, not again," Mr. Dodgson murmured, with an anguished look at Dr. Doyle.

153

Portman put his fears to rest. "Nothing at all like that, Inspector. Sammy lived a blameless life, as far as I know."

"Indeed." Inspector MacRae looked about the room again. "Someone must have hated him, that's for certain. Otherwise, why destroy all these things? I take it Mr. Basset was fond of hunting?"

"Only when we were together on our African adventure," Portman answered. His voice grew thick with emotion. "It was the most wonderful time of our lives! Poor dear Sammy never really got over it." He looked at the battered taxidermy and reached for a handkerchief, suddenly overcome with the enormity of what had happened to his friend.

Mr. Dodgson turned to Mr. Portman. "Sir, one hates to ask, but had Mr. Basset any expectations? Any heirs or other persons who might gain by his death?"

"In other words," Inspector MacRae was more blunt, "who gets his money?"

Portman looked blank. "Do you mean, who is his beneficiary under his will?"

"Did he have a will?" Mr. Dodgson asked.

"Oh, yes, my father insisted on it before we went off to Africa," Portman said. "Of course, that was some time ago, but I never felt any need to change my will, and as far as I know, neither did he."

"And who does benefit from Mr. Basset's death?" Inspector Calloway pressed on.

"I suppose I do. We made out our wills in each other's favor," Portman admitted. "We were young, we were friends, and we were about to go into places where there was a distinct possibility of not returning. Neither of us had much to leave, since my father was very much alive, and except for a small legacy from my mother's family, I had no money of my own at that time. As for Sammy, he was completely dependent on his own exertions to rise in the world."

"But circumstances change, do they not?" Mr. Dodgson was now peering at the objects on the late Mr. Basset's desk. "You now have a considerable income thanks to the legacy you inherited, as well as your share in *Youth's Companion* and the shop downstairs."

Mr. Portman nodded. "Sammy drew his stipend from the profits from the magazine," he explained. "What he did with it was his own concern."

"He had no wife or children?" MacRae had his notebook out and was scribbling notes to himself. "Any close relations, who might want to take a knife to him?"

"Not any of which I am aware," Mr. Portman said frostily. "When we were at school together, he never had visitors and often had to spend the school holidays with the staff. My father took pity on him and allowed him to make his Christmas holidays with us. My mother and sisters treated Sammy like a relation, although he was no such thing, of course."

"Hmmm." MacRae looked at Calloway, who shrugged.

"Sammy and I even took lodgings together when we came back from Africa," Portman went on, nostalgia welling up in his voice.

"But you did not invite him to share your flat at the Press Club," Mr. Dodgson commented.

"Well," Portman looked embarrassed. "One moves on. As I told you, I received a legacy that gave me enough to start the Press Club, and I decided to move there."

"But not with Mr. Basset," Inspector MacRae said, his eyes glittering behind his spectacles. "Now, why was that, sir? Considering that you two were once so close?"

Mr. Portman drew himself up haughtily. "I find that question impertinent, Inspector. My personal relations are none of your business. And if you are implying that I killed my friend in order to inherit his share of *Youth's Companion,* might I remind you that Portman Penny Press is an extremely lucrative concern, in which I own a considerable share, and that I am hardly in want of funds! In any case, I could not have stabbed Sammy. If Dr. Doyle is right, and Sammy was killed before four-fifty, I was not here. Mr. Levin will tell you that when he informed me of the sad death of my dear friend, I was in my rooms at the Press Club, dressing for dinner. What with the state of the roads, the snow, and the disturbances outside, it would have been impossible for me to get from St. James's to Fleet Street and back between four and five o'clock."

Inspector MacRae grimaced and acknowledged the logic of this. Mr. Dodgson had transferred his examination from the battered heads to the mess of papers on the desk. "Where is it?" he muttered to himself. "I thought I saw it . . . It should be here . . ."

"What are you looking for?" MacRae asked irritably.

"I don't know," Mr. Dodgson said, "but I will when I see it. Mr. Portman, where did Mr. Peterson and the others work when they were not invading Mr. Levin's office?"

"Oh, upstairs," Mr. Portman waved a hand in the direction of the ceiling. "They have their room upstairs, and Roberts does his engraving in the attic. You can do your interviews in the rooms upstairs, Inspectors. I'll need this one to put the next issue together. Levin, where are the stories for this week's issue?"

"I believe those are the ones Miss Harvey has just brought in." Mr. Levin scrambled about, picking up the papers that had been scattered about on the carpeted floor. "These are the manuscripts that were submitted to *Youth's Companion* for consideration for future issues."

Mr. Dodgson frowned. "Submissions?" He turned to Mr. Portman. "Did you not tell me that Mr. Basset wished the entire magazine to be written by his own staff?"

Mr. Portman nodded and turned his gaze to Mr. Levin.

Levin licked his lips and said, "That is true, sir, but I thought that the magazine was beginning to lose readership because the stories were, if I may say so, all of a piece. I suggested to Mr. Basset that perhaps a variety of styles and experiences might be better suited to today's youth."

"And you took it upon yourself to remedy the situation?" Portman asked sharply.

"I wrote to various persons associated with literature for children . . ."

"Including myself," Mr. Dodgson put in.

". . . Reminding them that *Youth's Companion* would value any contribution they might make," Levin continued, wilting under Portman's icy stare.

"Apparently Mr. Basset didn't think the same way you did," Inspector MacRae commented. "Isn't this a poem? What's that signature?"

"Mr. Stevenson," Levin said.

MacRae's eyebrows went up and his eyes glittered behind his spectacles. "Now there's a name a Scotsman can recognize," he said.

Portman accepted the handful of manuscripts and gathered up more from Basset's desk. "I'll go over these myself," he stated. "Levin, you've gone overboard on this, but I'm sure it was with the best intentions. Now, send Miss Harvey in to me with the typed manuscripts."

"Then we are going to press?" Levin asked, a worried frown marring the marble perfection of his features. "It may seem callous, but the distributors and subscribers will be unhappy if we are late with their issues."

"In that case, I'll have to go over the copy," Portman reminded him. "Mr. Roberts, have you a cover illustration ready?"

"I was working on one," the lanky artist said, flipping over another sheet on his sketchpad. "Only the room upstairs was so cold, I couldn't do anything yesterday." He scowled at Levin, who pointedly refused to look back at him.

Miss Harvey had left Mrs. Peterson to sniffle into Howarth's shoulder. Now she trotted in with the pile of typed sheets. "Here are the manuscripts," she said. "You may look them over before they go down to the compositors."

Levin was still picking up papers, while Portman went on. "I have no idea what Sammy was planning to put into this week's issue. He usually went over things with me at our Wednesday meetings, but of course, he never got to tea yesterday. I only hope we have enough material. David could fill in almost anything if I decided not to use a piece, but now he's gone . . . what are we to do?" Mr. Portman looked helplessly at the pile of papers scattered over the floor of the office.

Miss Harvey took over. "Perhaps I can help," she said sweetly, taking the manuscripts from Levin's shaking hands and placing them on the desk. "I used to assist my father in preparing his articles, proofreading, and so on."

"I could not ask you to remain here," Mr. Portman protested. "What about your mother?"

"I can send a note to my mother, explaining why I am detained," Miss Harvey said, taking off her hat and gloves. "My goodness, what an odd desk! It has drawers on both sides!"

Portman looked at the battered relic. "Yes, that's the desk Sammy and I worked at when we started *Youth's Companion*. It's a partner's desk, you see, so that one of us would work on one side, and one at the other. Now, let's clear away some of this stuff and make a start. Levin, has Hannegan come over from the Penny Press?"

"I believe there are five men and the apprentice boy in the printing room," Levin said. "They refuse to work unless there is a fire."

"Then get them one!" Portman snapped out. "Put it in one of those iron barrels we use for ink. And tell them that O'Casey's being held at Bow Street, but there is a solicitor working for him, paid for by the Portman Penny Press. We take care of our own," he admonished the secretary.

"Before all this gets started, I want a word with each of you," Calloway said ominously.

"Should I call in my solicitor?" Howarth asked half-jocularly.

A double knock at the office door interrupted him. A helmeted constable poked his head in.

"Sorry to bother you, Inspector MacRae, sir," he said, "but it's started again. There's a gang of toughs out of Whitechapel come into the Strand, and they've called out the Force to protect the shops."

MacRae said something under his breath that made Miss Harvey's cheeks redden. Calloway supressed a grin.

"You 'avin' this 'ere riot on your 'ands, Inspector," Calloway said officiously, "per'aps I can get on wif these statements. And then we can put our 'eads together, and see wot we makes of 'em."

MacRae glared around the room, his eyes lingering on Mr. Dodgson and Dr. Doyle. "None of you is to leave London until you have given your statements to Inspector Calloway," he ordered.

"Oh, we shall all be here," Portman assured him. "We've a magazine to put out!"

158

CHAPTER 16

I nspector MacRae was on the horns of the proverbial dilemma. On the one hand, he had all the suspects in the Basset murder case lined up, ready for questioning, with the possibility of winding that knotty problem up neatly before the Coroner's Inquest; on the other hand, his primary objective in Fleet Street had been the control of the dissatisfied workers rampaging through the streets. The idea of leaving the all-important interviews to the likes of Inspector Calloway galled him, but duty, in the form of Constable Ramsbotham, called him away from the murder to protect the West End from the mob.

He frowned at the constable. "Who else is out there?"

"There's a squad come in from Kensington. Shops in Southwark and the East End are boarding up, and there's word on the streets that the Militia is to be called up," the constable reported.

MacRae swore under his breath again. He looked at Mrs. Peterson, who had stopped screaming and was now crying silently into Mr. Howarth's shoulder. He regarded the dandified Mr. Monteverde and the slovenly Mr. Roberts and decided that Mr. Levin was the least obnoxious of the lot. Finally, he looked through the open door at Mr. Portman, who was by now checking the typewritten pages, with Miss Harvey hovering at his shoulder.

"Ahem!" MacRae coughed loudly to get Portman's attention. "I have been called away on an emergency. . . ."

"More Fenian rioters?" Calloway asked sarcastically.

"Rioters, yes. Fenians, perhaps. But whatever they may be, they must not be allowed to repeat last night's offenses." MacRae settled his bowler hat firmly on his head. "Inspector Calloway, you are in charge here. You will take down these people's statements and bring them to me at Scotland Yard."

"And then wot?" Calloway asked, gleefully relishing MacRae's discomfort at having to leave the scene of an investigation in any hands but those of Scotland Yard.

"And then we shall have more information." MacRae braced himself for the cold, buttoning his long overcoat tightly about his throat, and followed the constable down the stairs, forgetting the bloodstains in his haste to get back to the riot.

"I'm glad he's out of the way," Portman said, rubbing his hands together. He beckoned the two writers and the artist into the room, leaving Mrs. Peterson to the tender mercies of Mr. Levin and the constable left on duty in the anteroom.

Mr. Dodgson drifted out of the office, leaving the *Youth's Companion* staff to their conference. He beckoned Dr. Doyle to his side and murmured, "One usually finds that murder is done for money, but in this case, there seems to be no monetary motive. I am at a loss to understand why the man was killed."

"There are other motives," Dr. Doyle suggested. "Passion, for instance."

"But Mr. Basset had no wife, no sweetheart, and, apparently, no private life at all," Mr. Dodgson complained.

Inspector Calloway did not waste time on idle rumination. He barked at Levin, "Where's this 'ere room wot I'm supposed to 'ave fer interviewin'?"

"Up these stairs." Levin led the way up a flight of stairs, lit by the feeble rays that found their way through the skylight above them, to the second story, where the staff writers of *Youth's Companion* were supposed to court their muses, to provide the youth of England, Scotland, Wales, and the Colonies with entertainment and enlightenment in equal portions.

It was almost a duplicate of the floor below in reverse, in that the smaller room was the one just above Mr. Basset's sanctum, while the larger room was the one that contained two desks instead of one. Clearly, it was Mr. Peterson, the chief writer, who was given the larger windows and the view of Fleet Street below, whereas the other two men had to share a fireplace and a view of the paved yard behind the building, which included the shed used by the watchman and the convenience used by the staff.

Mr. Dodgson looked over the room and shivered involuntarily. The small fires that had been laid in the two fireplaces that corresponded to the ones in Mr. Levin's and Mr. Basset's offices had only just started to warm the barnlike room. There was frost on the inner surfaces of the windows, which lacked curtains to block the draft that whistled through the minute gaps in the ancient window frames. The furniture consisted of mismatched desks and chairs, corkboards to which illustrations and notices had been affixed with pins, and a large and libelous caricature of the late Mr. Basset that had been used as a darts target. Mr. Dodgson peered into the second, private office and found that Mr. Peterson had been allowed the luxury of a scrap of carpet under his chair and a fireplace of his own. Otherwise, the chief writer shared the privations of the other two.

Dr. Doyle stepped over to the nearest gas jet and lit it. The lamp flared, augmenting the watery sunshine filtering through the windows.

"I can see why Mr. Peterson felt ill-used," Dr. Doyle commented. "It would be difficult to write of sunny African climes in this icebox!"

Mr. Dodgson sat in the chair vacated by the late David Peterson and proceeded to pick up and read every item on the surface of the desk. There were many scraps of paper with cryptic notes; newspaper cuttings of strange occurrences and quaint old sayings; odd drawings and diagrams; handwritten stories, much corrected; letters from young subscribers to *Youth's Companion* requesting information about some character or another in a story.

" 'Ere! Wot d'ye think yer doin?" Calloway demanded, while Mr. Dodgson continued his search of Mr. Peterson's desk. "Yer muckin' about wif evidence!"

"What are we looking for?" Dr. Doyle asked, after watching Mr. Dodgson put the papers into separate piles.

"I'm not sure," Mr. Dodgson said. "But Mr. Basset was killed with something long, thin, and sharp. Where is it?"

Dr. Doyle frowned. "The murderer could have taken it outside and dropped it into the snow," he suggested.

"But Mr. Basset was ahead of him in the stairwell, and the rest of the staff were about to descend," Mr. Dodgson objected. "He could not have gone down the stairs and thrown the weapon out the door because Mr. Basset was in the way."

"I see," Dr. Doyle said slowly. "Then the dagger, or whatever it was, must still be in this building, for the murderer would have had no time to remove it."

"So it would seem," Mr. Dodgson said absently, scanning Mr. Peterson's manuscripts. "Mr. Peterson wrote a clear, neat hand. Very useful when editing manuscripts; printers are notorious for getting things wrong. There was a certain scholar at the House who had written a paper on a subject in which he mentioned the Sixth Commandment. The printer left a word out, and the text of his sermon read, 'Thou shalt commit adultery.' The result was not what had been intended." Mr. Dodgson chuckled at his friend's discomfort and went on reading.

Dr. Doyle peered into the second room. "These must be Mr. Howarth's and Mr. Monteverde's desks," he said. "Which is which?"

One was meticulously tidy, with pens lined up in the inkwell, pencils sharpened to a point, a blotter neatly lined up with the edge of the desk, and three manuscripts crossed one over the other. The other desk was a welter of paper, pens, newspaper cuttings, picture postal cards of exotic shores, and paper wrappings that smelled strongly of fish.

Mr. Dodgson had finished with Mr. Peterson's desk and now came into the second room. "Mr. Howarth is quite tidy in his dress," Mr. Dodgson noted. "Whereas Mr. Monteverde's hair is worn long, his trousers need pressing, and he has a stain on his very dashing waistcoat. I suspect that Mr. Howarth's is the tidy desk, and Mr. Monteverde is the one who has the desk nearest the back window."

Inspector Calloway had mounted the stairs and was now making himself at home in the writers' office. "I'll take the tidy one then," Inspector Calloway decided, sinking into Mr. Howarth's chair, which creaked ominously under his bulk.

"What were they working on, I wonder, when they were driven downstairs by the cold?" Dr. Doyle asked, not expecting an answer.

"Mr. Peterson appears to have been writing a continuation of the adventures of Robinson Crusoe," Mr. Dodgson told him. "Not quite in the style of Defoe, but certainly readable and moderately entertaining. I expect Mr. Basset would have insisted that certain geographical facts be inserted into the narrative, but otherwise, I find it unexceptionable."

"It certainly would fit Mr. Basset's criteria for his magazine," Dr. Doyle agreed. He checked the topmost item on Mr. Howarth's desk. "I see Mr. Howarth has been to the theater. This is a scenario for a Christmas pantomime."

"But that is not what we are looking for," Mr. Dodgson reminded him. "Nor is this." He offered a small bottle clearly marked BRANDY to Inspector Calloway.

"For medicinal use, I suppose." Inspector Calloway commented.

"Or to stimulate the brain cells," Dr. Doyle responded. "Do you suppose the murderer hid the weapon up here?" Dr. Doyle probed into Mr. Howarth's desk and came up with a packet of biscuits and a corkscrew.

"It is possible, but not probable," Mr. Dodgson said. "For if the murder was done between the time Mr. Levin told the staff they could leave and the time they all gathered in his office, none of the staff could have left without the others seeing him."

"What about that artist? Edgar Roberts?" Dr. Doyle pointed out. "Granted, none of the writers could have left early without the others seeing him, but the artist works up the stairs in the garret. He could easily have nipped down the stairs, stabbed Mr. Basset, put the knife somewhere, and nipped back up to Levin's office. He's a long-legged chap and looks very fit. What's more," Dr. Doyle warmed to his subject, "he's got a nasty temper, and Basset had gone out of his way to be provoking."

"Quite so," Mr. Dodgson said. He would have said more, but Inspector Calloway was now settled, with a sheet of Mr. Howarth's writing paper and a sharpened pencil in his hand.

"Since you are 'ere, gentlemen," Calloway said, scowling fiercely at the other two, "you can give me yer statements. 'Ow did you come to be 'ere yesterday?"

Mr. Dodgson said testily, "I have already told you that I am the Reverend Mr. Charles Lutwidge Dodgson of Oxford. I was here yesterday on business. . . ."

"Wot business?"

"Literary b-business." Mr. Dodgson's stammer began to manifest itself, never a good sign.

Dr. Doyle stepped in. "May I speak for us, sir?"

Mr. Dodgson nodded mutely. Dr. Doyle tried to explain. "Mr. Dodgson is a well-known author under another name—"

"A halias, hey?" Clearly Inspector Calloway was not impressed with literary eminence.

"Under the name of Lewis Carroll, Mr. Dodgson sent some items to this publication," Dr. Doyle persisted. "And because I, too, have written some short stories, he asked me to join him in calling on Mr. Basset. Mr. Basset was not accommodating, and we left at four o'clock. We did not see Mr. Basset again until the gentleman was already dying. So you see, Inspector, Mr. Basset's death was none of our doing."

"Then wot's yer interest in it?" Calloway demanded.

"Mr. Portman asked me to assist the p-police, as I have d-done once before," Mr. Dodgson sputtered.

"Oh, did 'e?" Calloway's voice could have cut glass. "Well, Mr. Dodgson, or 'ooever yer are, the perlice can do wifout yer interference or yer assistance. Get off and let us do our job!"

With a wave of his hand, Calloway shooed the two of them out and called, "Next!"

Mr. Dodgson was shaking with rage when Dr. Doyle and he were left on the landing of the stairwell. "How d-dare he!" he gasped out. "I thought Inspector MacRae was d-dense, but next to this . . . this . . ." Words failed him. "Inspector MacRae is willing to admit to being wrong. This C-calloway p-person is imppossible! He is convinced that he can discover who killed Mr. Basset by himself and refuses assistance when it is offered."

"In that case, we will have to uncover the murderer ourselves, as Mr. Portman has requested," Dr. Doyle said.

"And to do that, we must examine the entire premises," Mr. Dodgson insisted, taking a deep breath to recover his composure.

Once again they mounted the stairs. Edgar Roberts's studio had been the attic when the house was new. It was now a single bare room, with one tall table for layouts and another for sketching. Engraving equipment had been laid out on a long shelf against the inside wall, where jars of acids, metal plates, and fine tools were lined up, together with zinc pans for washing the plates and buckets of water for final rinsing. The two fireplaces were empty. Apparently, no one had thought to lay coals for a fire for the staff artist.

Mr. Dodgson eyed the room with approval. "Mr. Roberts knows his craft," he said. He looked over the sketches laid out over the wooden blocks. In a larger establishment there would have been a battery of underlings, each responsible for a section of the final piece. Here, Mr. Roberts was clearly in sole charge of the woodcuts.

Mr. Dodgson looked over the sketchbooks that had been left on the large table. Mr. Roberts's pen had a wicked edge to it. Here were Mr. Peterson's features attached to a porcine body. Mr. Monteverde appeared as a dandified billy goat, while the late Mr. Samuel Basset had a devil's horns and tail. Even Mr. Dodgson's features fluttered out of the sketchbook, adorned with the ears and whiskers of the White Rabbit.

One face seemed to recur, an elfin creature, with a tip-tilted nose and pointed ears, who looked familiar somehow. Only when he saw the same face under a flat tam-o'-shanter (made of a mushroom cap), did Dr. Doyle recognize Miss Helen Harvey as the sprite.

He pointed this out to Mr. Dodgson, who nodded and said, "It would be interesting to know whether Mr. Roberts and Miss Harvey met before and under what circumstances."

"He might have known her father," Dr. Doyle said, as Mr. Dodgson proceeded to count Mr. Roberts's wood-cutting tools.

"True," Mr. Dodgson agreed. "The late Mr. Harvey seems to have made his mark in the artistic world. This is very vexing. All Mr. Roberts's tools are here."

"You would hardly expect a man to use one of his own knives if he's going to stab someone in the back," Dr. Doyle said, as he led Mr. Dodgson back down the stairs. "Although, if this is a crime of passion, one might use any tool that came to hand."

"How very melodramatic," Mr. Dodgson murmured. "But you may be right, Dr. Doyle. I am a dry old bachelor, and passion is not an emotion that is known to me. I do not feel comfortable with it. What is more, I cannot find anyone who felt such an emotion towards Samuel Basset. His best friend was lukewarm towards him, he had no wife or sweetheart, his staff treated him with disrespect and contempt, when they were not in actual conflict with him. He left little money—"

"How do we know that?" Dr. Doyle interrupted the flow of chatter. "Mr. Portman has said that he did not know how Mr. Basset spent his stipend. For all we know, he could have been some kind of miser, squirreling his savings into a mattress in his lodgings, wherever they are."

"I believe Mr. Levin said Mr. Basset lived in Baker Street." Mr. Dodgson let Dr. Doyle back into Levin's office. The secretary was hovering at the door to the inner office, where Mr. Monteverde and Mr. Howarth had joined Mr. Portman in organizing the next issue of *Youth's Companion* while Miss Harvey hovered in the background, picking up papers and sorting them out.

Mr. Portman frowned to himself. "Levin!" he called out.

"Did you call me, sir?" Levin popped his head in the office door.

"Yes. I want to see the books, and the list of subscribers and distributors. And have the presses warmed up. Has Hannegan got here yet?"

Before Levin could respond to the verbal barrage, Mr. Dodgson poked his head into the office and coughed gently. "Mr. Portman, you offered me a commission last night. On due consideration, I shall undertake to do what you asked. However, in order to do so, I shall have to visit Mr. Basset's lodgings. Can you give me his direction?"

"Of course. 331-B Baker Street. It's a lodging house, run by a Mrs. Bering. And perhaps you could accompany Mrs. Peterson home? If there are still rioters about, I'd feel better if she had some male company. Inspector Calloway will wish to interview her before she leaves, of course, but once that's done, she can go back to her own house."

"Will she have to, er, identify the, er, remains?" Mr. Dodgson asked delicately.

"Oh, I don't think she'll have to do that," Mr. Portman said. "We've already told them all they have to know. It's Peterson, I will swear it."

"And what of Miss Harvey?" Mr. Dodgson asked.

"Oh, she's staying here," Mr. Portman said carelessly. "She's going to help with the proofs so that Monte and Win can get on with the layout."

Miss Harvey's smile was not at all wistful. She was clearly enjoying herself immensely. She had removed her jacket, revealing a dark tartan dress with a modest bustle and long sleeves. The other three seemed to have accepted the fact that there was a female in their midst.

Mr. Portman produced his purse. "See if you can find a cab," he instructed Mr. Dodgson and Dr. Doyle. "Spend what you need and give me the reckoning later. Poor, poor Sammy!" He sighed deeply, then turned back to his newly augmented staff.

"As soon as the printers get the presses ready, we can block out and set type," he said gleefully. "I'd forgotten how much work this is, but once it's done, you have something worthwhile!"

"Until next week," Howarth reminded him.

"It might be more convenient if Miss Harvey were to type the manuscripts here," Roberts blurted out. "A typewriting machine could be brought in, and she could use part of Levin's office."

Mr. Portman nodded slowly. "That had occurred to me," he said. "Although it would be even more convenient if all authors typed their own manuscripts."

"Perhaps in the future, all manuscripts will arrive ready for the press," Monteverde said. "David had a story about the future in which the writers send their stories in by a sort of airwave."

"Right now, we've got these," Miss Harvey told him, patting her stack of typed pages. "And if you like, I can sort them out by type: adventure tales, fairy stories, and so on."

"A good idea," Portman said. "Levin, take Mrs. Peterson up to Inspector Calloway."

Ten minutes with Myrna Peterson convinced Inspector Calloway that she knew nothing about Mr. Basset's death. According to the grieving widow, David Peterson must have been in the wrong place at the wrong time and had been waylaid and robbed by some unknown cutthroat during the riot. She knew of no one who would harm her beloved David and no reason why he should have been in the Strand in a snowstorm when she was waiting dinner for him in Holbein Street.

Calloway looked at the mass of material in front of him and groaned inwardly. He would now have to go back to Jewry Street and consider the evidence before him, which amounted to five people stating that they did not know how Mr. Basset could have been stabbed while they were in the building, and one person who could be crossed off because he was definitely elsewhere.

"You can go 'ome, ma'am," Calloway told Mrs. Peterson gruffly. "There'll 'ave to be an inquest, but yer 'usband'll be turned over to yer as soon as may be."

Myrna sniffled into her handkerchief. Mr. Dodgson and Dr. Doyle were waiting by the stairs to escort her down to the office.

Mr. Portman emerged to wave the widow on her way. "Mrs. Peterson, I cannot express how sorry I am to have lost David," he said. "He was a grand fellow and a good writer. I've asked Mr. Dodgson and Dr. Doyle, here, to see that you get home safely, and I have sent a note to David's brother, giving him the sad news."

"That is very kind of you, Mr. Portman." Myrna took a deep

breath to try and control her tears. "I only hope they find the ruffian who did this to David."

Calloway had descended from the upper rooms and shook his head behind her, as if to say, "Not likely."

Mr. Dodgson allowed Dr. Doyle to lead Mrs. Peterson down the stairs and into Fleet Street. "I only hope we can find a cab," Mr. Dodgson fussed. "Once we get Mrs. Peterson to her home, we can get about the business of discovering who killed her husband . . . and why!"

"Until then," Mr. Portman said, "we have work to do!" He bustled back into the office, leaving the others to pursue their investigations.

CHAPTER 17

The fog had lifted a little when Mr. Dodgson and Dr. Doyle looked out into Fleet Street and flagged down a growler.

"Sloane Square," Mr. Dodgson ordered, handing the grieving widow into the cab, while Dr. Doyle negotiated with the cabby.

Myrna Peterson had regained some control over her overwrought emotions. "It is very kind of you to come with me," she said, wiping her eyes on her sodden handkerchief. "I don't know what to say to the girls."

"Your children?" Mr. Dodgson's ears seemed to perk up at the thought of little girls.

Dr. Doyle said gallantly, "You seem scarcely old enough to be the mother of two children, ma'am."

"Flora is five," Mrs. Peterson said, with a watery smile. "Susanna is only two, hardly old enough to realize her loss. And now . . ." She lay her hands across her midsection.

Dr. Doyle felt compelled to change the subject. "Not much traffic on the roads," he commented.

It was true; the only vehicles on the move were cabs and omnibuses. The owners of private carriages had apparently decided that this was no day to call out the horses for mere pleasure. Between the fog in the air and the slush underfoot, the going was treacherous for both man and beast.

The passersby on the Strand were not the working men and women who had formed the bulk of the crowd the previous night. The hardy souls who had braved the elements and glowered at the shopkeepers on the Strand and in Piccadilly were tough-looking men, dressed in heavy woolen coats and bowler hats, who swaggered along as if daring anyone to stop them. The icy slush had melted into a disgusting species of muck that was churned up by the wheels of the passing cabs and omnibuses to coat the trouser cuffs or skirts of the passersby. Crossing sweeps plied their trade, hoping for a penny for their trouble. The toughs ignored these pitiful creatures, secure in the knowledge that none of them would ever descend to such demoralizing work.

The cab made its way along the Strand and into Trafalgar Square. After a moment's hesitation, the cabby decided to take the Whitehall route, on the theory that if any road would be cleared, it would be the one in front of the government buildings.

Mrs. Peterson accepted a fresh handkerchief from Dr. Doyle, as the cab marched along past St. James's Park, unable to respond to the eerie beauty of the winter scene in her personal distress.

"Who could have done such a thing?" she moaned. "It must have been one of the rioters."

"Did your husband have any enemies?" Mr. Dodgson asked.

"Of course not!" Mrs. Peterson stopped moaning long enough to be outraged. "Everyone loved David!"

"Someone did not," Mr. Dodgson remarked. "What were his relations with the men at the office?"

Mrs. Peterson wiped her eyes and gave the matter some thought. "David made it a point to give a hand up to people like Win Howarth and Monte Monteverde," she said. "When he got the position at *Youth's Companion,* he insisted on bringing them over from the Penny Press."

"Indeed. I trust they were suitably grateful," Mr. Dodgson murmured.

"They all got along, if that is what you mean," Mrs. Peterson said. "Of course, I knew Win before I met David. In fact, he introduced me to David."

Dr. Doyle frowned. "A rival in love? And they worked together all this time?"

"Win and David were the best of friends. Win even stood up for David at our wedding." Mrs. Peterson smiled happily into the darkness of the cab.

"And Mr. Monteverde?" Mr. Dodgson broke into her reminiscent mood.

"Monte? Oh, there was some foolishness, about a story David wrote. Monte has some relations who were with Garibaldi in South America, and he told David about them, and David put it into a story, and the relations were upset about it."

"Italians?" Dr. Doyle asked eagerly. "The Italians are passionate people, are they not?"

Mrs. Peterson sniffed into her handkerchief. "Monte has a temper, but it all blew over. David pointed out that no one would know who he meant by the story, since he'd changed everyone's names, and in any case, the only people who read *Youth's Companion* are far too young to do any mischief to Monte's relations in Italy or anywhere else."

"What about the hot-tempered Mr. Roberts?" Dr. Doyle asked.

Myrna shook her head again. "He's Welsh, of course, and David would make jokes about the Welsh and how they love to sing. Mr. Roberts was not amused, but even he couldn't stay angry with David for long. No one could."

They had reached the King's Road and Sloane Square. Dr. Doyle hopped out of the cab to hand Mrs. Peterson out.

Dr. Doyle looked up and down the street. There were no cabs to be seen. "Hi, cabby," he called out. "Do you hire by the day?"

The cabby, a wiry little man with a good-humored expression, shrugged. "I own me own cab and 'oss, guv'nor," he said. "I do oblige, from time to time."

"Mr. Dodgson," Dr. Doyle turned to his older companion, "perhaps we should hire this fellow for the rest of the day, since

172

we have several errands to do and there do not seem to be many other cabs available."

"Do you think so? We may be some time at each place," Mr. Dodgson said.

"That is true, but we will spend less time in searching for transportation," Dr. Doyle pointed out. "In the long run, it will be more efficient."

The cabby put in his mite. "There's a mort of bad'un's out there, and not many of us is out today." The cabby touched his hat with his whip and gathered the reins, as if preparing to move off in search of another fare.

Dr. Doyle put forward the clinching argument. "You know, sir, this cabby is sure to know where we are to go, which we may not. We have no idea what we will find out at Mr. Basset's lodgings. What is more, sir, he is quite right about the men on the street. I had no fear last night when I was with honest working men who were only demanding what was theirs by right and by law, but those fellows we saw in Piccadilly today were not of that stamp. I doubt that any of them's done an honest day's work in their lives."

"As always, Dr. Doyle, you are a fountain of good sense." Mr. Dodgson turned back to the cabby.

"My good man, what is your name?" he called up.

"Jerry will do, sir." The cabby touched his hat with his whip in a genial salute.

"Very well, Jerry, you may wait here until we are done, and we will use your services for the rest of the day." Mr. Dodgson looked at the cab horse, a black stallion with a blaze on his forehead and scarred knees. "I see you take good care of your animal, cabby."

"Aye, sir, Black Jack's a fine horse."

Mr. Dodgson nodded as if to say that a cabby who takes care of his horse will take care of his passengers. "You may have to walk the horse, Jerry, but we should not be above half an hour."

Jerry saluted again, and Mr. Dodgson followed Dr. Doyle and Mrs. Peterson up the steps into the brick row house, where the unsuspecting Peterson ménage waited for the mistress.

Mrs. Peterson was greeted by her maid, who stared at the unexpected midday guests.

"Millie, bring Cook and Nanny here," Mrs. Peterson ordered. "And the children. It would be better that you should hear this from me than read it in the newspapers."

"Ooh, ma'am, whatever 'as 'appened to the master?" Millie gasped out. "Was it them Red Commonists, wot Cook says is out fer blood?"

Mrs. Peterson said solemnly, "Mr. Peterson has met with a fatal accident."

Millie screamed. The cook, who had come upstairs from the basement kitchen, caught the end of this conversation.

"The master's dead?"

Mrs. Peterson could not go on. "Would you explain, Dr. Doyle?" she asked piteously, resorting to her handkerchief once again.

" 'E's 'ad a doctor to 'im?" Millie was confused.

"Mr. Peterson was attacked during last night's disturbance," Dr. Doyle explained. "This is Mr. Dodgson, who is a friend of Mr. Peterson's employer, Mr. Portman." A slight exaggeration, since the two men had only met that morning, but Dr. Doyle did not feel he could explain the exact relationship. He didn't understand it himself.

"Mama!" A dark-haired girl of five ran to her mother. "Nanny says something has happened to Papa, and he's not coming home!"

Mrs. Peterson's sobs grew more intense. That set off the roly-poly two-year-old in her nurse's arms. Nanny did her best to comfort them, while Mr. Dodgson drew Miss Flora aside. "How do you do," he said seriously, offering her his gray-gloved hand.

She took it and bobbed a curtsey. Clearly, she had been taught proper manners.

"I am not supposed to speak with strange men," she said. "Do you know my papa?"

"We met but yesterday," Mr. Dodgson confessed. "However, I know that he cared very much for you and your sister and your mama for I saw your photograph on his desk at his office."

"That was taken on my birthday," Flora said. "What happened to my papa?"

Mr. Dodgson chose his words carefully. "He was hit upon the head."

"Who did it?"

"We do not know," Mr. Dodgson said. "Perhaps you can help us find out."

"Me?" Flora considered it, then shook her head. "Papa didn't know any people who hit other people on the head. He said that violence was no way to solve problems."

"Did he, now."

"Yes, for when Baby took my doll and I hit her, Papa made me sit in the Angry Corner for a whole hour looking at the wall. He said I was to picture on that wall the consequences." She stumbled over the word. "Papa was funny, always telling stories." Flora's eyes filled with tears. "Do you really mean that he is never coming home again?" Tears began to leak out of her eyes as the true enormity of the situation came to her.

Mr. Dodgson felt in his pockets and produced his handkerchief, which he passed to Flora. "Your papa told very clever stories," he said. "I tell stories, too. In fact, your papa asked me to give you a copy of one of my stories. You are a very clever girl and will soon be able to read it for yourself. I shall sign it for you, so that you will remember who gave it to you."

Mr. Dodgson pulled the objectionable copy of *Alice's Adventures in Wonderland* out of his overcoat pocket. He did not like giving out bad copies, but it was the only one he had with him, and he liked the little girl.

"Where is your papa's desk?" he asked Flora gently. "I wish to use a pen to sign the book."

Flora led Mr. Dodgson from the beruffled and bedecked front room through the house to a back study, a dark room filled with books that looked out on a paved yard, now filled with grimy snow.

"This is Papa's room," Flora told her new friend. "Baby was never allowed in here, especially after she ate one of Papa's papers." She sat on a little chair that had been placed beside the

175

fireplace. "This is my chair, where Papa told me my letters. Soon I shall be ready for lessons," she added with pride.

Mr. Dodgson lit the gas and looked around the room. He could feel at home here among the artifacts of the working writer. Pens, pencils of two colors, a ruler, a letter opener in the shape of a medieval sword, a pair of scissors, a kneaded rubber eraser . . . any or all of these could be found on any desk in Oxford.

He examined the papers littering the desk. Peterson's work habits at home were no improvement over those at *Youth's Companion*. He wrote notes to himself on odd scraps of paper, including a laundry list and the back of a tract from the Church of Latter-day Saints.

"Interesting," murmured Mr. Dodgson, as he read several notes on King Arthur and his knights. Clearly, Mr. Peterson had not been mistaken when he said he had been working on a modern version of the Arthurian legend.

Mr. Dodgson turned his attention to Peterson's home library. "Dictionary, of course. Mr. Roget's *Thesaurus*. The *Encyclopaedia Britannica*." He read the titles aloud.

Flora watched him with large dark eyes. "What are you looking for?" she asked.

"I do not know," Mr. Dodgson replied. "Perhaps I am looking for a reason why someone would wish to knock your father on the head. Did he get angry often?"

"Oh, no," Flora assured him. "Papa liked to joke, and laugh, and play games. Even when Mama scolded him for coming home late, he would laugh and tell her that he was working out ways to make us all rich."

"Would you like to be rich?"

Flora considered the question seriously. "I'm not sure," she said at last. "I have a cousin who is rich. Her papa keeps a carriage."

"Then he must be quite rich," Mr. Dodgson commented.

Flora went on. "It must be nice to have a carriage to take one about, but Uncle never smiles, and he calls Papa a 'scribbling fool.' We spent Christmas Day with them, and Cousin Elsie wore a red velvet dress; but she was not allowed to eat ice cream because she might spill it on the dress. I ate ice cream and did not spill any," she added proudly.

"You are a very clever girl then," Mr. Dodgson said. He sat at the desk and found a pen.

"I shall sign this book, 'To Miss Flora Peterson, a clever girl,' " he told her, dipping the pen into the inkwell.

Flora watched as he signed it, then scrutinized the signature carefully. "I thought that doctor man said your name was Dodgson," she said accusingly.

"It is."

"But you signed this book 'Lewis Carroll.' "

"So I did. I am Lewis Carroll."

"But your name is Dodgson," the child persisted.

"That is my baptismal name. Charles Lutwidge Dodgson."

Flora shook her head. "You can't be both," she decided. "You must be one or the other."

Mr. Dodgson smiled and handed her the book. "That is a most profound statement, Miss Flora. Now I must speak with your mama. You must be very kind to your little sister, and even kinder if the angels bring you another one. Your mama is going to need you."

Flora tucked the book under her arm. "I shall be good," she promised.

Mr. Dodgson found Mrs. Peterson with Dr. Doyle in the dining room, partaking of cold chicken, warmed-up soup, and dried apple pies.

"Do sit down, Mr. Dodgson," Mrs. Peterson offered. "Dr. Doyle reminded me that I had had nothing to eat all day, and that I must sustain myself. I have sent Millie to the telegraph office to notify my parents of David's unhappy death. By now Mr. Portman's note must have reached David's brother, George, in the City. They did not get on well, but I know George will see to the funeral arrangements."

"I am relieved to hear that you will not be totally alone in the world," Mr. Dodgson said, refusing the offer of clear soup. "I shall have a cup of tea, if you please, and some bread and butter, if there is any."

This meager luncheon being provided, Mr. Dodgson went back to the subject of David Peterson. "What else can you tell me about your husband, Mrs. Peterson?" Mr. Dodgson asked between bites of bread and butter.

Mrs. Peterson sighed as she thought of her courtship days. "David was writing penny dreadfuls for Portman Penny Press when Win Howarth introduced me to him at a lecture," she said. "We soon found we had much in common, and we managed to be married, although my family was not pleased that I had married into his, and vice versa."

"There was a disparity there?" Mr. Dodgson hinted.

"Well, my father is schoolmaster in a village school, and his brother is something rather important in banking." The widow started crying again. "In fact, it was my father and his brother, both, who insisted that David take the permanent position at *Youth's Companion* when it was offered."

"Offered by Mr. Basset?" Mr. Dodgson asked.

"Offered by Mr. Portman," Mrs. Peterson corrected him. "You see, it was one of the conditions of our marriage that David should have a permanent position that would enable him to support a family. My father and David's brother, George, were both agreed on it, and so David took the position."

"And I am sure he never regretted it," Dr. Doyle told her.

The doorbell rang. Millie answered it and came into the dining room looking flustered. "Ma'am, it's Mr. Jenkins, the gentleman from next door. It seems he's read in the newspapers that the Lord Mayor's Fund is very low, and he's taking a subscription of all the houses here on Sloane Square. Would we wish to contribute?"

Mrs. Peterson swallowed hard and said, "I suppose I can spare a few shillings of the housekeeping money. If you will excuse me, gentlemen, I will attend to this."

"Considering that one of them murdering ruffians might 'ave done for the master, that's very good of you, ma'am," Millie said, following her mistress up the stairs to the small room next to the nursery that was used for household management.

Mr. Dodgson swallowed the last of his tea and wandered

178

through the long hall to the front room, where he stood staring out the bow window at Sloane Street. "None of this makes any sense," he complained. "From all I have heard and seen, Peterson was a jolly, friendly sort of man, who might be careless with money but would not harm a fly."

"There was the brandy in his desk drawer," Dr. Doyle hinted.

"There was that," Mr. Dodgson agreed.

"And he was not above pinching another man's young lady," Dr. Doyle went on. "Or appropriating a good story."

"None of which is cause for murder," Mr. Dodgson said. "Let us suppose that Mr. Peterson was one of those chaps who does not become thoroughly intoxicated, but who enjoys a small libation now and again."

Dr. Doyle nodded, as Mr. Dodgson continued his discourse. "Are we agreed that Mr. Basset was stabbed on the stairs at close to four-fifty yesterday afternoon?"

"That would appear to be the most logical time for the murder," Dr. Doyle stated.

"Very well. Is it possible that Mr. Peterson saw or heard something that led him to suspect one of his fellow sufferers at the hands of Mr. Basset?"

"It is certainly possible."

Mr. Dodgson sighed. "In that case, our theory that the death of David Peterson is directly related to the death of Samuel Basset is probably the correct one. When we find the murderer of one, we will find the killer of the other."

"But we are no closer to finding that person than we were twenty hours ago," Dr. Doyle complained.

"Not quite," Mr. Dodgson corrected him. "For we have eliminated a large part of the population of London, limiting it to those men who were in the *Youth's Companion* offices at four-fifty yesterday afternoon."

Dr. Doyle shook his head. "I still find it hard to believe that any of those men could murder his employer and follow it up with an attack on someone with whom he has been working side by side for years. It would mean someone in that office is mad!"

Mr. Dodgson nodded. "Passion can be a kind of madness," he

reminded Dr. Doyle. "And I believe we are dealing with a person who has succumbed to that sort of madness."

His thoughts were interrupted by the arrival of a large carriage with a liveried coachman on the box and a footman up behind. From the equipage emerged an elaborately dressed lady and her large and imposing male counterpart.

"Ah," Mr. Dodgson remarked. "Mr. George Peterson must have received the news of his brother's demise."

The elder Peterson was let in by Millie, who exhibited the deference due to the wealthy relations visiting the poor ones. Mrs. George Peterson descended on her sister-in-law with all the force of a gale.

"My dear Myrna! What a tragedy! I was never so shocked in my life as when I got the message!" The elder Mrs. Peterson embraced her sister-in-law.

"It has been dreadful," Myrna sniffled into her handkerchief. "This is Mr. Dodgson and Dr. Doyle, who are assisting the police in their inquiries."

Mr. George Peterson regarded the two would-be detectives coldly. "I assume it was one of the cutthroats who were out last night," he said. "They will have gone back to their lairs in Southwark or Whitechapel. We will never find them. I warned David about the company he was keeping and look where it got him."

"Sir!" Dr. Doyle protested. "Mr. David Peterson's death was not the fault of those poor souls who were protesting their wretched lot. Mrs. Peterson, Mr. Dodgson and I have pledged ourselves to find your husband's murderer, and that we shall do!"

"And now, ma'am, we must take our leave," Mr. Dodgson said. "Your sister- and brother-in-law will see to your comfort, and we will do what we can to see that the murderer is brought to justice."

"Thank you, sir, for all you have done and are doing," Myrna said, clutching his hand. Mr. Dodgson eased gently out of her grip.

"Whoever did this is guilty of the most depraved indifference to life," Mr. Dodgson said severely. "I will surely find him and deliver him into the hands of the law."

He bowed to Mrs. Peterson, and allowed Millie to help him on with his coat and hat, while Dr. Doyle shrugged himself into the plaid balbriggan. Together they left the house of mourning and stepped into Sloane Street, where the cabby with the black horse had pulled up behind the elegant carriage.

"Where to, gentlemen?" the cabby asked.

"Baker Street," Mr. Dodgson ordered. "Perhaps we will find out more about Mr. Samuel Basset in his own surroundings."

CHAPTER 18

By midday the fog had lifted from the London streets, revealing the full extent of the damage to the shops and hotels along the route to Baker Street. The panes of the upper stories of the elegant buildings in Pall Mall had been an irresistible target for stones, bricks, and wooden paving blocks. The glass flower boxes that adorned the windows of the Piccadilly hotels and stores had been especially marked for destruction. Jerry edged his horse carefully around the broken glass, taking the time to avoid the knots of men who gathered at the street corners to confer in lowered tones then shout obscenities at the carriages and cabs that passed by.

"Pack of fools," was the cabby's opinion, shouted down to his passengers, as they stopped to let a trio of constables oust a quartet of tough-looking characters in velveteen jackets, cloth caps, and bright neckerchiefs from their post in the middle of the road.

"Surely not," Dr. Doyle chided him. "Workingmen, honest laborers, who only want employment."

"Not that lot," the cabby said, with a wave of his whip. "Layabouts, that's wot they are."

"Dr. Doyle, your sentiments do you credit, but Jerry is correct.

The men on the street today are not the ones who were picked up last night." Mr. Dodgson peered through the murky window of the growler. "I see Inspector MacRae has been diligent in this, if nothing else. There is a very large police contingent out this afternoon."

"Let us only hope that Inspector Calloway has been as energetic." Dr. Doyle did not sound hopeful. "I'm sure if he questions the staff at *Youth's Companion* closely, he'll come to the same conclusions we have. One of them must have stabbed Mr. Basset, although I must admit I can't believe any of them would do such a thing. As for bashing poor Peterson . . ."

"Baker Street, gentlemen." The cabby had reached their destination, a thoroughly commonplace street of small shops and lodging houses. Baker Street had been laid out in the previous century to accommodate the growing population of middle-class householders who preferred to move away from the crowded streets of the older parts of the city but were not in the category of those who built fine mansions in Mayfair and Belgravia. Number 331-B was a narrow brick building, wedged in between three others on either side, with a modest doorway that was entered directly from the street without the elegance of a set of stairs. Only a single railing separated the building from the street.

Mr. Dodgson stepped up to the front door and knocked. A neatly dressed plump woman in a brown dress, apron, and cap appeared. "May I help you, gentlemen?" she asked, her accent holding the slight trace of a Welsh intonation.

"We have news regarding Mr. Samuel Basset," Mr. Dodgson announced.

"Mr. Basset is not at home," the landlady said.

"We are aware of that," Mr. Dodgson told her. "If you had read the morning newspapers you would have learned that Mr. Basset died last night, quite suddenly."

"Oh, no!" Mrs. Bering gasped. "I thought there was something amiss when he did not come home last night."

"Mr. Basset was a man of regular habits then?" Mr. Dodgson asked.

"Mr. Basset was a gentleman, no matter what sort of company he kept," Mrs. Bering said. "Are you from the police?"

"We are here on behalf of Mr. Nicholas Portman," Mr. Dodgson explained. "He has asked us to investigate the sad demise of Mr. Basset and has given us permission to examine his rooms. May we come in?"

Mrs. Bering looked the pair over. Dr. Doyle smiled reassuringly. "I expect Inspector MacRae will be along as soon as he has dealt with the, er, persons out on the streets," he said. "It can do no harm to let us look at Mr. Basset's lodgings."

Mrs. Bering stepped aside, to let the pair into the small vestibule, on the theory that if Mr. Portman had sent them, they must be worthy gentlemen who would do Mr. Basset's reputation no harm.

"It must have been them nasty rioters." Mrs. Bering shook her head, sending the frill on her cap into a flapping frenzy. "Scarin' honest folk on the streets, makin' speeches, and where does it get 'em, I'd like to know?"

"Into the Bow Street jail." Dr. Doyle answered the rhetorical question. "But the circumstances of Mr. Basset's death are such that we do not think it was one of the rioters in the street who caused it."

"Unfortunately, the police are, ah, otherwise occupied," Mr. Dodgson said. "That is why Mr. Portman has given us permission to examine Mr. Basset's lodgings to see if there is some indication of whether anyone had some animus against Mr. Basset."

"Mr. Portman, is it? He were just Nicky when he lived here," Mrs. Bering said, as she led Mr. Dodgson and Dr. Doyle up the stairs. "Nicky and Sammy, they called each other. Like brothers, they were. Here you are, gentlemen, just as Mr. Basset left it, barring that I redded up the rooms, as I do each morning."

The rooms were two: a small sitting room with two easy chairs drawn up to the fire and a low table between them, a shelf crowded with books, a desk placed under the window that looked out onto Baker Street, and a bedroom, with a four-poster bed, washstand, and wardrobe.

The walls were adorned with covers and drawings clearly taken from past issues of *Youth's Companion.* A plaster model of Michelangelo's *David* stood on the mantelpiece, on one side of an American clock. A pile of correspondence was stacked on the table in front of the fire, ready to be dealt with by the absent master of the establishment.

"Was Mr. Basset an easy lodger?" Dr. Doyle asked, while Mr. Dodgson poked about the sitting room, picking up papers and scanning the books on the shelves.

"A quiet gentleman," Mrs. Bering said, with some pride. "Paid his rent on the quarter, kept regular hours. I'd provide his breakfast and his dinner, should he be dining in. Most evenings he dined out, but there were times when he'd dine in or have a visitor."

"Visitors?" Mr. Dodgson turned around and approached the housekeeper. "Did Mr. Basset often have visitors? Did he, for instance, give card parties or other entertainments?"

"Visitors?" Mrs. Bering sniffed loudly. "There you have it, sir. It's not my place to object to a gentleman's guests, but some of those young men of Mr. Basset's were not gentlemen, and nothing you can tell me will make me think otherwise." She folded her hands at her waist and gave Dr. Doyle a knowing look. "They were a strange lot, sir. Not what I would have expected a gentleman of Mr. Basset's profession to entertain."

"Mr. Basset was a literary gentleman," Mr. Dodgson commented. "I have had some acquaintance with literary gentlemen, and some of them are, er, eccentric in their dress and exaggerated in their behavior."

"Eccentric?" Mrs. Bering considered that for a moment. "When Mr. Portman was here, we had literary persons up to tea, which was all well and good. And I will say, sir, that some of them were very odd. There was an American, Mr. Clemens, which Mr. Nicky said was also called Mark Twain. Now he was a loud one!"

Mr. Dodgson nodded in agreement. "I was once introduced to Mr. Clemens," he remarked. "One could scarcely breathe with him in the room. One of the sort who seems to absorb all the oxygen," he explained to Dr. Doyle.

"Yes, indeed," Mrs. Bering said. "And there were others who would come for tea or dinner, and very odd they looked, all hair and wild beards and no cravat, but a neckerchief instead. But Mr. Basset's guests were of a different stripe altogether. By the way they dressed and the way they acted, I'd call them common. Downright common, they was, and not at all what Mr. Portman would have had."

Mr. Dodgson frowned. "In addition to his odd friendships, our Mr. Basset seems to have been an eclectic reader, Dr. Doyle. I see Sir Richard Burton's *Thousand and One Nights,* alongside Sir John Speke's papers on his explorations in Africa. There are a number of volumes of zoological information, and Mr. Darwin's *Origin of Species.* I see there the *Household Tales* by the Herren Brothers Grimm, and also several books of lore collected by my friend Lang. Clearly, Mr. Basset was a man with wide-ranging interests." He drifted over to the writing desk and began to sort through the selection of letters, manuscripts, and cards stacked thereon, placing them into small piles automatically.

"And an odd selection of friends," Dr. Doyle added.

"Is this the entire establishment?" Mr. Dodgson asked. "It seems rather small for two gentlemen."

"Well, this is the way of it," Mrs. Bering explained. "The house was taken by Mr. Nicky, when he came back from Africa with Mr. Sammy. He took the rooms here, and Mr. Sammy had the upstairs bedroom, which is now kept for anyone who might need it, as a spare room, you might call it. Mr. Basset took the downstairs room when Mr. Portman moved into his new flat at the Press Club, and Mr. Basset told me to leave the spare room for anyone to spend the night."

"And did Mr. Basset have such visitors?" Dr. Doyle asked.

Mrs. Bering's rosy face betrayed her inward struggle. "It sometimes happened," she said at last, "that when I brought up breakfast, a young man was there. Not very often," she hurried to add, "and Mr. Basset explained that the young man had missed his train or that the weather had been bad. And this was usually so."

Dr. Doyle took a deep breath, let it out, and glanced at Mr. Dodgson, who was examining the bookshelves again. "I don't suppose you could recognize any of the young men should you see them again?" he asked. Mrs. Bering shook her head. "That I could not say, sir."

"Of course not, Mrs. Bering. You are discreet, as all good landladies should be." Mr. Dodgson looked down into the street.

"Someone appears to be at the door," he said, just as the knocker was applied.

"Not the police?" Mrs. Bering's cap began to flap with her excitement.

"I do not see a helmet," Mr. Dodgson said. "I suggest you answer the door. Dr. Doyle and I will respect Mr. Basset's privacy to whatever extent we can, but the police will shortly arrive. You must tell them exactly what you told us."

"I know better than to tattle," Mrs. Bering said.

Once the landlady was gone, Mr. Dodgson handed Dr. Doyle the pile of letters from the mantelpiece. "One may learn a great deal about a person from his correspondence," he pointed out. "Mr. Basset has several friends with whom he exchanged letters. In them he appears to be encouraging certain young men in their literary ambitions."

"Nothing wrong there," Dr. Doyle said with a smile. "I have had several letters from you with the same sort of advice and encouragement."

"Indeed," Mr. Dodgson said gravely. "But I do not use quite so fulsome a tone. And, I might add, I hope I have a better sense of judgment than Mr. Basset. He did, after all, reject your stories. Now, here are some tradesman's bills. What do you make of that?" He handed Dr. Doyle a letter, apparently from a Saville Row tailoring establishment, requesting payment.

"I did not think Mr. Basset's taste ran to quite such expensive attire," Dr. Doyle commented. "Let's see . . . one frock coat, one embroidered waistcoat, six linen shirts, one sack suit with jacket, trousers, and waistcoat. I wonder if Mr. Basset owned a sack suit."

He shamelessly entered Mr. Basset's personal quarters and opened the wardrobe. Samuel Basset did not favor sack suits or dittos. The wardrobe held the garments deemed appropriate for a man approaching his middle years: two frock coats that dated to the previous decade, a summer-weight linen suit, two pairs of trousers, and a cutaway coat similar to the one in which he had died. The lower drawers of the wardrobe told the same story. This was a man of neat and modest habits. He wore clothing of good but not superlative quality.

"And yet," Mr. Dodgson said, after Dr. Doyle pointed this out to him, "he has paid a tailor's bill for a flowered waistcoat, a suit of dittos, and five linen shirts."

"But not for himself," Dr. Doyle said. "For one of the young men mentioned by Mrs. Bering? A charitable gesture?"

"A very generous gesture," Mr. Dodgson said with a frown. "I have, on occasion, assisted my young relations who have been financially embarrassed, but not to this extent."

"What other charitable gestures did Mr. Basset make, I wonder?" Dr. Doyle returned to the pile of correspondence, while Mr. Dodgson dealt with the papers on Mr. Basset's writing desk.

"My goodness!"

Dr. Doyle stepped over to see what had caused such a reaction from his usually silent mentor.

"A tract? From the Church of Latter-day Saints?" Dr. Doyle examined the leaflet. "Considering his attitude towards women, Mr. Basset is the last person I would expect to be interested in the Mormon religion."

"Polygamy is not the entire compass of the sect," Mr. Dodgson stated primly. "But I have seen something similar at the offices of *Youth's Companion*. Mr. Peterson had written some notes on a tract very much like this one."

"I am still confused," Dr. Doyle said. "Where would Mr. Basset have come by such a thing? I know the Mormon sect sends missionaries into London to convert us Gentiles, but would Mr. Basset have been the target of their efforts?"

"Perhaps he found them at Toynbee Hall," Mr. Dodgson mused. "Here is another tract, a sort of prospectus, if you will. Mr. Portman mentioned that his friend had taken to charitable work when he decided to remove himself to the Press Club. I have heard Canon Barnett speak of his scheme to bring university men into the slums of London and other cities to treat the oppressed people of those areas much like the African heathen tribes with which Mr. Basset had become familiar."

Dr. Doyle pulled at his mustache. "I'm not sure I like where this is leading us, sir."

"Nor do I." Mr. Dodgson's usually serene face screwed into a frown. "It would appear that Mr. Basset sought out young men, befriended them, paid for their clothing. I strongly suspect that his intentions were not completely honorable."

"Surely, sir, you don't mean . . . ?" Dr. Doyle was aghast.

Mr. Dodgson's face was set in lines of deep distaste. "I do. Buggery is not unknown at Oxford, Dr. Doyle, although it is a grave sin. There have been unpleasant stories put about of abuses at certain boys' schools, and the students who came from those schools brought those crimes with them. I prefer not to be involved with such tittle-tattle and spiteful gossip. However, one cannot ignore such things. It is possible that Mr. Samuel Basset was one of those unfortunates who prefer their own sex to the fair one, and that his charitable efforts had a less salubrious motive than pure altruism. We shall have to go to Toynbee Hall to find out."

Mrs. Bering interrupted the discussion, bringing Inspector MacRae up the stairs to join the other two men.

"That were Mrs. Varney, who keeps rooms down the street. We're making up a subscription for the Lord Mayor's Fund to send for the poor women and children of Whitechapel," she said breathlessly. "And here's Inspector MacRae, just as you said."

MacRae was not pleased to find Mr. Dodgson and Dr. Doyle ahead of him. "What're you two doing here?" he barked.

"Mr. Portman sent us to inform Mr. Basset's landlady of his, er, sad death," Mr. Dodgson explained.

"I hope you had the good sense not to disarrange anything," MacRae snapped, looking around the room to see if evidence had been removed.

Dr. Doyle stepped between Mrs. Bering and Inspector MacRae, as if to protect her from persecution. "Mrs. Bering has touched nothing," he declared. "Mr. Dodgson and I have sorted through

Mr. Basset's personal effects and checked over his correspondence, but we have removed nothing, I promise you," he said. "You may draw the same conclusions from what you see that we have."

"Have your investigations revealed anything new?" Mr. Dodgson asked, arranging Mr. Basset's letters and bills into neat piles and patting them into place.

"Calloway's interviewed that lot of writers at *Youth's Companion*," MacRae said, with a grimace of disgust at the slovenly procedures of the City of London Police. "Not that any of them knew anything or would tell us if they did. Well, we've got the Irishman, and he'll do for a start."

"If you mean O'Casey, he did not kill Mr. Basset," Dr. Doyle stated, mustache bristling pugnaciously.

"I never said he did. It's the other one, Peterson, that's going to hang O'Casey."

"But we have conclusively proven—" Mr. Dodgson began.

MacRae cut him off. "He may not have done the deed himself, but he and those other two set the mob on fire, and that led directly to Peterson's death, as I see it. As for Basset, that's a puzzle, I grant you, but we'll get to the bottom of it as soon as we clear out those rioters in Trafalgar Square. They've called another meeting!" MacRae gave a snort of disdain at the tactics of radical workingmen. "As if that's going to get them anywhere!"

"If you refer to the men now gathering in the streets, I wish you good luck with your mission." Mr. Dodgson turned to Dr. Doyle. "Our cab is waiting. We must be off."

"What shall I do about Mr. Basset's things?" Mrs. Bering asked, as Mr. Dodgson and Dr. Doyle arranged their hats before going back out into the cold.

"Mr. Nicholas Portman is the executor of Mr. Basset's will," Mr. Dodgson told her. "He will be around shortly to take charge of Mr. Basset's affairs. Good afternoon, Inspector. I see you and your men have been most assiduous in clearing the streets of the rioters."

"If by that you mean that I've got the rabble where they belong, then you are right," MacRae said. "And if that fool Tom Mann and his Fair Trade League thinks he's going to start up again, he'll find himself in Bow Street along with the rest of 'em!"

"I wish you success in both your endeavors," Mr. Dodgson told him. He hustled Dr. Doyle out onto the street before the young doctor could say another word.

"Mr. Dodgson," Dr. Doyle sputtered, "what is the matter with you? MacRae and his men will destroy every clue Basset left . . ."

"Not so," Mr. Dodgson. "Here is the tract from the Mormon missionaries and the one from Toynbee Hall."

Dr. Doyle frowned at his mentor. "That's twice you've removed evidence, sir. A very grave offence!"

Mr. Dodgson put the two tracts into his pocket. "Nonsense. The scarf was not evidence. It was put into my hands, and I returned it to its rightful owner. As for these tracts, there are two others on the desk. I only took this one so that we may have the correct direction." He looked up at the cabby. "Jerry?"

"Aye, sir?"

Mr. Dodgson consulted the tract from Toynbee Hall. "Can you find Commercial Road in Whitechapel?"

The cabby sounded dubious. "I can find it, but what would a gentleman like you want in the East End? It's rough there, sir, very rough; and on a day like this, with the mobs out, it might be worth your life to go there. I wouldn't do it, sir. Even the coppers don't go to Whitechapel alone."

"There is an establishment called Toynbee Hall on Commercial Road," Mr. Dodgson said, consulting the tract once again. "Do you know of it?"

"I 'ave 'eard of it," Barker admitted. "A fine plan it is to set up schools and suchlike for the poor folks, but what good it may do I do not know. Fine gentlemen come down to teach, but will them street children learn? And why should they, when all that will come to 'em is to work in sweating shops or factories or, for the girls, to go out on the streets?"

"But if education will help a young person escape the streets, should they not have it?" Dr. Doyle demanded.

"That is exactly Mr. Barnett's point," Mr. Dodgson said, as he heaved himself up into the cab and pulled Dr. Doyle in with him. "Jerry, we shall go to Toynbee Hall."

"And what do you think we will learn there?" Dr. Doyle asked.

"If nothing else, we will find out what Samuel Basset did with the copies of *Alice's Adventures in Wonderland*," Mr. Dodgson said, settling himself into the cab for another long ride through the freezing streets.

CHAPTER 19

D r. Doyle waited until the cab was underway again, taking the long road around the major shops, from Euston Street to Gower Street, skirting Bloomsbury and the British Museum to High Holborn, and back to the City of London. Then he vented his feelings. "How do you come to know about Toynbee Hall?" he exclaimed. "I thought you rarely left Oxford."

"Toynbee Hall was widely discussed when Mr. Barnett conceived the idea," Mr. Dodgson told him. "Mr. Barnett is an Oxford man, although not from the House. When he was appointed Canon of St. Jude's in Whitechapel, he put forward this effort to educate the lower classes of London. He thought that as these miserable people are as devoid of Christian knowledge as are the heathen tribes in Africa, missionaries should be sent, even as we send our good people to those far shores. Furthermore," Mr. Dodgson added before Dr. Doyle could comment, "Mr. Barnett spoke before our undergraduates, urging young men to settle in these slums, as do missionaries in Africa or Asia, to share the lives and deprivations of the poor."

"And did anyone accept this offer?" Dr. Doyle asked.

"I believe one or two of our young men have seriously considered joining Canon Barnett in his work," Mr. Dodgson said. "Toynbee Hall has only been in existence two years, and there is much to be done. Mr. Barnett can be a most persuasive speaker, and the need for such a settlement house, as he calls it, is pressing."

Dr. Doyle was still puzzled. "I suppose Mr. Basset might have sent copies of *Youth's Companion* to Mr. Barnett in the name of charity, but I'm not sure I understand why he should go there in person to do so. It seems most unlike what we have heard of him. Except for those young men whom he befriended, he did not strike me as a philanthropist."

Mr. Dodgson said nothing. Dr. Doyle concentrated on the passing scene. The ice had thawed into a slushy mire, through which the gallant black horse stepped carefully, testing his footing, as the broad highway of High Holborn led back into the city. Dr. Doyle recognized the dome of St. Paul's and the walls of the Old Bailey as they went farther and farther eastward. They passed the great financial institutions, the Bank of England and the Stock Exchange, and trotted around the grim bulk of the Tower looming over Tower Bridge. From there, the streets grew dark and narrow, as Barker plunged into the heart of the ancient City of London.

On the far side of the old London Wall lay the worst of London's slums, the East End. Here the streets were filled with pushcarts and barrows, carrying anything and everything for human consumption: old clothes, new vegetables, books, shoes, household goods, and much, much more. Dr. Doyle drank in the aroma of frying fish and chips, and more exotic odors, even as his ears were assailed with street cries in a dozen languages, none of which remotely resembled the English or even the Scottish dialects he had grown used to.

The snow that had blanketed the rest of London lay on the roofs of the brick tenements, which had been built in the last twenty years to replace the decrepit wooden structures that had so outraged Mr. Dickens. The tenements were hardly an improvement; they lined up in rows, two rooms upstairs, two down, with a paved yard in the back and one outside privy to serve every pair of houses. Water could be had from a communal tap in the back of these houses, making washing a major event.

At that hour of the afternoon, the men of Whitechapel were either looking for work or plying what trades they had, some in sight of possible customers, some behind the doors of shops or small factories. Knots of unemployed day laborers stood in the doors of tumbledown taverns, smoking fiercely and muttering to each other. Stout women carried baskets of meager provisions back to their squalid lodgings, while ragged children capered up and down the street at will, with little or no adult supervision.

Cabs were scarce here, and this one drew unwelcome attention as it stopped in front of a set of small brick buildings on a street off the Mile End Road, one of which bore the painted sign TOYN-BEE HALL to distinguish it from the warehouses that surrounded it. As soon as it stopped, the careworn women and children gravitated to it, certain that whoever had arrived in such a vehicle must be a source of largesse.

One look at the crowd was enough for Jerry. He waved his whip at the beggarly horde and hoped that whatever business it was that would bring the likes of two gentlemen to a place like Mile End Road would finish quickly. He did not like the looks of Whitechapel, and he especially did not like the idea of one of these ragged urchins being unkind to his horse. The horse, on the other hand, seemed to take the grubby hands that reached out to pat him in stride, bobbing his head up and down, and occasionally tapping a foot on the snowy street.

Mr. Dodgson seemed to ignore the crowd. He turned to speak to Dr. Doyle as they surveyed the doors of Toynbee Hall. "Dr. Doyle," Mr. Dodgson said softly, "I feel we must be circumspect here."

"Precisely what I thought, sir. One does not like to mislead people, particularly those who are attempting to do good, but we have no idea what Mr. Basset's connection with this place was."

"I think we may be excused a small subterfuge," Mr. Dodgson decided. "I shall engage the Reverend Mr. Barnett in conversation, whilst you do the same with some of the younger persons."

Mr. Dodgson swallowed hard. "There may be some boys here. I do not get on well with boys, but you, Dr. Doyle, being nearer their own age, may be able to speak with them on more equal terms. You have a way of making persons of all orders feel comfortable."

Dr. Doyle smiled under his mustache. "Perhaps I ought to remain out here with the cab. That way I can converse with some of these people, especially the young ones," he suggested. "Meanwhile, you can speak with Mr. Barnett as one Oxford man to another."

"I am glad you understand," Mr. Dodgson said. "Although, I must admit I would feel safer if you were with me. These people look quite unpleasant." He glanced at the tatterdemalion children, the grim-faced men, and the careworn women and hurried into the building.

Toynbee Hall itself was a converted warehouse, with no pretensions to architectural splendor. Inside, the utilitarian motif continued. The walls had been painted a particularly nasty shade of brown, the better to hide the dirt, and the floors were covered with linoleum in lieu of tile or carpet. Photographs of some of the sites of London had been hung on the walls, the better to decorate the entry, but the result was not as lively as the decorators had intended.

Mr. Dodgson's black overcoat and top hat attracted attention from the uniformed porter at the door, who stepped forward to demand what business the gentlemen had in this institution.

Mr. Dodgson offered his card. "I am Mr. Dodgson of Oxford come to speak with the Reverend Mr. Barnett, if he will see me."

The porter sized Mr. Dodgson up with a practiced eye. Gentlemen of his stamp had come to observe the Reverend Mr. Barnett's experiment in social reform several times since its founding and had usually left a generous bequest when Mr. Barnett had finished with them. He beckoned to a shabbily dressed youth who was lounging in the doorway. "Dolittle, you take this gentleman up to the Warden's Office, right smart now," he ordered.

"Right-ho, guv!" The youth grinned, displaying teeth that would never see a dentist.

Mr. Dodgson followed the boy up a flight of stairs, past a large room, full of young men in baggy drawers doing calisthenics, and another room, where young girls sat sewing while a severe-looking woman read to them, to a corner office that overlooked the fluttering garments that marked Petticoat Lane, the used-clothing center of London.

"There's a gent to see the Warden," Dolittle announced, as he opened the door.

"Have you an appointment?" The stout man behind the barrier of a desk asked, glaring at them through pince-nez.

Once again Mr. Dodgson produced his card, and once again the magic words CHRIST CHURCH, OXFORD produced the desired result. Mr. Dodgson was ushered into the inner sanctum, a small room filled largely by the Reverend Mr. Barnett, a tall clean-shaven man dressed in frock coat and clerical collar and vest, who embodied the phrase "muscular Christianity."

"Mr. Dodgson," Mr. Barnett caroled, bounding forward with outstretched hand. "This is indeed an honor! I have sent some literature to each of the colleges, and I had hoped to encourage more interest in our undertaking, but I admit, sir, I did not expect to have a man of your distinction take the time to inspect our institution in person. What brings you to our doors, sir?"

Mr. Dodgson smiled gently. "I was up for the day, but the snow stopped the trains. I found one of your prospectuses at the offices of *Youth's Companion* and recalled the talk you gave at the House last year."

Mr. Barnett accepted the explanation and went burbling on, "Were you, perhaps, considering giving us the benefit of your wisdom by lecturing? I am afraid most of our young men would not appreciate your system of logic. They are of a more practical bent." Mentally, he congratulated himself on having attracted the attention of so noted a scholar as Mr. Dodgson, the author of *Euclid and His Modern Rivals*. It was also an open secret in Oxford that Mr. Dodgson had written a few books for children and that he was especially generous to any charity concerning juvenile education.

"I noticed several *boys*," Mr. Dodgson seemed to shudder as he pronounced the word, "engaged in physical activities. And I see you also have opportunities for girls."

"I will give you a tour of the facilities if you like," Mr. Barnett offered. "The London City Council has made every effort to assist me in helping these young people, for it is only by education that we can become better, more moral persons."

"A worthy aim, indeed," Mr. Dodgson murmured.

Mr. Barnett's enthusiasm was undeterred by Mr. Dodgson's tepid response. "We try to bring these young people the benefits enjoyed by happier children, whose hours are enhanced by play and not toil in gardens and fields, and not in filthy hovels or streets. You have already noticed our gymnasium, where the young fellows may enjoy healthful exercise. We are even planning to build a swimming bath, and a true People's Palace, a place where young and old can receive the benefits of health and education."

"I hope you do not neglect the minds of these young persons," Mr. Dodgson said. "By that, I mean their imaginations."

"Indeed we do not," Mr. Barnett told him. "We have a library, where young persons of either sex may find works of instruction and entertainment in equal measure. But you must excuse my enthusiasm, Mr. Dodgson. I believe in what I am doing, and I find much satisfaction in knowing that the young men who come here may find the means to better their position in life, to rise above the miserable streets of Whitechapel. Urban settlements are as necessary as those of our brothers who toil farther afield. Mr. Booth and his Salvation Army have acted as scouts, so to speak, but the Church of England cannot permit Dissenters to take the high ground, while we cower in the trenches!" Mr. Barnett glowered at the imaginary enemy.

"I see you borrow your military terminology as well as your sentiments from Mr. Booth," Mr. Dodgson said. "I am sure that my friend Mr. Samuel Basset would concur."

Mr. Barnett's face lost its rosy glow of self-satisfaction. "I was shocked to read of Mr. Basset's death in this morning's newspapers," he said slowly. "He was most active in promoting our activities, particularly the library."

"I should very much like to see the library," Mr. Dodgson said. "And I would like to speak with some of your students, if I may."

"Of course, Mr. Dodgson." Mr. Barnett called out, "Dolittle!"

The enterprising youth had been lingering outside the door of the office waiting for the chance to hit up the toff for a tip.

"Yer called, sir?"

"This is Mr. Dodgson, Dolittle. You are to show him about and especially show him the library." Mr. Barnett turned to Mr. Dodgson. "I would come with you, but today we are somewhat busy. I have been receiving subscriptions for the Lord Mayor's Fund all day. No matter how desperately poor these people are, they will still advance a penny or two for those still less fortunate than they."

"I have noted that many people have been reminded of their duty towards those less fortunate than themselves," Mr. Dodgson said.

Mr. Barnett's habitual smile faded into a worried frown. "It is truly unfortunate that it took a riot, and the loss of a life, to bring people to own up to their responsibilities."

"Surely you do not refer to the death of Mr. Basset," Mr. Dodgson demurred. "That occurred well before the events in Trafalgar Square."

"I read in this afternoon's newspapers that the body of an unknown man was discovered in the snow during the riot," Mr. Barnett said. "However, Mr. Mann is holding another meeting in Trafalgar Square tonight."

"I sincerely hope it will not produce the same disturbance as last night's riot!" Mr. Dodgson looked alarmed. "My friend Doyle and I were caught up in it. A dreadful scene, Mr. Barnett."

"Tonight's event will be properly run, I assure you," Mr. Barnett said firmly. "Mr. Mann, who leads the Fair Trade League, has applied for their permit. According to the newspapers, the Metropolitan Police have already got the perpetrators of last night's disgraceful upheaval under lock and key." He tapped the afternoon *Standard,* which lay open on the secretary's desk.

"In that case, I will not detain you from your good work," Mr. Dodgson said. "I only wish to assure myself that Toynbee Hall is all you have said it is, and I will most certainly discuss your efforts in the Senior Common Room at the House."

The two men shook hands ceremoniously, and Dolittle led Mr. Dodgson through the halls, where he could see small classrooms filled with children of various ages, in varying states of cleanliness, reading aloud or doing sums on slates. Eventually they got to the library, a small room filled with bookshelves but not with books. Only half the shelves were covered, and many of those wore the yellow bindings of the Portman Penny Press. Mr. Dodgson scanned the shelves and wondered if Dr. Doyle had learned more than he had.

Dr. Doyle had drawn quite a crowd by virtue of his dashing balbriggan coat, his cab, and the cab horse, who regarded the children clustered around him with a mild interest.

"That's a fine, gentle animal," Dr. Doyle commented, as the horse picked up one foot and then another, so as not to step on the very small child who had got under the cab.

"Now, if that creetur could talk, it might tell a tale," Jerry agreed.

"It must be an interesting life, driving a cab about London," Dr. Doyle went on. He kept a wary eye on the men in the tavern on the corner of the street, who kept just as wary an eye on him.

Jerry pulled his coat higher around his ears. "It's a 'ard life," the cabby said. "O' course, there's some as takes to it and some as don't. We gets all sorts as thinks they can tool a cab, but the London streets flummoxes 'em. Once we even 'ad a Yank."

"An American?" Dr. Doyle asked.

"Aye. 'E were good wif the 'osses, but when it come to finding 'is way about London, 'e were 'opeless. Jest 'opeless!"

Jerry sighed, then flourished his whip at a pair of nattily dressed young men who were approaching the cab with a predatory look in their eyes. "Be off, you! This 'ere cab's engaged!"

"No it ain't, for we've got it," the darker of the two declared. His fairer friend agreed, and tried to wrench open the door. Jerry stepped down from the box ready to defend his client's prerogatives.

Dr. Doyle stepped between Jerry and the two young men and looked the two of them over. "I do believe we have seen each other before," Dr. Doyle said, with sudden insight. "You were at the Café Royal last night with Mr. Wilde."

"And wot if we were?" The dark one glared at him suspiciously.

"I know you," the fair lad said. "You was wif that old gent in the tile 'at, looked like some sort of vicar." He turned to his friend. "I told yer I'd seen that coat afore."

"It ain't the thing," the dark one objected. "Are yer on the game?"

"I don't think—" Dr. Doyle began.

" 'Cos if yer goin' on the game, yer better lose the soup strainer," the fair lad instructed him.

Dr. Doyle's hand involuntarily found his mustache. "What's wrong with it?"

"Makes yer look old," the dark youth said. "Marks likes 'em young. Not too young, mind. That's sinful, that is."

"And wot would a nipper do wi' the coin anyways?" The fair lad shrugged. "Now, me an' Ern, we knows 'ow to do fer ourselfs." He adjusted his derby hat to a more flourishing angle.

"If you dine with Mr. Wilde of an evening, you must be quite the lads," Dr. Doyle commented. "And at the Café Royal, too. Are the rest of the, er, marks so generous?"

"You are a right Jock!" Bert mocked Dr. Doyle's Scottish burr. "Aye, they're good fer a meal, and sometimes a bit more, eh, Ern?"

"I don't suppose you'd take money . . . ," Dr. Doyle began.

Bert bristled. "Wot d'ye think we are? 'Ores?"

Ern tried to mollify his friend. "Don't take on like that. 'E's new on the game, Bert. Y'see," he turned to Dr. Doyle, "a little present, like a tip, that's all right, something just to tide us over till we can find something else. Or a present, like. But money . . . that's low. That's trade, that is."

Dr. Doyle was fascinated by the delicate gradations of the underworld. "If someone were to pay for a suit, now, would that be acceptable?"

Bert and Ern consulted in whispers. "Is that a hoffer?" Ern's dark eyes were bright at the thought of the acquisition.

"I just wondered, because I knew Samuel Basset, and he might have paid someone's tailor . . ."

The name Basset acted on the two young men like a dose of very unpleasant medicine.

"Sam Basset's dead," Bert said with a grimace. "Good riddance."

"Really? I thought he was well-liked hereabouts. He brought books to the library and assisted some of the young people here. Who was it? Oh, yes . . . Levin. That was the name, I think."

"Levin? Haw!" Ern guffawed. "Aaron Levy, settin' 'imself up. Sam Basset come 'ere and took to our Aaron, only now 'e's Andrew and Levin, not Levy. Got 'imself a job o' work, a position!" He uttered the last work with a scornful grimace.

"Arf a crown a week and fer wot? Sittin' in a hoffice on Fleet Street, runnin' herrands like a bloody fool? Puttin' on a clean shirt an' collar every day, so's 'e could say 'e's a gent? We knows different, we do!" Bert snorted his opinion of such pretensions.

"Still, 'e says 'e's got hexpectations," Ern said. "An' 'e gets ter meet nobs."

"So do we," Bert said with a knowing grin. "Ern, let's you and me leave this 'ere Jock to 'is old geezer, wot's gettin' the spiel from old Barnett."

"And where are you off to then?" Dr. Doyle asked.

"Doin's on Trafalgar Square," Bert said with another grin. "Plenty of cash for those 'oo knows where it's 'id." He twiddled his fingers and winked knowingly.

"Just you be careful, Jock," Ern warned him. "Them old geezers is the wust. Aaron's not the first lad old Basset took on. D'yer mind the bloke wif the 'air?"

"But 'e'll be the last," Bert said. The two youths winked knowingly again at Dr. Doyle and headed for the City, leaving Dr. Doyle to ponder what he had learned and wonder if Mr. Dodgson was getting anything more from Mr. Barnett.

Mr. Dodgson had tested the contents of the little library and found it wanting. However, he did not make his displeasure evident to Mr. Barnett, who bounded into the library exuding confidence in his creation. "How are you getting on?" Mr. Barnett's enthusiasm filled the small room.

"I wondered how you selected which books to use in your library," Mr. Dodgson said, his eyes roaming the empty shelves.

"We wish to provide those books that the children most need," Mr. Barnett told Mr. Dodgson earnestly. "The schools here are inadequate, to say the least, and many of the children in this district do not attend school at all. They are constrained by circumstances to earn their living, either on the streets or in a sweatshop. We have night classes, for those who wish to attend them, in such things as accountancy and bookkeeping, as well as such fine trades as engraving, watchmaking, and so on. We also give instruction in housewifery, cooking, and sewing. Some of these girls do not know one end of a needle from another!"

"I sincerely hope you do not neglect the children's souls in your efforts to improve their minds," Mr. Dodgson said sharply.

"Of course not," Mr. Barnett hastened to reassure him. "There are church services every Sunday, and we have had many worthy persons to speak here. General Booth and his daughter have come, for instance."

"That is not what I meant," Mr. Dodgson reproved him. "Children need laughter and nonsense as well as cold facts."

"Well," Mr. Barnett said defensively, "we have some charming stories brought in by Mr. Basset. He came every week with copies of *Youth's Companion* to distribute to the children. He even gave us a copy of *Alice's Adventures in Wonderland*, and nothing is more nonsensical than that!"

Mr. Barnett waved the volume in front of Mr. Dodgson's nose. Mr. Dodgson took the book and said, "The first printing. I am gratified that Mr. Basset did not attempt to suborn every copy that was given him for distribution."

"Sir, I do not understand. . . ."

"It is quite all right, Mr. Barnett. You may have heard that I am the author of this work, and I had specifically indicated that this printing was to be reserved for charitable organizations like this one. I was quite upset when I thought that Mr. Basset had failed in his trust by selling copies that were to be given to institutions."

Mr. Barnett was speechless with embarrassment. "I had no idea that Mr. Basset was that sort of man," he said. "He took such an interest in the young people, especially the young man who assisted him."

"Mr. Levin?"

"A Hebrew, of course. There are many who take advantage of our educational work without necessarily belonging to our church." Mr. Barnett considered Mr. Levin briefly, then said, "Mr. Bassett thought he had promise. He even offered him a position when his former clerk moved into another place."

"Indeed. Mr. Basset's death will be a double loss, then, since he was such a benefactor to this institution." Mr. Dodgson offered his hand to Mr. Barnett, who bowed and shook it heartily. "I shall certainly send another contribution to your excellent institution," Mr. Dodgson said, as the warden accompanied him down to the street door. "Thank you for your tour. It has been most educational."

Mr. Dodgson found his cab under siege when he emerged from Toynbee Hall. Both Jerry and Dr. Doyle were engaged in keeping the children away from the horse, who had had enough petting and clearly wanted to move on. "Now where to, gentlemen?" the cabby asked.

"Back to Fleet Street, I think, and then you may take yourself and your noble steed home," Mr. Dodgson told him. "You have done good service, Jerry."

"Thankee, sir!" The cabby flourished his whip and the crowd parted so that the horse could make his way back to the City and civilization. Inside the cab, Dr. Doyle and Mr. Dodgson exchanged information.

"Apparently, Mr. Basset was in the habit of befriending some of the more intelligent of these young men," Dr. Doyle summed it up. "Especially one Aaron Levy, alias Andrew Levin."

"In that case," Mr. Dodgson said, "I believe it is time we had a word with the staff of *Youth's Companion* and especially with Mr. Andrew Levin. He clearly knows more than he is willing to admit about the private life of Samuel Basset."

Once more they headed to Fleet Street, into the setting sun, leaving the grimy slums behind them.

CHAPTER 20

While Mr. Dodgson and Dr. Doyle were following the trail of Samuel Basset from Baker Street to Whitechapel, the offices of *Youth's Companion* had been gripped by a creative frenzy.

Once the weeping widow had been escorted off the premises and Inspector Calloway had decided to take his men back to Jewry Street for further consultations with authorities, Nicky Portman had assembled the two writers, the artist, Miss Harvey, and Mr. Levin in his office. He had even included Hannegan, the chief printer hastily summoned from Portman Penny Press at the Farringdon Road end of Fleet Street, who would, presumably, transmit the words of wisdom and encouragement from management to labor.

"My dear friends," Mr. Portman began with a deep sigh, "Mr. Samuel Basset is dead." He sighed again and looked around the room at the staff, who looked back with appropriately grave expressions. "This magazine was his life. The best memorial we can give him is to bring out this issue, as he would have wanted it, on time." Portman pounded his right fist into his left palm for emphasis.

"Hear, hear," Howarth applauded him.

"Now, I know you are as shocked as I to learn that our good friend and colleague Mr. David Peterson was attacked in the riots last night and is also dead. This magazine depended on him for much of its content. The best memorial we can give to him is to continue his work," Portman went on. "Howarth, Monteverde . . . or may I call you Win and Monte? We must all be friends here." Nicky Portman grinned boyishly at his staff. "I want you to use your talents to the best of your abilities so that this issue will be a fitting tribute to your fallen friend. Hannegan, I depend on you and your men to do your very best."

The brawny printer began to speak, but Portman went on before he could have his say. "O'Casey is still being held at Bow Street. I have my solicitor working to get him out, and I have two investigators looking into the matter of Mr. Basset's death. They will surely clear O'Casey of these baseless murder charges."

"Thank'ee, sir." Hannegan, as short and squat as O'Casey was tall and muscular, touched his forefinger to his paper cap.

"Now, Hannegan, you get the presses ready. I shall be sending down copy to be set, and I expect galleys within the hour." The printer saluted again and left the office to the writing staff.

Portman now turned his attention to the papers scattered about on the floor and piled untidily on the desk.

"What is all this?" he asked.

Levin pointed to various items around the room. "I believe these are some of the galleys of stories that Mr. Basset had already approved. Miss Harvey's manuscripts are here, and here are some other materials that Mr. Basset was in the process of correcting."

"I see. Miss Harvey," Portman turned to the young woman, "will you please sort these out, as you suggested? Levin, you can take the corrected manuscripts down to the compositors as soon as Miss Harvey gives them to you. Roberts," he turned to the artist, who had retreated to a corner and was glowering over his sketchpad, "have you got the illustrations ready yet?"

"I can't illustrate if I don't know what the story is," Roberts objected. "It was too cold to work upstairs yesterday. I'm a man;

I'm not a machine!" He glared at Portman as if daring him to replace human fingers with mechanical ones.

"In that case, I strongly suggest that we get you a fire, and that you get up to your garret and get back to work on whatever you can. Use filler, if necessary. I understand Furniss sent over some small pieces. Use those."

Roberts gave his new editor a look that would have killed him dead had Portman not been involved with something else by then. With a final snarl, the tortured artist strode out of the inner office. His feet could be heard resounding on the stairs as he bounded up to his attic workroom.

Monteverde and Howarth looked at their new editor in chief, expecting more orders.

"As soon as the columns come up, you chaps will have to help with the, er . . . ," Portman struggled for a word.

"Mock-up," Howarth supplied it.

"Meanwhile, I shall be reading through these manuscripts. Eventually I shall have to find someone to fill Sammy's shoes, but for now, I shall do my best." He turned to Miss Harvey and gestured helplessly at the mess on the desk. "I could never get Sammy to clear his desk, and now I never will." He sighed mightily.

Miss Harvey said, "I understand completely, Mr. Portman. My poor father used to keep his papers in just such a muddle, and he always said that he knew where everything was. I shall go through these piles and sort them out, and then you can deal with each pile in turn."

"Excellent idea," Portman said, pulling Mr. Basset's grand chair up and taking the seat of power.

"Mr. Basset would not have approved of a female in the workplace," Levin said, with a poisonous glance in Miss Harvey's direction.

"What nonsense!" Portman exclaimed. "Miss Harvey's father wrote several monographs on ancient art for Portman Penny Press, and Miss Harvey served as her father's amanuensis. A person with Miss Harvey's experience should be invaluable as copyreader. Now, Levin, take these down to the compositing room and bring back the galley sheets from yesterday."

"There were no galleys yesterday," Levin reminded him. "The men were called out on strike by that murderer, O'Casey."

"He's not a murderer," Portman protested. "At least, Mr. Dodgson doesn't think so. I wonder how old Dodgson is doing?"

"Halloo, Nicky!" A mellifluous voice interrupted the conversation.

Mr. Levin opened the office door and peered down the stairs to see who was causing the disturbance.

"Mr. Wilde?" Levin stared at the tall man who swept into the office with his slouch hat, fur coat, and nonchalant attitude.

"Oscar!" Portman was by this time the picture of a busy journalist, his hair on end and a pencil mark on his shirt cuff. "Oscar, what are you doing here?"

"I am applying for the position left vacant by the late Samuel Basset," Wilde said.

"Oscar!" Portman exclaimed, scandalized. "The man's not even buried yet!"

"He's unable to edit this magazine, in any case," Wilde pointed out. "Unless you were planning to give that fellow Peterson the job. Were you?"

"Unfortunately, Mr. Peterson also met with a fatal accident last night," Levin said solemnly.

"I am sorry to hear it," Wilde said. "In that case, you may be right, Nicky. There is definitely something amiss here. I should not be happy in a position where my two predecessors met violent ends."

"Nevertheless, I'm glad you're here," Portman told him. "We've only got half this magazine ready for printing, and Sammy would have wanted us to get to press on schedule."

"In that case, my dear fellow, I am all yours." Wilde removed his coat to reveal an elegantly cut suit of a delicate blue, better suited to May than to February.

Mr. Levin cleared his throat expectantly. Portman looked up and realized that the young man was standing in front of the desk waiting for orders.

"Oh, Levin. Here are some stories to be set. Take them down to Hannegan. Then get up to the garret and fetch whatever Roberts has and bring them down here so that we can fit them into the, er, mock-up. Now what?"

Another knock on the outer office door interrupted the group.

Levin ran to answer the summons. "Mr. Furniss?" He allowed the rotund cartoonist to poke his head into the private office, then trotted off on his errands.

Furniss recognized one member of the group in the office at once. "Hallo, Wilde. Did Mr. Dodgson ever find you?"

"Of course he did, Furniss. Whoever sent him off to Chelsea?"

"Oh, that was Tenniel and du Maurier. I knew where you were, but those two old fogeys thought the poor old fellow would have some sort of seizure if he set foot in the Café Royal. He is all right, isn't he?" Furniss sounded worried.

"Of course he is. In fact, he's out proving my innocence." Wilde smirked. "That is, innocence of murder. Anything else, I freely admit to. What are you doing here, Furniss? Not up for Basset's position, are you? There's definitely danger in assuming it. Basset's dead, and so's the chap who would have taken the chair."

Harry Furniss's cheerful face darkened for a moment. "In that case, the chair is yours, Wilde. No, I'm here about another matter entirely. Tenniel's dead set against those poor souls out in the street, but the rest of us at *Punch* thought we'd get up a subscription in the name of all the journalists on the Street to send to the Lord Mayor's Fund to help them out. After all, we're better off than they. We may be wretched scribblers, Wilde, but we're being paid enough to keep body and soul together, and we've got roofs over our heads. A shilling apiece wouldn't do us any harm and might help the women and kiddies. What do you say, Portman?" Furniss turned to the publisher-turned-editor.

"If one of those roughs killed old Peterson, I'm all too willing to let them starve," Portman growled. "But it's not right that the women and children should go hungry and cold because their men were foolish enough to go on the rampage last night."

"There's another meeting called for tonight," Furniss said. "I'll be on the scene, of course, along with everyone else on the Street."

"I thought they had Hyndman and Burns locked up," Portman said.

"Oh, they're still in Bow Street jail," Furniss told them. "Along with an Irishman who insists he's innocent of murdering anyone or inciting anyone else to do so."

"That's O'Casey. He's our printer," Portman said, fumbling in his pockets. "Have you been down to the Penny Press yet?"

"If you mean have I seen your revered father, Burnard's working on the bigwigs," Furniss said. "I'm taking the Strand end and working down."

"Here's ten shillings," Wilde said, handing his offering with the air of King Cophetua doling out largesse to the beggar maid.

Howarth and Monteverde donated a shilling each. Miss Harvey shook her head sadly. "I really wish I could contribute," she said.

"I shall have to stand your banker yet again and make another small loan," Portman said gallantly.

"But you've done so much already!" Miss Harvey protested.

"Nonsense!" Portman found his pocketbook. "Here is five pounds, and tell my father that I expect him to double it at the very least."

Furness accepted the offerings and clattered down the stairs, forcing Levin to stand aside to let the larger man pass. Furniss headed down Fleet Street, and Levin trotted back up the stairs, a freshly printed set of galleys in hand.

"Here you are, Mr. Portman," Levin said breathlessly, handing him the papers, carefully touching only the margins.

"Aha!" Portman handed the papers to Monteverde and Howarth. "Now if you two will be so kind as to check these for errors, we can get to press."

"We can do better upstairs where we can spread out," Monteverde pointed out. "Win and I usually go over each column, then we send them up to Eddie for the mock-up. Mr. Basset would have the final say as to placement."

"It's important, placement," Howarth explained, seeing Portman's puzzled frown. "One wouldn't like to have an unfortunate meaning attached to something. Remember the bird?"

Monteverde began to chuckle to himself. "We had a cut of a Bird of Paradise, with a crest on its head, over an article about exotic birds of Australia. All well and good, but the story in the next column was about the Royal family, and the queen's birthday celebrations; and the leader, which was right next to the picture of the bird, read, 'Victoria Regina et Imperitrix.' I don't think Her Majesty was amused."

"I see what you mean. Very well, go to it. Miss Harvey and I will go over these contributions that Mr. Levin solicited and see what nuggets we can find in this pile of dross. Oscar, if you care to stay, your advice would be invaluable."

"In that case, I shall demand payment," Wilde warned, pulling one of the leopard-skin chairs closer to the windows overlooking Fleet Street.

The rest of the morning was spent in scanning galleys, sending them back for corrections, scanning them again, and fitting the result into the framework of a four-column page, with space for Roberts's illustrations and appropriate leaders.

Luncheon was called at one. Monteverde and Howarth headed for the Punch Tavern, while Mr. Portman debated about Miss Harvey. Clearly, a tavern would be out of the question, and it would be difficult for her to leave at such a delicate time in the proceedings. In the few hours she had been there, she had brought order out of the chaos of Samuel Basset's papers. The ledgers were now neatly stacked on one side of the desk, while the piles of new manuscripts, corrected manuscripts, and rejected manuscripts had been sorted out.

Levin had been kept trotting back and forth from the printing plant in the basement to the artist's garret. Now he glared at Miss Harvey, as he requested leave to go to his midday meal.

"Oh, of course, Levin," Portman said carelessly. "I am taking Miss Harvey to luncheon. We shall be back at two, when we shall resume our labors. Miss Harvey, will you join me? I usually eat at the Press Club, but today that would be difficult." He thought it over. "Perhaps there is a private dining room at Ye Olde Cheshire Cheese."

"I really should be getting home, Mr. Portman," Miss Harvey demurred.

"But you can't leave us now!" Portman exclaimed. "Your mother knows where you are, after all. In fact," he seemed to gain momentum as he spoke, "I do not think I could have managed without you this morning."

Miss Harvey flushed prettily. "Mr. Levin would have been quite adequate to the task, Mr. Portman," she said.

Portman shook his head. "I need Levin to run errands," he decided. "And Howarth and Monteverde may have to write something quickly to fill up space. Besides, Miss Harvey, if I may say so, you are far more decorative than Mr. Levin."

"That is unkind to Mr. Levin," Miss Harvey said. "He is quite good-looking, is he not, Mr. Wilde?"

The aesthete had been seated near the window, using its light to read the contributed manuscripts. Now he looked at Levin for the first time. "He certainly is," Wilde said. "In fact, I do believe I have seen this young man before, although I cannot recall where."

Levin's classical features were tinged with pink. "I could not say that we had ever been introduced," he said. "Mr. Portman, if you like, I could escort Miss Harvey home." He hesitated, then added, "If it were known that Miss Harvey was alone with you in a private room at a place like Ye Olde Cheshire Cheese, her reputation might suffer."

Portman frowned. "I hadn't thought of that. Well, she's got to stay here until we can get at Sammy's keys to unlock his cash box, and we can't get the keys until that Scotland Yard man gives permission for me to claim poor Sammy's body and take charge of his possessions." Portman let Levin help him on with his coat and overcoat. "What we need is a chaperon. Oscar, you come with us and play Mrs. Grundy. No one can object to Miss Harvey dining with two gentlemen, with heaven knows how many other people about."

There was a thunderous knock on the downstairs door. "Now what is it?" Portman shouted into the outer office. "Levin!"

Levin bolted down the stairs and back up. "It's Inspector Calloway, sir, with some of his men. He wants another look round to find the knife or whatever it was that killed Mr. Basset. And the men are here with the paper for the printing. And Mr. Roberts is not satisfied with the woodcuts and wants them run again."

Sounds of battle filtered up from the press room, as Roberts and Hannegan shouted at each other.

"In that case, you'd better stay here, Levin, and take care of things. I'll see to it that something is sent in for you from Ye Olde Cheshire Cheese. Oscar, Miss Harvey, shall we go?"

The trio exited into the foggy streets, leaving Levin to cope with the policemen, the galleys, the dray with the paper for the new issue, Roberts and his woodcuts, and a growing sense that he was being shoved aside.

CHAPTER 21

M r. Dodgson and Dr. Doyle arrived at the offices of *Youth's Companion* just as Mr. Portman, Mr. Wilde, and Miss Harvey were making their way up the hill from Ye Olde Cheshire Cheese. Theirs had been a long and hilarious luncheon, during which Wilde had held forth on every subject under the sun, while Miss Harvey and Mr. Portman allowed themselves to forget that Samuel Basset lay at St. Bart's awaiting the decision of the coroner as to the disposition of his remains.

Mr. Dodgson paid off the cabby, who touched his hat in response.

"Thank'ee, sir," Jerry said with a grin and a flourish of his whip. "And should you be needin' a cab for the day, just ask for Jerry Barker. They know me at all the cabstands in the City." He started to move off, but his cab was immediately claimed by two men in sack suits covered by shabby overcoats.

"Trafalgar Square, cabby, and make it quick!" One of the men waved a handbill, while the other looked down the hill at a contingent of men marching doggedly along, holding placards and banners. Clearly, the Fair Trade League was going to make another attempt at venting the grievances of the workingmen of London, and the press had to be on hand to record the event.

The acting editor in chief of *Youth's Companion* appeared to be blithely unaware of the unrest in the streets. "Mr. Dodgson!" Mr. Portman greeted him. "Where have you been? Have you learned anything more about who might have killed poor Sammy?"

"I have been to many places, Mr. Portman, but I cannot discuss them here on the street," Mr. Dodgson said testily. He scowled disapprovingly at Mr. Wilde, who ignored him.

"Do come up, sir, and tell me what you know." Portman led the way back to the office, passing Levin at his desk. The secretary leaped up when he saw his employer. "Mr. Portman, may I have a word?" he asked.

"Not too long a word, Levin. I have to get back to work. Have the fresh galleys come up yet?"

Levin helped Mr. Portman out of his overcoat and hat and hung both on the rack near the wooden settle as he reported on midday events.

"The expressmen brought more paper," Levin reported, "and Mr. Roberts has had his illustrations redone to his satisfaction. Mr. Howarth, Mr. Monteverde, and Mr. Roberts are upstairs in the art studio putting the final touches on the mock-up for you to look over before it goes to the press. And Inspector Calloway and his men have been over the offices again." His icy tone showed what he thought of this second invasion of the offices.

"Calloway? Who is he?" Wilde asked. "I thought the fellow in charge was that Scottish policeman who doesn't like me."

"Inspector Calloway is with the City of London Police," Mr. Dodgson explained. "There is something of a jurisdictional dispute, since Mr. Basset met his death on Fleet Street, which is, but only just, within the boundaries of the City of London."

"And what did Inspector Calloway find out this time?" Portman asked.

"Nothing of consequence," Levin said with a sniff of disdain. "I don't think Inspector Calloway knows any more than he did this morning. He searched all the offices, including the pressroom downstairs, and the, um, necessary. He found nothing."

"Then I hope Mr. Dodgson can enlighten us," Portman said. "Levin, as soon as I have seen the mock-ups, run them down to the pressroom and wait until the first run is off, then bring it up to me."

"Yes, sir." Levin watched as Miss Harvey followed the others into the private office.

"That chap looks very familiar," Wilde murmured. "I do wish I could remember when and where I've seen him before."

Mr. Portman took the center chair as if by right. Miss Harvey and Mr. Wilde ranged themselves on either side of him as honor guard. Mr. Dodgson removed his hat and opened his ulster, while Dr. Doyle shrugged himself out of the balbriggan greatcoat, glad to be out of it.

Mr. Dodgson cleared his throat with an embarrassed cough. "Perhaps Miss Harvey should leave," he suggested. "What Dr. Doyle and I have to say may be painful, Mr. Portman, and it is not for the ears of young ladies."

Miss Harvey smiled sweetly. "My father's circle of friends included some very, um, eccentric gentlemen," she reminded them. "He was not a charter member of the Pre-Raphaelite Brotherhood, but he was familiar with many of that circle. I assure you, Mr. Basset's private life will not shock me. I had thought he was a bachelor, but that does not mean that he would not have kept a female companion in a private establishment."

Mr. Portman gave a crack of laughter. "Sammy? I don't think he's so much as looked at a woman since we left school!"

Mr. Dodgson reddened at such ribald raillery. Dr. Doyle took over, since Mr. Dodgson seemed unable to continue with so frank a young woman in the conversation. "It seems, Mr. Portman, that your old friend found his, um, companions in some very unsalubrious parts of London."

"Meaning, I suppose, he went to Toynbee Hall for more than charity work," Mr. Portman sighed. "I can't say I'm surprised. I did warn him, when I left Baker Street, that one of those young thugs would do him a mischief some day."

"But none of those young thugs, as you put it, were in this office yesterday," Miss Harvey objected.

"As to that," Dr. Doyle said, "certain facts have come to light that make it imperative that we have a word with each of the staff concerning the events of yesterday afternoon. Mr. Dodgson has come to some conclusions. Mr. Dodgson?"

Mr. Dodgson had been staring at Mr. Basset's desk. Thanks to Miss Harvey's efforts, the muddle of papers had been neatly sorted and arranged: one pile of manuscripts to be accepted; one to be rejected; a stack of ledgers to be read; a pile of correspondence to be answered; and a pile that had already been answered that was now to be filed. The pens were set up in the penholder, the inkwell was filled, the pencils had been sharpened, and even the African paperweights were now lined up like specimens in an exhibit case, instead of being tossed onto different stacks of paper, helter-skelter.

"I see someone has been busy here," he stated.

"That's Helen. I should say, Miss Harvey," Portman corrected himself. "She's a wonder. I wish I could have her here every day."

"My mother might not like my going out to work," Miss Harvey reminded him. "Today was, after all, an emergency. I shall have to get back to her quite soon." Her voice held a note of regret. Miss Harvey had been enjoying her excursion, playing in the boys' games.

"Mr. Dodgson," Dr. Doyle tried to bring the scholar out of his reverie. "What do you see?"

"It is not what I see. It is what I don't see. How many of those knives did Mr. Basset have on his desk yesterday? Were there three or four?" Mr. Dodgson turned around to face his young friend.

Dr. Doyle closed his eyes and tried to visualize the desk as it had been. "Four, I think. Yes, I am certain of it. There were four."

Mr. Dodgson pointed one gray-gloved finger at the line of daggers. "There are now three, Mr. Portman. The conclusion to be drawn? One of those daggers was used by the murderer to kill Mr. Basset."

"The longest, thinnest one," Dr. Doyle declared. "There was

one that looked just like an Italian stiletto. I wondered that it should be amongst those African artifacts."

Portman blinked at the collection of knives. "That was Sammy's fancy. He bought it from some peddler just as we were boarding the ship to go home. The rest of these we got on our safari from native tribes on our route."

"Why do unpleasant people insist on collecting weapons?" Mr. Dodgson murmured to himself. "Is it for the sole purpose of providing their enemies with the means to remove them?"

"In Sammy's case, it was nothing more than curiosity," Portman said. "He wanted a souvenir of our African adventures, just as he liked having the heads of the animals we shot placed here instead of at Baker Street. There really wasn't enough room in the digs, in any case."

"We visited Baker Street, and you are quite right, the rooms are small," Dr. Doyle said. "The flat at the Press Club is quite spacious. Forgive me for asking such a personal question, but was it Mr. Basset's choice to remain at Baker Street, in sole possession, as it were?"

Mr. Portman shifted uneasily in his chair. "I have said it before, and I will tell you one more time: There was no quarrel between Sammy and myself. I came into some money and decided to move out. I couldn't throw Sammy into the street, so I told him to keep the rooms for himself. That is all there was to it." He looked at the two investigators. "What did you find there, besides the fact that Sammy went to Toynbee Hall?"

"Ah, yes," Mr. Dodgson fumbled in his coat pocket. "We found these tracts at 331-B Baker Street." He displayed the Mormon pamphlets. "And we saw a similar tract at Mr. Peterson's residence, with some notes on it for future stories."

Wilde laughed when he saw the tracts. "Nicky, I don't see you marching off to Utah to marry five wives," he chortled.

"Of course not," Portman snapped. "I can only assume that Sammy must have picked them up at Toynbee Hall. Mr. Barnett will show his establishment to anyone who asks. As for Sammy, he had no interest in women at all."

"As we have discovered," Dr. Doyle said, glancing at Miss Harvey, who seemed amused by their care for her supposed innocence.

"As for his choice of companions," Mr. Dodgson said with a disapproving frown, "that may or may not be of consequence. I must speak with your staff, Mr. Portman. Dr. Doyle has a very good idea of how the deed was done, and when, and where, but by whom is another matter."

"And why," Portman added.

"Yes, indeed. That was what Mr. Basset asked as he lay dying. He was staring at the door to this building and at the people who were leaving, and he asked, 'Why?' Miss Harvey," Mr. Dodgson turned to her. "When did you leave this office?"

Miss Harvey frowned slightly. "I remained until Mr. Basset had come out of his office again," she said. "I thought I might be able to get my payment if Mr. Levin could get to the cash box. Unfortunately, Mr. Basset was very much out of sorts, and I felt that perhaps I should stay out of his way."

"So you were still here when Mr. Levin told the staff to go home?" Mr. Dodgson said. "Can you recall the exact movements of the people in the office after Mr. Basset left?"

Miss Harvey's frown deepened, as she concentrated. "Let me see. Mr. Basset had had a very painful scene with Mr. Levin. We could hear him roaring right through the door."

"We?" Mr. Dodgson pounced on the pronoun.

"Well," Miss Harvey explained, "there was I, and Mr. Peterson, and the other two gentlemen, and Mr. Roberts. Then Mr. Levin came out of Mr. Basset's ofice very upset, and Mr. Peterson went into the office to try to get him reinstated."

"Did he have so much influence?" Mr. Dodgson asked. "From what we saw and heard, we did not think that Mr. Basset valued any of his staff. He called Mr. Peterson a hack in our hearing."

Mr. Wilde shrugged. "He also called me a mincing mannequin, who could not write a story to save his soul. The late Sammy had the literary acumen of a brick."

Mr. Portman shook his head at the lack of judgment of his late partner. "Sammy and David had worked together at Portman

Penny Press when David was one of the main writers and Sammy was his editor. He'd shout at David, but he'd never have let him go; and sometimes he did listen to him. And, of course, David could charm birds off the trees. If Levin and Sammy had had some sort of tiff, David would be the one to put things right."

"In the interests of the publication. I see." Mr. Dodgson nodded, then said, "Continue, Miss Harvey. Mr. Peterson went in to remonstrate with Mr. Basset. Did he succeed?"

"Mr. Levin declared that he would not stay where he was not wanted and so the matter stood when Mr. Peterson and Mr. Basset came out of the office."

"Levin told me nothing of this last night," Portman said with a frown.

Miss Harvey took up her narrative. "Mr. Levin assisted Mr. Basset on with his coat and handed him his hat and accompanied him down the stairs to open the door. I could hear them speaking on the stairs, but I could not tell what they were saying. At least, Mr. Basset was not shouting."

"And what about the rest of them? Mr. Roberts, Mr. Howarth, and Mr. Monteverde?" Dr. Doyle asked.

Once again Miss Harvey tried to picture the scene. "I believe Mr. Howarth followed Mr. Levin and Mr. Basset down the stairs, but Mr. Roberts, Mr. Peterson, and Mr. Monteverde might have gone up. I remained in the office alone."

"The necessary is in the basement next to the printing plant," Portman explained. "One or more of the staff may have, ah, felt the call of nature, especially after all that excitement."

"And with Mr. Basset gone, I realized that I would get no money besides what Mr. Levin had given me for my fare for the underground. I decided to take Mr. Levin's advice and go home to type the manuscripts over again."

She looked from Mr. Dodgson to Mr. Portman. "If that is all, Mr. Portman, I really must get back to Chelsea. My mother will be wondering what has become of me."

Before Portman could speak, Oscar Wilde said, "My dear Miss Harvey, I insist on accompanying you. My charming Constance is having one of her tea parties this afternoon, which is why I decided to come here. However, I now see that I must come to your rescue. Your dragon of a mama must be fought at all costs, and I am the man to do it." He struck a mock-heroic pose, drawing a giggle from Miss Harvey.

"I would be very glad of your company, Mr. Wilde," she admitted. "I saw some men on Fleet Street going towards the Strand when we came back from our luncheon. They looked quite fierce."

"In that case, Nicky, you may add 'bodyguard' to the character reference you are about to write for me," Wilde said. "And by the by, I have looked over that stack of submissions. Most of them are dreadful, but there are a few that warrant attention. This one, *Captain of the Polestar*. Marvelous atmosphere!"

"I wrote that one," Dr. Doyle admitted. "Mr. Basset refused it."

"Which only goes to show how little Sammy Basset knew of literature," Wilde said, looking around for his hat and coat. "If this is a sampling of your style, sir, all I can say is, keep at it!"

Dr. Doyle flushed with pride, then remembered why he was there. "There is a large police presence in the West End," Dr. Doyle said. "Inspector MacRae and his men must be doing double shifts tonight to prevent another outbreak like last night's riot."

"In that case, I insist that you let Oscar see you home, Miss Harvey. And I hope I may be allowed to call on you quite soon." Mr. Portman bowed briefly over Miss Harvey's hand.

"Are you asking for my services here at *Youth's Companion* or in a more personal context?" Miss Harvey asked with that elfin smile.

"Possibly both," Mr. Portman said. The young lady put on her woolen hat and jacket, while Oscar Wilde donned his dramatic slouch hat and fur coat. Their departure was marked by a sigh from Portman and a loud "Ahem!" from Levin, who had been standing at the door waiting to be admitted during the last part of the interview.

"Hannegan has made his final run and would like your approval before the magazine goes to press," the secretary announced.

The writers and artist marched into the office with the finished product: eight pages, four columns each, with a tasteful selection of stories, factual articles, puzzles, and suggestions for handicrafts, all illustrated with carefully hand-lined woodcuts. Mr. Dodgson and Dr. Doyle stepped out of the way into Levin's anteroom.

Mr. Dodgson muttered to himself as he moved from the inner office to the stairwell. "Let us see: Mr. Basset is alive and quite well enough to shout at poor Peterson at four forty-five. He leaves the building at four-fifty. He is accosted by O'Casey at four fifty-five. We see him at five o'clock, and he is dead by five-fifteen. The bloodstains show that he was stabbed on these stairs, and the only time it could have happened is between four-fifty and four fifty-five. The office staff were given permission to leave at five o'clock."

Dr. Doyle's frown matched that of his mentor. "How do we know that Basset didn't wait a few minutes here in the vestibule until the next omnibus should come along? It would be more practical than waiting out in the snow."

Mr. Dodgson nodded in approval. "That would give our murderer time to come down the stairs, do the deed, and trot up again. . . . But then would not Miss Harvey have heard him? She could hear the footsteps on the stairs."

"And what about that dagger? Where could the murderer have put it?" Dr. Doyle asked. The two of them gazed up and down the shaft, seeking an answer.

The stairwell was lit by the last rays of sunlight finding their way through the skylight. As they stood on the upper landing, Mr. Dodgson gazed down the stairs at the front door. A shadow caught his eye. He blinked, then looked again. He was right; something had been perched precariously on the lintel over the front door, something that was thin enough to fit on that narrow wooden ledge.

"Dr. Doyle," Mr. Dodgson ordered, "come here, and see if you can reach the top of this door."

Dr. Doyle obediently stretched his arms to their greatest length, standing on tiptoe to reach to the edge of the lintel. "There's something up there!"

"There is indeed. I suspect it is the missing knife, although we will not know until we get it down. I begin to understand what happened. The murderer must have followed Mr. Basset down the stairs, knife in hand, and struck while on the stairs. The blade did not reach any vital organ, as it would have had they been level. Instead, as you noted at St. Bart's, the blade nicked the renal artery, and Mr. Basset bled to death internally.

"There was not a lot of blood," Mr. Dodgson went on. "However, the murderer did not wish to bring the weapon back into the office. He could not drop it into the street, since Mr. Basset stood in his way."

"Couldn't he have waited and dropped it into the street when Mr. Basset left the vestibule for his omnibus?" Dr. Doyle played devil's advocate.

Mr. Dodgson demurred. "I think not, Dr. Doyle. Remember, that night the street was full of people; not only the usual crowds, but the unemployed ruffians who were being incited to riot by Mr. Hyndman. If, as you say, this is a crime of passion, the perpetrator would not have wished to face that mob while holding a dagger in his hands."

"So," Dr. Doyle picked up the thread of the argument, "he had to put it where it would not be seen, that is, on the lintel. And that means that this murderer is quite tall, with long arms."

"Like Mr. Roberts," Mr. Dodgson said. "What is more, I found this in the wastepaper in Mr. Roberts's attic." He drew a sheet of paper from his overcoat pocket. The face was that of Mr. Samuel Basset, but the features had been elongated and twisted into an expression of lustful malevolence. "Clearly Mr. Roberts was not fond of Mr. Basset."

Dr. Doyle examined the drawing. "Should we not bring this to the attention of the police? If we can show that anyone else had better cause and a better opportunity to remove Basset, O'Casey will be let go."

"Unfortunately, O'Casey has let his Irish tongue get away from him. He will remain in custody, along with Mr. Hyndman and the Scotsman Burns, until they can be arraigned for the crime of Inciting to Riot," Mr. Dodgson said with a sigh. "It would be all too easy for the good inspector to allow this misguided man to be tried for the murder of Mr. Basset and chalk the death of Mr. Peterson up to a misadventure."

"Surely not!" Dr. Doyle was indignant. "No jury would convict a man on such specious evidence, particularly when there are other suspects."

"None of whom have made themselves so visible as Mr. O'Casey," Mr. Dodgson said sadly. "Even if he is acquitted, which may not necessarily be the case, there is the disgrace brought upon his family. No, Dr. Doyle, we must persevere until the true criminal is brought to justice to the satisfaction of the police."

"And how are we to do that?" Dr. Doyle asked with a hint of sarcasm.

Mr. Dodgson gave the matter some thought. "The murderer must realize that the dagger will be found shortly. He will come to retrieve it. Dr. Doyle, you must remain in the outer office, within sight of the doorway, to see if anyone tries to remove that dagger from its hiding place, for that will be the person who put it there."

"And what will you do, sir, while I am staring at this door?" Dr. Doyle's sarcasm sharpened.

Mr. Dodgson remained serene. "I shall have a word with Mr. Howarth, Mr. Monteverde, and Mr. Roberts," he stated. "But first, we shall join Mr. Portman and his staff for tea."

A knock on the door heralded a veritable procession from Ye Olde Cheshire Cheese: a large man carrying a tea urn and a stand on which to set it up and two more with trays of sandwiches and fresh cakes.

Mr. Dodgson and Dr. Doyle led the way up the stairs and into the anteroom, where the caterers set up their offerings to the intense disgust of Mr. Levin and the unabashed joy of Messrs. Monteverde, Howarth, and Roberts. The tea urn was soon bubbling merrily away, and the waiters handed out slices of cake and small egg-and-cress sandwiches. The staff eagerly fell on the food as if they had had nothing since breakfast, while Mr. Portman beamed paternally and munched along with them.

"Now this is more like it!" Roberts decided, tossing back his chestnut tresses.

"Good show!" Howarth crowed.

Mr. Monteverde simply filled his mouth with cake and followed it with a swallow of tea.

Mr. Levin did not join in the merriment. "Is there anything else you wish, Mr. Portman?" he asked with a look of disdain at those who would shirk their duty to fill their bellies.

"Yes, Levin." Mr. Portman handed his secretary the final copies of *Youth's Companion*. "Run these down to the printing plant and wait until the first run is completed. I want copies for myself, then send a note over to the Penny Press for the drays to come and pick up the copies for distribution tomorrow morning. And then, all of you, if you will just give Mr. Dodgson a few minutes of your time, he may be able to discover which of you killed poor dear Sammy. And if he does," Portman's genial manner hardened into a fierce determination, "I shall personally see to it that whoever it is pays the supreme price for it!"

With which Parthian shot Mr. Portman went into the inner office, leaving Mr. Dodgson to drink tea, Dr. Doyle to stand by the office door, and the rest to stare uneasily at each other.

CHAPTER 22

M r. Dodgson looked about the office at the tea drinkers. Then he said, "Perhaps it would be better if I spoke with Mr. Howarth first, then Mr. Monteverde, then Mr. Roberts, and then Mr. Levin, if Mr. Portman can spare him from his errands. Would you gentlemen prefer to do this individually, upstairs, in your own rooms?"

Monteverde and Howarth exchanged glances. Then Monteverde spoke up, "Win and I usually work together. We have no secrets from each other. I didn't kill old Basset Hound, and as for poor David, he must have been caught by one of the looters last night in the Strand."

"Besides," Howarth pointed out, "our fires are nearly out, and it's freezing up there. At least here we're warm." He stretched out his hands towards Levin's fire, which was still emitting enough heat to keep the room tolerable for human habitation.

"Dr. Doyle and I have already established that Mr. Basset was killed in the stairwell, probably as he was leaving the building," Mr. Dodgson said. "However, we are of the opinion that Mr. Peterson's death was not the result of some random violence connected with last night's disturbance, but a deliberate attack."

"You mean, something David saw or heard made him suspect one of us?" Howarth considered that for a moment.

"It is possible," Mr. Dodgson admitted.

"And it would be just like him to twit whoever did it," Monteverde said with a wry smile. "He liked to ferret out little things about people, nothing criminal, you understand, just things people wouldn't like known."

"Indeed? And what had he found out about you?" Mr. Dodgson asked.

Monteverde shrugged. "Only that I've got a cousin who spent time in South America with Garibaldi and wound up in an Italian prison for fomenting rebellion. David came to dinner at my father's restaurant, got to chatting with Cousin Guido, and got the whole tale out of him. Of course he used it in one of his stories, just to show me that he knew all about it."

"A literary blackmailer. Quite unique," Mr. Dodgson commented. "You seem to lead a blameless life, Mr. Howarth. Surely you have no reason to dislike either Mr. Basset or Mr. Peterson."

"Although," Dr. Doyle put in from his station at the door, "it must have been difficult to work with the man who stole your sweetheart away from you."

Howarth blushed under his straggling beard. "It's true, Myrna preferred David to me," he said. "But that was six years ago. We're all good friends now."

"Nevertheless . . . ," Dr. Doyle said meaningfully.

Howarth nodded. "David was starting to treat Myrna abominably. Staying out till all hours, drinking and carousing. . . ."

"Carousing?" Mr. Dodgson echoed. "With whom?"

Howarth shrugged. "Oh, just other fellows from the Street. I don't think he'd been after any other women, if that's your drift. David wasn't that sort; just careless."

"And if he had been, um, unfaithful?" Mr. Dodgson hinted.

Howarth's usually mild expression darkened. "I'd have had a word with him," he said slowly. "I don't think I could have tolerated it. Bad enough that he made such a point about his domestic bliss! Photographs of his children on his desk, knowing that all I have to come home to is Post-Office Polly. My dog," he explained hurriedly.

"Not much meat for a blackmailer there," Dr. Doyle put in from his place at the door.

"And you, Mr. Roberts," Mr. Dodgson went on, "what did you think of Mr. Peterson?"

The artist scowled and showed his sketchpad. Mr. Peterson's rotund features were attached to the body of a plump and satisfied pig.

Mr. Dodgson chuckled. "You have an excellent pen, sir, and a good eye for a likeness." He tapped another sketch on the page. "However, you have it wrong. I was not the White Rabbit. That was Dean Liddell. I was the Dodo." He unfolded the sheet of sketches he had abstracted from the wastebin to display the goatish head of the editor in chief. "Was this your opinion of Mr. Basset?"

Roberts shook the hair out of his eyes. "He came into the shop where I was 'prenticed," he said. "He said he liked my style, and that I could better myself if I went to work here."

"And did you?" Mr. Dodgson asked.

"I may not be London-bred, sir, but I know what's toward. I let him know straight out that I wasn't the sort he was lookin' for." Roberts consulted with some inner muse, then continued. "He took me to dinner one time at the Café Royal, and that was that."

"But he kept you on," Mr. Dodgson said.

"Oh, aye, he did that. He knew he'd get no one else, not at his wages, and he needed me as much as I needed him." Roberts looked at the other two, who nodded in corroboration.

"Eddie's got a real touch," Howarth praised his friend.

"And his cuts are far and away better than anything else on the Street," Monteverde added.

"And Basset let you use the premises for your own work," Mr. Dodgson said. "You have access to the attics, do you not?"

Roberts nodded. "Aye, I could get into the place should I need to touch up one of the cuts." He looked at Mr. Dodgson with sudden suspicion. "Meaning, that I could have come in and pulled those heads off the walls?"

"It is possible," Mr. Dodgson said.

"And I suppose you wouldn't care to listen if I told you I did not?" Roberts retorted truculently.

"You would say that, of course," Mr. Dodgson continued his questioning. "Did Mr. Basset approve of your taking outside work?"

"What business is it of yours what I do with my time?" Roberts snarled. "I don't have to answer to anyone for every minute. I do work here and there. All of us have something on the side. David used to write funny squibs for whoever would take them. Win writes sketches for variety acts."

All eyes turned to the bearded writer, who flushed under the scrutiny. "Why not?" he defended himself. "It's jolly good fun, and I get theater tickets for nothing."

"And you, Mr. Monteverde," Mr. Dodgson asked. "How do you supplement your income?"

Monteverde had been gazing into the fire. Now he spoke up. "You know, I just had a thought, Win. What do you think of a guide to good eating in London? A sort of Baedecker for travelers that tells which restaurants are worth patronizing and which are only indifferent? Perhaps with a rating system . . . ?" He let his voice trail off, as he followed this thought to its natural conclusion.

"That might be quite useful," Howarth said, animated at the prospect of a new project. "And you could follow it up with similar books for other cities in England and extend it to the Continent . . ."

"But we'd have to do it right," Monteverde said. "We'd have to eat at all of them." The thought seemed to cheer him up.

Mr. Dodgson interrupted this speculation. "So all of you had other work besides this position, and you could, if necessary, go elsewhere. Why did you stay?"

Monteverde looked at Howarth; Howarth looked at Roberts. Then they all smiled sheepishly at one another.

Roberts spoke for the group. "The work was fun, especially with David in the office. He could jolly us all out of our black

230

moods, ease Basset out of his tempers, even cope with Levin when he got that high-and-mighty-look."

"David really made this place go," Howarth said, his voice starting to choke. For the first time that day, the full enormity of their loss penetrated to the three men. "He had such a sense of the ridiculous."

"The summer picnic was his idea, not Basset's," Roberts said. "And there would be a little something at the Christmas holidays, too. David was the real soul of this magazine."

"And yet someone thought he was dangerous," Mr. Dodgson pointed out.

"Surely not!" Monteverde protested.

"It is becoming more and more apparent to me that Mr. David Peterson was killed by the same person who stabbed Mr. Basset because Mr. Peterson indicated that he had seen or heard something that led him to suspect that person of the crime." Mr. Dodgson gazed at the trio as if they were misbehaving undergraduates. "He should have gone directly to the police!"

"The police?" Howarth scoffed. "Not David!"

"You saw those two coppers," Monteverde added. "David wouldn't give them credit for a pennyworth of brains between them. Calloway's off chasing pickpockets, and MacRae's looking for Fenians under the bed."

"David would be more likely to keep what he knew to himself," Roberts declared. "Only he'd let whoever did it know that he knew. Then he'd put it into a story and send it off to one of the magazines that takes crime stories, just to let on that he knew."

"Then he wrote for other publications?" Dr. Doyle stepped away from his post to join the discussion.

"Of course he did. You can't turn creativity off and on like a tap. David's mind was always going in five directions at once," Howarth said. "And Basset never read any other magazines but ours, so he'd never know. Not that it mattered; none of them ever use bylines."

Dr. Doyle nodded. It had always bothered him that his name was not put under the title of any of the stories published by *Cornhill* or *The Boy's Own Paper.*

"Oh, we're used to it," Monteverde said with a shrug. "At Portman Penny Press, half the works are under pen names anyway. Heaven forfend that your future readers should learn that you got your start writing penny dreadfuls and shilling shockers!"

There was a general laugh at the idea of any of them having a future audience at all, let alone one that would care how they got their start in artistic or literary pursuits.

"Ahem!" Mr. Dodgson brought them back to the reality of their situation. "I should like to understand what, exactly, happened after Dr. Doyle and I took our leave of this office at four o'clock yesterday. According to Miss Harvey, there was some sort of altercation between Mr. Basset and Mr. Levin."

Howarth and Monteverde exchanged looks again. Then Howarth said, "I don't know what he'd done that put Basset over the edge, but whatever it was, it must have been the straw that broke the camel's back because Basset sacked him."

"I beg your pardon?" Mr. Dodgson put a hand to his ear.

"He discharged him, fired him, let him go!" Howarth's voice rose. In a more conversational tone, he went on, "Monte and I had seen it coming for a while. Levin was like the camel in the tent."

"Another camel?" Mr. Dodgson looked confused.

"An old tale," Monteverde explained. "First the camel put his nose in, then his head, and so on, and by the time he was finished, the camel was in the tent and the driver was outside. That's what was happening, only Basset was too besotted to see it."

"Besotted?" Mr. Dogson echoed. "Do you mean to tell me . . . ?"

Howarth nodded; Monteverde shrugged.

"It was obvious from the minute he walked in that Levin was one of Basset's pets," Roberts said bitterly. "There's some as will marry a pig for the muck!"

"Dear me." Mr. Dodgson digested this information. "To return to our muttons, as they say, where were all of you when Mr. Basset left?"

Howarth frowned. "I had to go downstairs," he said diffidently. "Basset's tantrums work on my insides sometimes."

"And David and I went upstairs because he wanted to see the cuts we already had," Roberts said.

"And you, sir?" Mr. Dodgson turned to Monteverde.

"Me?" Monteverde's nonchalant attitude cracked slightly. "I went upstairs to get my coat. It was damned cold in here, even with Levin's little fire."

"So none of you were in this office . . . ," Mr. Dodgson summed it up.

"Miss Harvey was still here," Roberts recalled. "The poor girl was still waiting for her money. Levin gave her some when he came back up the stairs to close up."

"Is that when he sent you home early?" Mr. Dodgson asked.

"Must have been," Howarth said. "I saw him when I came back. He was heading up the stairs ahead of me."

"And Mr. Peterson . . . ?" Mr. Dodgson's usually unlined face was marked with a thoughtful frown.

"David was just coming down as Levin and I were coming up," Howarth said. "Monte was in the office with Miss Harvey . . . Eddie, where were you?" He turned to the artist, who shook his hair back and frowned.

"I don't remember," he said. "David and I had looked over the cuts, and he'd picked out one for the cover, and then he went down, and then I think I went all the way down the stairs to fetch up some water from the yard."

"And that is when Mr. Levin decided that all of you were to leave early due to the inclement weather and the incipient mob outside," Mr. Dodgson summed it up.

The three men nodded in agreement.

Mr. Levin himself interrupted the conference. He popped his head into the office. "I wanted to tell Mr. Portman that the presses are rolling, and the next issue of *Youth's Companion* will be off the presses momentarily."

"Good show!" Howarth crowed.

"May we have a word, Mr. Levin?" Mr. Dodgson asked. "You have been in and out all day, and I have not had the opportunity to ask your opinion of all this. . . ."

"Meaning, the murder of Mr. Basset?" Levin's cheekbones flushed, while the rest of his face seemed chiseled in stone.

"Meaning, all of the events of yesterday," Mr. Dodgson said. "I would prefer to discuss these matters with you in private, since they concern your, um, personal relationships."

Mr. Levin's classical features were tinged with pink. The other three men shared glances; then Mr. Roberts strode to the door. "I've got to clean my tools before we leave," he announced.

Monteverde and Howarth followed him out the door, murmuring excuses, while Dr. Doyle resumed his post.

Levin remained standing, like a schoolboy being ticked off by the headmaster.

"I have heard differing versions of how you came to be employed here," Mr. Dodgson began. "Perhaps you can clarify the issue. Did you come in answer to an advertisement?"

Levin cleared his throat. "Mr. Basset and I met through a . . . a charitable event," he said at last.

"Indeed?" Mr. Dodgson's expression was blandly benign. "I had not thought Mr. Basset to be a charitable man."

Levin's voice took on an edge, and his accent sharpened. "Mr. Basset 'ad . . . had interests in several charitable institutions, connected with books mostly."

"Including Toynbee Hall?" Mr. Dodgson suggested.

"Mr. Basset came down in answer to Mr. Barnett's request for books for the library," Levin said defensively.

"I would not have thought that a young man named Levin would have any interest in Canon Barnett or St. Jude's," Mr. Dodgson commented.

Levin's cheekbones flamed and paled. "St. Jude's Library was open to anyone who wanted to improve himself," he said.

"As you wished to do. Most enterprising of you." Mr. Dodgson nodded his approval. "So Mr. Basset came down to Toynbee Hall to assist Mr. Barnett in his endeavors. You were there, he was there, and you met. Was that the first time you had encountered Mr. Basset?"

Levin took a deep breath, then let it out. "This is very difficult," he said. "Mr. Basset was . . . he took an interest in me. When I told him that I'd been studying accountancy through St. Jude's, he said that I might come here to take a position that might, in time, lead to better things in the publishing business."

"And so you came to *Youth's Companion*," Mr. Dodgson summed it up.

"Yes, sir."

"And did Mr. Basset keep his word?"

"I beg pardon?" Levin looked confused.

"You seem to have had several different functions here. You open the doors, lay the fires, and run the errands, but you also keep the books, which is the work of an accountant or clerk; you write letters to contributors, which would be Mr. Basset's domain; and you also seem to be conversant with the work of the printers."

"I wanted to learn the business," Levin said. "Unfortunately, I 'ave never 'ad . . . had the time for literature." His accent was becoming more pronounced as he became more agitated.

"And what did you think of Mr. Basset as a person?" Mr. Dodgson persisted.

"It wasn't my place, was it?" Levin's voice took on an edge. "Mr. Basset could be quite genial when he wished to be. He was pleased to offer me this opportunity, and I took it."

"You did not, for instance, meet him after business hours?" Mr. Dodgson asked casually.

"After business hours?" Levin's voice shook.

Mr. Dodgson leaned forward with the expression that had daunted an entire generation of undergraduates whose work had been found wanting. "I think you had best tell me the whole, young man. There were meetings, were there not? Perhaps he took you to dinner?"

" 'E were . . . he was," Levin corrected himself, "a gentleman who liked the company of younger men. Not boys but, like, young."

"Young men of the sort that congregate at the Café Royal." Mr. Dodgson's expression was one of extreme distaste.

Levin nodded. "I 'ave a few chums 'oo told me about the

goings-on at the Café Royal," he admitted. "They said it was an easy way to earn a quid . . . that is, to earn a pound or two. That all I had to do was let 'im pat me about."

"But you did not wish to join their company," Mr. Dodgson prompted him.

"I'd met Mr. Basset at St. Jude's, and he told me I could do better with him." Levin leaned forward, pleading. "I only wanted to improve myself! Nothing more than that! A man may improve 'imself! Basset did!"

Mr. Dodgson regarded the young man and nodded. "Samuel Basset was befriended at an early age and wished to pass on some of his good fortune to a likely young man. I agree, Mr. Levin, the circumstances are such that a certain interpretation could be put on his actions. I assume you have done nothing for which you may reproach yourself."

"I only wanted to help," Levin repeated.

"Of course, Mr. Levin. Quite commendable." Mr. Dodgson stood, as if to dismiss his student. Then he asked, "What did you think of Mr. Peterson?"

"Mr. Peterson?" Levin looked confused. "He was a gentleman with a strange sense of humor. He could be quite clever, with his stories and his jokes, but if he thought you held a secret, he'd never stop until he had it out of you. And he thought himself better than the rest of 'em because of his writing."

"It seems to have been common knowledge in this office that you and Mr. Basset were, ah, intimate." Mr. Dodgson winced at the necessity for mentioning the relationship.

"I cannot 'elp what other people may think," Mr. Levin said primly.

"And there was a certain surprise that you had been discharged," Mr. Dodgson went on, ignoring Mr. Levin's interruption.

"I was not pleased," Levin said. "He called me Judas and said I was trying to take his place, but I was not!" The last words were an anguished wail.

"I understand that Mr. Peterson tried to intercede for you," Mr. Dodgson said. "That was kind of him."

Levin swallowed hard. "Mr. Peterson could be kind. He and Mr. Basset began at Portman Penny Press together. Mr. Basset told me that he had depended on Mr. Peterson for good stories from the first issue. It's not going to be the same here without him."

Mr. Portman stepped out of the inner office. "Levin, are the presses rolling?"

"Yes, Mr. Portman." The secretary turned to Mr. Dodgson. "If you are quite finished, sir, I believe Mr. Portman wishes to consult me."

He bustled into the office, leaving Mr. Dodgson and Dr. Doyle to check the stairwell again. In the gloom of the darkening sky, the shadows cast by the gaslight danced and flickered. Mr. Dodgson glanced at the lintel, then looked harder. One shadow was missing.

"Dr. Doyle," Mr. Dodgson pulled the young doctor over to the edge of the stairs and pointed. Dr. Doyle looked chagrined.

"It's gone!" Dr. Doyle exclaimed.

"I thought I told you to watch that door carefully," Mr. Dodgson hissed.

"I did, except for the times that I had to let people by," Dr. Doyle protested. "Levin was in and out, and Roberts just ran down. I think he had to fetch some water from the spigot in the yard."

"Levin and Roberts. The two tall men, either of whom might have had reason to kill Basset," Mr. Dodgson muttered to himself. "Come with me, Dr. Doyle. We must find that dagger before someone uses it again!"

The last rays of the setting sun were making their way through the skylight as the two men walked up the stairs and into the artist's studio.

The gas had been lit, but the artist was absent. A glance out the window confirmed that Mr. Roberts was at the spigot, holding a pail under the frigid trickle of water.

"We must work quickly before he returns," Mr. Dodgson stated. Once more he examined the inks, the woodblocks, the acids, and the plates that were ready for the etcher's touch. Dr.

Doyle took on the task of sorting through the pile of papers on the central table.

"Aha!" Dr. Doyle crowed triumphantly.

"You have found it?"

"Right under these proof sheets." Dr. Doyle pointed to the dagger, now clearly seen to be coated with something brownish.

"Roberts is tall and muscular," Mr. Dodgson mused. "He has a violent temper, as we have seen. He disliked Mr. Basset intensely, he had the opportunity to remove the knife from Mr. Basset's desk, and he could have nipped down the stairs in time to stab him. But why, then, should he bludgeon poor Mr. Peterson, who, as far as I can tell, respected his artistic talent and wanted to include him in his latest venture?"

"Of course, someone else could be trying to pin the blame on Roberts," Dr. Doyle pointed out.

"In that case, we have a madman on our hands," Mr. Dodgson said. "Dr. Doyle, I think the time has come to summon the police before this lunatic has the opportunity to move that knife and use it again."

"Let us only hope that Inspector MacRae will have the time to listen to us." Dr. Doyle followed his mentor, determined that he would not fail him again.

Mr. Portman had assembled the staff in his office. Now he beamed at Mr. Dodgson and Dr. Doyle with the enthusiasm of one who has completed his task and is ready to celebrate the event.

"Mr. Dodgson, have you completed your inquiries?"

"I have found the murder weapon," Mr. Dodgson said carefully. "I have examined the evidence and come to certain conclusions. I must have some time to think, Mr. Portman, but I believe I can name the murderer tonight. Perhaps you should inform Inspector Calloway and Inspector MacRae and have them present when I do. And I should like Miss Harvey to be present as well."

Mr. Portman frowned for a moment. "I was going to invite you all to dine at the Press Club, but it would be most improper for Miss Harvey to attend such a party. I do not think her mother would permit it."

"Invite her, too," joked Howarth.

"I suppose I must," Portman said with a sigh. "One can hardly ask a lady to join a party consisting entirely of gentlemen without some sort of chaperon. I know," he decided. "We shall meet at the Café Royal. I shall bespeak one of the private dining rooms. There should be one available tonight since the newspapers will have everyone running for cover."

Mr. Dodgson frowned, then decided that a private room was quite different from the public Grill Room. "I strongly suggest that Mr. Levin should be present as well, since he was here during that fatal afternoon."

"In that case, gentlemen, you are all dismissed for the day," Portman said genially. "I will be waiting for you at the Café Royal at eight o'clock."

"And I sincerely hope that was no idle boast," Dr. Doyle murmured, as the staff of *Youth's Companion* made their ways up the stairs to retrieve their outdoor garments. "Do you really know who killed Mr. Basset and Mr. Peterson?"

"Oh, dear me, yes," Mr. Dodgson said. "The difficulty will be in proving it. Logic, Dr. Doyle, and a careful examination of the evidence will unmask the killer."

CHAPTER 23

As the staff of *Youth's Companion* prepared to celebrate their triumph over adversity, Inspector MacRae faced his counterpart from the City of London Police in one of the few private offices in the newly reconstructed Scotland Yard. The damage done by the Fenian bomb two years previously was still being repaired. Eventually, an entirely new building would be erected next to the old site, but for now the work of the Metropolitan Police had to be done while masons, bricklayers, plasterers, carpenters, and painters were wielding their tools, yelling their opinions of the bobbies, and generally causing havoc.

Inspector MacRae had managed to wangle this cubicle on the strength of his vital role in the defense of the nation in searching out Irish terrorists. Now he scowled over his desk at Inspector Calloway, who had wedged his bulk into a corner of the tiny office, making it even more impossible to move about. MacRae read the sprawling handwriting on the sheets before him carefully, trying to decide if Calloway was really trying to catch the killer of Samuel Basset or if he had already written it off as just another street hooligan out to grab a wallet. He himself had reluctantly come to the conclusion that the interfering scholar from Oxford and his annoying Edinburgh companion were right, and that this was one death he could not lay at the feet of terrorists, much as he would like to. MacRae's innate sense of justice would not let him hang a man for a crime he did not commit. The printer O'Casey may or may not have been a Fenian, but he could not have stuck a knife into the back of Samuel Basset. Neither did he bash in this Peterson fellow's head with a brick, MacRae thought gloomily, as he read Calloway's notes.

Calloway watched the Scotland Yard man peer at the reports through his spectacles and wondered how such a puny specimen had survived as a policeman all these years. In Calloway's opinion, a policeman's duty was to intimidate, and a scrawny bit like this MacRae would never deter a lawbreaker. As for MacRae's obsession with Irish terrorists, that was all nonsense. Calloway's grandfather had come from Belfast, and as far as he was concerned, the Irish could keep their miserable little island.

MacRae put down the papers with a disgusted snort. The autopsy report from one Dr. Angus Ogilvie declared that Samuel Basset had died of a stab wound to the back, which had nicked the renal artery and caused massive internal bleeding. The blow to the head was immaterial. The murderer of Samuel Basset had to have been behind him, ergo, he had to have been one of the people inside the building at 4:45 in the afternoon. Since Oscar Wilde had been at the Café Royal from 4:30 onwards, that eliminated him.

MacRae glanced up at Calloway. The Londoner glared back at him, as if daring him to find anything against procedure in the carefully written reports. According to Inspector Calloway, the City of London Police had conducted the investigation into the murder of Samuel Basset in the manner indicated by regulations. They had searched the premises of *Youth's Companion* in an attempt to find the murder weapon, but no murder weapon had been found. Calloway himself had interviewed the staff of the magazine to no avail. No one would admit to stabbing Samuel Basset, and all of them expressed deep concern at the demise of their dear friend and colleague, David Peterson.

MacRae felt frustrated. Every time he set out to conduct a

proper investigation, he was called away to do something else. He had been on the scene at a murder and had been hauled off to deal with a riot. He had been at Bow Street early to give his evidence, and before he could wind up the case properly, he was sent back to Fleet Street. Before he could delve into the intricacies of the *Youth's Companion* staff and who did or did not wish to remove Mr. Samuel Basset from his position, he had been summoned back to Scotland Yard to direct the action against the latest wave of protesters marching down the Strand towards Trafalgar Square. It meant leaving the investigation in the hands of Inspector Calloway, a galling prospect to Inspector MacRae, who considered the whole notion of a separate police force for a square mile of territory in the heart of the city to be a medieval holdover unworthy of the nineteenth century.

However, he had no choice. In the eyes of the Metropolitan Police, two dead bodies lying in the morgue at St. Bart's were not as important as several thousand live ones shouting slogans and waving cudgels at the windows of the clubs in St. James's Square.

It was into Calloway's huge hands that MacRae had put the case, and those hands seemed to have managed to destroy evidence, let possible suspects slip away, and generally botch the job, in MacRae's estimation.

"Why didn't you question that clerk Levin?" MacRae demanded, as he flipped through the sheets of paper looking for the missing interview.

"I tried," Calloway protested. "Every time I got near 'im, 'e were off wif some errand fer this Portman, wot 'as took over from Basset."

"Hmmm. Portman had rooms with Basset on Baker Street."

"Aye, them two were batchin' it," Calloway said. "But Portman moved out five year since."

"I've been there and had a word with the landlady," MacRae told him, handing him a neatly written report. "It seems that our Mr. Basset had a fancy for young men."

Calloway sniggered. "One of them sort, were 'e? Weren't that feller Wilde seen 'angin' about? Maybe it wos 'im wot slipped the knife inter Basset."

"Oscar Wilde was nowhere near the place when Basset was stabbed," MacRae said with a touch of regret.

"Which were when?"

"We arrived just after five o'clock, and the man had just died, according to Dr. Doyle," MacRae reminded him.

"Doyle? That Scotty wif the big plaid coat?"

MacRae tried to overlook the ethnic reference and continue his summation of the case. "Autopsy report has the knife going in at an acute angle, meaning the killer was much taller than he . . ."

"Or on them stairs," Calloway pointed out. "I don't like to say it, but yon Scotsman were right. It 'ad to be one of them writers inside."

"And now what?" MacRae asked the universe. The universe did not answer. Sergeant Hoskins did, summoning the two of them to attend a general meeting in the chief commissioner's office at the very top of the building.

Chief Inspector Warren shot a warning glance at Inspectors MacRae and Calloway, the last of the inspectors and superintendents to arrive. Chief Commissioner Henderson, the august head of the Metropolitan Police, appointed by Her Majesty herself, was waiting for the group to assemble. Chief Commissioner Henderson was not pleased with them.

Chief Commissioner Henderson had been reading the afternoon newspapers, which were spread out on his desk. He eyed his troops with a steely gaze.

"Do you know what has been going on?" he asked in a deceptively mild tone. "Are you aware of the state into which our city has fallen?" He tapped the newspapers. "According to the *Times,* last night's disturbances were worse than the Chartist riots, a harbinger of things to come, and possibly the next step that will lead to a commune, like Paris in 'Seventy."

"I doubt that, sir," MacRae ventured to say.

It was not a good idea. Henderson turned to see who had spoken.

"Inspector MacRae, Special Branch, sir." MacRae saluted smartly.

"In that case, Inspector MacRae, let me inform you that the

London populace reads the *Times*. They believe the *Times*. And when the *Times* informs the London populace that the police are doing nothing, that is not good news for anyone. Are you aware that certain schools have closed and are sending their pupils home? There was a rumor bruited about that a mob is marching through the Commercial Road to Fleet Street to continue last night's entertainment. The Southwark shopkeepers are boarding up their establishments. I hear the theaters are even canceling tonight's performances."

This, more than anything, struck home. If the theaters were closing, matters must be serious indeed.

"The Metropolitan Police are the officers of the law, but more than that, we are here to keep order," Henderson declared. "I want every available man out on the streets tonight. There is to be another of those rabble-rousing meetings in Trafalgar Square, called for seven this evening. I do not want a repetition of last night's fiasco. There will be no violence!"

"We can't arrest Englishmen for listening to a lot of hot air," someone commented from the back of the crowd. "If these so-cialists or Fair Traders have been given official permission . . ."

"We cannot stop them from speaking," Henderson allowed. "But we can stop them from acting on that speech. There will be no riot tonight, is that understood?"

"Sir," MacRae interrupted the tirade. "Begging your pardon, sir, but Inspector Calloway and I were in the middle of a murder investigation . . ."

"It can wait," Henderson decided. "The man won't be any less dead in twenty-four hours. I have requested assistance from the City of London Police, to bring in extra constables and sergeants to protect South London, while the Metropolitan Police concentrate their attention on this meeting in Trafalgar Square. There are rumors of mobs gathering everywhere, in Bethnal Green and Camden Town, even Kentish Town. I wouldn't be surprised if the artists in Bloomsbury and the, ah, ladies in St. John's Wood were up in arms. I want you all to be ready for anything."

"Yes, sir!" Chief Inspector Warren saluted and turned to his men. "Dismissed!" he ordered. "We will convene in Trafalgar Square!"

The policemen shuffled out of the chief commissioner's office thinking bleakly about another night spent in the cold and fog. MacRae and Calloway trudged down to MacRae's office, where they gathered their reports together and looked at each other in bafflement. For once the two of them were in agreement. Their murder case was being put to the back of the fire just when it was getting interesting.

A uniformed constable poked his head in at the door. "Inspector MacRae? Message for you."

MacRae accepted the folded note, scanned it, then tossed it to Calloway. "And what do you make of that?"

Calloway read aloud, " 'Mr. Nicholas Portman requests your presence at a dinner party at the Café Royal at eight o'clock tonight. Mr. C. Dodgson will speak on the subject of the deaths of Mr. Samuel Basset and Mr. David Peterson.' Is the bloke barmy? Don't 'e know there's a riot on?"

MacRae scowled at the note. "If Mr. Portman wants policemen, he will have to wait in line," he said. The thought of a dinner at the Café Royal reminded him of something else. "Have you had your tea?" MacRae asked his Cockney colleague.

"I 'ave not. Nor 'ave I 'ad me luncheon, barring a bite o' veal and 'am pie bought off a stall in Fleet Street."

"Then we'd best have something now before we're put out on duty again. It's going to be another long, cold night."

MacRae led Calloway to a small pub, where they ordered hot pies and pots of stout and compared notes in relative amity.

"It 'as to be one of 'em, but I'm blasted if I know why," Calloway said between bites.

"I had a look at Basset's personal accounts," MacRae offered. "He'd been buying some men's suiting, but not for himself. Find the fancy boy, I say."

"Shershay ler fammie?" Calloway's French accent was atrocious, but the sense was plain. "Which of 'em were in that office?"

"The Italian with the fancy vest? The artist with all the hair?" MacRae shook his head. "And that other one . . ."

Calloway considered his mental notes. " 'Owarth," he supplied.

"And then there's that secretary or clerk or whatever he is." MacRae scowled.

"Except that 'e's afraid of 'is own shadder." Calloway dismissed them all with a wave of his hand. "Pity we can't mark it down to the mob an' let it go at that."

MacRae shook his head. "That would not be right," he stated. "And that Irish printer didn't do for that fellow Peterson in the Strand either. Nor can we hold Hyndman or Burns responsible for what some lunatic does on their behalf." He sighed and took another bite of steak-and-kidney pie.

"Then wot do we do about it?" Calloway asked.

"We do our duty in Trafalgar Square," MacRae said, throwing coins onto the table. "And then we go back to Fleet Street tomorrow morning and find the murderer. Most murders are solved in the first twenty-four hours, in my experience," he added, as the two men settled themselve into their bowler hats, wrapped scarves around their necks, and set off for another night of coping with the unemployed.

It was dark when the two of them got to Trafalgar Square. Torches had been brought to augment the gaslight. The air was cold and damp, and puffs of steam punctuated the speakers' exhortations as they declared their determination to wrest a decent day's wages from their employers, as well as such luxuries as Sundays off, a week's holiday in the summer, medical attention in case of an accident on the job, and some sort of pension plan for those too old to work.

"Move along there," MacRae ordered. "Sergeant, no more than ten people may listen to any one speaker at any time." The sergeant looked about him. There were ten constables to the right of him and another ten to the left. There were, by this time, several hundred men gathered in the square. Most were dressed in flashy suits of dittos, covered with dramatic greatcoats or overcoats, with a cape or two swirling about for variety. There were few men in workers' corduroys out on the streets this night and fewer in the high collars and sack suits of shop clerks. Those worthy gentlemen had assessed the damage done to their establishments, mopped up what they could, and gone home to avoid the mobs rumored to be descending once again on the West End.

The sergeant looked at MacRae again. "Move them off, sir?"

MacRae's Glasgow burr sharpened. "Did ye no hear me? Move them off!"

The sergeant squared his shoulders and prepared to do his duty. "Move off, then," he ordered.

The men with the banners paid no attention to him. The men with the capes flung them back to reveal stout clubs and coshes.

"I said, 'op it!" The sergeant raised his baton.

"We are doing no 'arm," the speaker called out. "We 'ave grievances, and we will be 'eard! The bosses, the capitalists, those who sit in the 'alls of power will listen to the voice of the masses!"

A full-throated roar of approval punctuated the statement.

MacRae squared his shoulders. It was going to be another long night. "The Riot Act was read last night," he told the speaker. "It is still in effect. You may have permission for a meeting, but it will be held with order!"

"Riot Act or no, we will be heard!"

The blue-clad policemen moved forward. So did the crowd.

In a moment, the scene changed from one of wary confrontation to one of armed conflict. Clubs and batons were used with vicious abandon. The slushy remains of the previous night's snow made for treacherous footing, and one man went down, shouting that he'd been murdered.

MacRae's troops were outnumbered. The police fell back, while the protesters surged forward, banners waving, towards the clubs in the rarified sector of London.

They were met by a second squad, batons at the ready and Black Marias open to haul away those who could not escape.

MacRae watched with satisfaction as the organized protesters deteriorated into another mob. He had always known that London held the scum of the earth and here was proof of it. Clearing this lot away would be jam, he thought, as the Metropolitan Police fought the good fight, and the police vans carried load after load of protesters to the Bow Street Police Station.

From the windows of the clubs, restaurants, and hotels, reporters looked on the scene and scribbled their cryptic notes. These would be conveyed back to the night editors to be rewritten into workmanlike journalese. The morning editors would carry the news to all corners of London: The Masses Are on the March!

The echoes of the second riot in Trafalgar Square did not reach as far as the outer boroughs of London, where the staff of *Youth's Companion* were preparing for their victory dinner.

In the flat above the Ristorante Monteverde in Saffron Hill, Roberto donned his most decorative waistcoat and preened before a mirror, while his mother urged him not to venture out when the armed mobs were ready to attack and his father demanded that he discover as many of the secrets of the Café Royal kitchens as he could.

In Pimlico, Winslow Howarth unearthed his dress suit, last worn at the wedding of his two dearest friends, David and Myrna Peterson, and informed Post-Office Polly that she must be a good girl and wait until he came home from Regent Street before she could get her nightly walk.

In Bloomsbury, Edgar Roberts shrugged himself into his least objectionable velvet jacket, soft shirt, and loosely tied cravat, and smirked at the preliminary sketches he had made while Miss Helen Harvey had been working at the office. With or without her approval, he was going to get his Queen Mab on canvas!

In their rooms off King's Road, Miss Helen Harvey shook out her only silk dress and prepared for a night of festivity.

"You cannot possibly attend a dinner at the Café Royal," Mrs. Harvey stated flatly. "The place is notorious. What your father would say . . ."

"If he were alive, he would be the first to accept the invitation," Helen said. "And you will note, Mother, that you are included in the invitation. Mr. Portman is not totally lost to propriety."

"I cannot go. I am ill." Mrs. Harvey coughed delicately into her handkerchief to prove it.

"Then I will go alone," her rebellious daughter said with a decided toss of her head.

"Helen! Think of your reputation!"

"Mother, I am nearly twenty-five. I am as good as an old maid. I am not in society, and the few friends we have left will hardly be shocked to learn that I have dined with a party of gentlemen at a public restaurant."

"In a private room!" Mrs. Harvey reminded her.

"Precisely," Helen said. "I've already decided. With you or without you, Mother, I am going to the Café Royal!"

At the Press Club, Mr. Dodgson fussed about, muttering to himself. He had not expected to spend one night in London, let alone two. He had not expected to dine in public, even in a private room, and certainly not at the Café Royal. He felt uncomfortable in his borrowed dress suit and said so.

Dr. Doyle was more sanguine. "I only wish Touie were here," he said. "I must tell her all about it when I get back to Southsea. She will be so disappointed to have missed our adventure."

"I would have preferred to do without it," Mr. Dodgson said. "This is a dreadful business. I am truly sorry to have dragged you into it."

"I'm not," Dr. Doyle said with a gleeful grin. "I've been speaking with some of the gentlemen downstairs. There's a wild chap downstairs, an Irishman named Shaw, who's got the most unusual views. And I believe you mentioned the collector of folklore, Mr. Lang . . ."

"Is he here? I thought he belonged to the Athenaeum." Mr. Dodgson fiddled with his cravat.

"He was very interested in my idea for a historical novel," Dr. Doyle went on, oblivious to his older companion's disinterest.

"Indeed." Mr. Dodgson had completed his toilet and now faced Dr. Doyle. "I believe I am dressed for dinner, Dr. Doyle."

Dr. Doyle agreed. "And are you ready to reveal the name of the murderer, sir?"

Mr. Dodgson nodded. "Oh, that is quite obvious. Almost elementary. The difficulty will be in proving it to the satisfaction of the police."

"I am sure you will be able to do it," Dr. Doyle said, as the two men prepared to meet their colleagues in the lounge below.

"And then," Mr. Dodgson continued, as they descended the stairs, "we can both return to our homes and our own work."

CHAPTER 24

The threat of mob violence may have led some of the hotels and restaurants in the West End to bar their doors and shutter their windows, but the Café Royal remained open for business. Mr. Daniel Nichols, the determinedly royalist émigré who owned the Café Royal, had staunchly refused to give in to the *canailles* who rampaged in Trafalgar Square. He had decided that the Café Royal would remain open, defiantly and aristocratically, until he was carted off in a tumbril!

His patrons had other ideas. They were not so willing as their host to lay down their lives in defense of good living. For the first time in many months there were tables to spare in the Grill Room, and private rooms were available upstairs. It was with great delight, therefore, that Mr. Nichols was able to accommodate Mr. Nicholas Portman in his sudden request for a small private room and dinner for a party of ten that would include two ladies. Accordingly, a small room was prepared, and the chef was alerted. The dinner would be arranged, and Mr. Portman would be pleased.

Mr. Portman had been to some pains to see to it that his female guests should not be put to the necessity of finding a cab in Chelsea. The Portman carriage had been dispatched to fetch Miss Harvey and her redoubtable mother to the Café Royal, while he waited with Mr. Dodgson and Dr. Doyle at the Press Club. There they stood in the lounge, discussing the events of the day and deploring the violence of the previous night, until Norwich entered with the expected message.

"Mr. Portman," the superior butler informed him, "the carriage has arrived."

"Good!" Mr. Portman gathered his two guests and herded them away from the rest of the gentlemen in the lounge. "We shall dine capitally at the Café Royal." He peered into the carriage. There was only one other occupant.

"Miss Harvey?" He checked again. "Where is your mother? I made certain to ask her to join us."

Miss Harvey's face could not be seen in the darkness of the carriage, but her voice had an edge to it as she replied, "Mother would not come out in this weather."

"I am surprised that you would attend a dinner at which you are the only lady," Mr. Dodgson said, hesitating at the carriage door.

"I have been the only female in male company before," Miss Harvey reminded him. "My father was used to having several students, young men who enjoyed his company and conversation, who would meet of a Sunday afternoon. I was often allowed to participate in the gathering."

"I see." Mr. Dodgson edged into the carriage and took the seat opposite her, with Dr. Doyle next to him, leaving Mr. Portman the honor of sitting next to Miss Harvey.

Thomas made his way carefully around the crowds gathering in Pall Mall and skirted Trafalgar Square, muttering to himself about the foolishness of his master's whim to dine out on this of all nights. Mr. Dodgson peered out through the fog at the gathering mob, while Mr. Portman chattered amiably with Miss Harvey, and Dr. Doyle drank in the excitement of the moment.

The doorman at the Café Royal was always ready to turn the great revolving door for a party of three gentlemen and a lady, all in evening dress. He was, however, less cordial to the tall man in artistic dishabille and the man in the frock coat and florid vest who accosted the larger party just as they were coming in the door.

"Mr. Roberts, Mr. Monteverde," Mr. Portman greeted them with a cheerful wave of his hand that indicated that here were persons to be allowed into the lobby with the rest of his guests. "I see you managed to find the place."

"Hard to miss it," Roberts said. He looked lost without his ever-present sketchpad and pencil.

Monteverde assessed the establishment with a practiced eye. "A little overdone, but not bad," he pronounced.

The revolving door turned once more. Mr. Howarth had arrived, looking somewhat harried. "Have you seen the crowds in Trafalgar Square?" he demanded. "It was all I could do to get the cab to go through them."

"Oh dear," Mr. Dodgson fussed, "I sincerely hope we will not have a repetition of last night's disturbance."

"And I hope we can find Inspector MacRae if we need him," Dr. Doyle muttered.

"I sent the good Inspectors MacRae and Calloway invitations to our dinner," Mr. Portman said genially. "However, under the circumstances, I will not hold it against them if they do not attend. Their duties may take them elsewhere tonight."

A scuffle at the door drew their attention. "I thought I told you lot to hop it!" The doorman tried to thrust Mr. Levin, resplendent in a brand-new evening suit, back through the door and into the crowd of youths in loud check suits and slightly shabby dress coats who persisted in hanging about in the street outside.

"Levin!" Mr. Portman protested. "Hi, doorman, that's my secretary you have there! Let him in!"

Mr. Levin turned the revolving door once more to place himself firmly in the lobby, with all the aplomb of one who knows he is an invited guest and not an interloper. He rubbed his hands together and looked at the rest of the party in anticipation of the evening's entertainment. "I thought I'd be late," he said with a gasp for air. "I see we're all here."

"Except for Miss Harvey's mother, who was indisposed," Mr.

Portman said. "And the policemen, who are otherwise occupied."

Levin's face turned pale, leaving two red patches on his cheeks as if they had been painted on. "I was not aware that any policemen would be joining us," he murmured.

"And Oscar's in the Grill Room, but he said he'd look in," Portman went on carelessly, as one of the page boys approached to relieve them of their overcoats, which were taken off, to be stored carefully against their owners' return. Miss Harvey's gray cloak was removed to reveal her evening dress of half-mourning, a pearl gray silk with a modestly high neckline and elbow-length sleeves, trimmed with silver braid caught up with black beads. Another of the page boys arrived to lead the group up the magnificent staircase, down the halls, and to the small room that had been assigned to them.

As they started the procession up the stairs, Oscar Wilde emerged from the Grill Room looking thoroughly upset in spite of the elegance of his evening dress, complete with green carnation thrust through his buttonhole.

"I'm so glad you're here, Nicky," he said, sailing through the lobby like a ship in full steam. "That old f——." he noticed Miss Harvey and amended his statement.

"That old fright, Whistler, has gone his length. I knew he was jealous of my genius, but he has no right to be disgusting about it." Wilde fairly quivered with indignation.

"Disgusting?" Portman echoed.

"He just said that I had regurgitated his thoughts and placed them before the public as if they had been original!" Wilde's face twisted in revulsion at the imagery.

"Oh dear," Mr. Dodgson murmured. It seemed inadequate to the occasion.

"I shall not sit in that man's company," Wilde decided. "I shall dine with you instead."

"I thought you were going to your wife's tea party," Dr. Doyle said, as they followed the page boy up two pairs of stairs to one of the small rooms on the upper floors of the building, where intimate parties could be held in comparative secrecy.

"I did. I was polite to Constance's friends, all of whom are crashing bores, with little to say and a great many words to say it in. I then dressed and told her that I had a very important dinner engagement and not to wait up for me," Wilde said with an expansive smile that included Miss Harvey and Mr. Levin, who was lagging behind the rest of the crowd.

"How fortunate that Mrs. Harvey could not join us," Mr. Portman said. "We have a spare place at the table for you, Oscar."

"Oh, there's always a place at the table for me," Wilde said with another of his expansive gestures.

"Right 'ere, sir." The page boy indicated the door and allowed the dinner party to pass through. The private rooms at the Café Royal echoed the luxury of the more public rooms downstairs. The table was of the best mahogany; the chairs were comfortably upholstered; the table linen was of the finest; and the table settings were discreetly elegant. The service was equally discreet. Woe to the waiter who even breathed a hint of what he had seen or heard in one of the private rooms at the Café Royal! He would shortly find himself without a position and effectively blackballed by every elegant establishment in London, forced to retreat to the bywaters of Birmingham or Manchester.

The dinner party for *Youth's Companion* might not have matched that for *Punch* in wit, but the conversation was kept going by Oscar Wilde, whose sallies had the rest of the company laughing through the various courses. True to his democratic sentiments, Mr. Portman had requested a round table, so that there was no distinct head or foot. Nevertheless, there was a certain air of precedence. Mr. Portman sat facing the door, with Miss Harvey at one hand and Oscar Wilde on the other. Mr. Roberts sat next to Miss Harvey, with Mr. Howarth next to him. Mr. Dodgson had the place next to Mr. Wilde, while Mr. Levin had his back to the door, between Mr. Monteverde and Dr. Doyle.

The dinner was as delectable as expected. Mr. Dodgson devoted his attention to it, while the rest chattered happily, forgetting both Samuel Basset and David Peterson until the cloth had been cleared and the fruit and cheese set out. Then Miss Harvey attempted to rise, as the sole female in the group, and do her social duty.

"I must thank you, Mr. Portman, for the opportunity to enjoy an evening out," she said. "But I know that you gentlemen are probably about to smoke and drink port, and while I may be in your company for dinner, I really must leave you to it."

"Miss Harvey," Mr. Dodgson said, "we are not going to smoke or drink port. It is quite imperative that you remain at this table until I have finished speaking."

Miss Harvey looked surprised but resumed her seat. Whatever call of nature would take her out of the room would simply have to wait. When Mr. Dodgson spoke, it behooved her to listen.

"Mr. Portman, last night you requested that I discover what had happened to your dear friend Samuel Basset," the scholar went on, as Miss Harvey's brows went up in a quizzical stare. "I have a certain hypothesis to put before you all. To do that, I must have present all who were in the offices of *Youth's Companion* yesterday."

"That excludes me," Wilde said with a wave of his hand.

"On the contrary, Mr. Wilde. You have a certain knack for observation," Mr. Dodgson told him. "And you were in the office for a small time."

"May I also be excused?" Levin asked. He had sat silent during dinner, conscious of his ambiguous place at the table.

"Oh no," Mr. Dodgson said, at his most professorial. "Mr. Levin, I insist that you remain here until I have finished. Your testimony will be most necessary before this business is finished."

Levin sank into his seat, his dark eyes fixed on Mr. Dodgson's face.

Mr. Dodgson took a deep breath and turned to Mr. Portman. "Last night there were two deaths," he stated. "One was that of Mr. Samuel Basset. The other was that of Mr. David Peterson. Both were perpetrated by the same person."

"Are you certain?" Monteverde asked. "I thought that policeman said that David had been set upon by the mob last night."

"That is what we were supposed to think," Mr. Dodgson said. "But as I shall demonstrate, that is not the case.

"Mr. Basset had been upset when Dr. Doyle and I saw him. He had been very unjust to Mr. Wilde . . ."

Wilde waved his hand in dismissal. "It was only to be expected," he said grandly. "I shall soon find a position, one way or another."

". . . and to my friend Dr. Doyle," Mr. Dodgson ignored the interruption. "He dismissed Miss Potter's work out of hand. He also insulted his own staff and revealed that he had stolen an idea from his chief writer, who was one of his few friends from his youth. One would think that Mr. Basset would have had more sense."

Mr. Dodgson took a sip from his water glass and continued. "As I understand it, Mr. Basset left the offices at four forty-five to attend his regular meeting with Mr. Portman, leaving Mr. Levin to lock up."

"That is correct," Levin said.

"But you took it upon yourself to allow the rest of the staff to leave an hour early," Mr. Dodgson said. "Considering that you had just been, as Mr. Howarth said, sacked, was that not somewhat presumptuous?"

"Mr. Peterson had told me that he'd see me right," Levin protested.

"Ah yes, Mr. Peterson." Mr. Dodgson sighed. "He had gone up the stairs to Mr. Roberts's attic studio to look over the illustrations for the next issue. Mr. Howarth was downstairs." He tactfully did not say why. "Mr. Monteverde was also upstairs at his own desk. You, Miss Harvey, were alone in the office."

"Yes, I was." Miss Harvey looked around as the rest of them stared at her. "Well, I couldn't very well leave until I had my money," she exclaimed.

"Indeed. Now, I must ask you a very important question, Miss Harvey. What did you hear while you were alone in that office?" Mr. Dodgson's eyes were no longer those of a mild gentleman who delighted little girls. He was now the churchman, the deacon, ferreting out sin.

Miss Harvey thought hard. "I heard Mr. Levin and Mr. Basset going down the stairs," she said carefully. "Then I heard the noise in the street. That man shouting about something . . . you could scarcely miss it. And people shouting back at him."

"Hyndman," Dr. Doyle said, with a nod. "Inciting the likes of O'Casey to riot and rebellion."

"And what else?" Mr. Dodgson persisted.

Miss Harvey frowned in concentration. "It's hard to tell," she said at last. "Between the wind outside, and that man, and the crowd . . . ," she ended in confusion. "I thought I heard some sort of argument, but I couldn't tell you whether it came from outside or inside the building."

Mr. Dodgson nodded. "That is what I thought. Mr. Basset was stabbed as he stood in the vestibule with the door open. The murderer was standing behind him with one of the knives taken from Mr. Basset's own desk.

"The murderer did not know that he had not killed Mr. Basset outright. He had to find a place for the knife, and he heard a sound behind him, so he placed it where he was certain no one would find it, to wit, on the lintel over the doorway."

"What? Up there?" Portman exclaimed.

"A most precarious spot," Mr. Dodgson agreed. "Very much in the manner of Mr. Poe, hiding it in plain sight, as it were."

"He'd have to be tall," Howarth said.

"With long arms," Monteverde added, conscious that he and his friend were now excluded from the list of suspects. They stared at Roberts, who scowled back at them.

"Yes. Well," Mr. Dodgson sipped more water. "What our murderer did not know then was that someone was coming down the stairs at that moment. Mr. David Peterson was returning to his own office to retrieve his outer wraps and perhaps, to, er . . ."

"Have a snort," Howarth said. "Oh, well, it doesn't matter now. The poor chap's dead."

"He is indeed." Mr. Dodgson sighed. "Because, you see, he did not realize what he had seen."

"Which was . . . ?" Howarth asked, intrigued.

"The back of a tall man with his hand upon the lintel," Mr.

Dodgson said. "It was not until much later, perhaps after he had had another drink or two, that he understood what that position must have meant. And, as ill-luck would have it, he met that very person, who had had an errand that brought him into the Strand, as he was making his way home. I can only surmise that Mr. Peterson took the opportunity to twit the other man, indicating that he knew what had been done, and that he could identify Mr. Basset's murderer."

Portman's expression became distinctly unfriendly. "So this murderer of yours bashed Peterson with a brick to keep him quiet?"

"Oh yes," Mr. Dodgson said. "And now, Mr. Levin, I think you should tell us the answer to Mr. Basset's question. I know why you killed Mr. Peterson. He had seen you with your hand on the upper lintel when you put the knife there. He taxed you with it in the Strand during the riot, and you hit him with whatever you found to hand. But Mr. Basset had befriended you. He had dined with you. He had taken you out of the slums of Whitechapel and given you a position. Why did you kill him?"

"I?" Levin stood up on shaky legs and stared around the room. Howarth and Monteverde stared back. He got no more help from Roberts, while Miss Harvey's expression was one of dismay tinged with horror.

"Why should I kill him? He was my employer, nothing more!"

"Nothing more?" Mr. Dodgson repeated. "When you were seen dining with him here at the Café Royal?"

Wilde regarded Levin carefully. "Of course!" Wilde looked around at Portman. "That's where I saw him! You're one of Ernie's friends!"

"I'm sure you're mistaken." Levin edged closer to the door.

"I seldom forget a face, especially not one so very handsome as yours." Wilde turned to the rest of the company. "I'd been dining with Whistler, and he pointed out Basset and this young fellow off in a corner, and made some remark about young sprouts and old shoots."

Roberts regarded Levin with contempt. "I turned him down," he said pointedly.

Levin stood up, eyes blazing with fury. "It weren't like that!" It was a cry of anguish. "He said he would bring me into the business. 'E told me to wait, and wait, and wait . . . that 'e 'ad to be careful of 'ow we were seen together . . ." Levin's accent was pure Whitechapel by now. " 'E told me 'e'd see me right, but 'e never did! 'E used me! And when I tried to do something on my own, 'e sacked me! Told me to clear out!"

Levin approached Mr. Portman, pleading with every step. "I put it to you, sir, what was I to do? I was facing ruin! I couldn't go back. . . . I wouldn't go back to Petticoat Lane!" He took another step and trod on Miss Harvey's train.

"Mr. Levin, you are tearing my dress!" Miss Harvey tried to pull her skirts aside.

"Your dress! Take that for your dress, you . . ." Levin's voice rose to a shriek, as he roughly grabbed Miss Harvey by the shoulders and shook her violently. "You don't belong here! Sammy wouldn't never allow a female to take my place! Why didn't you stay home where you belong!" Miss Harvey shrieked as Levin threw her against the wall and stepped forward again.

Mr. Portman rose to defend himself. Roberts and Monteverde tried to block Levin's path, while Howarth ran to help Miss Harvey. The room seemed to be too small to hold all the people in it as Levin dodged around the table, scattering chairs in his wake, trying to find the exit in a room that suddenly had none.

Dr. Doyle was caught between the desire to chase the criminal and the necessity of performing his duty as a physician. He bent over Miss Harvey, gently touching her temple where it had connected with the wainscoting of the wall, while Mr. Dodgson tried to make sense of this descent into melodrama.

Howarth and Monteverde moved in on Levin from opposite sides of the table. For a moment there was a confused tussle as the two shorter men tried to hold onto the taller one. Then Levin shook them off, wrenched the door open, and bolted down the hall.

"I'll get him!" Roberts shouted, loping down the hall after Levin.

Dr. Doyle made a quick assessment of the situation. "Miss

Harvey is not badly hurt," he pronounced. "She appears to me more shaken than bruised."

Mr. Dodgson looked thoroughly shaken as well. "I blame myself," he whispered.

"Nonsense," Portman told him. "None of us suspected that Levin, of all people . . ."

"I suspected him," Mr. Dodgson said miserably.

"He can't have gotten far," Monteverde said. "Eddie's after him."

"I think you had best send for your carriage, Mr. Portman, and get Miss Harvey home to her mother," Dr. Doyle decided.

"But what about Levin?" Portman protested.

"Your Mr. Roberts has already gone after him," Mr. Dodgson said. "Mr. Monteverde, Mr. Howarth, please help Dr. Doyle take Miss Harvey downstairs."

"And what will you do, Mr. Dodgson?" Mr. Portman interrupted this flow of instructions.

"I shall consider where Mr. Levin might find refuge and inform the police so that they may capture him before that unhappy young man kills someone else."

CHAPTER 25

W hen he ran out of the room, Levin tried to get his bearings. The private rooms of the Café Royal were on the third story, along a corridor that led to the grand staircase at one end.

Levin looked down the corridor, seeing nothing but closed doors and electric light fixtures. Behind him he could hear the rest of the party tripping over chairs and each other in their haste to get to him. Ahead of him lay freedom . . . but where?

For a moment he forgot about escape in his indignation at the treachery of the woman. Helen Harvey! It was just as his mother had told him. Women were no good! He had only meant to be kind, to make the magazine better, and see what it had got him! That little minx! Trying to take his position with Nicky Portman, doing his work! *He never should have let her into the office,* Levin thought. It was all of a piece! Just because he wanted to improve himself, get out of Whitechapel, away from the crowd that hung about the doors of the Café Royal . . .

He looked about, his eyes darting here and there. Somewhere along this corridor was a private stair, used by the staff as they brought food up and took away the dirty dishes. He knew all about it, had even used it once or twice before Sammy Basset had taken him in. . . . Ha! Taken him in! If he had the time, he would laugh about that. Basset had taken him in all right; made him into a drudge, used him, and not given him the position he'd been promised. Oh, there had been a few perks, a new suit or two, and a dinner at the Café Royal, but what of that? He could have had that if he'd stayed with Bert and Ern and the rest of that lot.

He had wanted more. He had wanted to rise, to be respectable, to be deferred to like Sammy Basset. He had wanted authority, power even. Sammy wouldn't let him do anything, not read contributions or ask for them, not even correct the proofs. Sammy had the power, and Levin wanted it; and when he tried to take what he deserved, what did he get? The sack! Thrown out after all he'd done!

Levin heard the door open behind him. He looked back and saw Eddie Roberts, his face set in lines of grim determination, hands ready to wring the neck of one Andrew Levin.

Levin sought some hiding place, trying each door in the corridor. Two doors were locked. *No parties in those rooms tonight,* Levin thought. He opened two more doors. One room held a man and a woman in a fond embrace; the woman shrieked, the man swore loudly, and Levin backed away. Another held two men too busy to notice an intruder. Levin closed the door quickly and quietly, breathing hard and trying to forget that he might have been in the same position at one time.

Levin headed for the grand staircase, then backed away. Roberts must have summoned reinforcements. Two large and muscular waiters had mounted the staircase at the end of the hall, cutting off Levin's escape. Roberts was closing in, and the Scottish doctor, Doyle, had come out of the room and was heading towards them. Levin thrust a hand out. . . . Aha! The service stairs! He bolted through the door set into the woodwork of the hallway, papered over, and nearly invisible to any but those who had free access to the back passages of the Café Royal.

Behind him, Roberts shouted, "He's here!"

Monteverde and Howarth followed Roberts and Levin down the service stairs. Dr. Doyle joined the chase, leaving his patient in the hands of Mr. Dodgson and Mr. Portman.

The stairs wound down behind the dining rooms, leading into the kitchens, where the cooking stoves were full and the chefs were concocting the delectable dishes for which the Café Royal was famous. The room was full of steam and fury, bubbling out of pots and chefs in equal measure. The table in the middle of the room held the remains of vegetables, scraps of meat, even odds and ends of pastry shells and fruit. Tables near the swinging doors that led into the public dining rooms held trays full of covered dishes, waiting to be delivered to the tables of the celebrated diners at the Café Royal.

Levin's arrival went unnoticed at first in the hurly-burly of the kitchen. Sous-chefs were working madly, waiters were dashing here and there, while assistants were waving various implements, and the master chef swore loudly at all of them. There was a veritable Babel of epithets when Levin burst into the kitchen, thrashing his arms madly, with the rest of the *Youth's Companion* staff in hot pursuit.

Levin dodged here and there, scattering the kitchen staff in his panic. He blundered against a table where one of the underlings was chopping vegetables, sending a cascade of greenery onto the floor and under the feet of his pursuers. He dodged around a table filled with elaborate pastry, crashed into a waiter bringing in a load of dishes, and fairly flew into the dining room.

The rest of the *Youth's Companion* staff followed Levin through the kitchen, sliding on the remains of lettuce and spinach, splashing through the ruined pastries and stumbling over the broken crockery, muttering apologies as their progress was marked with crashes of chinaware, clashes of pans, and loud curses in three languages.

Levin's departure from the kitchen had led into the Grill Room. The hum of conversation was disturbed by the entrance of one overwrought young man being chased by four more, all of them spattered by whipped cream, vegetables, and béchamel sauce.

Levin dodged around the tables as Monteverde and Howarth tried to corner him. Waiters converged upon him from three corners of the room, but Levin wriggled around them, leaving Monteverde and Howarth to apologize to the diners whose dinners they had interrupted. The elegant Mr. Whistler shouted in exasperation as the chase interrupted one of his best witticisms. Two young men from the provinces yelled, "Tally-ho!"

Dr. Doyle yelled out, "He's getting away!" and pointed at the door to the lobby. Dr. Doyle and Mr. Roberts charged after Levin, past the affronted headwaiter and into the lobby. "Stop him!" Dr. Doyle gasped out, waving madly at the doorman, who put himself directly in the path of the fugitive.

Levin looked wildly about the lobby, breathing hard. A gentleman in the dress uniform of Her Majesty's Navy and his highly painted female friend were being let into the Café Royal just as two gentlemen in evening dress and two ladies in cloaks were trying to leave. Levin sized up the situation, while Dr. Doyle and his cohorts regrouped. Then Levin dashed for the door as the naval gentleman removed his cape.

Levin was caught in the folds of the cape. The doorman struggled to seize him, while the naval officer yanked at the enveloping cape. Levin writhed out of the cape and wriggled into the revolving door, leaving the naval officer to air his nautical vocabulary and the doorman to face the pursuers.

"Call the police," Dr. Doyle gasped out, as Mr. Roberts and the rest tried to maneuver their way outside, where the crowd waited on Regent Street.

" 'Ere, wot's the matter?" someone asked, as Levin dashed past.

"Stop him!" Dr. Doyle called out, as he emerged from the revolving door.

"Wot's 'e done?" That was Ern, the young man with the smoldering eyes and dark curls, apparently waiting for someone to invite him to dine inside.

"Killed two men, and just tried for another," Roberts said breathlessly.

"Cor!" Ern exclaimed.

"Walk-er!" Bert chimed in.

"Somebody call the police!" Howarth yelled, as the group tried to locate Levin in the crowd.

"They're all at Trafalgar Square!" Ern yelled back. "Wot d'ye think, Bert?"

"I think our Aaron's done it this time," Bert said. "We better go after 'im, afore 'e does any more damage." They joined in the chase, leaving any hope of an evening's entertainment behind them.

The fog was now drifting in patches, settling back over the streets. Howarth and Monteverde clutched each other, gasping for breath.

"Not as . . . fit . . . as I used to be," Howarth confessed.

"Get back to the Café Royal and tell Mr. Portman that Levin's headed for Trafalgar Square," Dr. Doyle told them. "Mr. Roberts and I will try to find him."

"Good luck!" Monteverde said. "You'd think people would stay indoors in this fog!"

"Not bloody likely," Roberts swore. He peered through the murk, then pointed to a tall man well ahead of them. "There he is! Come on, Doyle! With all these folk about, he'll have to stop, and we'll have him then!"

Dr. Doyle joined Mr. Roberts as Howarth and Monteverde made their way back to the Café Royal with the news that Dr. Doyle and Mr. Roberts were after Levin and there was another mob out in Trafalgar Square.

By that time Levin had reached Piccadilly and was casting about looking for somewhere to run. Dr. Doyle pointed him out to Mr. Roberts.

"We've got to stop him before he reaches Trafalgar Square," he panted. "He'll be able to lose himself in that mob."

Roberts's face was set in lines of grim determination. "That little bastard killed David," he rasped out. "I found the knife he stuck old Basset with in my papers. Try to frame me, will he?"

The fog had settled in over London, turning the gaslights to mere blobs of luminescence and nearly drowning the torches carried by the protesters in Trafalgar Square. There was barely enough visibility to make out some sort of torchlight procession winding its way up Fleet Street and through the Strand towards the square.

Dr. Doyle and Mr. Roberts joined the press of people that had taken possession of Trafalgar Square. Their quarry had been swallowed up in the mass of bodies. Nevertheless, the two men pressed forward, following the rest of the crowd into Trafalgar Square, where the fog swirled and eddied around the speakers, the listeners, and the police, while omnibuses, cabs, and carriages tried to make their way through the crowd and into the West End.

The mood of the gathering had changed. The most violent of the protesters had been hauled off to Bow Street to face the magistrate in the morning. Now Tom Mann, the leader of the Fair Trade League, could finally make his official plea for more work, and make it he did, at great length, while the torchlight procession came closer.

"Isn't that Inspector MacRae?" Dr. Doyle recognized the small, spare figure in the long overcoat.

"Something's happening," Roberts observed, pushing forward towards the line of policemen, who were forcing a passage for the procession through the crowd by the simple act of poking anyone who got in their way with their batons. Dr. Doyle and Mr. Roberts were in the front rank as the police shoved them aside to make way for the procession. They could only stare helplessly across the passageway made by the City of London Police, as Levin stared back, unable to move through the crowd that pressed in on him from behind.

The parade was led by a stout man in the anachronistic garb of a beadle of the previous century, complete with knee breeches, velvet coat, and cocked hat. He was followed by two smaller men in the magnificent robes of the aldermen of the City of London.

"We can't get through this," Dr. Doyle fumed, as the larger of the two aldermen mounted one of the soapboxes and roared out, "My good people!"

This was greeted with jeers and catcalls and cries of, "Let 'im speak!"

"We have good news for you!"

More jeers, more catcalls. "I wish he'd get on with it!" Roberts tried to get around the large policeman in front of him and was blocked off with a well-placed shove to the shoulder.

"Let 'Is Honor speak!" the constable ordered, as Dr. Doyle and

Mr. Roberts watched Levin, and Levin stared helplessly at them.

"It will be in tomorrow's newspapers." There was a general muttering and a respectful silence, so that the alderman's voice could ring out across the square. The reporters in the crowd reached for their pads and pencils. Something was in the wind, and each of them wanted to be the first with the story.

"The people of London have responded to the distress of the poor," the alderman announced. "We have been receiving donations all day from all sorts of our citizens. Some of the members of Parliament contributed a subscription for the relief of the indigent . . ."

"And not before needed!" someone in the crowd shouted, echoed by similar sentiments.

The alderman raised his hand for silence. "If you please!" He cleared his throat and continued, "Thanks to the generosity of the populace, the Lord Mayor's Fund has tripled in the last twenty-four hours."

There was a general cheer at this news. The alderman went on: "Therefore, the City of London, in collaboration with the councils of the City of Westminster and the other boroughs of London, will be able to offer work to any able-bodied man who desires it. Be at the Guildhall tomorrow morning at eight o'clock."

"Wot sort o' work?" someone in the crowd wanted to know.

"The recent fall of snow and the, er, disturbances have left the streets blocked with mud and, er, other things," the alderman explained. "Any man who reports for street-cleaning duty at the Guildhall tomorrow morning will receive a shilling for the day, with the promise of more if the man is married with children dependent upon him."

There was a general cheer. Suddenly the mood of the crowd changed from sullen anger to jubilation. They had gotten what they wanted. Work would be forthcoming, and spring was right around the corner.

None of this made any difference to the miserable Levin. He was trapped in the crowd, unable to break out of the press of people around him.

"Let us through!" Dr. Doyle ordered the constable in front of him. "We have important information for Inspector MacRae of the Metropolitan Police!"

"Do you now?" The constable looked the two of them over. Robert's artistic velveteen jacket was covered with the remains of their excursion into the Café Royal's kitchens. Dr. Doyle's evening clothes looked battered, in more ways than one. Neither of them wore overcoats or hats.

"Wot's your business with Inspector MacRae?" the constable asked, certain that two such vagabonds were up to no good.

"We've got information about the murderer of Samuel Basset," Dr. Doyle said.

"He's right there!" Mr. Roberts pointed to Levin. Levin turned and tried to work his way through the crowd.

Dr. Doyle did not wait for the constable to answer. He darted across the aisle, right in front of the astonished alderman, shouting, "Levin! Give it up!"

Levin scrambled through the crowd with Dr. Doyle behind him. The protesters protested as their toes were trampled and they were roughly shoved out of the path of the fugitive.

"That man's a killer!" Dr. Doyle shouted, plunging after Levin.

Roberts wasted no time in dodging through the crowd. He made a quick calculation and headed towards the Strand, hoping to cut the fleeing Levin off as he emerged from the crowd.

The aldermen were marching in stately fashion through the path cleared for them by the police, when Levin broke through the line of constables.

"Stop him!" Dr. Doyle gasped.

Levin looked wildly around, saw that he was the center of attention, and dashed through the line of policemen towards the carriages ranged at the Strand.

"Who's that man?"

"Wot's 'e done?" someone else shouted out.

"He's killed two men," Dr. Doyle told them. The aldermen uttered cries of horror. The constables muttered amongst themselves. The crowd was ready to turn into a mob again. There was a general murmur that grew into a roar as the men in Trafalgar Square moved in on the hunted man. Levin saw the mob and veered eastward, down the Strand, into the fog that was gathering at the Strand end of the square.

The mob surged forward. Levin turned to look behind him, when out of the fog loomed the last omnibus of the night, making its final run before the weary horse headed for its barn.

There was a sickening crunch, a jolt, and a whinny from the horse, which reared and pawed the air in alarm. The heavy hooves landed twice on the body under the wheels of the omnibus.

There was a positive symphony of tweets from the whistles of constables and sergeants of two police forces. Inspectors MacRae and Calloway were drawn away from their attendance on the alderman by the commotion at the Strand. By the time Mr. Roberts and Dr. Doyle arrived, Levin's body had been pulled out from under the horse's feet, and the horrified driver had been taken in hand by Inspectors Calloway and MacRae.

"I swear to you, Inspector, I never saw 'im coming! 'E were right in front o' me . . . ," the driver blubbered.

"That's all right," MacRae soothed the driver. "We saw it all. It's no fault of yours."

Dr. Doyle bent over Levin's broken body. "He's dead," he pronounced. "As for the victim," he glanced at Levin, then faced the policemen, "this man was a fugitive, a murderer fleeing the law."

"Wot's this?" Inspector Calloway rumbled.

"If you had taken the time to attend Mr. Portman's little party, you would have learned that Mr. Levin is the one who killed both Samuel Basset and David Peterson," Dr. Doyle informed him.

Inspector MacRae digested this, then turned to the driver of the omnibus. "We'll need your number, and you'll give a statement to Inspector Calloway here, but you may rest easy, my man."

"You've saved the Crown the cost of a trial and the trouble of 'angin' 'im," Calloway added. "Nasty little bugger. 'Oo would've thought 'e 'ad it in 'im?"

The thought was echoed by Mr. Roberts and Dr. Doyle as they slowly made their way back to the Café Royal.

"Poor Levin," Roberts sighed, as they turned up Regent Street.

"To tell you the truth, Doyle, I didn't think he had the nerve. He must have been desperate."

"There's no excuse for murder," Dr. Doyle declared.

There was a brief note waiting for them at the Café Royal. Dr. Doyle read it as he and Mr. Roberts retrieved the dramatic cloak and balbriggan greatcoat that they had forgotten in their haste to find Levin.

"Mr. Portman has taken Miss Harvey back to her mother," Dr. Doyle told Mr. Roberts. "He says we're all to meet back at the Press Club. He won't like what we have to tell him."

"It'll all be in the newspapers tomorrow," Roberts reminded him, as they hailed what must have been the last cab on Regent Street. "I wonder how your Mr. Dodgson managed to work it all out."

"That," Dr. Doyle told him, as they gave the directions to the cabby, "is what we are going to find out."

CHAPTER 26

Peace had been restored in Trafalgar Square. The protesters had dispersed, jubilant at the announcement that work for street laborers would be forthcoming and aid to the indigent was to be doled out from the Guildhall. The reporters had it all in their notes: the procession, the announcement by the aldermen, and the reaction of the crowds. The odd behavior of the young man who was subsequently run down by the omnibus was dealt with by Inspector MacRae, who issued a modest statement to the effect that the young man had apparently lost his way in the fog and that further information on the sad accident would be forthcoming from Scotland Yard when the young man had been identified. There was no mention of the murder of Samuel Basset.

MacRae and Calloway faced each other in Trafalgar Square as the reporters hustled off to Fleet Street to get their notes to their editors in time for the morning editions. The body of Andrew Levin had been taken off to St. Bart's to join those of Samuel Basset and David Peterson, waiting for inquest.

"Now wot?" Calloway asked hoarsely.

MacRae adjusted his spectacles. "Now we make out our reports," he stated.

"Hullo! Inspector MacRae! Inspector Calloway!"

The two policemen looked around to see who would address them at this hour of the night.

They were beckoned over to a cab that had been stopped at the Whitehall end of the square. Dr. Doyle leaned out the door, the better to see in the fog.

"We're going to the Press Club. Mr. Portman wanted you to be there when Mr. Dodgson explained about Levin," Dr. Doyle said, somewhat incoherently.

MacRae looked at Calloway, then back at Dr. Doyle. "It was you chased that young man under the omnibus," MacRae said sternly.

"I didn't chase him," Dr. Doyle retorted. "He ran. And if one of your constables had done his duty and stopped him, he wouldn't have gotten that far."

"This don't get us nowhere," Calloway said, heaving himself into the cab. "Come on, MacRae. I'd like to 'ear this Oxford perfesser explain 'ow 'e knows wot we don't."

MacRae summoned one of his constables. "Tell the chief inspector that I'm continuing the investigation into the death of Samuel Basset," he said. He turned back to Dr. Doyle. "This is all very irregular," he complained.

Calloway wasted no time. He hauled MacRae into the cab and ordered the cabby to continue to St. James's. "At least we'll be warm and dry," he said. Calloway hoped the gentlemen in the Press Club would be quick about their business so that he could get on home, where his stout wife waited for him with a late supper of cold meat and ale.

MacRae frowned into the darkness. He hated the idea of amateurs meddling in police business, especially when it led to tragedy. He was certain that, given time, he would have been able to collar Levin without loss of life or limb to anyone.

Dr. Doyle sighed to himself and tried to decide if he had actually caused Levin to bolt or if the high-strung young man would have killed someone else if he had not been stopped.

Mr. Roberts tried to visualize the exact angle of Levin's head as he lay on the ground, and the glaze in his eyes. He could use that, perhaps, in another painting . . . Saint George and the Dragon? Or Gawain and the Green Knight?

All ruminations stopped as the cab pulled up to the Press Club. Norwich, the superior butler, led the group to the private elevator. "Mr. Portman is waiting for you, sir," he pronounced, addressing Dr. Doyle, who was clearly the only one of the four who could be considered a gentleman by a respectable butler.

The glum group in Mr. Portman's sitting room was not the same jolly crew that had laughed so heartily over dinner. Mr. Wilde and Mr. Portman sat on one of the long sofas, while Monteverde and Howarth, the two writers, perched unhappily on the other. Mr. Dodgson stood in front of the fire staring into the coals.

"I've brought Inspector Calloway and Inspector MacRae," Dr. Doyle announced, as the two policemen were escorted into the private sitting room, hats in hands, and Mr. Roberts took his favorite position propped up against the mantelpiece. "How is Miss Harvey?"

"I have sent my own doctor around to attend her," Mr. Portman said. "She is a very brave young woman."

"And a very determined one," Mr. Dodgson murmured.

"And where is Levin?" Portman demanded, looking past Mr. Roberts and the two policemen.

" 'E's gone," Calloway said bluntly.

"Gone?" Mr. Dodgson inquired. "Gone where?"

"Gone under an omnibus," Roberts said, tossing his hair back. "He ran right under the horse and was trampled before we could stop him."

There was a hushed silence. Then Mr. Dodgson said serenely, "Perhaps Divine Providence works in mysterious ways. Mr. Levin alive would have been disastrous."

"What do you mean?" Portman's attention was drawn back to the tall scholar who stood before the fire ready to lecture.

"Mr. Levin's relationship to Mr. Basset may have been quite innocent," Mr. Dodgson said. "However, there are other interpretations of their friendship, if one may call it that."

"Friendship?" Wilde's voice rose in pitch. "How can you call a relationship between two souls a mere friendship?"

273

Mr. Dodgson shook his head. "Mr. Wilde, I doubt very much whether Samuel Basset considered Andrew Levin a soul mate."

There was a general hubbub as the rest of the staff of *Youth's Companion* added their own comments to Wilde's.

Portman raised his hands to call for quiet. "Mr. Dodgson," he said, "how did you come to suspect it was Levin who stabbed poor Sammy in the back? And why did he do it?"

"In the first place, I did not suspect Mr. Levin of anything more than intrusiveness," Mr. Dodgson said. "He was officious, but many clerks are. It is sometimes a part of their duties to sift through their employer's letters, to bring those that are important to the attention of a busy man and answer those that are not with a polite but meaningless reply. Mr. Levin, however, had begun to encroach upon Mr. Basset's prerogatives, and this Mr. Basset would never allow."

"How do you mean, 'encroach'?" MacRae asked, notebook at the ready.

"He had written to various well-known authors, myself included, requesting contributions," Mr. Dodgson told him. "You yourself noted a small item from Mr. Stevenson. My friend Harry Furniss had contributed a few illustrations."

Portman looked around at the rest of the staff. "How did Levin think he could get away with it?"

Mr. Dodgson said, "There are no bylines in your publication, Mr. Portman. If one of my small offerings was included on a page, for instance, it might well be attributed to one of the staff writers. The fee for such a contribution may have been taken from the magazine's profits.

"Levin kept the books, of course, and he would have had to deduct the fees paid to contributors. He may well have deducted other sums for his own use. You will have to have one of your own accountants go over the ledgers very carefully, Mr. Portman. And while you are doing so, you might check the cash box."

"Eh?" Portman frowned in confusion.

"Mr. Levin was so insistent that there was no other key to the cash box than the one on Mr. Basset's watch chain that I suspect he might have had one made."

Portman's face grew crimson at the implications of this. "But that would mean that he had access to Sammy's watch chain . . ."

"Which, under normal circumstances, would not be removed in the office," Mr. Dodgson said. "Another indication that the relationship between Mr. Basset and Mr. Levin was one of great, ah, intimacy."

"So Sammy discovered that Levin was corresponding with contributors on his own," Portman said hurriedly, obviously uncomfortable at the public revelations of his friend's private life.

"That was my fault. I deeply regret any harm I may have done," Mr. Dodgson said with painful honesty. "I only wished to assist my friend Doyle by introducing him to some of the people who might take an interest in his work. I may have precipitated events."

"It would have come out sooner or later," Howarth said, consoling the distraught scholar. "And when Basset went over the books, he'd have found out what Levin was up to."

Monteverde shrugged expressively. "But that wouldn't make Levin want to kill the old hound," he objected. "Unless this was more than just the usual lovers' quarrel."

"Surely," Portman said, ignoring the implications of the last remark, "Levin could have found another position."

"But not that one," Mr. Dodgson said. "What Mr. Levin wanted was what Mr. Basset had promised him, without, as my theatrical friends have it, paying one's dues. He wanted the editorial position now, not in twenty years. Young people can be very impulsive." He shook his head sadly.

"You still haven't told us how you worked it all out," Howarth said.

"How did you hit on Levin?" Monteverde added.

"And why did Levin hit poor old Peterson?" Wilde asked.

"Actually, there were two persons in the office who drew my attention." Mr. Dodgson took a deep breath, to control his stammer.

"Two?" Calloway had his own notebook out.

"Mr. Roberts had several grievances against Mr. Basset. He is a man of strong passions with a hot temper. I saw him handle the fatal dagger during the argument in Mr. Basset's office that afternoon. What is more, he was in the Strand that night, he had keys to the building, and he is a tall man with long arms. And to clinch the matter, as my students would say, Dr. Doyle and I found the bloodstained dagger amongst his papers after we interviewed him this afternoon."

"What?" Roberts strode forward, ready to throttle the scholar.

Mr. Portman stepped between them. "Easy on, Roberts." He turned to Mr. Dodgson. "What drew your attention off Roberts and onto Levin?"

"I would have dismissed Mr. Levin as another officious clerk, as I said, except that he seemed to know a great deal more about Mr. Basset than any clerk had a right to know, such as his flat direction on Baker Street. And then, the following day, when Mrs. Peterson came into the office, what was it that Mr. Levin said?" He turned to Dr. Doyle.

"To tell the truth," Dr. Doyle admitted, "I didn't pay much attention to Levin, what with Mrs. Peterson having hysterics."

"I do not hear well, but I certainly heard Mr. Levin remark that Mr. Peterson had been, in his words, 'left in an alley in the snow,'" Mr. Dodgson said. "But the police had not said anything about the particulars of Mr. Peterson's death, and there was nothing about it in the newspapers."

"No need to tell a pack of meddling reporters wot they 'ad no reason to know," Calloway said defensively, reddening under the sudden scrutiny of so many pairs of eyes.

"And then I spoke to Miss Flora Peterson, who is a very clever child." Mr. Dodgson took back the center stage. "She remarked that one cannot be two people. However, it struck me that there are certain persons who hide their true nature, who are indeed two people. Mr. Basset seemed to have a double life. Could not there be another person in that office, someone with a secret to hide?

"As Dr. Doyle and I continued to discover more about Mr. Basset, we kept running into Mr. Levin. He had been known to the people at Toynbee Hall and St. Jude's in Whitechapel. He knew the young men who haunt the Café Royal, and although he had been the one to hire Miss Harvey, as soon as she appeared to make herself at home at the office, he evinced clear signs of jealousy."

"Of Miss Harvey?" Portman exploded.

"Miss Harvey was taking on the position of executive assistant that Mr. Levin considered his own," Mr. Dodgson pointed out. "Whereas you relegated Mr. Levin to the position of errand boy, sending him to fetch and carry."

Portman looked embarrassed. "I couldn't stick him," he admitted. "There was something about him that made me uneasy."

"He was certainly nervous," Mr. Dodgson said. "As well he should have been. He was holding onto his nerves with both hands, as it were."

"And I suppose he was the one who took the animals off the wall in Mr. Basset's office and messed up the papers," Dr. Doyle said. "But why?"

Mr. Dodgson sighed. "Undoubtedly, Mr. Levin removed the mounted heads before he locked up the office for the night in anticipation of taking possession of the office for what he was certain would be his own occupation of the position."

"But that's nonsense," Mr. Portman burst out. "Levin was never even in the running for that position!"

"But he did not know that," Mr. Dodgson went on. "I suspect that one of the reasons he killed Mr. Peterson was because Mr. Peterson made it clear that he, and not Levin, was the most likely prospect for the chair."

"I saw David in the Strand," Roberts said. "I should have said something. . . ."

"I doubt that you could have known what Mr. Levin was about," Mr. Dodgson consoled him. "There is the true tragedy. Like the rest of you, Mr. Peterson thought that Mr. Levin was a person of no account, a worm who had turned but would turn no more. He did not know that Andrew Levin would literally do anything to gain what he thought he had earned through his, ah, relationship with Mr. Basset.

"It was bad enough that he should stab his benefactor, but to destroy a man with whom he had worked for several years, a man with children . . . I am only sorry that he will not hang. Divine Providence has taken that responsibility from us." Mr. Dodgson stopped, overcome with indignation.

"What about the knife?" Monteverde asked. "When did he pick that up?"

"He must have taken it during his final argument with Mr. Basset," Mr. Dodgson said. "He could have seen me discover the knife over the lintel while he was running to and from the printing plant in the cellar. He had to find another hiding place for it and chose to incriminate another of the staff, one who may have derided him in his illustrations."

Mr. Dodgson shook his head as he contemplated the duplicity of the clerk. "That, of course, was the final error, the one thing he could have done that would eliminate you, Mr. Roberts, as the murderer."

"Eh?" Calloway was trying to follow Mr. Dodgson's reasoning. "How do you know that?"

"Because Mr. Roberts was in his garret with Mr. Peterson while Mr. Basset was being let out by Mr. Levin," Mr. Dodgson explained. "Miss Harvey confirmed what I had already surmised. Neither Mr. Roberts nor Mr. Peterson could have come down the stairs without being seen by Miss Howard, who was in the office with the door wide-open.

"Miss Howard heard the voice of the street corner orator and the sounds of the crowd; therefore, the front door must have been open, for the street noises were not apparent when the door was shut. She heard Mr. Basset cry out and thought it was one of the rioters in the street.

"Mr. Basset must have known who had stabbed him. That is what he was trying to tell us when he died. He was looking at Mr. Levin, who had just closed the door." Mr. Dodgson stopped for breath.

Dr. Doyle shook his head. "The man must have been mad," he whispered.

"As I said, obsession is a kind of madness," Mr. Dodgson agreed. "Mr. Levin was obsessed with the need to put his past behind him, and to take on responsibilities for which he was in no way suited."

Inspector MacRae was still unconvinced. "Just how did Basset make the acquaintance of this Levin?"

Mr. Dodgson looked into the fire. "I think, Inspector, that you will discover that Mr. Levin, or Aaron Levy, was one of those young men who hang about places like the Café Royal hoping to attract the attention of a gentleman like Samuel Basset. They were seen dining there at least once, possibly more than once. Mr. Levin's features are quite striking, and Mr. Basset is not unknown."

"I can vouch for that," Wilde put in.

"I must now depart from fact and descend into supposition," Mr. Dodgson went on. "I cannot tell whether Mr. Levin placed himself in Mr. Basset's orbit by deliberately going to Toynbee Hall before or after their first meeting. What *is* certain is that the two men did become acquainted and, perhaps, intimate." Mr. Dodgson swallowed hard, then forged ahead with his speech. "Mr. Levin may have affected an interest in Mr. Basset's work. Mr. Basset, to his credit, offered to train the young man. He probably offered to pay for some clothes that would be more suitable to an office position than the garments worn by the, um, young men at the Café Royal. However, there was a price to be paid for Mr. Basset's patronage. Mr. Levin was to be berated in public, made to work like a drudge, and generally treated like a servant."

"We always wondered why he took it," Monteverde said, shaking his head. "David would have his opinion, of course. He'd known Basset since they were both at Portman Penny Press, and he knew the kind of company Basset kept. Begging your pardon, sir," he turned to Mr. Portman.

Portman sighed. "You see, Mr. Dodgson, I was right. It was one of those young thugs after all."

"Indeed it was," Mr. Dodgson said. "And now, Mr. Portman, you see your dilemma."

"My dilemma?" Portman echoed.

"It is quite bad enough that Mr. Basset should have died at the hands of an employee with a grudge. If the exact nature of the grudge became common gossip, parents may well refuse to let their children read *Youth's Companion*. Your publication would be considered tainted because of the editor's, um, peccadilloes."

Portman turned to the two policemen. "We must keep this quiet," he said urgently.

Inspectors MacRae and Calloway looked at each other, then at the rich and influential publisher.

"This has been a difficult day for all London," MacRae said slowly. "What with the riot last night, and more of the same tonight, it's possible that someone might have gotten carried away."

"This 'ere Levin, 'e might 'ave 'eard yon socialists on their soapbox and taken 'em literal," Calloway conjectured.

"And the writer, Peterson?" MacRae shrugged. "As we said before, a man in the wrong place at the wrong time. With your Mr. Levin gone, who's to say differently?"

"I shall have to make a statement to the press," Portman said. "I shall express deep regret at the loss of my dear friend Sammy Basset and I will be equally unhappy at the loss of David Peterson, a valued member of our little family at *Youth's Companion*. And I will be quite shocked to hear that Andrew Levin, Mr. Basset's confidential secretary, was run down by an omnibus in the fog tonight."

Dr. Doyle listened, appalled. "You are going to perpetrate a fraud on the public!" he exclaimed.

Mr. Portman eyed the young doctor with a look of experience. "It will do no one any good to vilify poor Sammy now," he said. "David's family need not know that he was capable of blackmail, and Levin . . . I don't even know if he had a family."

"I suspect the young men at the Café Royal will know," Mr. Dodgson said. "As for Mr. Peterson's wife and children, they will remember him as a loving father and husband. There are times, Dr. Doyle, when the truth is best left unsaid, and this is one of them."

"Thank goodness this week's issue is printed up," Monteverde said. "I don't know what we're going to do about next week though." He glanced at his comrade-in-arms. "Win is the writer; I'm the editor. David could do it all, of course, but he's not here. What do we do now?"

Portman frowned, then said, "I think tomorrow the offices will remain closed so that we may attend the inquests on our dear friends Samuel Basset and David Peterson, and also on Mr. Andrew Levin, who was, after all, a person employed by Portman Penny Press. After that, I may have to take up the reins until we can find someone else."

"Not Mr. Wilde?" Mr. Dodgson asked innocently.

"Definitely not Mr. Wilde," Portman stated firmly.

"Why not?" Oscar protested. "I can choose a story as well as Sammy Basset could, and I'm a much better writer."

Mr. Portman shook his head and smiled at his friend. "Oscar, you are a good chap, but I do not think you are really a suitable editor for a magazine for young persons. No, I had another thought. I shall speak to Miss Harvey as soon as she is recovered from her distressing adventure. She appears to be a young woman of amazing good sense, with a talent for bringing order out of chaos. Women are good with children. It would be a real innovation for a woman to assist in a publication devoted to children. I must think about it."

"A most interesting idea," Mr. Dodgson said. "And now, if you please, Mr. Portman, I must seek my bed. It has been, as you have said, a most eventful day, and I must take the early train back to Oxford."

The scholar and the others bowed themselves out of the room, leaving the two policemen to consult with Mr. Portman as to the time and place of the inquest on the staff of *Youth's Companion* and the disposition of the body and personal effects of Mr. Samuel Basset.

"And that's that," MacRae told his City of London Police colleague, as they were shown out by the supercilious butler. "Mob's gone, murderer's taken care of. Now we can all go home."

CHAPTER 27

F riday dawned bright and fair, a positive relief after the snow and fog of the previous two days. The February sky overhead was blue, and the chilly air held a promise of spring.

The streets of London rang with the sound of workmen plying their many trades. The Guildhall had fulfilled the promise given by the Lord Mayor and aldermen, and an army of sweepers were busily removing the debris of the last two days' riots. Bread and milk were being doled out to small children, and ragged women lined up to receive a few pennies each, which would buy enough stringy beef or suspiciously pungent fish to keep the men at their labors. Clearly, God was in his Heaven, all was right with the world, and London was itself again.

The morning newspapers were full of the dramatic events of the previous night. The speeches were described in detail, as was the aldermen's announcement of the replenishment of the Lord Mayor's Fund. Nothing was said about the unfortunate young man who had run under the omnibus in the fog.

Mr. Dodgson and Dr. Doyle met Mr. Portman at breakfast in the dining room of the Press Club. Mr. Portman had taken great care with his toilette this morning. He had to walk the fine line between extravagant mourning and businesslike attire fit for the halls of justice.

"You need not attend the inquest," Mr. Portman explained to his overnight guests.

"We may be called upon to give testimony on Mr. Basset's demise," Mr. Dodgson pointed out. "I can only hope that the press will find the arraignment of Mr. Hyndman and Mr. Burns more entertaining than an inquest on the editor of a publication devoted to children. I should not like Dean Liddell to find out how I spent the last two days."

Portman laughed heartily. "I don't see what difference it could possibly make to Christ Church if you chose to stay in London," he said, digging into a plateful of ham and eggs.

Mr. Dodgson sighed. "You are relatively young, Mr. Portman, and you associate chiefly with literary persons. I can assure you, sir, that Dean Liddell does not look favorably on my recent endeavors to further the literary ambitions of some of my younger colleagues." He looked hard at Dr. Doyle, who was cheerfully boning a kipper. "As for the last two days, I can always explain that I was detained in London because of the weather. First the snow and then the fog made any railway travel out of London well-nigh impossible."

"And you don't have to mention the Café Royal, or Baker Street, or Toynbee Hall," Dr. Doyle said. "However, I mean to tell all of it to Touie as soon as I see her. My wife," he explained to Mr. Portman.

"Of course," Mr. Portman said.

Mr. Dodgson drank his tea and swallowed carefully. Then he cleared his throat and asked, "How did you get on with the, er, editing yesterday?"

Portman beamed. "Quite interesting. So many people trying to get their stories published and in quite the wrong place, too. I never knew there were so many writers in London, let alone England."

"And Scotland, Ireland, and Wales," Dr. Doyle put in. He

fidgeted in his chair, then blurted out, "Mr. Wilde said that he liked my stories. Have you read them yourself?" His voice rose in anticipation.

Portman stopped beaming. "Ahem. Well, actually, yes, I did."

"And . . . ?" Dr. Doyle leaned forward eagerly.

Portman's face twisted in an agony of indecision. "I thought they were very . . . interesting," he said at last. "But Sammy was right about one thing. They were not what we want for *Youth's Companion.*"

Dr. Doyle's face fell. Then he asked hopefully, "Perhaps they could be used in another publication of the Portman Penny Press?"

Portman took a deep breath. "The difficulty," he said at last, "the difficulty is the length of the tales. They are too long and complex for *Youth's Companion,* but they are too short to be published by themselves. What we need," he said, warming to his subject, "is a good shilling shocker, some story that will grab the reader, with a set of characters who can be used in several novels, in a series. A mysterious death in a strange and unusual place, a heroine in danger, and a dauntless hero . . ."

"A gothic romance?" Dr. Doyle shook his head. "I think not, Mr. Portman. What would be truly interesting to the public would be a perfectly ordinary setting, like London, and a detective who uses the latest scientific knowledge to solve his cases. That, sir, would be new and exciting."

"I would like to see a story like that," Mr. Portman said. "Norwich, what is it?"

The butler was summoning him to the door. "There are some persons outside, Mr. Portman. I did not wish to permit them farther than the vestibule."

Mr. Portman's curiosity was aroused. He led Mr. Dodgson and Dr. Doyle down to the anteroom where Bert and Ern, the two young men from the Café Royal, were waiting. They had covered their loud checked suits with long black coats and substituted broad-brimmed black hats for their rakish billycocks to match their serious expressions.

Ern bowed to Mr. Portman and nodded affably to Dr. Doyle,

as to a comrade-in-arms. "We was in Trafalgar Square last night," he began.

"And we saw how Aaron, which you knew as Andrew Levin, were run down by the homnibus," Bert went on. "And we saw them coppers took up by a cab and brought over 'ere by yon Jock in the plaid coat."

"And we wants to know," Ern took up the inquisition, "wot's toward wif our Aaron?"

"He was trying to escape capture by the police," Dr. Doyle explained. "My friend Mr. Dodgson had proof that he murdered two men, one of them his employer, Mr. Basset."

Bert and Ern exchanged meaningful glances.

Dr. Doyle added, "I assure you, there was nothing we could have done. It was a dreadful accident."

The two youths nodded silently as if to say, *If you say so.*

"There is to be an inquest at Bow Street this morning," Mr. Portman told them. "If you have any evidence, you may give it there."

"Thank'ee, but Bert and me stays clear of the perlice," Ern said.

"I allus told Aaron as 'ow 'e shouldn't 'ave pushed it," Bert declared. "But 'e 'ad ambitions."

"And wot's done is done," Ern decided, philosophically. "I'm 'is cousin. Wot we wants ter know is, where is 'e? So's we can see 'im 'ome, so to speak."

"I believe the body of that unfortunate young man is still at St. Bart's," Mr. Dodgson told them. "Once the verdict has been handed down at the Coroner's Inquest, you may inter him as you see fit."

With this information in hand, the two young men left on their melancholy errand. The Portman carriage was ready to transport Mr. Portman and his two guests to Bow Street, around knots of workmen clearing off the debris of the last two nights of snow, slush, and rioting.

The Bow Street Police Station was, if anything, even more crowded than it had been on Thursday morning. Mr. Gosport had taken his cold home and was replaced by Mr. Hampton, a relatively young and jovial justice, with a waggish turn of mind.

He gazed at the assembled riffraff and decided that it was to no one's interest to keep any of them in custody. "Get on home," he ordered, "and find yourself better occupation than listening to lunatics, Socialists, and Trade Unionists."

The men dispersed, grateful that they had not been fined and making up stories to tell their wives and mothers as to where they had been all night.

"And now, let's have the ringleaders," Hampton said. "Burns, Hyndman, O'Casey. How plead you?"

Hyndman stared grandly about the courtroom. The only people left to impress were the gentlemen of the Fourth Estate. He raised his head and declared. "I am guilty of demanding justice! The workingmen of the world will not be denied their rights!"

Hampton shrugged. "What about you two? Do you want to spend the next year in prison, or will you go back to your own families and stop this ceaseless bawling and brawling in the streets?"

Burns scowled. O'Casey looked at his employer, then at his newfound comrades-in-arms.

"We stand united," Burns stated. O'Casey nodded in agreement.

"This won't do," Hampton scolded them. "O'Casey," he consulted the notes laid before him by O'Casey's solicitor (provided by Mr. Portman), "you're the only honest workingman in this lot. Do you really think you can change the world by going to jail for a year?"

O'Casey looked at Burns and Hyndman, then at Portman. "I been talking to John here, and he's right. Us workingmen have to stand together. I'll go to jail if I have to, but I won't go back to what I was."

"Then so ruled." The magistrate slammed his gavel down, and the three men were led back into the cells.

"It's a pity O'Casey has no thought for his family," Mr. Dodgson said. "His wife must be quite upset. There are children, too, I understand."

"I'll do what I can," Portman promised him. "But a man who turns his back on a good position to join the likes of Henry Hyndman and John Burns must be as mad as Levin."

Hampton looked around to see what was next on his agenda. "Coroner's Inquest?" he asked, looking at his papers. "Whose inquest?"

"A result of two nights' riots." Inspector MacRae stood up, with Inspector Calloway at his side. "Three deaths: Mr. Samuel Basset, on Fleet Street; Mr. David Peterson, in the Strand; Mr. Aaron Levy, also known as Andrew Levin, in Trafalgar Square."

Hampton examined the reports in front of him. "Aha. Basset . . . stab wound? That doesn't sound like the result of a riot. People don't go stabbing other people in the middle of a riot."

"The murder may 'ave been committed by Mr. Andrew Levin, 'oo was inflamed by the speeches and took a knife to 'is employer in consequence," Calloway said ponderously. "Which Andrew Levin, also known as Aaron Levy, were run down by a homnibus in the fog last night."

"How providential," Justice Hampton observed. "What proof do you have that this Levin stabbed his employer?"

"We have the knife used for the purpose. We also have evidence provided by Mr. Dodgson here," Inspector MacRae said, indicating the shrinking scholar, "that places Levin at the scene of the crime with sufficient motive and with the means to do it. That would have placed him in the dock had he not had the fatal accident."

"As for Mr. Peterson," Calloway went on, " 'e were 'it by a brick in the middle of Wednesday night's snow. Death by misadventure, if ever there was one."

"Don't presume to do my job for me, Inspector." Hampton looked about the nearly empty courtroom. The press had followed Hyndman, Burns, and O'Casey in hopes of getting more rhetoric to pad out their stories. Only two women sat in the Public Gallery: a careworn Irishwoman in a hand-knitted shawl of the same pattern as O'Casey's woolen scarf and Myrna Peterson, draped in black.

287

"Is there any evidence to the contrary?" Justice Hampton asked sharply. There was no answer.

Dr. Doyle opened his mouth, then closed it again as he met Mr. Dodgson's accusing gaze. Should he mention the fact that Levin had not worn gloves last night, although he was otherwise elegantly dressed? Should he tell the police to look for those gloves, which may well be soiled with brick dust and the remains of David Peterson?

Dr. Doyle closed his mouth and shook his head. Perhaps there were some things that were best left undeclared. It would do no one any good to reveal Mr. Basset's secret vice, or David Peterson's brief attempt at blackmail, or Andrew Levin's sordid youthful indiscretions. Better to let these sleeping dogs lie and go back to Southsea.

"Then it is the opinion of this court that Samuel Basset died at the hands of Andrew Levin, also known as Aaron Levy, who was himself killed in a street accident. David Peterson was the victim of a felonious attack by persons unknown as a consequence of the riot on Wednesday night." The gavel came down sharply, and the magistrate looked about for the next case.

Myrna Peterson stepped up to Nicky Portman as he was preparing to leave the Bow Street Police Court.

"Mrs. Peterson," Mr. Portman greeted her. "I am truly sorry the murderer of your husband could not be apprehended. . . ."

Myrna put her veil aside. "I understand," she said. "However, I had to speak to you about something quite different. I know this is not really the time to discuss business, but I have to think of my children. . . ." She took another breath, then said, "I have several manuscripts, written by my husband, for publication. They were never submitted to Portman Penny Press, or anywhere else, because he had not quite finished the stories to his own satisfaction, but . . ." She stopped, peering up into Portman's face.

"I shall publish them, never fear," Portman promised her.

Mr. Dodgson coughed diffidently behind them. "Ahem. May I point out that Mr. Samuel Basset's new volume, *King Arthur in London,* was taken from an outline submitted by Mr. Peterson. Perhaps this fact could be incorporated into the title page, and

Mrs. Peterson could be given a portion of the royalties? This, with the royalties from Mr. Peterson's other works, might provide a small income for Mrs. Peterson and her children."

Portman nodded. "Of course, Mr. Dodgson. An excellent idea. And I shall attend the funeral, Mrs. Peterson. I am truly sorry for your loss. David was a good writer. He shall be sorely missed at *Youth's Companion.*"

Mr. Portman turned to Mr. Dodgson and Dr. Doyle. "I do wish I could have been more helpful about printing your stories, Dr. Doyle, but you see how it is. I would be quite happy to read any of your new writings, should you send them." He smiled briefly at Dr. Doyle, then went on. "Mr. Dodgson, thank you for your efforts in uncovering the truth about poor Sammy's death, but you are quite right when you say that it would be best for all concerned if the events of the last two days never came to light. Good day, gentlemen!"

He put on his silk hat, strode out into Bow Street, and mounted his carriage, leaving Mr. Dodgson and Dr. Doyle to seek a cab for themselves.

"I must get to Victoria," Dr. Doyle told his mentor.

"And I must get to Paddington," Mr. Dodgson said.

"Do you suppose Mr. Portman was right? That I should give up my idea for a historical novel and try my hand at a mystery story instead?"

Mr. Dodgson considered and said, "I think you should write what suits you, Dr. Doyle."

"In that case," Dr. Doyle decided, as he flagged down a cab, "I shall take this tangled skein of ours and weave a shilling shocker out of it that will make Mr. Nicholas Portman sit up and take notice!"

"And I shall look forward to reading it," Mr. Dodgson said. "I should expect no less of Dicky Doyle's nephew."

AFTERWORD

Youth's Companion continued to be published under the imprimatur of Portman Penny Press. Mr. Nicholas Portman took on the editing chores for a year, then passed them on to his able assistant, Miss Helen Harvey, when he inherited Portman Penny Press on the death of his father. They were married in the spring of 1887. While Mr. Portman expanded the Penny Press into a publishing empire, Mrs. Portman ruled the world of the children's literature until after the Great War, when she reluctantly retired from active participation in publishing. They died within a few months of each other in the influenza epidemic of 1920, leaving the Portman Penny Press in the hands of their two sons.

The painting of Miss Helen Harvey as *Queen Mab*, by Edgar Roberts, was one of the sensations of the Royal Academy Salon in 1887. As a result, Mr. Roberts became one of the most popular painters of the fantastic, with a great vogue in the 1880s and '90s. Although the market for fairy painting slackened after the turn of the century, he continued to paint scenes of fairy palaces and strange landscapes that no one wanted to buy until he died of malnutrition in 1930. His works are now coming back into style; one recently sold at auction for $20,000.

Roberto Monteverde and Winslow Howarth continued at *Youth's Companion,* with Miss Harvey (later Mrs. Portman) at the helm. They also collaborated on the *Monte Winslow Guides to Fine Dining,* published annually by the Portman Penny Press.

Myrna Peterson managed to live on the royalties left by her husband's books until she married Winslow Howarth after her year of mourning was over. Their marriage was long and happy, and Howarth was a kind stepfather to his old friend's children, as well as fathering several of his own.

The autographed copy of *Alice's Adventures in Wonderland* remained one of Flora Peterson's prized possessions, handed down from mother to daughter for four generations. It was only after the Second World War, when the Howarth-Peterson family fell on hard times, that the book was offered for auction. It was sold to a private collector for $250,000.

Seamus O'Casey never went back to the printing plant. Instead, he became a professional rabble-rouser and trade union agitator, much to the despair of his wife, who was left to raise the children on the salary she earned as a cleaner at *Youth's Companion.* (See Historical Notes).

Mr. Dodgson returned to Oxford and explained to Dean Liddell that he had been unavoidably detained because of the bad weather. He did not mention the riots, the Bow Street jail, or the Café Royal.

Dr. Doyle regaled his wife with the story of his adventures, and then drew up the plot of a new story, to be called "A Tangled Skein." He later changed the name of the story, the name of the chief characters, and some of the plot . . . but that is, in itself, another story.

HISTORICAL NOTES

❧❧❧

The Trafalgar Square Riots of February 9, 10, and 11, 1886, are a matter of public record, leading off what amounted to a decade of social unrest. Henry Hyndman and John Burns led a group of dissatisfied unemployed workers to Trafalgar Square through the Strand, where they met the Fair Trade League, led by Tom Mann, who had been given permission to hold a meeting protesting the lack of employment for unskilled workers. The two groups fought each other, the police fought all of them, and through it all, a heavy snow fell, making it hard to tell friend from foe. The following two days were filled with fear for the upper and middle classes and hopes of mob action for the working classes. The matter was resolved, as I have shown, by private contributions to the Lord Mayor's Fund, a discretionary fund that provided some sort of relief to the indigent. This proved to be only a temporary stopgap. There was labor agitation through the 1880s and '90s until legislation was passed guaranteeing workers some basic rights. Henry Hyndman and John Burns were tried for sedition in April of 1886, and were acquitted.

I have taken certain liberties with the actual events, by moving the day of the riot from Tuesday to Wednesday, mostly to save

Mr. Dodgson and Dr. Doyle a long and ultimately pointless journey to Maida Vale to interview John Tenniel, and including a more dramatic conclusion to the event than was reported at the same time.

The Wednesday-night dinners at *Punch* were occasions of great hilarity, with food brought in from the best restaurants, and fine wines to accompany the meal. This was a "working dinner," strictly stag, after which the following week's issue would be lined out, and the subject matter for the "big cut," i.e., the political cartoon on the front page, would be given to Tenniel, who would then come up with the required illustration. The big cut for the week of February 12 showed the allegorical figures as I have described them.

The printing history of *Alice's Adventures in Wonderland* is complex, partly because there were two first printings. The first run of the book did not pass the stern eyes of either Tenniel or Dodgson, who saw minute discrepancies in the illustrations. That run was to be discarded, and the books were sent to such institutions as could not afford better copies (at Mr. Dodgson's expense, since he was paying for the printing). The few copies of this run that survived are now museum pieces and are literally priceless.

The Café Royal still stands in Regent Street, although under different management. Oscar Wilde held court there in the Grill Room, as I have described, throughout the 1880s and '90s, until his arrest on a charge of Gross Indecency in 1896. Wilde held an editorial position at a magazine for women from 1886 to 1887, when he began to write for the theater.

Oscar Wilde and Arthur Conan Doyle actually met at a dinner party in 1889. They never became intimate associates, but each read and respected the works of the other.

Toynbee Hall was established by the Reverend Samuel Augustus Barnett in 1884 in Whitechapel as the forerunner of the settlement-house movement that inspired such social reformers as Jane Addams in Chicago and Lilian Wald in New York. The early buildings have been replaced by an education complex, and the institution now encompasses social services for all ages, from the very young to the very old.

Baker Street still lies between Euston and Oxford Streets, south of Regent's Park.

The clubs still occupy Saint James's Square and Pall Mall, but the Press Club is not one of them, since it is my own invention.

Mr. Dodgson and Dr. Doyle never met. This story is an exercise in "What if . . ."

ACKNOWLEDGMENTS

★

Information about the February riots came from two sources: *Outcast London: A Study in the Relationship Between Classes in Victorian Society*, by Gareth Stedman Jones (Pantheon, 1971), and *The Journals of Beatrix Potter* (1995). Miss Potter was nineteen at the time, very politically aware, and gives a full account of the incident and its repercussions among the moneyed classes. Mr. Steadman, writing from the perspective of a century later, puts the incident into the larger context of Victorian society and quotes extensively from contemporary sources.

I found photographs and maps of Victorian London in Charles Viney's *Sherlock Holmes in London* (Smithmark, 1995) and photographs of London working people in John Thomson's *Victorian London Street Life* (Dover Publications, 1994).

In addition, I would like to thank the following people for their kind advice and information: Mr. Fred Wharton, Head Custodian at Christ Church, Oxford, and ex-policeman, who put me right about British police procedure; Dr. Gayithri R. Keshav, M.D., who spent several hours on a plane to Chicago explaining the finer points of back stabbing; Mr. John Hale, of Robert Hale Publishing, who explained about British office life and allowed me to use his desk; Ms. Stella Wilkins, of Abner Stein, my London agent, who took me to lunch at a perfect restaurant; Mark, the doorman at the Café Royal, who gave me a brief history of the place. And, as always, Keith Kahla, my faithful editor at St. Martin's Press; Cherry Weiner, my ever-helpful agent and mentor; and my husband and biggest fan, Murray Rogow.